She was the most infuriating woman...

She licked her lips and gazed up at him, and really, he thought suddenly, for a plain woman her eyes were ridiculously fine—brilliant though they were gray, almost silver in color, and fringed with long dark lashes. Dew clung to her skin, giving it the sheen of nacre, and her pink tongue, darting out to wet her trembling lips, was a silly little enticement. Irritation waged war with rationality, but irritation won. He could not turn her over his knee to teach her to mind her own business, so... he grabbed her around the waist, hauled her into his embrace, and bent her backwards with a hasty and impetuous kiss certain to silence—and possibly confuse—her. A servant who had approached at their entry gasped and backed out of the hallway.

But it did not daunt her. The moment he released her, she slapped him. Hard. The sound echoed to the upper reaches of the third floor. "How dare you, sir?"

He planted his hands on his hips and laughed out loud...

Lady Anne

AND THE

HOWL

IN THE

DARK

Lady Anne
AND THE
Howl
IN THE
Dark

DONNA LEA SIMPSON

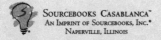

SOURCEBOOKS CASABLANCA™
AN IMPRINT OF SOURCEBOOKS, INC.®
NAPERVILLE, ILLINOIS

Published by Sourcebooks Casablanca, an imprint of
Sourcebooks, Inc.
P.O. Box 4410, Naperville, Illinois 60567–4410
(630) 961–3900
FAX: (630) 961–2168
www.sourcebooks.com

Library of Congress Cataloging-in-Publication Data

Simpson, Donna.
Lady Anne and the howl in the dark / Donna Lea Simpson.
p. cm.
1. Nobility—England—Fiction. 2. Country life—England—
Fiction. 3. Werewolves—Fiction. 4. Yorkshire (England)—
Fiction. I. Title.
PR9199.3.S529L325 2009
813.'54—dc22

2008041431

Printed and bound in the United States of America.
QW 10 9 8 7 6 5 4 3 2 1

One

WHAT WAS IT ABOUT LYDIA'S LETTER THAT WORRIED
Anne so deeply?

Lady Anne Addison clung to a handle on the
interior wall of the Royal Mail coach as they jounced
along a Yorkshire highway in the fading twilight, and
thought about the letter that had sent her scurrying
north. Lady John Bestwick—Miss Lydia Moore before
marriage to Lord John Bestwick, younger brother of
the Marquess of Darkefell—was desperately unhappy.
As charming as Lord John had been prior to their
marriage four months before, now he was horrible and
left her alone for hours with her mother-in-law, who
despised her, Lydia claimed in her latest letter to Anne.
She hinted at worse; her husband had faults she hadn't
known of when she said her vows. Anne wondered
what those faults could be. She feared the worst, abuse
or perversion, and would let her dear friend Lydia,
who hadn't sufficient strength of character to assert her
own will, suffer from neither.

With a long knowledge of Lydia's tendency to
dramatize herself and her sufferings, (Anne had once

been engaged to Lydia's beloved brother, though poor Reginald had died in a military engagement), Anne would not necessarily have given credence to those afflictions, but something in the letter made her uneasy. It was, she thought, something *between* the words… something *underlying* the sentences. Lydia truly was desperately afraid, but it was impossible to discover the source of her fear without direct questioning, which could not be done by letter.

Still, Anne would have used her own carriage and driver, a slower but more comfortable way to travel all the way to Yorkshire, but for Lydia's horrified assertion that a werewolf haunted the Darkefell estate grounds at night. During the full moon, the beast had been witnessed standing on two legs and speaking English.

Utter tripe, Anne reflected, primming her mouth and staring out through the carriage window at the wild, rocky landscape. Fairy tales told to frighten little children into behaving. But still… she was intrigued, the fantastical tale slicing through the tedium of days that had become a little humdrum of late.

The full moon was just days away. The letter had been bleak and despairing enough that Anne had set out immediately, committing her safety, if not her comfort, to the Royal Mail. So she hurtled along this northern road using the latest madness in travel, the swift but jarring Royal Mail run. Fast it was—she had left London only the day before at four in the afternoon, and already she was in Yorkshire—but exceedingly uncomfortable, too.

The slanting rays of sunset poured through the glass and directly into her eyes as they bumped over every rut in the indifferent road. Wedged in by her seat companion, an enormous, snoring woman, she could not reach over to draw the curtain. Ill with fatigue and trying to quell her nausea, Anne took a deep breath and regretted it immediately. The snoring woman reeked of heavy perfume, the stinking scent battling the fetid aroma of body dirt, the flatulent eruptions from the sleeping gentleman opposite her, and the stench of sour milk from the slumbering child next to him.

They could not arrive at Staunby, her destination, quickly enough for her. Her maid, Mary, and her trunks would follow, but she would be on the scene, at least, before the full moon.

The clarion call of the post horn indicated either an inn or a tollgate was imminent; Anne fervently prayed it was the post-house at Staunby. It was, and with blinding swiftness, Lady Anne and her portmanteaux were deposited with less consideration than the bag of mail, to stand bewildered and disoriented near the post-house door.

"I beg your pardon," she said politely to the rotund little fellow who was lugging the heavy canvas mail bag toward the post-house. "Is there a carriage to meet me?"

"Carriage, miss?" the postal employee absently asked, blinking at her and scratching his behind. The post-house was a small cottage just a few yards from him, within ames ace; the interior, visible through the open door, was warmly lit with inviting lamplight. He shrugged, then turned away and continued pulling.

"My name is Lady Anne Addison," Anne said through gritted teeth, following him, "and I believe my friend, Lady John Bestwick, has arranged transport for me to Darkefell Castle. Where is my carriage?"

"Darkefell Castle?" With a swift burst of strength, he hauled the mailbag up over his shoulder and scuttled into the post-house, slamming the door shut. There followed the unmistakable sound of the bolt being shot.

Lady Anne was left gaping in confusion in the twilight on the side of the lonely highway. It took a full thirty seconds for outrage to boil up in her heart. She strode to the door and pounded. "Is this how you treat your paying passengers, sir?"

No answer.

"I demand assistance!" she shouted, pounding again on the thick plank door.

"Not an inn, madam, not an inn!" his voice sang out from within.

"I don't want to *stay* here, I want to *go!*"

Silence.

Befuddled by the resolute lack of response, queasy from the journey, and exhausted beyond calculation, Lady Anne shouted, "I shall have the local magistrate down upon you, sir, and if there is no crime with which to charge you, I shall invent something. I have absolutely no sense of fairness where I have been injured."

The only response to that was a rustling sound. A folded slip appeared from under the door, visible in the faint fan of light from the lantern above the door in the gathering gloom. One final little push, and the paper popped out and wafted in the breeze. She picked it up and held it toward the light.

It was a crude map on a dirty scrap of paper. She could just make out a road indicated, with what looked like rocky hillsides, a vague sketch of something labeled "*cassel*," and the plea "GO."

"Go?" she shrieked, turning back toward the closed door. "Do you expect me to walk? It's almost dark!"

But did she have any choice? She gazed around, a chill racing down her back at the lonely desolation of this spot, a crossroads. Rocky hills tumbled upward away from the highway, which was now just a dark stretch of winding road that dwindled in the distance. Stunted trees near the post-house huddled in stygian shadows, and shutters blotted out any light from the interior fire and lamps.

She pounded on the door again. "Do you have a carriage I could hire?" No answer. "Or a cart? Or even a horse?"

Still no answer. She looked at the crude map again, holding it slanted to the light, and then gazed around her. It appeared that the road indicated was the one that ran at a 90 degree angle from the highway, just beyond the post-house. It had a definite slope, but a lady as fit as she could manage it. She was going to have to walk. Perhaps the carriage to pick her up was on its way; if she started walking, she would meet it.

However, she could not possibly carry her portmanteaux, which held everything she would need until her trunks arrived. She dragged them over to the cottage and hammered on the door again. She could hear him scuttling around inside. "Listen to me!" she said, loudly. "I'm going away. I ask only that you look after my bags until I can come back for them on the morrow."

Nothing. But he was on the other side of the door; she could hear him wheezing. Snuffling little badger of a man! She hammered on the door again with even more vigor. "Sir, I will *not* go away until I have some affirmation that you will take care of them for me! I'll stay here and pound and call out until—"

The door swung open, and one stubby hand was stuck out; she looped the leather straps of her portmanteaux over the hand, and he hauled them into his burrow. She then settled her plumed bonnet on her head, lifted her skirts, and started up the sloping byway, feeling a trickle of trepidation in her stomach. It was getting dark, and she had to pick her way carefully. "This is not how one treats a guest," she exclaimed aloud, in part to ward off a lingering childish fear of the dark. "If I turn my ankle, I shall be most put out."

As he strode from the twilight coolness of the outdoors into the great hall of Ivy Lodge, dower house of Darkefell Castle, the Marquess of Darkefell briefly considered how feminine a place it had become under the influence of his mother, *insidiously* feminine, with light-paneled walls, flowered paper, and soft carpets everywhere but the entrance. He glanced around as he entered; no Andrew in sight. The head footman should be immediately there to see to his needs, but the place felt oddly deserted.

He poked his head into the door of the formal drawing room, immediately off the great hall. Ah, only his sister-in-law, Lydia, reclined within; it was no wonder the place felt deserted. She would have to do, though, in the absence of an intelligent servant. "Where is the marchioness this evening?" he inquired.

Lydia rested on a sofa near the fire. Wide-eyed, she stared at him through the dimness and shook her head.

"Then where is John?" he asked, naming his younger brother, her husband of four months.

She shook her head again.

He closed his eyes and counted, containing his irritation against his sister-in-law's overwhelming uselessness. Vapid, but wellborn, Lydia had been fortunate that intelligence did not rate as an important quality in a wife among most men, and certainly not for his brother.

He would have throttled her after a se'nnight, but then he was not John. Her loveliness had quite faded from his sight, while her idiocy remained painfully evident. Having reached a count of thirty, the number required before he could civilly address Lydia again, he opened his eyes. "Think! Where is John? I have something of import to discuss with him, and Mother, too. Osei follows after a time with some papers that I need John to glance at after we speak."

"I don't know, my lord," she said, her voice faint. "I have been most cruelly deserted tonight, and—"

"Then I shall send John to you once I find him and we've spoken," he said, wheeling and exiting. Pausing for a moment in the great hall to collect his thoughts, he heard a sound that crawled up his spine; that damnable howling again, piercing even the thick walls of Ivy Lodge! He stood, undecided, then strode down a hall toward the housekeeper's private domain.

Mrs. Hailey was more likely than anyone else to know where his mother or brother were.

As Anne walked, the darkness gradually became more profound, progressing from charcoal murk to pitch blackness. Trees overhung the road, and newly sprouted leaves whispered in a strengthening breeze; despite the steady scuffle of her footsteps, Anne heard the faint rustle of animals in the bushes that encroached onto the narrowing road. On the wind the mingled scents of smoke from hearth fires and the green aroma of growing things drifted. Her pace slowed and became uncertain as darkness closed in. It occurred to her for the first time that she had only the badger's word for it that this *was* the road to Darkefell Castle. Surely, if it was, she should be there by now? Lydia claimed in her letter that the castle was only a mile from Staunby. She had gone that and more. But why would the fellow at the post-house lie?

Clouds had closed in as the breeze sprang up, but now a faint silvery glimmer displayed the cloud shapes and then broke through, the rising half moon lighting the landscape in tones of gray—dove, charcoal, slate, and smoke. The road ahead rose, misty, ahead of her, so she gathered her courage and strode onwards, upwards, grateful for the faint glow of moonlight. At least walking would keep her warm. After another half mile the night noises ceased, and the only sound was her sturdy traveling shoes scuffing the hard-packed road surface. It was silent until a howl cut the hush;

the eerie blade of sound sliced through the night, a preternatural wail that crept up her back and caused the skin on her arms and neck to pimple in shivery waves under her cloak and shawl.

"I am not afraid," she said aloud, her voice strong and steady.

The baying echoed again through the night, and Anne forced herself to walk on more quickly. Dogs—the howling must be dogs, for there was no other rational explanation. Dark shapes loomed some distance ahead—shadowy, blocky squares that were likely buildings, and black masses that might be trees. The surface under her feet had changed, subtly. Was she still on the roadway or lane or whatever it was? Her pace slowed, and her foot caught on a tuft of grass; she stumbled, then righted herself, stopping to try to get her bearings. It was too dark, but some of the shapes did appear to be square, and she thought she could see a glimmer of light in the distance.

Beyond the other shapes it appeared that a tower pointed to the heavens, blotting out the shred of moonlight she had been depending upon for courage. The square shapes ahead *must* be the buildings of Darkefell Castle or Ivy Lodge, she cared not which, but even if they were farm buildings, she would cast herself upon a farmer's mercy and sleep by his hearth until morning. She crept forward, hoping that a faint glimmer of what looked like a lantern was not an illusion brought about by her exhaustion. She was on grass now, and dew dragged at her cloak and skirts, coated her stockings, and even seeped through the sturdy leather of her shoes.

Another howl, an eerie sound like a blend of human voice and animal clamor, tore though the night, and she hastened her step, calling out, "Hello… is anyone there?" She staggered down a bit of a hill. "Hello? I fear I'm lost! Hellooo!"

The only answer was a scream—a sharp shriek of fear or pain, Anne thought, and then silence. Utter, dead silence. Trembling, she stopped, hearing only the blood pounding in her ears and the ragged gasp of her breath. Her eyes wide, she stared into the night, waiting. As her heart calmed, she could hear a rustling sound, then footsteps retreating, a wheezing breath sighing on the stiffening breeze. She staggered into motion again, heading in the direction of the scream. It had been a woman's cry, of that she was sure. Whoever made that sound was in dire need of assistance.

She lurched into longer grass, wet, tangled, and dew laden from the heavy mist of evening. Drifting on the night air was a sound. *What was that? A moan of pain? Oh, no!* The landscape was hilly, and Anne tumbled to the ground, turning her ankle and wrenching her shoulder. But she staggered to her feet, gathered up her cloak and skirts, and stumbled on toward the sound. The moaning was faint now, as if the woman was giving up the ghost.

"I'm coming!" Anne said out loud. "Where are you?"

A soft moan nearby was her only answer. Blindly, Anne turned toward the sound and, arms outstretched, felt past some bushes. The glimmer of lantern light had disappeared, and darkness had closed in again as she wandered close to a brushy area. "Where are you? Help me, so I can help *you!*" Her voice echoed in the darkness, and she suddenly felt silly, with a growing conviction that there was no one; it was her fatigued imagination working. But no, she was not that inventive. There *had* to be someone there! Buoyed by her own common sense, she moved forward, steeling her mind to think rationally.

But all sound had hushed. Slowly, carefully, she moved forward, hands still outstretched in front of her. Impatient with the slow pace, she began to walk more quickly and stumbled through some bushes and over something, falling to the ground and crying out in pain. "What on earth did I trip on?" she said, feeling under her feet.

It was something soft… an animal? The smell of blood filled her nostrils. A *dead* animal? Taking a deep, shuddering breath, she felt the form; it was *not* an animal. There was cloth. Clothing. Skirts. It was a woman!

"Hello? Are you all right? Are you well?" She groped around in the dark, warding off branches from some thorny bush as she tried to find the woman's face. "Of course you're not well, but are you ill or injured?" she babbled. Anne took in a deep, shuddering breath, filled with the conviction that there was no point in speaking to the woman. She was dead.

Anne staggered to her feet again, a fierce pain shooting through her ankle, but she could not stay where she was. "Help!" she cried, shoving and pushing away branches, then scaling the low hill that was topped by the road. "Help, someone, anyone!"

She spotted the dark shape of a building ahead and limped toward it, encouraged by the lamp that glowed above the door. "Help me!" she cried again. The house was a large, long ornate building of dark brick with a doorway that opened directly onto a crushed gravel drive. She edged along the low stone fence that lined the property, found the wrought iron gate and the latch in the center, undid the catch, and hobbled up to the double doors, her limping footsteps scraping through the gravel. She hammered on the door, grief for the poor unfortunate she had left behind in the dark welling up within her.

The door swung open, and a footman in livery and a powdered wig bowed low, his face barely creased with puzzlement as he stared at her. "Madam?" he said.

Fury filling her, Anne drew herself up and clasped her damp hands in front of her, saying, "Is this Ivy Lodge? I'm Lady Anne Addison, expected by Lady John Bestwick."

He simply stared at her and then down at her dress and hands. "This is Ivy Lodge, but we are expecting no one, madam."

"Let me in. There is trouble in the park!"

"No, madam, I cannot allow—"

"Stop blocking me, you imbecile," Anne said, pushing him out of the way. He shrank from her in disgust. "There's a woman in trouble out there. Where is your mistress?"

There was a clatter in the hall, and a light voice said, the tone fretful, "Who is it, Andrew?"

"Lydia!" Anne exclaimed. She pushed past the footman and saw her friend paused in the hallway by an open door that gave onto a fire-lit reception room; the lamplight in the entrance hall gave her complexion a sallow cast. "Lydia, it's me!" With the appearance of her friend, the awful treatment she had received rushed back to dominance in her mind. "Whatever has happened? Why was I not met at Staunby Post-house?"

Lydia took two steps into the hallway, staring at her, went pale and screamed, then crumpled into a heap.

"Lydia!" A young man strode toward them from a long hallway beyond the entrance, followed by someone else. "Lydia," he repeated, racing to her side and kneeling by her, raising one hand to his lips. "My dear, what's wrong?"

"Who the devil are *you?*" a new voice demanded.

Anne whirled to face her inquisitor and found a darkly handsome man staring at her from the shadows. "I am Lady Anne Addison, and I've come to visit Lydia," she stated, imperiously.

"And do you always come visiting at all hours and covered in blood?"

Blood? Anne looked down at her hands and dress. In the golden pool of lamplight, crimson stains sullied her best traveling cloak and her gloved hands; she was daubed in red, the blood of the unfortunate in the dark.

Two

"Oh," Anne said faintly, gazing down at her hands. "Lord help that poor girl!"

"What poor girl?" the younger man said, looking up from Lydia's prone form on the marble floor of the spacious entrance hall.

"The girl… the dead girl… oh, it *must* be a female, for the body wore skirts," Anne muttered, still staring at the crimson smears on her dove gray gloves.

The older, bolder man strode toward Anne. "Andrew," he said, over his shoulder to the footman, who hovered in the shadows near the door. "Have a maid get a basin of hot water for this woman and call Lady John's abigail. Tell her to bring smelling salts. My sister-in-law has fainted again." To Anne, he said, "Let me remove these gloves and your cloak and shawl." He unbuttoned her cloak at the neck. "They've gotten the worst of the gore. Now, what do you mean, a *body?* Where?"

Anne shrugged away from him and said, "I beg your pardon, but who are you, sir?"

He firmly took her hand and unbuttoned, then stripped off, one glove, casting it aside. "I could ask the same of you, but there are more pressing concerns. I surmise from the blood on you that someone is in trouble. What happened? Did your carriage overturn? Was there an animal attack of some sort? Tell me!"

He efficiently unbuttoned the wrist and stripped off the other glove as Anne reflected that he seemed well versed in unclothing a female. "I beg your pardon?" Her head swam. How odd, she thought, putting one trembling hand to her forehead. The entrance hall, lit by flickering lamplight, whirled above her, and the chandelier, centered in an ornate rosette in the coffered ceiling, spun. She shook her head and took a deep, trembling breath.

"Shall I slap you?" the man growled, grabbing her shoulders in his large, naked hands.

"*Slap* me? How *dare* you say such a thing!" Anne cried, focusing on his dark eyes and well-molded lips. She tried to twist out of his grip, but he was far too strong.

"Good." He gave her a little shake and released her. "I thought that would straighten you out. You have courage and are made of sturdier material than Lydia. You won't faint. Now, tell me, what happened? And where? We must get some men together and help whomever 'she' is whose blood you wear." He turned to the young footman who had just returned from his errands and snapped, "Andrew, summon Lisle and one of the grooms from the stable and have them meet me outside the front door immediately. There's a female in distress somewhere on the grounds who needs our assistance."

"No, I fear not," Anne said, her legs wobbly. Exhaustion and sorrow left her weak. She limped to a chair and collapsed on it.

"What do you mean, you 'fear not'?"

"She's beyond earthly assistance. I believe she expired just before I got to her."

"*Expired?*" he exclaimed. "If you mean she died, then say so!"

Anne looked up at the assertive gentleman, examining his gleaming dark eyes, and said through gritted teeth, "Expired, died, passed away, gave up the ghost. She is *dead,* sir, in any vernacular or common phrase you wish to hear it."

Unmoved by her stinging response, he asked, his expression skeptical, "Who is she?"

"How am I to know? I just this minute arrived. Even if I hadn't and was acquainted with all of the inmates of this house, it is dark as pitch out there. I couldn't see a thing. I could barely make my way here." She slipped off her cloak and carefully laid it aside, bunched with her shawl, unwilling to examine the gore. A maid bearing a basin of steaming water bustled in and set it down on a table near her, then uncertainly stood a ways away.

He stared at her. "You arrived on foot? How extraordinary. Do you make it a habit to drop in unannounced on friends on remote estates?"

"That's enough," Anne said, rising. "*That is enough!* I will not tolerate this treatment. There is a woman out there dead, not more than five hundred feet away. Levity ill becomes the situation."

"I was not being humorous but asking a question. I have only your word so far—a lady arriving alone, bloody, and disheveled—that there's a woman in trouble. So answer me; do you make it a habit to visit unasked? And did you indeed arrive on foot?" His dark eyes gleamed, and white teeth flashed.

Big white teeth… *the better to eat thee with,* as Perrault wrote. She felt faint. Wolves. The howl in the dark. A woman screaming, savaged. But no, there were no wolves in England. "No… no," she repeated, regaining her voice. "I do not make it a habit to visit unasked, and I did not do so this time. Lydia summoned me, and I'm still lacking an explanation as to why there was no carriage awaiting me at the Staunby Post-house."

"I would like an answer to that, too," he said, turning to the young man holding Lydia. "What's this about, John? Why would your wife invite Lady Anne and then fail to let anyone know about it?"

The young fellow gazed desperately toward the stairs that wound up from the entrance into the darkness of the next floor. "Where is Lydia's abigail?"

"Never mind that right now. Lydia will recover, but the girl in the park will not, if we are to believe this… lady."

Anne felt her hands curl into fists. "And who, sir, are you to question me?"

He met her angry gaze and, despite the awful situation, there was a hint of humor in his beautiful eyes. "I am the Marquess of Darkefell, master of all you survey," he said, spreading out his brawny arms to encompass all.

Anne stared at him, drawn into his gaze by the hypnotic force of his fine dark eyes. She turned away finally and stared down at the marble floor. "Then it truly is your concern to find that poor girl. Find her, my lord," she said, her voice cracking with sorrow. "I cannot bear to think of her out there alone."

Grimly, he answered, "If she's dead, then she'll not know if she's alone or accompanied. Are you certain she's dead?"

Anne nodded. "Yes. Oh, yes, I'm sure."

"Nevertheless, I'd like to find that out for myself." Two rugged men came to the open door, with hounds baying and torches flaming. "Finally!" he growled. He strode toward them, pausing only to look back at Anne and say, "Am I to assume I should be searching in the park toward the road, my lady?"

"Yes," she said. And then he was gone, and with him went all vitality in the room, for Lydia was still unconscious, and the fellow—presumably her husband, Lord John Bestwick—hung over her, the two immobile, like a marble statue of dying lovers. Anne limped to Lydia's side and knelt by her. "Does this happen often?" she asked the young man.

He was gazing down at his wife's pale face. "No... yes... only a few times. More lately." He looked up. "Where is her abigail? Where is Cecilia?" he cried, a hint of desperation in his voice.

Anne stood. A cowering maid stood in the shadows, but that evidently was not Lydia's abigail; a footman lingered near the girl, and she summoned him with a brisk wave of her hand. He moved forward, and she said, "Andrew, isn't it? Has Lady John's maid been summoned?"

"No one can find her, m'lady."

"That is unacceptable. Someone else, then, to help her ladyship... the housekeeper?"

"I've summoned Mrs. Hailey. She was out in the kitchen garden, m'lady, but she'll be here momentarily."

"Good. And where is her ladyship, the marchioness?" she asked about Lydia's mother-in-law.

The footman simply shook his head, unable or unwilling to answer that question.

"Well? Where is she?" Anne, accustomed to dealing with recalcitrant servants, would not be opposed.

"No one can find her, m'lady," the footman finally said.

Anne turned back, knelt again by Lydia, and examined the young man. He was a stout, well-formed fellow, a bit fleshy for Anne's taste, but solid and pleasant looking. "I take it that I truly was not expected by anyone?" she said. "I am, by the way, a good friend of Lydia's."

"My lady," he said, with a nod of acknowledgment. "I recognize your name—you were engaged to her brother at the time of his tragic death, and she speaks of you fondly. No, my wife told no one of your visit."

"How extraordinary." Anne sat back on her heels and examined Lydia. A nerve jumped below one eye, and her breathing was rapid, not like one in a swoon. "And yet her letter was quite specific as to needing immediate aid. I sent a reply by Royal Mail before setting out myself." The jumping nerve quickened. "She must have received my confirmation yesterday that I would be here today," Anne mused. "I traveled by the supremely uncomfortable but swift Royal Mail, simply because Lydia's plea for help was too pitiful to ignore."

"Help?" He frowned up at her, his smooth, pale forehead wrinkling. "Did she say why she required help?"

"Ooooh." Lydia stirred. She put one trembling hand to her forehead.

"Lydia, my darling," her husband said, bending over her and tenderly brushing back a lock of hair from her brow.

"What happened?" she murmured.

"You fainted." She stirred, and he put his hand on her shoulder in a quelling motion. "No, don't try to get up yet."

Anne watched with a skeptical eye. "Lydia, hello. Why did you not tell anyone I was coming? I had to walk all the way here from the post-house and had a dreadful experience on the way up."

Lydia's husband gave Anne a fierce look and shook his head.

"Anne!" That quavering hand touched her brow again, and she appeared bewildered. "I forgot to tell John that you were coming. It slipped my mind, and you see, I thought you were coming tomorrow."

"Did you receive my letter?"

"Yes, but—"

"It was quite specific as to my arrival this evening. How could you mistake it?"

"I don't know. I… " She trailed off, and her eyes fluttered closed again.

In the next moment several things happened at once: the door swung open, and the marquess, carrying someone, strode in; Lydia tried to get up, and a heavyset woman bustled in with a vial in her hand. Anne's heart thumped at the body in the marquess's arms. A female form drooped, the modest clothing rent. Blood saturated the cloth, but worse, much worse, was the raw, ragged flesh at the neck. She had been savaged.

Anne stood as Lydia screamed and fell into another swoon. The housekeeper—for so Anne assumed the plump woman must be—rushed to her and aided Lord John to lower his wife back down to the floor, and Lord Darkefell's steady gaze met Anne's eye across the limp body in his arms. No hint of levity danced across his face now. His expression was grim and filled with fury, which she judged was not aimed at her but at the perpetrator of such a foul deed.

"The poor girl," Anne said, swallowing back her revulsion at the gore. "Who is she?"

"Lady John's maid," the marquess said. "This is the earthly remains of Cecilia Wainwright." With that, he strode through, across the hall's marble floor, and directly toward some back room, kicking doors open ahead of him with one booted foot.

The next few hours were not as shocking as the first. Anne had been guided to her room, provided with hot water for washing and tea for drinking, and now she paced—albeit with a limp—wishing she knew what was going on. But the situation was complicated. She was an unexpected guest, putting the household to quite enough trouble without demanding information or making herself a nuisance, especially at such a time as this.

But finally she couldn't stand waiting. She ventured out and limped downstairs. The house was a Jacobean villa, small in comparison to the usual interpretation of the style, but exquisite in design. Anne descended to the second level, where (she had learned from a maid-servant) the family's living rooms were located. Painted wood paneling lined all of the carpeted hallways, and portraits adorned the walls, with lit lanterns on sconces between. It had been modernized, Anne had learned in a letter from Lydia describing her first visit to her new home, by the dowager marchioness, Lady Sophie. It was not clear to Anne why Lydia and John didn't live in the castle with the current marquess, since the man wasn't married and didn't have a family; but having met him, she could conjecture. Lord Darkefell was imperious and possibly unpleasant.

Anne ventured into a room that had been pointed out to her by a footman as the family's evening parlor and found that Lydia and John were ensconced by the fire. A graceful woman of middle years stood by a table nearby. "Pardon me," Anne said. "Am I intruding?"

"No, of course not, my lady," Lord John said, bowing. "Come, join us." He indicated the fireplace, where a cheery blaze glowed and flickered, warmth filling the wood-paneled room.

As Anne crossed the carpeted floor, the fellow continued, "Lady Anne Addison, this is my mother, the Dowager Marchioness Lady Sophie Darkefell."

"My lady," Anne said, offering her hand with a slight curtsey. The other woman briefly touched her fingers and then turned away. *Humph… some greeting.* "Lydia, how are you?" Anne asked, turning toward her friend, who was tucked into the chair with a robe over her legs.

"I should be asking *you* that, Anne, dearest, for what a welcome you've had!" The young woman held out her arms, and Anne leaned in for an embrace. "I'm sorry," she whispered in Anne's ear.

"For what?"

"For everything."

"Nonsense," Anne said, standing.

"I beg your pardon?" Lady Darkefell said, turning back toward her. "What is nonsense?"

Anne gazed steadily at the lady. There was something cold in the marchioness's gaze, a lack of welcome, perhaps, or a hint of aversion at Anne's appearance. Without her portmanteaux, the best Anne had been able to do was tidy herself. Her dress was still covered in road dirt, though her shawl and cloak had protected her dress from the worst of her awful adventure. "My friend was exclaiming at the poverty of my welcome, and I was saying nonsense, she must not apologize."

"Well, if one will make unexpected visits, one must not expect to be greeted appropriately."

A rush of anger kindled at the continuing misapprehension that she was not there by invitation. "I reassured her that an hour's walk in the wrong shoes, nightfall, and the hideous discovery of a gore-besmirched body in the park was no mean welcome at all, and if she had devised it as entertainment, she could not have pleased me more," Anne said. "That it was an awful tragedy was merely the sad conclusion to a diverting beginning."

The woman's face bleached under her paint, and Lord John gasped.

Lydia hastily said, "Now, Anne, I *am* sorry." She stood, her lap robe falling to the floor in a heap, and turned to her mother-in-law. "Lady Darkefell, Anne *was* invited, truly she was. I merely… forgot to say anything."

"Or to order a carriage to greet me, or tell anyone at all I was coming." Anne watched the dowager's expression, but it betrayed no more emotion. Turning to Lydia, she said, "You haven't explained the worries expressed in your letter——"

"Anne, please, let us talk in private later," she said hurriedly with a sidelong look at her mother-in-law.

Glancing from one feminine face to the other, Anne held her tongue. As Lydia was the only one of the three she knew, she would speak with her first before she decided what to say or ask. "I'm deeply sorry about poor Cecilia," Anne said with a gentler tone. "I know she's been with you since your coming-out season, and she always seemed to me to be a valuable help to you, and a quiet, unassuming girl."

Tears filled Lydia's eyes. "I cannot understand what she was doing out of the house after dark, especially with all that has gone on lately."

"Clearly she was having an affair with someone," Lady Darkefell said, trailing her fingers along a console table as she strolled closer to the fire.

"Why do you say that?" Anne asked, watching her eyes. It was a conclusion she had considered, for it explained what the young woman would be doing out of the house at dusk and beyond the immediate environs of the lodge, but it seemed to her there was no clarity in it at all, until they knew more. Perhaps the dowager marchioness *did* know more. If so, now was the moment to reveal it to the dead woman's mistress.

The marchioness merely shrugged, though, and said, "What other reason could there be for her being so far from the house? She was meeting a lover, an arranged assignation."

"Cecilia was not like that," Lydia said, her voice tight with tension.

"Mother is likely right," Lord John said with a serious frown that ill suited his round, pleasant face. "You said yourself she was acting different lately. You thought she was just lonely for home."

The young woman's eyes filled with tears as she stared at her husband. "But—"

"Lydia, enough," Lord John said with a quick glance at Anne.

"If you know something, Lady Darkefell," Anne said, staring at the woman, "you should say it. Where were *you* while this was going on?"

The marchioness's eyes widened, and her lips tightened into a slash. She shook her head. A footman opened the door, and the marquess strode in, jacketless, and stalked to the fire, warming his hands in front of it. Anne could see only his profile, but he appeared deeply troubled, not surprising given what his last few hours must have been like. He had sent for the local magistrate and had been closeted with him, presumably, for some time, while his men searched the grounds.

His dark sleek hair was tied back in a queue, confined at the nape of his neck with a black ribbon, but a stray lock fell loosely over his forehead, shadowing his deep-set eyes. His full lips were set in a grim expression. After a moment, he turned and surveyed them, his gaze stopping when he reached Anne. "I find it difficult to believe that, in walking up to the house, you managed to stumble across Cecilia's body among the hundreds—nay, *thousands*—of acres of land surrounding this lodge."

Stung by his cynical tone, Anne retorted, "I beg your pardon. Perhaps I didn't explain myself sufficiently. I did not *stumble* over her body in a stroll toward the house. First I heard howling, an eerie sound that cut through the night. Then I heard a scream. Then footsteps. I *then* heard moaning indicative of someone in trouble. I responded, followed the sound, crashed through some bushes, and *then* stumbled across the body of the girl."

She expected him to reply in kind, with a sarcastic tone, but instead his gaze sharpened.

"You heard footsteps? You didn't say that before. Human footsteps?"

"I was a little distracted." She could hear the soft sound of Lydia's weeping but did not take her eyes off the marquess's arrestingly handsome face. "Of course it was *human* footsteps."

"I've been searching, but so far, found nothing," he muttered, his gaze unfocused. "My first thought was that the attack was by an animal, but you say footsteps… " He trailed off and met her eyes once again, his brow furrowed, his expression deeply troubled. "Are you certain?"

"Yes, and I'm sorry I didn't make myself clear before," she said, employing a more conciliatory tone in the face of his understandable disquiet. "In the heat of the moment—"

"No, don't blame yourself." He smiled at her briefly, a dazzling grin of self-reproach; it disappeared as quickly as it appeared. "You did everything most correctly, and I commend you on your bravery and poise in a terrible situation. Not one woman in a thousand would have behaved as you did. I should have asked more questions before running off." He passed one hand over his thick, dark hair, sweeping the stray locks back from his broad forehead.

Anne had decided she didn't like the man, but she might have to change her mind. He seemed fair-minded and genuinely deeply troubled.

"Tony," his mother said, "could it be…?" She didn't finish but gave her eldest son a significant look that was meant to be understood by him and him alone.

"Could it be *what?* Or whom?" Anne said, unwilling to be left out of any discussion that held conjectures about the perpetrator of the deed. She looked to the marchioness and then the marquess. Neither spoke again, and the marquess gave his mother a stern look that seemed to hold a warning. Perhaps she was hasty in deciding she might have to like him. This was no time to be hiding anything from her, after what she had been through. After her ordeal, she was in no temper to be reasonable. "Do either of you know who may have done this awful deed?"

"Of course not," the marquess said. "I would shield no one who would do such a thing." He gathered them all in his glance. "It's late—I suggest to you all that you get some sleep. The men have been searching the grounds with the dogs for hours but have found nothing. The perpetrator is probably far off by now."

"Ah, so he arrived here just to murder the young woman and then conveniently left, did he?" Anne said. "Even though your estate is miles away from anywhere, as I have cause to know, having walked here from that desolate hovel masquerading as a posthouse. Do you expect me to believe that a complete stranger would have come so far, found a maid wandering about in the night, attacked her, and then disappeared without a trace?"

Lydia was sobbing again, and her husband murmured, trying to soothe her, but Anne had no time for her hysterics. She was not about to let the marquess go without answering.

"I'm suggesting nothing of the kind," he said, his mouth tight with repressed fury.

"Then what *are* you saying?"

"I have no answer, my lady, nor do I owe you an explanation."

Shouts in the corridor outside the parlor door drew all of their attention.

"Good heavens. What is that commotion?" Lady Darkefell asked.

The door flew open, banging against a table and rocking the vase upon it, and a man strode in. He was slender and very dark skinned, wore gold-rimmed spectacles, and carried a sheaf of papers clutched in one fist. "What is this about?" he cried. "I just heard that Miss Wainwright was hurt! I heard... what is going on?"

Lydia gasped and put one hand over her mouth, and Anne's gaze, drawn to her friend, passed over Lady Darkefell, noting peripherally that the woman's mouth drew up slightly in one corner.

"Osei," the marquess said, his tone fraught with tension. "Calm yourself, man!"

The fellow stood stock still and stared at Darkefell. "Where is she? I was just walking with her in the garden not more than three hours ago—what has happened? An accident? Let me see her." For a long moment, tension tightened the very air of the parlor, and no sound cut through it. His dark eyes were wide with horror, and the sheaf of papers quivered. "Tell me," he pleaded, looking from face to face.

Darkefell walked slowly over to him and put one hand on his shoulder. "Osei, I have sad news."

"About Cecilia? What do you mean?"

"Not here—let's go back to the castle."

"No, *tell* me!"

"Tony, tell him. He looks ghastly, but I'm sure he can handle the truth," the marquess's mother said. She turned. "Cecilia is dead, Mr. Boatin, murdered. While she was out of the house *with* someone, it is conjectured."

Even if Lady Darkefell had not mentioned the possibility just moments before, and even if he had not said he was walking with her just hours before, Anne would have known that the man had a personal interest in Lydia's unfortunate maid. His face twisted in anguish, and he fell to his knees, releasing the papers in his hand; they scattered in a drift, like rustling autumn leaves. "No!" he shouted. "How is that possible? How—"

Darkefell gave his mother a disgusted look and grasped the other fellow by the shoulder. "Osei, come with me this instant." He pulled the fellow to his feet, but even as the man turned away, doubled over in agony, Anne could see the tears streaming down his cheeks, the dark skin ashen in cast. "Wait for me in the hall!" Darkefell ordered, giving him a shove toward the door. The fellow stumbled out on stiff legs.

The marquess turned back to them all. He gave his mother a long level look then included them all in his scanning gaze. "I will be searching for the perpetrator of this outrage all night. Do *not* discuss this terrible event with anyone until I've had time to investigate thoroughly."

"You cannot forbid us from discussing it among ourselves, my lord," Anne said.

"I mean what I say—not a word, not even to one another!" he commanded, one finger raised. "I will be most harsh to *anyone* who disobeys me! I include you in that, Lady Anne."

"That is unforgivably high-handed, my lord," Anne said, "but given the circumstances, I will forgive your severity. However—"

"Good evening," he said loudly over her last words, and then he bowed, whirled, and left.

Anne, in a fit of pique, excused herself and made her way back upstairs. From her room, she gazed out the window over the landscape and could see, in the waning moonlight, the marquess, his white shirt glimmering, striding up a hill with his arm over the shoulders of the unusual Mr. Boatin. Infuriating fellow, the marquess. On the morrow she would have to demand answers from him, but tonight she would speak to Lydia. There had to be something going on besides all of the superstitious nonsense in her letter, and that "something" had perhaps ended in murder.

Three

LORD JOHN REFUSED TO ALLOW HIS WIFE TO BE
disturbed, claiming she was tucked in her bed, dosed
with laudanum, the housekeeper at her bedside. He
then retreated to his own room and would not answer
Anne's questions, though she spent half an hour at his
door, knocking and entreating him to be reasonable.
She desperately wanted to know what was going on,
but no one would tell her a thing.

Disgruntled, she finally decided to retire, even
though her exhaustion had transformed into a frenetic
vigor. The housekeeper, still closeted with Lydia,
would not come out even to bring order to the
chaotic household, so Anne was on her own. She
went through a few awkward contortions—ladies'
clothes were not intended to be managed without
help—pulled off her dress and summoned a maid
to take it away for brushing, and then removed her
mangled hat, the plume damaged beyond repair,
tossing it on the vanity table.

She tugged a brush through the tangled mass of
her heavy curls and stared in the mirror at her ghostly

gray eyes, underlined by dark smudges. When she finally did climb into bed, scandalously clad only in her shift, she was furious and wide awake. She blew out her candle and stared through the darkness at the ceiling, reciting the calumny of the household, until the memory of a pair of dark eyes intruded. She stared into the darkness and considered what she knew of the Marquess of Darkefell.

He had attained his title several years before, after his father's death, and held a string of minor titles as well, with estates scattered across England. Darkefell Castle was, however, the largest and was his principal seat. He was unmarried and the eldest of three brothers—one, Lord Julius Bestwick, had died just a year ago. There were ladies in society who kept a list of all eligible men, and he was on it, though never the first, for his abhorrence of marriage was well known and bruited about town as an example of his eccentricity. So he was known in social circles and journeyed to London for Parliament every year, but gossip damned him as reclusive and arrogant to the point of unpleasantness. Having met him, she couldn't say he was exactly *unpleasant*. He was arrogant, yes—commanding, intelligent, and enigmatic. Weaker people than she could be intimidated and find him disagreeable. In direct opposition to the favored pale, gentle, artistic youths beloved by many young ladies, the marquess was dark and bold. He was not a beautiful man in the modern sense, but he *was* dangerously compelling, with those fine eyes that would bore holes through a simpering maiden looking for an easy conquest.

But *she* was no wilting pansy either, not as she once was. She turned on her side, pounded her pillow, and thought of herself seven years before, a plain, awkward, and frightened eighteen-year-old girl in her first Season. She had been opinionated and clever, but her fashionable mother, training her for her Season, regally proclaimed that men did not like women they suspected were more intelligent than they; therefore, she must hide her cleverness. So she had become graceless and unnatural, afraid to speak lest it be discovered that she knew a few things.

Anne closed her eyes, but immediately the image of Lord Darkefell, his grim face pale above the bloody body of Cecilia Wainwright in his arms, assailed her. She would never go to sleep if she kept seeing that!

She went back to considering her past, a safe and boring subject. As desirous of all of the courting and fuss as any other young lady, she had gone along with the charade of idiocy. In elaborate detail, her mother had explained that, as Anne was "unfortunate" in appearance, she must make up for it by being the perfect model of ladylike behavior. Once she was married and had produced children, then she could become as original as she wished, exposing her intellect in public places.

So, imitating the most sought-after beauties of that London Season, she became vacuous against her natural intellect, vain in defiance of her plainness, and frivolous despite a desperate need to do something that mattered. In private she read Descartes and Mary Astell; in public she discussed face powder and the latest fashion in bonnets.

All the determined subduing of her natural personality, the deliberate downplaying of her intelligence and education, worked. Sir Reginald Gladstone Moore, a conceited and dim-witted captain in the Horse Guards—and Lydia's older brother—had taken an interest in her. Before long, in a bored and nasal tone, he made the appropriate requests of her parents, said the usual banalities, and they were engaged to be married without a murmur of protest from her.

The ongoing trouble with the American colonies escalated. He journeyed across the ocean with his regiment to earn glory on the battlefield and lost his life in the decisive American siege at Yorktown, in the colony of Virginia, in the autumn of '81. When the news reached her of Reginald's death, she was in London to bespeak a wedding trousseau. With her engagement tragically ended, she retreated to her home in Kent for a period of mourning and never came back out. The London Season had been a torture chamber for her at eighteen, and at almost twenty, her mourning done, she didn't think it would have improved.

In that intervening time, a year of quietude and reflection, she questioned whether marriage would provide her with the freedom for which she longed. It seemed to be a move from one form of imprisonment—the proper behavior expected of a young, unmarried lady—to another form, becoming one man's burden forever, bearing child after child to fulfill her marital duty. Her father was studious, quiet, and did not bother himself with her activities. As long as she observed society's dictates in matters of attire and public behavior, he was untroubled by the shame of a spinster daughter and quite happy for her to remain in his home forever, taking the place of her mother as nominal mistress of Harecross Hall. Her mother preferred the convivial social whirl of Bath, and lived there with *her* mother, the Dowager Viscountess Everingham.

Anne had received a bequest from her paternal grandmother upon her twenty-first birthday, and so was independently wealthy; with her father's amiable aid, she had access to her fortune. A husband would not be as understanding as her father, she feared. Her mother, though furious with her over her refusal to come back to the London Season after her period of mourning to try a second time to capture a husband, had no power to control Anne's life beyond the weight of guilt she tried to inflict on her daughter.

Guilt did not work. Anne had broken free of that burdensome emotion when she decided against marriage, at least for the time being. Someday she might meet the right sort of man, but until then, life as a spinster bluestocking suited her. She had no desire to be notorious, and so observed the proprieties—she always had a chaperone when at their house in London; Lolly, a dotty aunt, was happy to accompany her wherever she went—but there had been no time to acquire her aunt's services in this instance. Lydia's letter was quite specific as to the fear she felt and the anguish she suffered. This was the first time Anne had broken with convention to travel north to this wild place alone; it was a simple coincidence that she had immediately stumbled over a dead body, but she was sure her mother would see it as divine punishment. Anne turned over, still sleepless, turning her mind away from the brutalized maid and back to her own life, a safer subject to induce drowsiness.

Anne would have been unhappy as Captain Sir Reginald Gladstone Moore's wife; he was dreadfully vain and had chosen her deliberately, she now understood, because of her plainness, so his dandified looks would always outshine hers. Five years after his death, as little as she thought of her late betrothed, she would never interfere with Lydia's idealization of her brother as wonderful beyond words, and Anne as dying of love for him.

She turned over again and tried to sleep, but slumber was chased away by the awful memory of the evening's events. That poor girl, Cecilia Wainwright. To think she had heard the young woman's last cries and moans. *And* heard the footsteps of the perpetrator, whoever that was. Had she been out meeting a lover, as Lady Darkefell conjectured? And was that lover Mr. Osei Boatin, as seemed indicated by his highly emotional response to the news of her death? He had been out walking with her, he said, but his violent reaction to the news of her death meant he either had nothing to do with her murder or dissembled to appear innocent. The savagery of the attack, though, did not seem such as could be inflicted by a lover. And what creature had howled with such eerie wildness? With so much to wonder, she would never get to sleep. The house was dark and silent around her, and she stared up at the ceiling, feeling terribly alone.

But weariness won out, and she fell into Morpheus's welcoming arms. When she next became conscious, it was morning, and a young woman was setting a tray on her bedside table. Anne spied a glimmer of tears in the girl's red-rimmed eyes before she turned away to pull back the draperies.

"What's your name?" Anne asked, propping herself up on one elbow and examining the contents of the mahogany tray: a pot of steaming chocolate and a plain white china cup, a damask napkin, and a hothouse rose in a crystal vase.

"Ellen, milady," the girl said, turning away from the window and curtseying, her dull stuff gown silent, her neck and shoulders modestly wrapped in a neckerchief of snowy white. As with all good servants, she would not be heard arriving or departing and could move as a ghost through the house, unnoticed except when needed.

"Well, Ellen, in future could you ask Cook to send up a rack of toast with my chocolate? I'm often hungry first thing in the morning." Anne blinked and gazed out at the sun, now ascending over the spring landscape. "And could it be an hour earlier? I'm generally an early riser. I slept past my usual rising this morning."

"Yes'm," the girl said, turning away.

"Excuse me, Ellen," Anne said. When the girl turned back, her head hung, she continued gently, "I'm sure no one else has noticed that you've been weeping, and the tears still stand in your eyes. Were you close to the poor unfortunate who last night met her end?"

She nodded and snuffled.

"What was she like?"

The girl looked startled at her opinion being sought. "Milady?"

"What was Cecilia Wainwright like? If you are so deeply affected after presumably a short acquaintance, I must guess she was an engaging girl?"

Ellen nodded. "She were, milady." A shaky sigh ended with a sob. "Cecilia would do anything for anyone."

Anne examined the pretty, guileless face framed by blonde curls and a white lacy mob cap. The rosy cheeks were marred only by tear trails down them. "You mourn her, and yet you've known Cecilia only since she came here with Lady Bestwick?" That was a few short months before.

"Yes'm." She sniffed back tears. "Before that it were only Lady Darkefell and Lord John Bestwick in this house, you know. When Lady John came and brought Cecilia… why, it was like the house became sunny."

"So what was she like?" Anne repeated, swinging her feet out of bed and stretching.

"Cecilia? She were so very pretty and good-natured, not stuck on herself like Lady Darkefell's French abigail, Therese. Cecilia even give me a silk wrap her ladyship didn't want no more, and it only had two small rips in it!"

Anne sighed at such a vague answer. "Did she get along with the rest of the staff? Or did she put on airs?" A lady's maid was a superior servant and often felt the difference between herself and the others most keenly; abigails and valets were next only to the butler and housekeeper in importance at the servants' table. Divisions below stairs were as rigid as those above stairs.

"Oh, no, milady. Cecilia were pleasant to everyone." Ellen looked uneasy and began to glance at the door.

"Did she have a sweetheart?" Anne asked.

The girl shook her head but would not speak again. "Does that mean you don't know?"

"I'm sure I couldn't say," she said, a remote expression on her tearstained face. "If that's all?"

Anne sighed. Once a good servant had gone silent, there would be no opening her mouth until another emotional, vulnerable moment. "I shall need my portmanteaux retrieved from that unspeakable post-house. Until I have them, I must wear the traveling dress I wore yesterday. Has it been brushed?"

The young woman nodded. "Mrs. Hailey done it herself. She sponged it out, seeing as how… seeing… " She trailed off and paled.

Anne nodded. "I understand," she said. The sponging was necessary because blood had gotten on the skirts of the dress, though it had not been noticeable in the dim light of the previous evening. She turned her mind away from that dreadful thought. "Could you see that my dress is brought up to me and return to help me with it? I expect my abigail, Mary, to arrive some time tomorrow with my trunks, but until then I'll need someone's help. I don't wish to trouble Lady John or Lady Darkefell. Perhaps, if you're willing and Mrs. Hailey allows you enough time, you could try taming my hair," she said, putting up one hand and feeling the tangled mass. "It needs a stern hand. And could you see that I get hot water immediately?"

Ellen agreed and quickly returned with the garment, as well as the traveling cloak and shawl, which she hung up in the wardrobe in the attached dressing room. A younger maid carrying a ewer of hot water accompanied her and filled the washing bowl on the dressing table. Anne washed, then dressed with Ellen's help, and sat at the dressing table so the maid could do her hair. If Anne had her morning gown, a more relaxed style would have been appropriate, but with only her traveling attire, she couldn't leave her hair down. It would be most unsuitable.

"Do you like your position here, Ellen?" Anne glanced up at her face in the dressing-table mirror.

The young woman was pale but composed and said, "I do, milady."

Anne watched her in the mirror. The young woman frowned as she tugged at a recalcitrant lock of hair. It would probably have been better for her scalp's sake to have borrowed the services of Lady Darkefell's abigail, but that woman would have to help Lydia now, too, no doubt. She did have another purpose in retaining Ellen's services, though; Anne had already made inroads with the maid, as far as trust was concerned, and was determined to learn more about what was worrying Lydia. "Has it always been safe hereabouts, Ellen?"

"Safe?"

"Yes, safe. Do you all feel secure walking the grounds?"

"D'you mean, are we scared of ending up like Cecilia?"

"No, I didn't exactly mean that—I'm speaking of *before* last night."

"Well… " She sounded a little reluctant but then said, "Lately it's been a little anxious. We been told not to go a'walkin' out after dark."

"By whom?"

"Mrs. Hailey."

"Why is that?" Anne said, thinking that, considering what had happened, it seemed a prophetic instruction.

The young woman's eyes were wide, with an excited gleam in them, the first emotion other than sadness that Anne had seen. "The werewolf, ma'am!" she whispered, meeting Anne's reflected gaze.

Anne burst out laughing. "Werewolf?" Despite having been prepared by Lydia's letter for the absurdity, the notion still struck her as humorous.

Affronted into silence, Ellen continued work on Anne's hair, her lips primmed into a straight line.

"I didn't mean to laugh at you, but really, a werewolf? You're an intelligent girl and surely don't believe in such idiocy."

"I seen it with my own two good eyes." With a final tug, Ellen pronounced her task done. "How d'you like the style, milady? I never done hair before, but it seems passable good to me."

Looking at her reflection, twisting her head this way and that, Anne had to admit it echoed a truly classic Grecian style, even mythic; Medusa was, after all, a Greek mythic creature, and Anne's hair now resembled the snaky locks of the gorgon. "How interesting," she said faintly and turned away from the mirror. A woman of humble appearance needed all the help a talented hairdresser could summon, so her image at that moment was shocking to Anne's modest *amour propre*. However, she did have other things on her mind than her tortured hair. "You cannot make me believe that you saw a werewolf. What exactly *did* you see?"

"Well," Ellen said, frowning and staring at the floor, "I were out walkin'—"

"Alone?"

"Yes... nooo... I was... uh..."

"Never mind with whom," Anne said, watching the young woman's pale complexion burn cherry red on her high cheeks. "You weren't alone, but were out walking with a young man of the household. Have I guessed correctly?"

"Yes, milady," Ellen said. "We was walkin' near the tower—"

"The tower?"

"Yes'm. 'Twas built by the previous marquess when he was first raised up to be such. Before that he was the Earl of Staunby. The new title was given him after the trouble with Scotland."

"After the Jacobite rebellion?"

"Yes'm."

"About the time of Culloden Tower, then," Anne said, naming the tower built near Richmond forty years before to celebrate the defeat of the Jacobite rebellion.

The girl shrugged and said, "We ain't supposed to go near it, but…"

Anne eyed her with interest. "But it's a shadowy spot, and one is able to cuddle with a young man, and no one the wiser."

Ellen blushed and nodded, then looked away again. "Me an' Jamey—he's a groom, milady, one of the marquess's men—we was walkin,' when out of the bushes near the tower jumps this animal. On his hind legs! Never seen a dog do that!" She looked directly into Anne's eyes and whispered, "I were terrified!"

"What time of day was this?"

"Just on twilight, milady."

"How long ago did this take place?"

"Two months or more gone. 'Twas fearful cold, so we was seekin' shelter to talk."

"And what did you do when this creature jumped out at you?"

"I ran away," she said. She picked up a brush and began to clean the hair from its bristles.

"And what did Jamey do?"

"Followed me."

"Immediately?"

"Near enough," Ellen said. "A minute or so later."

"What delayed him?"

Ellen frowned and thumbed the brush, absently playing with the bristles. "I don't know, milady."

"What did he say when he caught up to you?"

She blushed and looked away, setting down the brush on the highly polished dressing table.

"I see. Probably nothing beyond some personal nonsense to comfort you."

She nodded. Anne watched her for a minute, but was satisfied that the young woman was telling the truth such as she knew it. The fellow's "comfort" was likely a few kisses and a cuddle. "You say it was an animal but that it stood on its hind legs."

Ellen nodded but didn't offer anything more.

"Did it growl or bark or make any other noise?"

"It howled, milady."

"Howled."

"Yes, the snout went up, kind of, and it howled. Jamey said since 'twas the night of the full moon, it must be a werewolf."

Anne pondered that, remembering the eerie howling she had heard the previous night. "And that is all you saw before you ran?"

"Oh, yes, milady. I ran toward the back kitchen garden and through the gate."

"And that's where Jamey caught up with you?"

She nodded.

"Ellen, I no more believe you saw a werewolf than I believe that people can sprout wings and fly. Your young man and a confederate are in the business of frightening young women into their arms, no doubt, a shabby trick but meant just as a lark."

"Oh, *no,* milady," Ellen said, sitting down on a nearby stool. Such a breach of proper behavior seemed out of character for the reticent maid and spoke to her complete absorption in the topic. "Others since have seen the werewolf, milady, and for longer'n me."

"Really?"

"Yes."

Anne again considered the howling she had heard, a precursor to the young woman's screams. "Ellen, tell me who else has—"

"Ellen!" A peremptory female voice from the hallway beyond the door harshly repeated the girl's name.

The maid leaped to her feet and rushed out to the hallway, where two voices, hers and the authoritative woman, could be heard, Ellen murmuring apologies and the other scolding.

Anne marched to the door and flung it open.

A plump woman with protuberant eyes whirled and adjusted her expression from one of command to a more complaisant look. "Milady," she said, softening her voice, "your portmanteaux have been brought to the lodge by a neighboring gentleman. Andrew will bring them upstairs momentarily."

Anne eyed Ellen, and then, noting the return of tears to the maid's eyes, turned to the housekeeper.

Levelly, she said, "You are the most excellent Mrs. Hailey, of whom I have heard so many good things. You were helpful to poor Lydia last night in her distress. Thank you for the loan of Ellen—I would not have been able to dress without her, and thank you for your own services in rendering my limited wardrobe wearable once again." She waved down at the skirts of her traveling dress.

The housekeeper curtseyed and said, "You're welcome, I'm sure, milady." She fingered her chatelaine and added, eyeing Anne's snaky hairstyle, "I was pleased to do it. I only hope Ellen has been helpful."

"She has, thank you. Is Lady John better this morning?"

"Poor lamb," the housekeeper said in a confidential tone as Ellen slipped away down the hall. "Still sleeping. Gave her another sleeping draught in the middle of the night, for she was having dreadful nightmares."

"Let me know when she's able to see me. Now, you say a neighbor has brought my portmanteaux to the house. May I express to this gentleman my personal gratitude?"

"Yes, milady—he's in the morning parlor with Lady Darkefell."

Anne found her way there and entered. It was an elegant room, the walls hung in yellow silk damask, and furnished in modern oriental style. The dowager marchioness was by a table in a bay window, earnestly speaking with a portly, jovial-appearing gentleman. "Good morning," Anne said to announce her presence to the oblivious duo.

Lady Darkefell straightened and moved away from the man, who turned and bowed low.

"Lady Anne Addison?" he said, his voice pleasantly timbered and musical.

"Yes, but I don't have the pleasure of your name, sir?"

The marchioness nodded to Anne. "Good morning. I hope you slept well."

"Adequately."

"Lady Anne Addison, may I introduce to you Mr. Hiram Grover?"

Anne nodded to the gentleman. "Thank you, sir, for bringing my baggage up to Ivy Lodge. How did you happen to find out from that villainous postmaster that they were to be delivered here?"

"I am the nearest neighbor to the lodge and the castle, and often bring the mail up—neighborly courtesy, you know. Jacob Landers, the postmaster, sent me the bags with a note, along with the mail for both myself and the castle."

"What an easy method for the post employee to slough off responsibility," she commented.

"Lady Anne," the marchioness said, "I had just invited Hiram to dine with us. Will you join us in the breakfast room?"

Nothing had been said of the awful murder, but Anne assumed that the marchioness had already filled in her neighbor. She was right. They removed to the breakfast room, a smaller octagonal room with cherry silk on the walls and various gilt-framed paintings of roses, and the servants had, at the marchioness's request, left them to their meal.

Mr. Grover said, "I am horrified that you were subjected to such an experience last night, Lady Anne, as finding that poor, unfortunate girl. The fragility of a lady should never have been put to such a brutal test—as the

Italians say, *una signora dovrebbe essere protetta*. I congratulate you on your hardiness, for I am in amazement that you should be on your feet and not prostrate."

Anne eyed him while she chewed a mouthful of eggs with mushroom ketchup. He was a fleshy fellow, porcine in countenance, with friendly features and a perfectly coiffed wig on top of an egg-shaped head. His cheeks were ruddy, the redness like a rash, but not from the cold; rather, it appeared to be redness associated with good food and drink, too much of both. And a choleric disposition? He seemed pleasant enough, so perhaps not.

Despite his words, he likely considered it no compliment to note that she was well after such an occurrence, and no doubt felt that Lydia was more the ideal of feminine fragility for keeping to her bed. "I'm stronger than that, sir."

"But to have stumbled over the bloodied body! It's dreadful." He shuddered delicately and bit into a forkful of ham. He chewed for a moment, while Lady Darkefell sipped a cup of tea and broke a piece of toast into bits on her plate. "Whatever possessed you to venture so far off the lane, my lady?" he asked.

"So far off the lane?"

"Why, you must have been quite a ways off the lane to have found the body, for I understand it was well concealed."

"Who told you that?" she asked.

He bridled. "My lady," he said, clearly insulted by her briskness, "I have heard all about it from Lady Darkefell."

The door to the breakfast room was flung open just then, and Lord Darkefell and Lord John entered, intent on some conversation.

"… insist she receive a proper burial in the servants' cemetery," the marquess rumbled, his handsome mouth pulled down in a scowl. "I'll not hear of any nonsense from Lydia about it."

"But Lydia's concerned about what the others will say, for with Cecilia being…" Lord John broke off when he realized they were not alone.

Anne watched the two brothers, but then focused her attention on the elder, the marquess. His eyes were on Mr. Grover, and his expression was not friendly. Grover, for his part, appeared completely at ease until Mr. Osei Boatin entered a few moments later. He then got up, pulled out a pocket watch on a too-short chain, examined it closely, then dabbed at his lips and bowed to the gathering. He took Lady Darkefell's hand, kissed the air above it, and murmured a farewell.

With a fulminating look, Darkefell watched him go.

"What is all of this nonsense?" Lady Darkefell demanded, glancing between her sons.

"It will keep until later," Darkefell said, grabbing a plate from the sideboard, filling it randomly with eggs, ham, and bacon until it was heaped high, and taking a seat by Anne. "How do you fare this morning, my lady?" he asked, casting her a sideways glance. He eyed her hairstyle with an awed expression and suppressed a quick smile. "You seem in excellent good looks this morning, none the worse for your awful experience."

"Your enthusiasm for my appearance is a paean to the lack of my lady's maid, Mary, who will arrive tomorrow, I hope," Anne said, her tone as dry as his was humorous. "Though if you think this style suits me," she continued, patting her snaky locks, "I'll be sure to have Mary copy its intricacies."

"I'm humbled by your reliance on my opinion of the mysteries of feminine hairstyling."

"What's going on, Tony?" Lady Darkefell pressed, impatient in the face of her eldest son's absorption in their guest. "Why were you and John arguing about where Cecilia will be buried?"

"I'd rather not go into it right now," the marquess said, then wolfed down a rasher of streaky bacon. His secretary, Mr. Boatin, was taking a plate from the sideboard and slowly adding a piece of toast to it. His expression was solemn. He didn't appear hungry but seemed to Anne to be focusing on the sideboard as a way of avoiding the others. That he ate with the family was no surprise, for though a secretary was a kind of servant in some households, he was also a valuable member of the household and privy to matters of the most intimate nature. No man kept secrets from his valet or his secretary.

"Mother, Lydia just doesn't think it's right for Cecilia to be buried in the castle graveyard with the other servants," Lord John said primly, sitting down at the table without taking any breakfast.

"Whyever not?"

"There's no need to answer that, John!" Darkefell said, mumbling around a mouthful of food.

"I'll answer if I want to!" the younger man said indignantly.

Darkefell glanced over at Boatin, who had paused, ham-laden serving fork in hand. The marquess swallowed and hastily said in a loud voice, "Shut your *mouth,* John, if you please!"

But he was overridden by his younger brother, who angrily said, "Why should I? All will know eventually, to the shame of our household. She is not *fit* to bury with the others, for she was carrying a bastard child."

There was a crash behind them, and Anne started from her chair and whirled. It was Mr. Boatin; he had tumbled to the floor, unconscious, spilling eggs and ham over his spotless waistcoat and frock coat.

Four

MR. BOATIN WAS REVIVED AND LED AWAY BY THE marquess, so Anne was unable to find out anything more of interest. Lady Darkefell and Lord John, too, melted away after the commotion. Left alone in the breakfast room, Anne finished eating as the maids, supervised by Andrew, the head footman, cleaned up the food and broken china spilled by the secretary. She pondered the events of the last twelve hours, but decided ultimately that the murder was unlikely to have any connection to what she had journeyed to Yorkshire to investigate on Lydia's behalf, the werewolf sightings.

But there was no way to be sure; Cecilia's murder did strike far too close to her friend. And there was a further mystery there—who was the father of Cecilia's unborn child? Did her pregnancy have anything to do with her tragic death? Anne could not rest easy and let other minds attempt to untangle it. If she was to find out anything, though, she would need to get each family member alone. That would take time and subtlety, difficult for an impatient and direct woman like herself.

It took Anne only an hour after the unpleasant-ness at breakfast to master the layout of Ivy Lodge. Curiosity demanded that she uncover the secrets of a place: its layout, how the family lived, where the private apartments were. Though her ankle was still aching from turning it the previous evening, she ignored the throbbing.

Ivy Lodge was modest in size, a three-floor, red-brick residence built in the early years of the previous century, she knew. The entry was the centerpiece of a marble faux-pillared front, carved deeply with orna-mental scrollwork and lozenges. All three floors were glazed with innumerable mullioned windows, and the whole was topped by a roofline made interesting by openwork parapets.

She would have known nothing about the exterior yet, having arrived so late the night before, but there was a detailed painting of Ivy Lodge hanging in the upstairs gallery hallway, above the entrance, along with a portrait of several Earls of Staunby and the first marquess. There was also an enormous painting of the dowager marchioness, her late husband, and their children. The current marquess, as the heir apparent, was holding the family bible open on his lap, with his left index finger pointing to his name inscribed. She frowned up at it. There was Lord John, the younger brother, just an infant in the portrait, but also another boy who looked exactly like the young marquess. Something teased at her memory but was not yet ready to come to the surface.

After her exploration, satisfied that she would not get lost again, she marched up to Lydia's chamber and stood before the door for a moment, thinking. She didn't want to knock, only to be ignored. Much better to simply slip in. She eased the door open, and there, on a Jacobean monstrosity of a bed—four heavily carved posts, a headboard that was deeply engraved with armorial patterns, and a ceiling that loomed over the poor girl like a coffin lid—was Lydia, sleeping, the dishevelment of the bedclothes a testament to the truth of Mrs. Hailey's assertion that the young woman had slept poorly before a draught had been administered.

But she had slept enough by now. Anne approached the bed, pulled a chair close, and sat down. She watched Lydia for a moment, observing the same jumping nerve in the neck as she witnessed during the previous night's swoon.

"Lydia, dear, it's me. I shan't leave until we talk, you know. I don't know why you invited me here if you're going to ignore me."

Anne's young friend stirred and yawned. She prettily "awoke," holding the back of one soft hand to her pale cheek. She really was a beauty, Anne thought, sitting back to watch the performance. Her chestnut curls tumbled about her bare shoulder, the white nightgown having slipped off one and draped her round arm. Her skin was pale as milk, her eyes dazzling blue, and her lips twin buds of cerise. Not being one herself, Anne had always admired beautiful women as one might admire a work of art one could never own.

"Oh, Anne, dear!" Lydia held out one fine-boned hand in a beseeching gesture. "How kind of you to travel all this way to visit me!"

"All very well," Anne said dryly, "but why, if you consider my visit such a kindness, did you warn no one I was coming?"

"It slipped my mind."

Anne sighed. Her hands folded on her lap, she said, "Now this is a pretty dance you've led me, Lydia, but last night was not entertaining. That poor girl!"

Tears welled in Lydia's blue eyes and dripped down her cheeks. Somehow she managed, even when sobbing openly, to appear lovely. She covered her eyes with both hands. "Don't be cruel, please, for I'm truly heartbroken. Cecilia was all I have here at this awful place. Everyone else hates me."

"Oh, come. You have John, and he loves you very much."

Lydia dropped her hands to her lap and brought her knees up to her chin, her tears drying. "No, he regrets marrying me—I'm too silly and stupid. The moment we came here, his awful mother and brother began to pick away at me."

This was not the topic that Anne wished to pursue, and she knew her friend well enough to understand that, once focused on her suffering, it required firmness to redirect Lydia's thoughts. "Who wanted to harm poor Cecilia? I remember her a little—she always seemed a nicely behaved girl to me. Had she gotten in trouble?" Anne asked, thinking of the shocking condition she apparently was in at death.

According to Lord John, Lydia knew all about it, but her expression was now veiled. "Trouble? I don't know what you mean."

"Lydia," Anne said, standing. "I'll just go home if you don't intend to confide in me."

"No! Don't go!" Lydia slipped from bed, donned a wrapper that was draped over the foot, and tiptoed to the door; she closed it tightly, then raced back across the room and jumped in bed, shivering. "I hate this place."

"Don't be childish," Anne replied, stern in the face of such a petulant statement.

"You don't know what it's been like." She pulled the covers up over her legs.

Cecilia's murder was a topic Lydia was clearly not prepared to tackle. All right, then. "I've heard stories of your werewolf from the maid who helped me this morning," Anne said. "But why don't you tell me about it?"

She took a long, trembling breath and began; at first she thought it a joke, one she and John laughed about. She blushed a little when she said that, and Anne suspected some husband and wife tomfoolery was involved, but she directed her imagination away from such a topic as the intimate details of a married couple.

"But then Therese, Lady Sophie's abigail, saw it in the flesh, too. And it ripped some sheep to shreds, up in the hills and down at Mr. Grover's. It's so terrible!" Lydia began to breathe quickly and paled.

"Lydia, calm yourself. There is no point in making yourself hysterical."

"That's so like you, Anne. As if I *choose* to become hysterical!"

"You *do* choose it," Anne said. "I see the signs and know the patterns. Women use hysteria as a retreat from difficulties. While you're indulging in hysteria, you need not handle anything and will be looked after by men and serving women."

Lydia, distracted from her mounting frenzy, eyed her with a pout. "You are so very unfeminine, Anne. No wonder you have not found another beau. Men would not like so unwomanly a woman."

Disregarding the insult, Anne went on, "I find it interesting that fainting spells and hysteria are the sole province of women of the upper classes. Farmers' wives, serving girls, dairymaids… you'll never see one of them swoon from hysteria."

"That's because they're less delicate. Really, Anne, that you would class us among such creatures!" Lydia fanned herself with one hand.

"Now, see, you're working yourself up this moment, and yet if I change the topic to, say, shoes, you would become quite calm again."

Lydia stared at her and shook her head. "I have never understood you."

"I note that you did not call any other woman to your rescue, not your sister nor even your mother."

"Why would I call upon them? They would be no help to me at all!"

"Exactly."

Lydia eyed her, brow furrowed in pretty confusion. "I don't think I understand."

Anne sighed. "No, of course you don't." Satisfied that Lydia showed no signs of lapsing back into a swoon, she said, "Now, about this werewolf nonsense—"

"But it's not nonsense, for even the marquess has not denied there could be one."

Anne thought of the man, bold as a pirate, dark and masculine, hardier by far than his pallid younger brother. "That interests me. I will have to engage him on the topic."

They spoke for a while longer, and Lydia told her all that had occurred in the last two months, the gutted sheep, the frightened village girls who had been chased by the animal back to Hornethwaite, the market town nearby.

"And does this latest attack upon poor Cecilia not prove the presence of a werewolf?" Lydia asked with a shudder. "No human would kill a simple maidservant!"

"There is no such thing as werewolves. The agent of that girl's destruction must have been either animal or human, not some frantic amalgam of the two." Anne paused but then approached a delicate topic. "I'm interested in Lord Darkefell's secretary, Mr. Boatin. Where is he from?"

"Don't be afraid of him, Anne. I was at first, you know—afraid of him, that is, because he's so dark and different—but he's very genteel and speaks just like any normal person."

Anne restrained a sigh. Sometimes she thought that Lydia needed to be shaken, with the hope that her brains would settle in a more sensible pattern than the one with which God had seen fit to gift her. "I have observed him and heard him speak and don't expect any wild behavior from him." She calmed the sarcastic edge to her voice—sarcasm was too sharp a weapon to wield against silly Lydia, like picking up a carving knife to cut butter—and went on with a gentler humor: "The marquess, I think, is much more likely to alarm me with wild fits, for he seems… hmm, hotheaded. But have you ever observed Mr. Boatin with Cecilia?"

Lydia shook her head.

"Did Cecilia have any beaux among the footmen or grooms?"

"Maids are not allowed flirtations!" Lydia said, eyes wide. "You should know better than that, Anne. Mother says in any well-regulated household, the behavior of the maidservants is a reflection on the propriety of the ladies of the house."

"I have always thought it unfair that maids, being young women, are not allowed their share of flirtations, for how can a female sustain life without them?" Anne smiled at Lydia, whose eyes were widening again. How *could* the girl continue to be so naïve, even after marriage? And given that Cecilia was with child, how could Lydia continue in the blithe assumption that the girl had no flirtations? It was not immaculate conception, and the alternative was that Cecilia became pregnant from a liaison with the marquess or Lord John. "The plain reality is, there would not be so many former maidservants hastily married to publicans and grooms, and bearing robust seven-month babies, if they did not engage in flirtation and something beyond."

Lydia blushed; Anne watched her with interest. Judging from the conversation between the marquess and his brother at the breakfast table, Lydia knew about Cecilia's state. She must have *some* notion with whom her maid was intimate.

Lydia, putting her hands to her flaming cheeks, asked, "Do you think she and Mr. Boatin… is that why you ask about him?"

"Please don't assume or insinuate until we know more, and do *not* share my speculation with anyone.

I just don't know, but the young man was deeply distraught at her death. Perhaps they had merely established a particularly close friendship." Anne paused then said slowly, watching her younger friend's face, "My dear, I know that you're aware of Cecilia's pregnancy."

Her lower lip trembled, and tears welled in her eyes. She turned her face away.

Anne sighed. "Do you know who the father was?"

"How can you ask me such a vulgar question?"

"It would help the magistrate if you did know and could tell."

"The magistrate?"

"Well, yes. Whoever the father is, if he had reason not to let anyone know, he could have killed her to keep her silent. After all, her condition would have soon become obvious."

Lydia paled and grasped the covers to her bosom. "I h-hadn't thought of that. No, she didn't confide in me."

"Is that the truth?"

She turned her face away and mumbled, "Of course."

"Are you sure?"

"Anne, please!"

From long acquaintance, recognizing that her friend would say nothing more, Anne let it go and stood, patting Lydia's soft hands fisted around handfuls of snowy bedcover. "You look a little peaked. Rest some more, my dear. I have much to find out."

"Please," she whispered brokenly, meeting her friend's steady gaze, "find out what killed poor Cecilia!"

"That's not what I'm here for, Lydia. You asked me to uncover the truth behind the werewolf story."

One lone tear trembled on Lydia's lush lashes then dropped onto her cheek and ran down, dripping off her chin. "I'm so frightened. Please, Anne, you're so brave and clever. Try. Perhaps it was the werewolf. It *must* be the werewolf. You can track it down."

Anne sighed. "I'm neither a magistrate nor a hunter."

"Just try!"

Anne descended, considering Lydia's sudden certainty that the "werewolf" killed Cecilia. Were the werewolf sightings and the murder tied together? It was possible. She set out to find Mrs. Hailey to apprise her of the imminent arrival of her maid, Mary Agnes MacDougall, and her tiger, Wee Robbie. They traveled north in her carriage driven by Sanderson, Anne's coachman. Though Anne didn't wish to put the household out by having to find room for them all, having her own carriage and driver there would offer her the best chance at quickly leaving, should she become weary of the place or if her presence was no longer needed. Having experienced the rude rapidity of the Royal Mail Coach, she was relieved she wouldn't need to travel that way again and could go at a more civilized pace on her return.

Following the delicious smells of roasting goose and venison haunch down narrowing passages toward the utilitarian back offices and kitchen, to the dismay of startled staff, who scurried out of her path, Anne peeked into various chambers: the buttery, the wet larder, and the dry provision room. She passed the butler's room, though since Ivy Lodge seemed to make do without a butler, it was more properly the head footman's room, where he would polish silver and decant the wine. Anne knew that she should have sent a message to the housekeeper by that footman, Andrew, saying she wished to speak with the housekeeper, but impatience was her second-worst failing, after curiosity. And she had ulterior motives in making this foray into the nether regions of Ivy Lodge.

Anne spied a small room off the dark hallway, away from the food and washing area. She peeked in; it was the housekeeper's office. "Ah, Mrs. Hailey," she said.

The woman looked up from a book on a pedestal, with a startled expression in her prominent eyes. "Milady!" she gasped, slipping down off her stool and curtseying.

"I'm sorry to burst in on you like this," Anne said, summoning up what charm she could and occasionally did use to soothe injured pride or hurt feelings. "I'm sure you're dreadfully busy, especially with the awful events of last night. I didn't wish to have you summoned all the way up to my room just to give you a bit of information you will find necessary for my stay." Anne entered the room as she spoke, though she really should have waited for an invitation.

The woman would be within her rights to ask her to leave and to complain about the intrusion to Lady Darkefell, but Anne didn't think Mrs. Hailey would. There was curiosity and intelligence in the depths of the woman's pale eyes, but she merely said, "What information would that be, milady?"

"I'm expecting my maid, Mary MacDougall, to arrive tomorrow and have imposed terribly upon this household by having her bring along my tiger, Robbie. Mary is a widow, and Robbie is her son. My coachman, Sanderson, will be driving them, and I'd like him to stay."

A housekeeper did more than keep house, she kept secrets, both ignominious and monumental; making friends with her would be vital to discovering what was going on at Ivy Lodge and Darkefell Castle. "I don't know who else to ask, and you know better than anyone, Mrs. Hailey," Anne continued in a tone that she hoped subtly flattered the housekeeper and magnified the importance of her position. "Will there be room at Ivy Lodge's stables for my equipage, or should I approach the Marquess about using his facilities?"

Mrs. Hailey blinked rapidly and then said, "The lodge stables are small, milady. If you wish your coachman and team to stay, you'll need to keep them in the castle's stable. I could have Andrew send a message to the marquess's coachman, Varney, if it pleases you? He'll consult with the marquess and tell us what may be done."

"I would consider that a great favor, Mrs. Hailey." Anne hesitated but then plunged in. "I'm still terribly shaken by that poor girl, Cecilia Wainwright's, tragic death. I can only imagine what those of you who knew her must be suffering!"

"Terrible!" Mrs. Hailey said, then glanced toward the door and lowered her voice. "But not surprising."

"Oh?"

"Considering how she did carry on with the gentlemen…" She trailed off with a significant nod and wink.

Anne watched her eyes. The woman's words were deliberately meant to entice conversation. There was a ghoulish delight that sat ill with Anne but might prove useful to encourage. "Really? Do you not think her death the result of a wolf attack?"

"Humph!" she sniffed, jingling her chatelaine, from which dangled a glittering charm on a short gold chain, likely a gift from her employer for long service, or some such thing. "No wolves around here, no matter what the silly girls say."

"I was told you were outside when I arrived last night, in the kitchen garden. Did you not hear a howl, as I did?"

The woman paled. "I did, but... but that was just one of the stable hounds, to be sure."

"It didn't sound like a dog to me. What were you doing out in the garden at that time of night?"

Mrs. Hailey bridled and clamped her mouth shut, but relented a moment later and said, "Lady John was a touch bilious. I went out with Cook to cut some mint and comfrey for a tisane, to settle her stomach."

Anne leaned forward. "So who *do* you think killed Cecilia Wainwright?"

The housekeeper folded her arms over her chest. "Find out who the father of her baby is, I say, and you'll find the murderer."

It was not at all surprising that the housekeeper should be aware of Cecilia's condition. Anne was just opening her mouth to ask who that might be when a shout echoed outside of the lodge, piercing even the thick walls, followed rapidly by an explosion that rattled the windows.

Five

"WHAT WAS THAT?" ANNE CRIED.

"Gardener," Mrs. Hailey replied stoically. She sighed. "Her ladyship is creating a rockery, so Gardener is using that devil's powder to shape a shelf of rock above the lodge."

"Good heavens! I'll go, now, Mrs. Hailey. I'm sorry to intrude on your day."

"I'll send the message to the castle stables about your carriage, ma'am."

"Thank you. By the way," Anne said as if it was an afterthought, "you conjectured the father of Cecilia's child may have killed her—do you know who that is?"

Mrs. Hailey shook her head. "No, milady. Just giving my opinion." Her eyes held a trace of belated wariness after her openness of moments before.

"Had you observed Cecilia with any particular young man?"

"D'you mean, Mr. Boatin, the last one to see 'er alive?"

Anne watched her eyes. A veiled satisfaction at having said the man's name seemed to tremble through her rigid frame. "I understand they were friends?"

"Threw herself at 'im, she did," the housekeeper said with a sniff.

"I see. And you didn't approve?" Anne wondered whether it was the man's color Mrs. Hailey objected to or his status as secretary to the marquess—that position put him well above a lady's maid—or Cecilia herself. That was answered by the housekeeper's next words.

"Not my place to say, but no maid ought to behave as she did. She an' some of the other maids… pure silly they are, 'bout men."

"The last person to see Cecilia alive was whoever killed her, Mrs. Hailey, and that person would likely not come forward with that information. Mr. Boatin openly stated that he and Cecilia had been out walking. Do you know of anyone else with whom she may have been?" Anne asked.

"No. If you'll excuse me, milady, I've got work to do if your maid and her boy are coming tomorrow. They'll have to share with the other servants."

Darkefell strode down the long hill toward Ivy Lodge, troubled by his talk with Osei. It had been evident, even to him, that Osei and Cecilia had some kind of relationship, but whether it was merely friendship or something deeper, his secretary was not willing to divulge. Osei was often lonely, Darkefell knew, and Cecilia was a pretty girl who may have been lonely too, coming into an insular family like theirs, with closed-mouth Yorkshire servants. Any man with eyes would have noticed the young woman's lovely face and form; even *he* had when she accompanied Lydia to dinner at the castle. What had occurred between his secretary and Cecilia during their off hours, he didn't know, beyond the fact that they had walked and talked, on occasion, when both had free time. But Darkefell knew Osei as well as he knew anyone and couldn't imagine his secretary hurting anyone, least of all a woman.

Nothing made sense at the moment. He trudged on down the green, sloping lawn, barely aware of the light spring breeze and birdsong around him. Every tragedy that befell his family increased his uneasiness, he reflected; it was as if a shadow hovered over the Darkefell name. But this... this was worse than thievery, sheep slaughter, and filthy gossip about him circulating in the village. This tragedy, Cecilia Wainwright's brutal murder, cut him to the quick. Was it related to the other torments, or was this an isolated incident?

He would find the perpetrator, but Lady Anne Addison's involvement was an unwanted complication. As grateful as he was that she had found the girl so soon after the attack, and as much as he admired her calmness in the wake of such a terrible experience, he wished her back in London or wherever she belonged. Even John didn't know why his wife had invited her friend without telling him. Lydia had given him some mumbled excuse that the lady was intelligent and would find out what was going on with the sheep killings and werewolf sightings.

But she would become a thorn in his paw, he sensed, unless he could convince her to leave. He reluctantly admitted her intelligence and courage—how many women would have been as steadfast as she in the face of murder? Still, she was too tenacious. He needed to get rid of Lady Anne and quickly find out who had done this most terrible deed; only then could he go on and figure out the rest of the mysteries that had lately plagued Darkefell estate.

He strode around the lodge toward the back garden. Though he had already sent a servant to warn his mother's gardener to stop blasting for her cursed rockery, the command had not been heeded. He stopped and looked around; where was Pincher, his mother's gardener? The man would listen to him or be expelled from the estate. The explosions were upsetting people. With everything else going on, he didn't want to cause any more anxiety than was already being experienced. Just an hour ago Dandy Lincoln, his home farm manager, had visited to complain that the ewes were upset and holding back on birth, a phenomenon the experienced farmer directly related to the explosions that echoed through the valley.

Dandy also took the opportunity to hint at his troubled thoughts about the "werewolf" and his superstitious dread that the lambs, once born, would be carried off by the creature or cursed in some inexplicable manner. Superstition it might be, but several of their sheep had been killed and gutted, as had Grover's and a few others nearer Hornethwaite. It had to stop.

"Hallo, Lord Darkefell!"

He looked around at the greeting. There, at the lip of the hill where the last explosion had broken away a chunk of rock and rubble, was Lady Anne, surveying the debris. Damnation. If he had seen her, he would have avoided her, for she was the sort of female who would demand answers of him, answers he didn't have. However, he did need to see her at some point to establish exactly what she saw and if she suspected anything. Taking a deep breath, he tried to settle his features in some kind of moderately welcoming expression.

She waited for him to join her and then remarked, looking at the scarred hillside and the dressing of dirt that a nearby grove of hawthorn bushes wore, "If you're looking for Lady Darkefell's gardener, you are too late. He's gone to the village for supplies from the blacksmith, he mumbled as he left. I had several questions for him, but he seemed in such a hurry to go!" She stared at the rubble. "I am told that this destructive fury is aimed at creating a rockery for your mother."

Hands on his hips, feet planted apart, he surveyed the scarred hill. It seemed a travesty to try to rearrange nature to suit oneself, though it had already been done to much of the estate by none other than Capability himself. "She's done what she wanted to the inside of Ivy Lodge and now wishes to beautify the outside," he complained morosely.

Turning away from the scarred rock ledge, Lady Anne said, "The inside of Ivy Lodge is lovely." She cocked her head to one side. "How grateful you—and everyone else—must be that she didn't use explosives to effect *that* change."

He laughed out loud; his dark mood lightened a shade. He hadn't expected to laugh on this grim day. Examining her, he began to reassess his first impression of a plain spinsterish woman of mounting years. She was probably only in her twenties, though it was hard to tell, for her face was shadowed by an ugly bonnet with broken feathers. The monstrous hairstyle he had seen at the breakfast table was covered, at least, and that was a good thing, for the snakelike locks were distracting. She gazed up at him from under her bonnet, and he noticed that her skin was good, her lips full, and her eyes a brilliant, clear gray. She fairly gleamed with health and vigor, and that made her as attractive as she ever would be.

He would take the opportunity to speak with her about the previous night. "May I show you some of the property, my lady?" he asked, offering her his arm.

"Certainly."

"Shall we walk toward the castle?"

"I'm at your command, my lord, so 'whither thou goest, I will go.'"

"Ah, quoting from 'Ruth'? I didn't think fashionable young ladies quoted from the Old Testament."

"I'm not a fashionable young lady, as you surely must have noticed," she replied calmly, matching her steps to his long strides.

"But you didn't have your bags until after breakfast. I expect to see you decked in silks and satins when next we meet, at dinner."

"After the events of the last twenty-four hours, my lord, I don't think I would garb myself in satin even if it was a part of my apparel."

Rebuked, he muttered, "You shame my light tone."

"Not at all," she replied. "I merely found a creative way to introduce the subject that is on both of our minds and the reason you have enticed me to walk with you."

There was no need to dance around the topic. "You're right, of course; Cecilia's murder. But first, let's walk. I'm so seldom home this time of year, and spring is, above all times at Darkefell, the season I love."

"Ah, yes… it's parliamentary season, and you should be in London," she remarked.

They set out, descending from the limestone cliff created by the explosion, and heading toward the unbroken sward of green grass that led to Darkefell Castle. The gravel drive was circuitous, and the grass more pleasant underfoot. "I have taken a leave from the Lords," he said, referring to the House of Lords, "to solve the problems plaguing my people."

"What do you think happened to Cecilia Wainwright last night?" she asked. "Is it related to this foolishness, this werewolf business?"

He hadn't intended to speak of it yet and deflected the question with one of his own. "Did Lydia really ask you to come all the way here to find out what is going on?"

"Now, should I ask another question, too?" she asked, glancing up at him. "Soon we shall have an assortment of unanswered questions between us, like a heap of refuse neither deigns to notice."

She was direct, and he was stymied. Obfuscation was a skill he had perfected in the last few months.

When he didn't answer, she said, "I propose that we each answer a question before asking one of our own. I'll start. Yes, Lydia asked me to find out what is going on. She's frightened and accustomed to having someone around upon whom she can rely."

"Why not rely on her husband?"

"I asked her that—to be blunt, she fears that he's regretting the marriage." She glanced up at him and seemed about to say something but then stopped. She cleared her throat. "Now I'm allowed another question. This is working out nicely."

"But my comment was not truly a question."

"But it was, my lord. You asked why she could not rely on her husband, and I answered." She smiled up at him, the sly expression and laughter in her eyes unexpectedly charming, even on such a plain face. "So," she continued, looking ahead as they strolled up the long sloping lawn that led to the rise beyond which Darkefell Castle loomed. "Lydia implied that you weren't discouraging talk of a werewolf. I don't for one moment think you believe in such drivel, so why do you not put a stop to it?"

"I choose not to engage in the discussion of werewolves at all. I don't encourage such talk, I simply say nothing."

She shook her head, appearing to reject his words, but didn't respond. It was his turn, by her rules, to ask a question. "Lydia seems to be frightened of me. I can't imagine why. I'm really the simplest of men with whom to speak."

Lady Anne snorted. He chose to ignore that.

"Has she confided anything to you?" he continued. "Anything about what she fears is going on or even anything about Cecilia, any relationships she might have had here since her arrival?"

"Oh, my goodness!" she cried, dropping his arm.

Her expression caught him off guard, and he stared at her in alarm. They had topped a rise and circled a grove of trees, and Darkefell Castle was in view for the first time as a whole. She was staring at it openmouthed. He crossed his arms over his chest; she would say something disparaging, now. His mother hated the castle, and any other woman who had ever expressed an opinion had deemed it hideous at best, terrifying at worst.

"It's glorious!" she said on a sigh, clasping her gloved hands together.

"Glorious?" He stared at her and then at the building.

It was huge, part of it in ruins. It truly was a castle, built in the fourteenth century, then abandoned, re-inhabited, then abandoned *again* in favor of the Jacobean Ivy Lodge, a more manageable household built by the third Earl of Staunby in the early years of the last century. His father had moved his family back into the castle and commenced rebuilding it, but soon after he died, his widow moved, as was her right, to what the late marquess had designated the dower house. He, as the new marquess, stayed in the castle.

"Yes, glorious," Lady Anne said. She strode toward it with single-minded intensity, picking up her skirts and climbing the last few feet of the rise with surprising hardiness, a brisk, chilly wind lifting the bent plumage on her hat.

He was taken aback for a moment, stunned and unmoving. Then he followed, catching up to her with three long steps. "You like it?" he asked, matching her pace.

"It's stunning! Beyond description. May I draw it?"

"Of course."

She stopped, and he bumped into her, but she seemed unperturbed. "From here," she said. She stared for a long moment. "Yes. From right here."

He looked at Darkefell Castle over her shoulder. "There," he said, pointing to the dark tower, a dry-moated, crenellated castle keep, "is the original section, the keep. It was built by Baron Geoffrey Destaun, my ancestor, from whom Staunby eventually took its name, which was kindly given back to us when a later ancestor was graced with the earldom."

She glanced over her shoulder at him. "A castle keep? Darkefell, how romantic!"

She had seemed so pragmatic, but he was delighted to find her otherwise. "Destaun was a follower of Edward of Woodstock until they had a falling-out, it was said, over a game of chance."

"Edward… the Black Prince," Lady Anne said, looking back toward the castle. "But… what do you mean, 'a game of chance'?"

"First," he said, holding up a quelling hand, "Edward was never, during his life, called the Black Prince. Anyway, he and Destaun gambled on a backgammon game, though I don't believe it was called that then, and quarreled. My later ancestors claimed the argument concerned something more noble, such as Edward's treatment of those over whom he had control—he was a cruel man—but from what I have been able to ascertain, it was that one simple game and Edward's charge that the baron cheated him."

"Really." She examined the castle and began to walk again, asking as she went, "So the castle keep is from those days, but what about the rest?"

It was a novelty, someone asking him about his family history, so he spoke while they walked, examining his home with fresh eyes. "The keep was to protect Geoffrey Destaun and his family. Or families. He had many children, not all of them with his wife."

"He was that kind of fellow, was he?"

He ignored her comment and pointed to the long wall to the left that merged into the ascending hill beyond the castle. "That is the ruined part of the castle from the earliest time. The wall joins with the keep and was part of the fortification. The dry moat—at one time it was a fully functioning moat fed by spring water—has been mostly filled in over the years with earth. Within the walls were the laundry yard, the butchery, the buttery, the milk shed, even the vegetable gardens, everything necessary to keep the family and servants fed during long sieges."

"Did your ancestors indulge in many quarrels with their neighbors?"

"Oh yes, they were a hot tempered, irritable lot." Grimly, Darkefell thought of his own problems of late and muttered, "Time changes nothing, it seems."

She glanced over at him. "I noticed this morning in the breakfast room that Mr. Hiram Grover, who so thoughtfully brought my bags up to Ivy Lodge, ignored your arrival. It must mean you two have nothing of which to speak—either that, or there is some barrier to conversation between you."

Sharp and sharper, he thought. Lady Anne was a noticing female, of all types the most inconvenient to have staying at Darkefell Castle right then. He had deep reasons not only to despise Grover, but also to dislike the man's friendship with his mother. "You're correct in thinking he and I have never gotten on," he said, keeping his tone light. "I corrupted his son when we were of an age in school, and I fear the man has never forgiven me."

"I think you are deflecting my curiosity, Lord Darkefell."

"And I think we have strayed from any topic in which you may have an interest, my lady."

Six

ANNE GAZED INTO THE MARQUESS'S DARK EYES. HOW amazing that chocolate brown could look so frosty! "I understand, my lord." She took a deep breath and broke the connection between them; if she stared into his eyes any longer, she feared she would just stop breathing altogether. The whole time he had her arm secured against his body, she had been fighting to keep her breathing even, for she was seized by an unlady-like urge to move even closer. He was attractive—intensely so—in a way she seldom saw. Intelligent. Forceful. Magnetic.

And her bodily perturbations were *completely* inappropriate.

Toward them, at a distance of about fifty feet, came Mr. Boatin with a troubled expression on his lean, dark face. He said not a word until he approached, then he swept off his hat, bowed, and said, "I beg your pardon, my lady, but I must speak with the marquess."

"Of course."

The secretary drew his employer aside and muttered something. The marquess, his expression dark and his mouth a grim slash in his face, angrily replied then clapped the other man on the shoulder. He turned toward her, strode three paces, and said, "My lady, I'm afraid you must excuse me, for some business has arisen that demands my immediate attention. If you do not object, Mr. Boatin will see you back to Ivy Lodge. Your exploration of the castle must be put off for today."

"Of course, but I can walk back on my own. Mr. Boatin," she said, meeting that man's calm gaze. "You need not concern yourself."

The man bowed but diffidently said, "I would deem it a favor, my lady, if you would allow me to accompany you."

Anne stared into his dark eyes, behind the gold-rimmed spectacles, and saw through the diffidence to how many times he had been rebuffed by unthinking folk since his arrival on the rainy shores of their island. She had not rejected his company for such a vulgar and thoughtless reason but merely because she would not trouble him to walk all the way back to Ivy Lodge with her if he had other duties. His concern spoke well of him, and so, for two reasons, she smiled and said, "Mr. Boatin, it would be my pleasure if you would escort me."

The first reason was satisfied when, relief on his face, a faint smile curved his lips upward. He was conscientious. After the horrors of the night before, his concern for any woman alone was not far-fetched, she supposed. But her second reason was, if she was to find out about his relationship with Cecilia, who better to ask than the man himself?

Lord Darkefell said, "I'm relieved you'll accept his company, Lady Anne. Nothing has yet occurred during daylight hours, but after last night, I'm not so sanguine that I would risk your safety. I must go—the magistrate awaits."

Anne glanced toward the castle and noted a phaeton with a standing horse; she hadn't noticed it before, as her attention was turned toward the ruined section. She was terribly curious as to what the magistrate's business was, or if the murderer had been seized, but since the marquess himself didn't know yet, she must satisfy her curiosity at some later time. "Good day, my lord."

"I will see you for dinner, my lady, at Ivy Lodge," he said and bowed.

Diffidently, Mr. Boatin held out his arm to her, and she took it as he clapped his hat back over his neat wig. She watched the marquess stride away, and then turned with the secretary and began to walk back toward Ivy Lodge. She glanced up at her companion. He was tall and thin, garbed in a dark gray frock coat and breeches, and walked with a slight limp.

Their stroll would likely take only fifteen minutes or so, and she must make use of each second. "I was alarmed, Mr. Boatin, by your reaction to the terrible news of poor Cecilia's death. You must have been fond of her." Interesting; even with his dark skin, she could see a blush mount his weathered cheeks.

"I knew her only a short time, but she was a kind young woman."

His tone was solemn and didn't invite further questioning, but she was not one to be put off. He had committed himself to walking her all the way back to

Ivy Lodge, and she judged he would never be rude to a lady.

However, a change of topic would set him at his ease, perhaps. "How did you come to be Lord Darkefell's secretary?"

He took a deep breath, and some of the tension left his thin frame. "It is a long and tedious story, my lady."

She paused, but then, judging that no story could be so long as to take fifteen minutes or more, said, "I have time and interest."

He smiled, a rare glimpse at a great deal of personal charm that he guarded carefully, doling out small amounts when least expected. "I was born on the African continent but sold into slavery in my sixteenth year."

"Oh, no! Sold by your own people?"

"No," he said patiently, "not by my own people. For some years our people had been struggling against others, for my race, like yours, is not united as one people." He showed a brief smile again. "I am of the tribe called Fante. The conflict goes back and forth, and one occasionally defeats the other. Our enemies— those your people call Ashanti—swooped down on us unexpectedly and defeated my village. They killed many, including my parents, and sold the rest of the men and some of the women to slave traders on the coast, keeping a select few for themselves. Those who sold me were *not* my people."

Subtly instructed, she appreciated the distinction he was making and how gracious he was. Having the same skin color did not make those who captured and sold him his own people any more than she was of the same people as an Italian or German. Excepting that they were all of the human race, each nation's people, each tribe's intimates, were accounted their own people. Had the English not been separating themselves into warring factions for millennia? And instead of uniting, they divided themselves into still smaller groups.

"I stand corrected," she said, gently. "So you were sold into slavery? How terrible, your family killed, taken from your home." Her voice broke, and she shook her head. "It's despicable."

"My sister was sold at the same time, but she was taken by a different ship. I do not know if she even survived."

"How awful."

He was silent for a moment then said, "I was on a ship. I had never seen such a thing before and thought we were to be sacrificed. I could not imagine what those white men wanted with us all, except perhaps as some kind of offering to their gods."

"Men who would do such a thing have no God... not truly," she said.

"Ah, but they claim to understand all about God and his wisdom and say that my people are not men but beasts of burden."

Anne was familiar with that argument. "I hope you know that most English citizens of thought and conscience do not believe that's so," she said with quiet ferocity.

"I know there is a mix of people here, some savage, some civilized, for I have experienced both. And I cannot claim that my people have superiority, you know," he said, anxiously gazing down at her, "for the richest among my tribe, and that was my own family, held slaves, too. Only now do I see the wrong in it, for at the time I merely accepted it as the way of life, as did we all."

"Your family owned slaves?"

"Yes. We are chieftains, royalty, you might say. The slaves did our work, cooked, planted. Much like slaves in Jamaica and America."

"I didn't know that."

"It is so," he said. "The difference, as I see it, is that somehow your people have decided that skin color determines a man's eligibility to be a slave. For why else do you not enslave a Russian or a Pole captured in war, as you do those of my color? I know of the system of indentured servitude, but it is not the same, for an indentured servant at least has the hope, however faint, that he or she will one day be free. Hope is a wonderful thing." He glanced over at her. "I confess I still do not understand why only dark-skinned people are to be enslaved among the people of your race, and not your own kind? If slavery is to be suffered, why not any man captured in war?"

"I can't answer that, Mr. Boatin. My only answer, I suppose, is that no man should be enslaved, nor any woman or child. Any lines we draw are surely artificial."

He guided her gently over a hillock. "Though we held slaves for the domestic chores and farm work, I was not raised in idleness but in warcraft, for it is an honorable occupation among us, like soldiers here, you see. Your royal dukes, some of them are warriors, and that is what I would have become in another year, with a wife and slaves of my own."

"I see." It was an adjustment, thinking of Mr. Boatin as a slaveholder. But her quick mind saw how it was, and she asked, interested, "How do you think of it all now, Mr. Boatin, having seen it from the other side, I mean slavery and such?"

"I thank the Lord that I have been shown how life is for those who have lost their freedom. It is a terrible thing, not worthy of humanity, and my one wish is that all people of the world will eschew it. I cannot be judgmental of your people, when mine are much the same. I fear for us all."

"But I have hope," she said, glancing up at him and lifting her skirts to step over a rocky outcropping. "I have hope, because where education shines a light on such a thing, it exposes it as beneath us all."

He smiled, briefly, radiantly, but then sobered. "I pray you are right."

"So you were on this slave ship… " she said, encouraging him to continue his story.

"I was. We were packed in so tight in the hold of the ship, and many were ill." He shuddered. "Even now I can smell the terrible odor of illness all around me, and I can hear the cries, the moaning, the sound of vomiting. I became ill myself, retching and shivering like the others." He sighed deeply. "We endured a long voyage. Many of the ill died and were thrown overboard, food for the sharks, no proper ceremony, no family to mourn them, just as if we were animals, our carcasses merely to be disposed of."

She took in a deep, shuddering breath; she could feel it, the heave of the waves, the creak of the wood, and the odors: vomit, diarrhea, the uncleanness. Mr. Boatin was fastidious, and it must have been wretched.

"I will never judge your people as I do the sailors on that ship, because if you knew what they did, how they treated us…" He trailed off and shook his head. "Our family slaves were at least properly buried when they died. But I cannot call that more than a faint vestige of humanity."

Mr. Boatin paused, his gaze set on the distant tree line on the ridge above Ivy Lodge. "I was close to death and welcomed it, for I could not imagine any good ending other than to join my ancestors and my parents beyond the veil. But many of us were then wrenched from the hold. The sailors left behind only those who were not yet ill. I thought, 'Perhaps these white devils will give us some fresh air and let us clean ourselves.' I felt hope. If I could only smell fresh air and drink clean water, I thought I would recover."

Anne trembled, and bile rose up in her throat as hot tears scorched her eyes; fear of what came next assailed her. She dropped his arm and stopped, facing him, willing herself to see his pain. She examined his face, shadowed as it was by his hat brim, the lines, the pitting of his skin, which should not be there in one so young, for he was younger than she, she realized with a start—probably only twenty-two or three. "What happened, Mr. Boatin?"

He met her gaze, his dark eyes curiously deep with knowledge. "When we were brought above board, I saw, for the first time the other ships with which we were sailing."

"Ships seldom travel alone, with all the trouble there

is on the high seas," Anne said, swallowing back her tears. "Do you know now where you were headed?"

"Yes. We were on our way to the West Indies, to labor at the sugar plantations, but were not yet in sight of land. One ship in particular was close to us, so close I could see the people lining the deck, the women in pretty, colorful gowns and with sunshades, both ships becalmed for the moment."

She swallowed again, gulping back emotion, willing herself to calm. "Go on, Mr. Boatin," she said, fearing the worst but ready to hear it.

He met her gaze. "You are a singular lady, to invite such a disclosure, for I believe you suspect what is coming. There has been only one other who heard my tale, and that was Cecilia Wainwright."

It was an opening, but at that moment she chose instead to listen to what needed to be said. "Tell me."

"The sailors were laughing and joking. I could not understand their language, but I remember their smiles. I thought, 'Ah, here are some good men who are going to help us.' Then I saw the first one of us go over. They took a frail old man—one sailor at his feet and one at his shoulders—grabbed him, swung him, and threw him overboard."

Anne felt her breakfast rise up. "How awful," she moaned, not even recognizing her own voice. She put one gloved palm over her mouth as tears burned her eyes, blurring her vision.

"After the second or third—at first I thought they were going to make us swim for a while and then pull us out—I realized they were disposing of us. I saw the people go under, flailing, drowning, and then it was my turn. I was thrown, so weak I could not even fight the sailors, and I felt the air, an odd feeling of weightlessness, and then I hit the water, and it was like hitting the ground. Who would think water could be so hard? I knew in that second that I wanted to live. I began to thrash about and call out to the others. Only some were Fante and could understand me."

"What did you do?"

"I think I would have drowned. I had been ill for days… weeks… I don't know how long. I went under, water closing over my head like dirt over a grave. Then someone grabbed hold of me, and I fought him. I thought, 'Now these devils are going to hold our heads under water,' but I soon understood that this one was trying to save me. It was Lord Darkefell who grabbed me and held me up, then took me back to the ship upon which he traveled, one of the convoy. He and his brother saved several of us that day, as many as they could before the waves and sharks claimed their victims."

"Lord John Bestwick?" Anne asked, trying to imagine the pale, plump young man she had met the previous evening leaping in the ocean to save lives.

"Oh no, not Lord John… it was the marquess's *other* brother, Lord Julius Bestwick. They saved seven, I think, between them. I was so ill, I will never know exactly, and the marquess does not boast of such things. It is perhaps hard to imagine," he said with a faint smile, "but the marquess is not a conceited man."

Anne smiled, too. Yes, the marquess could easily be thought of as conceited by people who mistook his confidence for vanity and his pride for arrogance. "How brave that was, to jump from so high up!" she remarked.

"Yes," Mr. Boatin agreed. "He and his brother sailed on a smaller ship than the one upon which I was captive, but the water was still a good many feet below. It took great courage and determination to do what he did. From what I understand now, Lord Darkefell took the initiative, as always, and his brother, Lord Julius, followed."

"Lord Julius," she said out loud. "Ah yes, his twin!" She remembered the painting she had seen; so that was Darkefell and his twin brother, Lord Julius Bestwick, as children, with Lord John the infant on his mother's lap. "I remember hearing something about him a year ago. He... disappeared, did he not? Then died?" After being charged with murder, Anne thought but did not say.

"Yes, there was some trouble, as you no doubt remember, and an unjust accusation of murder leveled against Lord Julius. He left England under a cloud and was next heard from in Upper Canada. But then he was killed in a tragic accident and buried there."

"How sad."

"He was a good man. Not so daring as his brother, the marquess, but good and lighthearted, the jewel of his mother's heart. She, poor lady, was devastated by his death."

"Were they identical? I saw them in the painting in the gallery at Ivy Lodge, and they looked alike."

"I suppose, as children, they did, but they altered as they got older, I think. Lord Julius was shorter than the marquess and... different. His hair, his smile, everything about him. I knew them both and would not consider them to be interchangeable. Lord Julius was a great loss to his family."

Anne went back to the story of Mr. Boatin's rescue by the marquess. "And so you came back to England. What of those dreadful sailors who threw you overboard—they were charged with murder, I hope?"

He met her steady gaze. "No," he said gently. "If you shoot your horse that is ill, are you charged with murder?"

It hit her then. "There was no legal recourse," she whispered, staring into his dark eyes. "None at all, was there?"

"None. The killings were not an illegal act, for we were considered chattel, not men. It was as if they had thrown overboard a set of chairs or trunks." They had walked on, in the meantime, and were at Ivy Lodge. "Here we are, my lady. I must get back to the castle," the secretary said with a bow, "for the marquess will need my services." He led her to the front door. "Good day."

Anne had no other avenue but to let him go. Mr. Boatin's tale had filled all of the time, and she had been unable to probe further about his relationship with Cecilia Wainwright. Perhaps that was his purpose?

She watched Mr. Boatin walk away but felt too restless to go in just yet. The secretary's story had affected her deeply. Though the sky was closing in, becoming a solid ceiling of dull gray and threatening rain, she walked along the gravel driveway and followed it back to the rear of the house, where a vista of bucolic tranquility greeted her.

The back of the red-brick dower house showed the same style of large, shuttered windows as the front, and the same elaborate, openwork parapets along the roofline, fanciful as fairy towers. But then the scene opened out onto vast gardens, arranged in linear patterns, as well as the kitchen plot and herbs in a knot garden; there she saw the dowager marchioness, in a faded bonnet, dusting dirt off her hands from replanting a perennial.

This was a side of the marchioness Anne had not expected to see, a woman of her rank grubbing about in the dirt. She was about to approach Lady Darkefell, hoping the informal surroundings would make conversation more natural, but a young man accosted the marchioness, and the two began talking. Rather than interfere in what might be estate or garden business, Anne decided to explore the grounds and wait until the marchioness was free, though there wasn't much to see this early in the season. April was a month of green shoots and rare blossoms.

Anne scanned the landscape; beyond the line of trees on the hill above Ivy Lodge, she spied what appeared to be the top of the tower folly Ellen, the maid, had mentioned. She would go to see that, as she was curious what secrets the folly might hold. She was just taking the first steps when she heard the marchioness scream.

Seven

ANNE WHIRLED AROUND AND SAW THE YOUNG MAN that she had taken to be an undergardener throttling the marchioness. "Stop!" Anne hollered. Holding her skirts up, she raced across the damp ground, her vision obscured by the first raindrops in her eyes, bounding over cultivated beds that still wore a topdressing of mulch.

The marchioness's choked screams were dying, and the young man, red faced and with a bulging vein at his temple, seemed oblivious to Anne's approach.

"Stop, I say," she cried as she reached them.

The woman was beginning to turn purple, her tongue jutting out, a fearful sight. Anne crashed into the young man, clawing at his hands and doing her best to break his firm hold on the older woman. Her bonnet was knocked askew in the fray.

A thudding sound made her turn; the marquess, on a dark gold stallion, leaped the last garden and threw himself off his horse, pulling the young man away. They rolled in the mucky, sodden earth, the marquess finally tossing him aside as if he were no more weight than a rag doll. The young man rose, shook himself, and, as Anne raced to the marchioness's side, began to shake and moan; he had smelled strongly of alcohol, Anne realized, watching him closely

The marquess turned toward his mother, but the young man suddenly wailed, a cry of pain so unutterably deep and a sound so piercing that it drew both Darkefell's and Anne's attention. The fellow fell to his knees on the damp grass.

"What the devil was going on?" Darkefell said, helping Anne raise up his mother, who, now that she was able to breathe again, was recovering apace. Bruises began to empurple her throat, but she gasped that she would be fine and shook away their helping hands.

The commotion had drawn attention from the house, and Andrew, the footman, was approaching with horror on his lean, handsome face.

"If that question was aimed at me," Anne gasped, hand over her heart, out of breath from the tussle, "I haven't a whisper of an idea. I was approaching to talk to her ladyship, saw the young man speaking to her, and turned away, but then heard her scream. I turned back and saw him throttling her. Who is he, and what shall we do with him?"

"What's going on, Mother? Why did young Allengate attack you?" the marquess asked, leaning over his parent.

She waved off his question, unable or unwilling to speak, so Darkefell motioned to Andrew and said, "Help her ladyship back to the house and summon her maid. I will be in once I've dealt with this."

The footman nodded and supported the marchioness toward the house. The marquess turned to the young fellow, who now stood, head bowed, awaiting the older man's attention. Anne watched the scene, puzzled. Why had the fellow not run away after such a crime as attacking the marchioness? It was a hanging offence to attack a woman, his superior, in such a violent manner and with the apparent intention of killing her.

Was that the face of a murderer? Anne examined the scruffy young man, his unshaven face and bleary gaze suggesting a worrisome combination of little sleep and the liquor consumption she had already detected. His clothes, she noted, looking him over, were very good quality but looked as if he had slept in them for some days.

Would the crime of the previous evening be so swiftly solved? Had this fellow been hanging about just waiting for another unwary victim? She was about to hint such a thing to the marquess, but he put his arm over the younger man's shoulders and led him a short distance away. Baffled, she watched them speak, then frustrated at being left out of the conversation, Anne moved closer.

To her utter amazement, Darkefell clapped the fellow on the back and shoved him away. Allengate, if such was his name, slumped away and then trotted, wobbling a little, across the gardens, around a garden shed, and disappeared.

"What are you doing, letting him get away like that?" Anne cried, striding over to the marquess and grabbing his arm. The limb was like steel under her fingers, no fleshy give at all under the fine linen of his besmirched shirtsleeve.

He turned and regarded her with calm, dark eyes. "Are you questioning my handling of this affair?"

"I am," she exclaimed, pushing her bonnet all the way off her head, allowing it to dangle by its strings on her back. "That could be the man who murdered Cecilia, for all you know! You must go after him, detain him, arrest him! The magistrate must still be at the castle. Go get him, for God's sake!" She shook him, or tried to, anyway.

He glanced down at her gloved hand clutching his arm, unmoved by her violent action. "Allengate is no murderer," he said.

"But he just tried to kill your mother!" She stared into his dark eyes, perplexed and infuriated.

"If my mother says he tried to kill her and wishes him to be arrested, I will know where to find him."

"But he may have killed Cecilia! Don't you need to question him or turn him over to the magistrate? You can't just let him go, after what he did to Lady Darkefell."

"On the contrary, I can do whatever I want," he said, insinuation in his soft tone.

She felt a shiver race down her spine. What exactly did he mean?

He turned her around and took her arm in his, seeming completely at his ease, despite the muck on his breeches and the rain dampening his linen shirt. A young stable lad had appeared, and Darkefell called over his shoulder, "Gilbert, see to Sunny. I will ride back to the castle in about half an hour."

Bemused and baffled, Anne allowed herself be led away by the marquess. Once again the sensation of his muscular form next to her left her a little breathless, and she searched her mind for the wit to say something, anything! "It seems," she said stiffly, "that there is much more going on here than the silly werewolf sightings and even the murder of poor Cecilia."

"Whatever do you mean, Lady Anne?"

"I mean, Lord Darkefell," she said, shaking off his arm and confronting him face on, blinking raindrops out of her eyes, "that I want to know why you let that fellow go, after he nearly strangled your mother to death."

"Do you not think," he said, "that I know better than you what my mother wishes in this case?"

"You cannot mean that she would let the fellow roam free to strangle some other poor woman?" She began to shiver. "You saw that girl, p-poor Cecilia. And after that, you can make light of it?"

"I am making light of nothing." The words were ground out of his handsome mouth. He grabbed her elbow in his steely grasp and began to march her, swiftly, around the lodge and toward the front door, his footsteps crunching on the graveled pathway. "Come, you're getting damp and cold. I'll not be responsible for your becoming ill. I think your concerns would best be put to rest if you hear from my mother how she wants me to deal with Richard Allengate."

She tripped and trotted, trying to keep up with his stride; though she tried to slip from his grasp, she couldn't. She kept casting him glances, his profile so arresting as to make her breathless, even if the pace had not. He was jacketless—shockingly so—and the muscles of his brawny shoulders were now delineated by the dampening affect of the mizzling rain that came down, plastering his shirt to his torso. She daren't look down to his chest, or she might not survive the sight. This was an exceedingly inconvenient time for her occasional attraction to a man to assert itself. He was not a man to whom she wished to be attracted; on the contrary, he was high-handed and supercilious and needed to be taken down a peg or two. Or three.

Darkefell fought to control his ire. Of all times for Allengate to pull such a boneheaded move, it had to be in front of this infuriatingly nosy woman. Lydia he could have intimidated. The servants he could command. But Lady Anne Addison? He threw open the door and hauled her after him; she squawked like a perturbed hen, and he chuckled mirthlessly. But entering Ivy Lodge had the effect of cooling his fury.

He released her, took a deep breath, and in the dimness of the entry hall, gazed down at her as she rubbed her elbow and undid the strings of her rain-soaked bonnet. She tossed it to a nearby table. Sense reasserted its dominion in his fevered brain; his best tack now was to flatter or coddle her into forgiving him for his violence. "I must apologize, my lady," he said with a deep bow, "for making so free with your person."

"You're unbearably imposing, my lord," she said, huffing and settling her dress properly about her person. "But you will not overcome my curiosity nor my determination to discover why you have handled such a vile crime, perpetrated upon your mother, in such a shocking manner!"

She licked her lips and gazed up at him, and really, he thought suddenly, for a plain woman her eyes were ridiculously fine, brilliant though they were gray, almost silver in color, and fringed with long, dark lashes. Dew clung to her skin, giving it the sheen of nacre, and her pink tongue, darting out to wet her trembling lips, was a silly little enticement. Irritation waged war with rationality, but irritation won. He could not turn her over his knee to teach her to mind her own business, so… he grabbed her around the waist, hauled her into his embrace, and bent her backwards with a hasty and impetuous kiss certain to silence—and possibly confuse—her. A servant who had approached at their entry gasped and backed out of the hallway.

But it did not daunt her. The moment he released her, she slapped him. Hard. The sound echoed to the upper reaches of the third floor. "How dare you, sir?"

He planted his hands on his hips and laughed out loud as his brother, John, raced down the steps, his pudding-pale face gleaming with perspiration.

"Tony, what's going on? This is no laughing matter! Mother won't tell me what happened with that poor fellow, young Allengate, but said I must ask you, and—" He stopped ranting finally upon seeing Lady Anne, who had been concealed from his view by Darkefell's own bulky form. John's breath still came in deep, gasping gulps as he stared from one to the other of them. "What's going on?" he wailed plaintively, hammering his fist on the oak banister railing.

"I would like to know the same thing," Lady Anne said, her cheeks pink from Darkefell's amorous assault. "Who is Allengate, and why did he attack your mother?" She looked from the marquess to his brother, but both men were silent.

Darkefell made a sudden decision. This was already too complicated, and he had much to do that did not include placating an irritating spinster with too long a nose and too sharp of a gaze. "I don't owe anyone an explanation, least of all you, my lady." He turned to his brother. "John, will you escort the lady back up to her room? I'm sure, now that her bags are here, she'll want to change her damp and soiled clothing. I will see you both at dinner, but for now, I do need to see Mother about something, which is why I was on my way here in the first place."

He turned back to Lady Anne. "I'll assure myself that she's well, I promise you. I value my mother very much, for all you may have doubts on that topic. Good afternoon, my lady—I will see you at dinner, no doubt."

Anne, after a couple of hours of rest and reflection in her room and clad in a more suitable dress of blue lustring, sat in the drawing room with her hands folded on her lap. Nobody would speak to her, not even the maid, Ellen, whom she had summoned to help her change out of her traveling dress, now ruined beyond redemption by the rain and muck of the garden. Her hair still looked a fright, but there was not a thing she could do about that. The maid had been resolutely silent, even when closely questioned, frightened into silence by the bullying marquess, Anne felt sure.

Lydia sat at the piano in the corner of the room, picking out a plaintive little tune. Either she truly did not know who Allengate was, or she had been warned not to speak about him, for she shrugged her shoulders when Anne pestered her about the garden incident, merely answering that, since her mother-in-law did not wish the fellow arrested, then she supposed that was the end of it.

But Anne must keep trying. Her frustration was mounting, and the only appeasement would be to learn something. It was either that or go back to pondering the feel of Lord Darkefell's too-perfect lips pressed against her own. And his too-perfect body against hers. He was entirely *too* perfect—if there was such a concept as overabundant perfection—in a physical sense and entirely too maddeningly imperfect in every other way. Especially evident was the imperfect transparency of his motives and character.

He was making a mockery of her with that kiss; he must have sensed her attraction and was using it to disarm and distract her. Her cheeks grew warm, and she fidgeted in place, pulling at the fingers of her gloves. It had worked too well, for even the memory of his shocking action caused her heart to race and her palms to perspire. Agitated, she burst into speech, saying, "I don't know how I'm to help you figure out what's going on, Lydia, if you won't speak to me!"

Lydia merely shrugged again, plinked a few piano keys, and sighed.

Anne narrowed her eyes, watched her friend, and said, "I shall just go home, then, when Sanderson brings my carriage tomorrow."

Her younger friend sniffed back a sob but said nothing. Anne stood and stalked over to Lydia, putting her hands over the other girl's on the piano keys and crouching down beside her. "My dear," she pleaded, staring up at her young friend, "please talk to me! I don't mean to badger you, but—"

"You don't understand at all what it's like to be married! How could you, a spinster likely never to wed?" She sobbed aloud, and her breath caught in tiny gasps.

"Has John been cruel to you in any way?"

"N-no," she said but then added, "but he's still a man, and men... oh, *why* do they kiss other girls and... " She trailed off and shook her head.

"Kiss other girls? What on earth do you mean?"

But Lydia shook her head and turned away. Anne asked again what she meant, but she wouldn't be drawn. Finally, she sighed and said, "I thought marriage would end all of my worries, and I did love... I *do* love John, but he has some secret that he's not willing to share, and how can we be truly married if he won't tell me what's troubling him?"

Nudging her aside gently, Anne sat down with her on the piano bench. Now that she had broken through the girl's silence, she must take advantage of her vulnerability to answer the nagging questions she had after the day's events. "Have you ever heard Allengate's name before today?"

"No," Lydia said.

"Did Cecilia ever speak of Mr. Boatin?"

"Not to me."

"Why does Mr. Hiram Grover not like the marquess?"

"I don't know."

Anne sighed.

"It seems my little sister-in-law is not as helpful in your snooping as you could wish, my dear Lady Anne."

Anne whirled and stared toward the door, where the marquess leaned against the doorframe, handsome in a dark blue cutaway jacket, richly embroidered waistcoat, fawn breeches, and stockings that outlined muscular legs.

"So," he continued, "you did not believe me when I said that Mr. Grover still holds an old resentment regarding my schoolboy corruption of his sainted son, Theophilus, whom I introduced to gin, rum, cards, tobacco, and women of ill repute?"

"Your school days are so far behind you, my lord," she replied stiffly, "that I merely doubt any sensible man would hold such a long resentment as that would imply."

He smirked. "Ah, yes, as you point out so cleverly, I am considerably older than you and more wise about the ways of men."

"Age and wisdom have so long been paired, I must gracefully admit that his lordship would seem to have the better of me in both," Anne commented, the waspish tone in her voice a deliberate reaction to the still-tangible quivering of her body at his appearance.

He threw his head back and laughed, then strolled into the room, prowling the perimeter and watching her like a handsome, sleek cat might watch a drab gray mouse, with much more interest than the rodent would seem calculated to inspire. "I must thank you, Lydia, for inviting such a fantastical creature as Lady Anne Addison, by whom I am entranced. She makes me laugh, and in such hours as these, with terror and sadness forever looming, that's a rare and wonderful quality."

Lydia merely snuffled and huddled in her own misery.

"I don't like to be laughed at, my lord," Anne said, her gaze following his progress. Every circle around the room brought him closer to her.

"Ah, but I'm not laughing *at* you, Lady Anne. You make humorous comments, and I laugh at your sallies, Lady Anne. May I call you my *dear* Lady Anne?"

She had regained her composure at last, determined not to allow the rogue dominance over her pulse, and inclined her head slowly as Lydia slipped away. "You may call me what you will, sir. And what shall I call you?"

He stood before her, too close, the buttons of his waistcoat inches from her nose, heat from his solid form washing over her in waves. "A woman I once knew called me 'Dark,'" he murmured, taking her hand, stripping off her glove, then turning her hand palm up and bending low over it. "I fear she considered it an endearment."

Tempting, oh, so tempting to slap his cheek again. He was being impertinent, deliberately so. "Or perhaps she considered it a description of your heart," she said softly, gazing up at him. If he would be insolent, then she would be daring. His breath was warm on the naked skin of her wrist, where he pushed back the edge of her sleeve. He pressed his lips to her pulse, thumbed her palm, then released it; her heart, after thudding heavily, raced once more as her glove fell, disregarded, to the polished marble floor.

"That's possible." He turned as the doors swept open, and Lady Darkefell, dressed in a gown with a fichu concealing her throat, strolled into the room on her younger son's arm and accompanied by another man, tall and thin with a small, round paunch under his waistcoat. The marquess advanced on them, bowed and murmured a greeting, then motioned for the other man to stroll with him. When they reached Anne, the marquess bowed to her and said, "Lady Anne Addison, may I introduce to you the magistrate, Sir Trevor Pomfroy. Sir Trevor, Lady Anne has some rather sharp questions for you, and I warn you, she's like a terrier with a rat once she is on the scent."

Eight

AFTER SUCH AN INTRODUCTION, THERE WAS NO
questioning the magistrate, of course. Lord Darkefell
had made certain of that by putting the man on his
guard. They were joined by the vicar, Charles Sydney,
a short, fiery gentleman, and his intelligent-looking
wife, Mrs. Philodosia Sydney. Dinner was long and
tedious, the conversation among the guests about
people Anne did not know and events about which
she didn't care. When conversation strayed toward
the previous night—not so much "strayed," as Anne
raised the topic—Lady Darkefell resolutely turned it
away from the murder, the throttling incident earlier
giving her voice a husky, pleasant tone. Anne, silenced
once more, sourly reflected that strangulation should
perhaps be introduced in London for girls in their first
Season, to give their voices that indubitably attractive quality. Given the other tortures of the Season, it
could make the experience no worse.

After dinner the ladies sat for a time in the drawing
room. Lady Darkefell took Anne aside, and in a stilted
fashion, admitted that she had said intolerable things

to young Allengate, things she now regretted; in his drunken state he had objected, which resulted in his attack. As wrong as his behavior was, she still wished to forget about the incident. Anne had no recourse but to nod and agree as the marchioness turned and stalked away.

They were then joined by the gentlemen, who smelled of port and cigars, not an unpleasant combination to Anne's sensitive nose. Especially not on the marquess.

But the evening was a waste of time as far as her investigative purposes went. Sir Trevor, her dinner companion, had been austere and remote, and in company, Anne could not ask what she wanted even if he had been more approachable. She sensed the marquess's mocking gaze on her often through the evening. Her frustration mounted; what were they all hiding, and why?

It had been a long, weary day. She slept soundly, awakening early the next morning just as the first hints of daylight filtered wanly through her bedchamber window.

Sadness filled her as she sat curled up in the window seat of her room. Her view was of the front of Ivy Lodge and the gravel drive disappearing up the hill, beyond which lay Darkefell Castle. Young Cecilia Wainwright, with a life blooming in her womb, would never greet another dawn, never love another man, never see her baby's face or hold it to her breast. All the glorious trouble and turmoil, joy and pain of existence was lost to her, gone forever, as was the life she was bringing to the world. Though the marquess appeared to be genuinely determined to track down the killer, and she had no wish to impede his progress, it frustrated her that he would not allow her to help. Instead, he blocked any attempt she made to join him in his investigation.

Why would he do that? Why, if he had nothing to hide, did he not just accept her help? Granted she was a stranger to him, and if she was fair, there was little reason for him to trust her, but still, a woman had been brutally murdered, she had found the poor soul, and she could not just let it go and leave it in someone else's hands.

She dressed in a morning gown as best she could without a maid to help her, twisting and turning and doing up laces meant to be tied by other hands; pulled back her abundant hair, securing it with a ribbon; then draped her warmest shawl over her shoulders. April mornings were cold and damp in Yorkshire. Pattens she eschewed, though she had brought them, for mud and muck were enemies of the elevating objects, clogging them and sometimes making them treacherously heavy, clumsy mechanisms. She would rather her hem be muddy than her footsteps be hampered. Also, the metal soles of pattens did not promote stealth. Though she didn't intend to creep around like a thief, she had no intention of signaling her whereabouts to anyone, neither man nor monster. A stout pair of half boots would suffice.

She slipped from her room and down the stairs. Life was just beginning to stir in the household. It was not even six in the morning, daylight still just a pearly gray, rose-tinted promise on the horizon, a hint of light soon to come. A young girl hunched on the front step, scrubbing it with a brush and a steaming bucket of water, but she scuttled away into the shadows with an alarmed look on her pinched face as Anne emerged from the house. Servants rarely saw their betters up and about at this time of day.

Anne wanted to retrace her steps of the night she arrived and see the scene of the crime. She glanced around in the misty predawn half-light, noting the stone wall and gate through which she had arrived that evening, two nights before. She headed toward it. The stable lad who had tended the marquess's horse the day before raked the gravel path and grubbed stubborn weeds that pushed up among the stones, tossing them into a barrow. He looked up and touched his forelock, ducking his head, but then bent back to his task. He likely needed to complete the whole path before he would be given any breakfast.

She took her time, stopping to examine the drive once she had closed the gate behind her and turned in the direction of the highway. There was a copse of trees to the left, from her vantage point now. Picking up her skirts, she left the path and followed the sloping grass down to a break in the shrubs and trees. Morning sun began to brighten the scene, and through patchy fog she could make out disturbed spots among the brush, leaves strewn 'round, and a couple of broken branches. That must be, she decided, where the dogs and men, including the marquess, had found poor Cecilia that night, blundering around in the dark until they happened upon her.

Anne paused and closed her eyes, picturing the scene, lanterns held high, the mournful baying of hounds, and Cecilia, lying alone and beyond earthly help, her throat savaged, whether by man or beast she had not yet decided. What else? She opened her eyes and advanced, making her way under the low branches and toward the spot where poor Cecilia met her end. There, she thought, finding a spot that still bore some evidence of the murder; that was it, where she had expired.

Crouching, she examined the spot, her sharp gaze following the path of the girl and murderer, possibly even as they staggered about in the auditory turmoil that had first drawn Anne's attention. Under the brush was a dark patch of splotches and drips; blood, Anne thought, a tremor of horror racing through her. After the turmoil of that night, with men and dogs searching for Cecilia, the dead leaves were scattered, no sense now from what direction the murderer may have come.

A tuft of gray drew her attention above where the girl's body must have come to rest, and Anne reached up to the thorny branch of a hawthorn shrub, where a hank of fur was caught. She examined it where it was, then pulled it off and rubbed it between her fingers, holding it briefly up to her nose. It was some kind of animal fur, no doubt, but it had a feel of age and decrepitude, not freshness, and it smelled of… she wrinkled her nose. Camphor? It did not seem as if it was pulled from a living creature.

But perhaps that was her own fanciful imagination. She was about to back cautiously out of the area when the silvery dawn light pushed fingers of brightness into the shadowed shrubbery and caught on a glint of gleaming metal. She reached out one hand, stretching deep into the shrub's depths.

"Halloo, there! Are you quite all right, miss?"

Startled, she fell backward, and her uncovered hair caught on a hawthorn, tearing one hank of it from its roots and pulling the rest from the ribbon. She scrambled from the bushes and beheld Lydia's husband, mounted on a russet mare and staring at her with alarm on his pale face, his hat under his arm.

"Lady Anne!" he exclaimed.

"I…" How to explain what she was doing? Anne could feel her countenance grow crimson with confusion.

He simply stared, awaiting her explanation.

"What is it, John? What on earth are you looking at?"

Her mortification quadrupled. That was the marquess's deep voice, and he rode up behind his brother on the grassy hillock and stared down at her, amusement lighting up his dark features. "Lady Anne," he said heartily. "An early riser, I see. But I suspect this was no morning promenade that brought you to this exact spot."

Aware of the fiery red spots on her cheeks and the state of her tumbled hair, she crawled out of the shrubbery and stood, rapidly concealing the hank of fur in her tucker under the guise of straightening her shawl. She plucked a thorn out of her hair and discarded it, and brushed leaves off her shawl.

The marquess's expression grew serious, and he gazed thoughtfully at the area she had been examining. Suddenly he leaped down from his horse, threw the reins to his brother, and followed her path, diving into the brush.

"Stop! Be careful," she insisted, following him and tugging on his jacket skirt.

"All right, all right," he said, irritably, resting back on his haunches in the grass and leaves. "It would help if you told me just what it is—other than these tragic blotches of blood—that caught your eye under here." He turned around to stare up at her from his awkward position. "Or have you already recovered the item?"

Cornered, she thought of the shiny object and said with all sincerity, "No." She followed him and crawled past, while Lord John plaintively asked what the devil they were doing. Both Anne and the marquess ignored him as she wiggled past the elder brother to where she had spotted the glint of metal. She reached out, gently pushed some twigs away, and found the treasure.

"While the view I have is most stimulating," Lord Darkefell said from behind her, "I would be more entertained if I knew what you've found."

She twisted around and abruptly ended up on her bottom on the damp ground, but held up the item. It gleamed dully, besmirched with some clinging debris. It was a couple of inches of heavy, gold, elaborately woven chain, likely part of a watch fob or some such thing. The marquess stared at the hank of chain for a moment then met her gaze.

"How did you ever see that among that tangle of brush?"

"Does that matter?" she asked crossly, crawling out from the brush. "What I want to know," she went on, staggering to her feet and dusting off her damp bottom—really, she would have to stop soiling her clothes, or she would have nothing to wear—and holding the chain up to the growing daylight, "is how it got there, and if it has anything to do with Cecilia's death."

Lord John stared down at them, blinking and frowning. "I don't understand," he cried plaintively.

The marquess ignored him and instead addressed Anne's query. "I think it must have something to do with it," he said, looking back at the brush. "That's exactly where we found Cecilia's body, and given that the gold chain was visible, it must not have been there too long."

"Yes, I had thought of that. It was just as if it had flown there during a struggle." She held it up and looked at it. The chain was thick and good-quality gold. It would not likely have belonged to any feminine object, nor would a maid, even a lady's maid like Cecilia, own anything so fine.

The marquess snatched it from her, saying, "I shall take charge of it and figure out where this came from."

"But, but—"

"No, don't thank me," he said, taking the reins of his horse from his brother and leaping up on the animal's back. "I may decide to let you know if I find anything. Have a good breakfast." He whirled and rode off, with his brother following at a more subdued pace.

"Arrogant! High-handed!" She huffed and stared after the marquess as he disappeared beyond the hill. It required another half hour of walking to regain her composure, but she eventually decided, as there was nothing she could do about his seizure of the chain, she must make the best of it. She did have the piece of fur, after all, and she had examined the gold chain closely and noticed how the last link was twisted, as if it had been ripped off of something.

Not that it would do any good to remember the details. Many people had items on gold chains: pendants, pocket watches, trinkets, seals, chatelaines. She thought back. A heavy gold chain on a chatelaine. Mrs. Hailey had one. Though she had thought the chain could not belong to a woman, she must not make such assumptions without investigation. A gift or an inherited piece could easily be so thick.

In her walk she came to a tower and realized that she had inadvertently found the folly Ellen had spoken of, as the place she had seen the werewolf. Anne examined the ground all 'round but found nothing, then stood back and examined the tower itself. It was tall, sixty feet at least, and had windows in an ascending pattern that likely corresponded with the winding staircase that would lead to the viewing tower at the top. A sweet conceit on the part of a newly elevated marquess many years before, Anne thought, the marquess's father, if she remembered right, a tall tower over which to view his vast estate but also a metaphor for his rise in status.

It was constructed of hard red brick, with prominent gray stone lines circling it every ten feet or so, all the way up to the gray stone parapet at the top. There must be a door somewhere, she thought, following the base around. A Romanesque arch with a plank door was on the lee side of the tower, and she pushed down the handle. It smoothly opened. It must have been used recently, or surely the latch and hinges would be stiff, not well-oiled and working.

She glanced around. No one would be out this time in the morning to see her... except for a meddling marquess and his brother, she amended. But they were long gone.

The interior was dreadfully gloomy and cold. She left the door open for light and air, wedging it with a stone. The morning sun had not yet pierced the gloom of the interior, so it took a few moments for her eyes to become accustomed to the dimness.

When they did, she saw that the inside was really just a tall hollow, with steps in a spiral going up the interior. And no railing. Against one curved wall, in an alcove under the steps, was a large trunk, but it was securely padlocked. There was nothing else, nothing to investigate but the tower itself. "However," she said aloud, her voice echoing strangely and then disappearing in the vertical tunnel, "I do not need to go up there this morning. What possible purpose would that serve?"

But that, she decided, examining the stair and tentatively putting her foot on the bottom one, was the whining voice of terror that had led to almost marrying Lydia's brother. Years ago she had been afraid what society would say of her, a plain woman and shamefully unmarried. Saved from a disastrous alliance by Reginald's untimely death, she had vowed never to listen to that inner voice of unreasoning fear again. Perhaps marriage and a steep ascent up a tower could not be compared, but then again, both could end in tragedy if one was not careful.

She looked straight up. The steps were broad enough, and she had never suffered vertigo. If she stayed by the wall, there would be relatively no chance that she would fall. How would she know what she might discover if she didn't go up?

She began, step by step, the dimness worse on the side away from the rising sun, and her progress there slower. Cautiously, she wound her way upward, her ankles beginning to tremble. She must not look down, she decided, for that was sure to frighten the unreasoning animal part of her brain, where nightmares and superstition dwelt. How she would descend thusly she had not yet worked out. Time enough for that conversation with herself once she got to the top.

It was a little warmer as she ascended, or perhaps that was her imagination. But it was getting lighter. She paused and looked up. Near the top was a semicircular platform, her goal, and she could see that the windows were larger, set around the wall within more arches. Finally, she reached the top, and it was well worth the nervousness the climb had inspired. She stepped up into the semicircular room and approached the windows, catching her breath from the long climb and the gorgeous view.

Darkefell. The Yorkshire landscape stretched out, the morning sun now rising in the sky. From the valley she could see a long line of hills to the north, spotted with wooded glades and topped by windswept trees. At quite a distance she could see some kind of rocky outcropping and a waterfall that sparkled and gleamed in the rising sun, rimmed by burgeoning greenery. A stream below the waterfall tumbled through the property, winding between groves of trees, disappearing from view, then reappearing; as she followed it down,

circling the room and gazing out, she saw more struc-
tures. At a distance of about a mile, in a farther reach
of the gentle valley, was a neat farm, with a patchwork
of fresh green fields and pasturage stretching out from
the stream in neat angular shapes separated by dry stone
fences and hedgerows. Cows lazily grazed near a byre,
and sheep cropped grass on a distant hillside. Just a half
mile from the farm nestled a tiny cottage.

She moved to another mullioned window. Closer
to hand was Ivy Lodge, with the stables and various
outbuildings behind, the marchioness's elaborate
gardens, workers now bustling from task to task.
Then, as she circled the tower room, in the distance,
on a prominence, was the castle. She took in a long,
deep breath. It was gothic and enchanting, the old
castle keep and stone wall that disappeared into the
hillside, then the more modern attached building,
glass gleaming in the rising sun, glittering panes like
diamonds, winking and blinking.

Looking toward the highway, down closer to the
road just beyond the estate property, which appeared
bounded by a low stone wall, was another house,
large but modern, too squat for its size. Perhaps Hiram
Grover's home?

Anne turned away from that and went back to the
view of the most distant reaches of the marquess's land,
preferring it for some reason. She couldn't think why.
She was pure Kentish, preferring marshlands and sea
views; the only wildness she liked was a crashing sea
or the flight of a tern overhead.

But this dark landscape, Yorkshire gloom, she
thought as a cloud blotted the sun for a moment and

sent dark shadows racing over the land. It sent a chill down her back, one that she didn't dislike. It was rather like the master of the estate, the dark and enigmatic marquess; he was a product of this place—the darkness of its name, and the darkness of its aspect were both an integral part of him and vital to discovering what lay behind his mysterious character. And he unfortunately sent those same thrilling chills down her back.

Movement in the distance drew her attention, and she squinted, leaning her elbows in the arched window opening. Two horsemen, the marquess and his brother, were still riding. Such muscle as the marquess was built of must be honed by many hours in the saddle, but his soft brother was not such a sportsman. Why, then, was he out so early and so far with the marquess?

She watched. They approached a building that looked to be no more than a one-room hut near a grove of trees low on the hillside, and one of them—the marquess, judging from the golden horse— dismounted. Another figure joined them, emerging from the hut. The person moved slowly, and it appeared that he leaned on a stick.

Nothing odd in a good landlord visiting a tenant. From the well-kept landscape, it appeared that the marquess was a very good landowner indeed. Anne's stomach growled loudly. She had not yet had break-fast, and she was about to turn away to descend, when something caught her eye. Beyond the hut on the hill, a creature loped away. It looked like a dog, but something about it made her think it was *not* a dog; there was something quite, *quite* different about the way it ran.

From her angle, Anne could see the back of the hut; a man crept out a door and began to run. The marquess caught sight of him and gave chase. Anne was watching avidly, clutching the cold stone sill of the mullion, when a creak and slam reverberated up to her, and she gasped, her attention drawn down to the interior of the tower. The door! That was the door to the tower slamming shut. How was that possible?

She raced over to another window and looked below, but caught sight only of the bushes at the base of the tower rustling back into place, as if someone had just gone that way.

What was going on? Was she locked in?

When she went back to look into the distance again, the landscape was calm, the marquess and his brother riding away from the hut, and not another soul—not even the animal—in sight.

Nine

GOING DOWN WAS MORE TREACHEROUS THAN GOING up, Anne found. Her ankles trembled, and she had to keep one hand on the wall at all times, for every step down felt as if it would bring her tumbling to the bottom. The thought, once it had invaded, left her quivering. Who would find her body if she fell to her death? The door, latched from the outside, would inspire no one to investigate further.

And who closed and latched it? She could eliminate the marquess and his brother, and whoever else was off in the distance with them. To distract herself, she pondered what she had seen from the top of the tower; what was the animal loping across the hills, and who was the person creeping out from behind the hut?

Finally at the bottom, she felt her way over to the door and rattled the latch. Secure. Her heart thudded, but imagining her skeletal remains being found shockingly garbed in a loosely fastened morning gown at some point in the next century would do no good. She took a deep breath and knelt to examine the latch. Daylight framed the door, and a dark patch that was the latch darkened a sliver of open space. If she had her chatelaine, she would have had tools enough to fish through and lift the latch, but she had nothing. She felt around on the floor for a thin stick. Nothing!

She rattled the door and hollered, "Halloo!" then waited. She did that over and over, hoping a groundskeeper or stableboy might hear, but no one responded. Climbing the stairs seemed the only solution, to see if she could catch a glimpse of someone and attract their attention.

The climb did not seem as bad this time, except her legs felt the wear of such an ascent twice in one morning. It was fortunate that she was a seasoned walker and had rambled over her family's Kentish home acres often in the last few months as she contemplated her future plans.

Her stomach, though, grumbled in an undignified way, complaining that she had not had breakfast nor even her morning chocolate. And that was a ray of hope, she thought as she ascended the last few steps. Ellen would have gone to her room with her before-breakfast toast and chocolate; perhaps she would report Anne missing. Not that anyone would think to look for her up the tower, but they might search the grounds, and she could get someone's attention.

She looked in the direction of Ivy Lodge. So far, no one was close enough to hail. She scanned the vicinity; the marquess and his brother approached, trotting down the sloping hill toward the low prominence on which the tower was situated. She would have to call out to them, and yet she dreaded the laughter her situation would occasion from the marquess.

She dithered for a moment, but as the two neared, she had to call out or risk being trapped for some time. Patience was not her strong suit, and this was by far the most expedient chance of escape. Embarrassment was the price, but mortification must not keep her from breakfast.

She leaned out the window as the men came through a copse of trees and shouted, "Halloo! Lord Darkefell, Lord John!"

The two men stopped, but only the marquess looked up to the heights of the tower. His face split in a wide grin. "Lady Anne! How delightful to see you again. And how is your morning progressing?"

"I'm fine, my lord, and enjoying the view. It's spectacular from up here. In fact, I spied you gentlemen on your morning jaunt into the hills."

Lord John stared up at her and said, "Good Lord, whatever inspired you to climb such a height? I haven't been up there since I was ten."

"Lady Anne is more energetic than you, John," the marquess said, still staring up at her. "Why, I'm sure she intends to run up and down the stairs a few more times before breakfast." He saluted and called out, "Have a good morning, my lady. Be careful descending." He turned his horse to ride away.

"Darkefell!" she shouted, irritated.

He turned back but did not speak.

"I would be grateful if you would unlatch the door at the bottom, please," she said, her cheeks burning with humiliation.

He didn't tease as she expected. Instead, his expression grew serious. "Am I to understand, since I have full confidence in your intelligence, madam, and do not think you locked *yourself* in, that someone closed the door on you and latched it?"

"Yes."

"Knowing you were up there?"

She was about to protest that she didn't know that but was arrested by his expression. Even from a distance, his fury was evident.

"This is too much," he said, vigorously throwing himself from the saddle and staring up at Anne. "Come down, my lady, at once."

Lord John, foreshortened in her view from on high, patted at his jacket and frowned, then glanced up at the sun rising above the trees. "It must be time for breakfast. I'll ride back, Tony, and tell Mother to wait for Lady Anne." He rode off toward the lodge.

Anne, her ankles now aching, made her way down the steps as the marquess unlatched the door. He opened it. Blinded by a stream of the rising sun, she stumbled directly into his arms and looked up. She jerked away, pulled her shawl closely around her, and limped out, trying to ignore the soreness of her ankles.

"Let me take you back," he said.

"I can walk," she replied.

"No need when I can carry you." He scooped her up and threw her onto his horse, then leaped up behind her.

She was seated sideways, so her hip was firmly pressed to an uncomfortably intimate part of the marquess. She had studied—covertly, of course—an aged copy of Cheselden's *Anatomy of the Human Body* in her father's library and knew precisely what was where. The only question left was how much of *what* the marquess had; if she discovered that, she was sure she would self-immolate on the spot in a blaze of heated conjecture. His lordship used a hunting saddle, she had observed, with a low pommel and cantle; so was that hardish lump against her hip his pommel or his lordship?

To distract herself from such indecent thoughts, she considered his behavior as he settled himself. He was unbearably commanding! "Please let me down, my lord," she said, her voice as steady and her tone as frigid as she could manage in such an intimate position. "I'm perfectly capable of walking."

"You were limping. Why walk when you can ride?" he said, putting his arms around her and taking up the reins. "Now, what were you doing up the tower?"

The smothering sense of attraction she experienced whenever she was near him annoyed her. When she was alone and a little cooler, she would ponder it, discover its genesis, and defeat it, she decided. "I was looking over your property, sir," she said, holding herself stiffly away from him but still terribly aware that her hip was settled firmly against his groin. "I saw you and your brother up on the hill, speaking with someone, while some kind of creature that was *not* a dog loped off into the distance and some man tried to sneak out of the back of the hut. What say you to that?"

He chuckled, and she could *feel* the sound of it rumbling through his broad chest and vibrating into her where her upper arm rested against his body. When he didn't answer, she looked up at him. His chin had beard stubble, and his dark hair was loose, curling deliciously against his thick neck, above a limp cravat loosely tied. She swallowed. "Why don't you answer?" she asked.

"Answer? But you didn't really ask a question, did you?"

"There we are back to unanswered questions piling up," she said, irritation threading through her voice. "Why are you trying to block me, my lord? Why not just accept my help in figuring out what is going on here?"

His grip around her became firmer, and he leaned forward, pressed more closely to her as his horse mounted a rise. "Just because my silly sister-in-law invited you here to calm her idiotic fears, it doesn't follow that I should enlist your aid in solving the tragedy that occurred. There's nothing going on, my lady, that should concern you *or* Lydia. The best thing you can do is tell her to mind her husband and take up a pastime. Needlepoint or whatever young ladies do to fill their days. Netting purses. Trimming bonnets."

She was speechless with anger. Just so was *her* entire life written off with such advice. No wonder she had no desire to marry.

They approached Ivy Lodge from the rear, and he leaped down, grabbed her by the waist with his iron grip, and lifted her off his horse then leaped back up. "Good day, my lady. And stay out of places where you don't belong, or I may not be around to rescue you next time."

He turned his mount and galloped away.

She stared after him, realizing that she hadn't asked him who he thought locked her in. But then, *he* didn't conjecture, either. Surely that was strange? Unless he thought he knew who had done it. With that disturbing thought, she walked up to the lodge and in, going directly to her room to dress appropriately for the breakfast table.

In a black rage, Darkefell rode back to the castle. Who had *dared* lock Lady Anne in the tower? Not John, at least, though his brother was keeping something from him, and Darkefell was dreadfully afraid it concerned the maid, Cecilia, and her death. Not Osei, who was being questioned by the magistrate; Sir Trevor persisted in believing that Darkefell's secretary killed the girl. Whether it was unreasoning prejudice or simply that Osei and Cecilia were walking together that evening, Darkefell didn't know.

However, Lady Anne was an insufferable snoop. Perhaps someone was as irritated by the woman as he was. And yet… with all the exasperation Lady Anne caused him, he could not stop thinking about her. Holding her close to his body as he took her back to Ivy Lodge, he had felt a wicked urge to kiss her again or to carry her off somewhere and make her pay attention to *him* rather than the puzzle of poor Cecilia's death.

Unaccountable and completely unsuitable.

Why had she even gone up into the tower, and what could he tell her to put her curiosity at rest about his and John's trip to Edward Carter's hut? He shouldn't need to say anything, but she was indefatigable when it came to the small mysteries of Ivy Lodge and the castle. It was vital that she not puzzle out the solution to *that* little enigma, even though it had nothing at all to do with the maid's murder. He would certainly tell her some lie—perhaps that the figure she saw was Daft Neddy and Bull, his dog. That would have to do, and to hell with her if she didn't believe him. But he would need to remember to tell John to go along with the lie.

He paused for a moment at the top of the rise and gazed at Darkefell Castle; when had he begun to do things he was not wholly proud of just to keep his family safe? He had compromised his integrity, and it shamed him. He had lied and worse, but would do it again, over and over, given the same circumstances. He pressed his heels in, and Sunny responded immediately, leaping into a gallop.

In a foul mood, he put his steed into his groom's trustworthy hands and hurled himself into his home, through the echoing halls of the modern section of the castle and up to his chamber. His mind kept going to Osei; if his secretary had not agreed to the solitary meeting with the magistrate, Darkefell would not have allowed it. His valet silently attended him as he changed from his morning riding gear into more presentable clothes, but as his mood ameliorated, he remembered Lady Anne's condemnation of his inability to allow her to aid him in the investigation.

He did have questions to which she was, perhaps, uniquely situated to find the answers. His sister-in-law Lydia was afraid of him. He had tried his best, but the silly chit still shied away from him like a nervous mare. He had tried gentleness, humor, even silence, but still she eyed him as if he would eat her if she came too close. But she trusted Lady Anne, apparently more than she trusted her husband. Lydia must know more about Cecilia's secret life than she was divulging, but she was stupid enough not even to be aware of what she knew. Lady Anne could, if directed properly, ask the right questions and give him the answers. But how to engage her help now that he had rejected it so boorishly?

Harwood finished with the cravat, and Darkefell gazed at himself dispassionately in the mirror. He was handsome. He wasn't vain about it; it was simply part of his life. With Lady Anne, he did have one tool at his disposal; she was physically attracted to him. He felt it, saw it in her eyes, could see her breath quicken, her cheeks pink. When he leaned against her in the saddle—more closely then he had needed to, certainly, even as he stifled the urge to do more—she had trembled. He was adept at exploiting such a rare thing as female passion, and he was not loath to do so, but he was surprised to discover ardor in her. She was intelligent, and he had always thought that clever women lacked the capacity for lust, and therefore would not experience animal attraction as lesser women sometimes did. But Lady Anne Addison was powerfully attracted to him. That, he had to admit, fascinated him.

He had been with passionate women. He had been with intelligent women. But one who was both? She intrigued him, and he was a little afraid of her for that very reason.

He descended and strode into his wood-paneled study to find that Osei and the magistrate were still there. It had been hours. Osei was wan and weary, as pale as he ever could be. His gaze, when it slued to his employer, held a hint of desperate entreaty in the dark brown depths glinting behind the spectacles.

"Sir Trevor," Tony said, stalking to sit behind his desk, "you will allow Mr. Boatin to rest. He's told you everything he knows."

"Ah, but that's the trouble, my lord. He has told me everything he *wishes* but will not divulge some key points. What am I to think?" Sir Trevor, his mobile, thin-lipped mouth drawn down in a frown, was clearly irritated by Osei's reticence. He paced to the window and back. "He was with Miss Wainwright just before her death but says that he saw her go into the lodge, and then departed. Now, since the maid was found outside, that is certainly false."

"Don't be ridiculous—Osei may well have seen Cecilia go into Ivy Lodge, but that doesn't mean she stayed there."

The magistrate was silent for a long moment, his brows drawn down. "I will grant you that point, my lord."

"Nor, even if she did stay there, does it mean that she was not accosted inside and dragged out! The doors were not yet locked. It was dark. It could have happened that way, though I make no claims to any knowledge on that point."

"Nevertheless—"

"No," Darkefell thundered, slamming his fist down on the desk. "Let him be!"

The magistrate, a severe and humorless man, stared at the marquess. "We're stuck on one point, my lord. Mr. Boatin is refusing to answer a couple of questions."

Osei turned to Darkefell. "I told Sir Trevor that I will not divulge Cecilia's private affairs, as she is not here to defend her behavior. It is not my place to speak of such things."

"I agree with my secretary," Darkefell said, turning to the magistrate. "He's defending the reputation of a friend who can no longer defend herself. I think that honorable behavior."

"If you support his intransigence, then I'm done," the man said. "If either of you feels like cooperating a little more fully, then I will come at a moment's notice. I can make no further inroads on the mystery if I'm not given all the information I require. Good day, my lord, Mr. Boatin." He departed in high dudgeon.

Osei bowed his head for a long moment then looked back up at the marquess. "Thank you, sir. I did not know how else to say I was not willing to answer for my poor Cecilia."

Darkefell watched Osei for a long moment. "I know you, Osei. I know with what horror you view violence. But others, particularly Sir Trevor, don't know you. People will look at you with suspicion, yet you will not do what you must to keep from being an object of that mistrust. Cecilia, of *all* people, would forgive you unveiling her secrets now that she's gone and can no longer be injured by cruel gossip. She was your friend, you've told me—she wouldn't want suspicion to fall on you. Why not just tell what you know if it will help to exonerate you?"

The secretary stood, his dark eyes behind the glinting lenses of his spectacles full of anguish. "I do not agree that she cannot be injured by gossip, sir. I wish her spirit to rest easy, and the spirit of the life she carried within her, too. My people say that as the mother cries, so weeps the unborn child. Death cannot change that."

The marquess had known Osei five years, and not once in that time had he ever found him to err when it came to matters of morality. If he could have said the same of himself, he would have felt more easy demanding answers. Darkefell knew from the magistrate that the villagers were perturbed. They had tolerated Osei since his arrival, but with the murder of a young woman and Osei implicated, how could Darkefell protect him if he wouldn't help? "I won't try to force you to speak."

"Thank you, sir."

"But I wish you would."

Osei inclined his head. "May I go?"

"Yes, yes, of course. Is all ready for tonight?"

"I have everything prepared."

"Good. You may go. Get some rest—you look dreadful."

Ten

It had been a disturbing morning so far, but upon attending the breakfast room and expecting to talk about her ordeal, Anne found no one and dined alone. Ellen, busy with her usual tasks, had been able to spare only a few moments to help with her dress, and none for her hair. In a miff and with nerves frayed to the nub, Anne stood staring out her bedroom window. But her mood lifted when she caught sight of her own carriage pulling into the lodge drive and back toward the stables. "Thank goodness!" she cried aloud as she wrapped her shawl around her shoulders and descended, then exited the manor house, hastening around back. Mary, her son Wee Robbie, and Anne's driver, Sanderson, would be invaluable support to her, stranger as she was to everyone else but Lydia.

"Mary, Robbie! How grateful I am to see you both. And Sanderson, of course," she said, striding toward them as they descended from the coach, Robbie first and then his mother.

"Aye, we're here. Finally!" Mary said, her steps wobbly. Her son, just nine but with a bright and intelligent gleam in his blue eyes, took his mother's arm and steadied her.

Then, from the open door, leaped Irusan, down to the gravel drive. Two large dogs, released from the confines of the stable by the grooms opening the door to temporarily house Anne's coach horses, tore out and into the open drive. Irusan arched his back, hissed, and leaped up into Anne's arms. She buried her face in his thick, long fur and hugged him. "How I've *missed* you all." The big tabby's throaty purr responded in kind.

The stable dogs leaping and barking, Mary trying to talk over them, her r's rolling in her agitation, and Robbie laughing at the dogs' antics, made a horrendous din. Lord John opened a window from a room on the second floor. "What's going on? Poor Lydia is trying to sleep."

"Come inside," Anne said, to her maid and Robbie. "Sanderson," she said more loudly, "the coach and horses will be housed up at the castle, so after you've unloaded my trunks and watered the horses, see to it." Taciturn as always, her coachman tipped his hat and nodded, then went about his work.

Anne edged close to him for a moment and said *sotto voce*, "Sanderson, when you get to the marquess's stables, befriend a groom by the name of Jamey—it's possible he and a confederate are behind the werewolf hoax."

He gave no hint of hearing her. Robbie and the stable lad eyed each other; the other boy—Bertie he introduced himself as—at the advanced age of eleven or twelve, must have decided Robbie was a harmless child, so he offered to show him around the stables.

Mary agreed, and the two boys ran off, his mother shouting a reminder not to stay out too long and not to keep the lad from his tasks, and to go to the servants' entrance when he was done.

Anne led her maid up to her bedchamber as two sturdy grooms carried up Anne's trunks and Mary's more modest bags. Mary unpacked Anne's clothing and necessities in the dressing room attached to her mistress's bedchamber while Anne sat on a low chair by the window and related what happened the night of her arrival: finding Cecilia's body, Lydia's lack of courtesy in not telling anyone of her arrival, and the odd behavior of Mr. Osei Boatin upon hearing of the maid's death. She went on to speak of her adventure that morning, being locked into the tower.

"Didya consider, milady," Mary said, shaking out a shawl, "that the tower door being shut and locked could've bin a mistake? P'raps someone, e'en the stable lad, saw it open and thought it should be locked, and did so."

"But I shouted down—I saw someone disappearing through the brush."

"If that was my Robbie, he would've been afeart that he was in trouble and cut oot. You dinna know how boys are."

"I hadn't thought of it being a simple mistake." She and Mary talked more, and all the while Anne stroked Irusan, her enormous, long-haired tabby, a cat renowned for his irritable temper and inquisitive disposition. Idly, she said, ruffling his fur, "I don't think I mentioned to Mrs. Hailey, the housekeeper, that you would be bringing Irusan with you."

Mary cast her a knowing look as she shook out a blue camlet gown that had a matching merino shawl. She picked off a couple of cat hairs and carried it over to the wardrobe. "I s'pose that wee task will be up to me, then? I'll no' have a moment's rest if she takes against me, milady."

Anne sighed deeply. "You're right, of course. I'll tell her about Irusan. I need you to be on good terms with the household staff—as much as any visiting maid can be—and find out more about Cecilia Wainwright's affairs, love and otherwise. Ellen, one of the chambermaids, seems to have been on particularly good terms with Cecilia, so I'd like you to get to know her."

"Aye, I thought as much—I'll be your ears and eyes belowstairs, just as I have in the past. Are ya for findin' out who done the turrible deed, then?"

Anne sighed and shook her head. "Lydia's upset. I made no promises, but if I find out, it would be a relief for all concerned."

"Aye," Mary said as she took a tabby silk dress from the trunk, brushed it, then hung it up. "An' yer ain curiosity willna stand the suspense 'til you do."

"How well you know me," Anne said tranquilly, rubbing Irusan under the chin. He purred loudly and sprawled on her lap. "How did this one behave on the way here?"

"Your feline companion? As well as you'd think," Mary responded, her tone clipped.

"Rather poorly, then."

"Aye."

"That's odd, he always behaves perfectly for me."

"He's no fool, that one. He knows who provides his catmeat."

Anne was silent as Mary continued with her tasks. Pelisses, capelets, shawls, dresses, bonnets, petticoats, night attire, chemises, stays, stomachers—all were carefully shaken, brushed, fluffed, then hung, folded, or otherwise disposed of. Brushes, combs, jewelry, lace fichus, gloves, fans—these Mary refolded or examined then tucked them back in the confines of the trunk drawer, which she locked with one key on her silver chatelaine. From the other trunk, Mary removed Anne's drawing paper and tools, and her travel desk, a cunningly constructed, latched mahogany box, fortified at the corners with brass plates, and with a sloped surface for writing. It had inside a multitude of drawers holding ink bottles, quills, sealing wax, seals, paper, a pounce pot, the sand to fill it with, and a penknife. These were dispatched to Anne's bedchamber on a table to the left of the window, situated perfectly for morning light.

"Your chatelaine reminds me of my discovery this morning," Anne called out as Mary set up the desk box in the bedchamber. "Or rather, my two discoveries." Her maid returned to the dressing room, and as she unpacked a case holding toiletries, Anne told her about the hank of fur and the bit of gold chain she found in the shrubbery that morning where Cecilia's body had been found two nights before.

"What d'you make of it, milady?" Mary asked, proceeding to unpack her own modest baggage, and Robbie's.

"I don't know. My first thought was that we were meant to believe Cecilia had been killed by the werewolf."

"And your second thought?"

"That it makes no sense. No one saw the werewolf that night, so what would be the point of leaving clues to indicate it was he, without a witness to that effect?" Anne retrieved the piece of fur and held it up to the light. "How did this fur get there?"

Mary leaned over and looked at it. "Looks to be cut from a tippet, or some such garment."

The hank of fur did seem straight cut rather than a tuft ripped from an animal. "And it smelled faintly of camphor, to me, at first."

"An' you have the most sensitive nose of any bein' on God's green airth," Mary said with a smile. "So, p'raps from a tippet or stole that'd bin stored?"

"You think it was placed there deliberately, then, along with the piece of gold chain?"

"Seems daft to go to so much trouble, though, milady. How would anyone see that in the drear night?"

Anne slowly said, "But, Mary, no one knew I was coming. The murderer thought Cecilia would be found in daylight and the two items discovered at the same time."

"You've got it, milady!" Mary exclaimed, her blue eyes wide.

"But in that case," Anne reasoned, "the murderer wanted the household to know that she was not killed by a real werewolf but someone pretending to be a werewolf—perhaps the chain was meant to point to one person directly." She stood, set Irusan down on the chair, and brushed the cat fur from her skirts. "Therefore," she said, "if I can find out who the chain and fur points to, then that person is the most likely to be innocent! I need to find out what's been going on around here."

"Aye," Mary said. "An' I must round up m'boy. I dinna care to have him keepin' the stable lad from his chores."

Though she had journeyed north in answer to Lydia's plea for help concerning reports of a werewolf, the murder of a helpless young woman was a far more serious and distressing matter, particularly as that young woman was so closely associated with Lydia. Investigating the murder might lead to solving the other mystery, Anne decided. Was the murder a passionate crime, or had poor Cecilia merely been in the wrong place at the wrong moment? Perhaps she knew something she shouldn't have about the werewolf? If Anne was right about the deliberate placement of the tuft of fur and chain, then her murder was planned *and* allied with the werewolf mystery.

"No one here is willing to talk. I need to go to the nearest village," Anne said, looking around. She was quite alone, except for the sleeping cat. "Well," she commented, "one can never be more sure of sensible conversation than when one talks to oneself."

Lydia arranged for a pony cart for Anne and directions into Hornethwaite, the nearest village, located just beyond the marquess's property. Robbie, garbed in his dark gray livery, was enlisted to go along, both to hold the pony and to carry packages should she buy much. The day was bright, the air sparkling, and Anne was invigorated by new hope that she could find answers in the village. But first she went only a short way, her excellent sense of direction leading her to the house that she had seen from the tower. It was oddly close to the marquess's property and must be the estate of Mr. Hiram Grover. Anne wondered if the marquess had ever tried to buy it.

She reined in the pony as she mounted the short drive to a square, modern building. What excuse could she possibly use now that she was there? "I can't think of a single reason to be here now that I have pulled up. What do you think, Robbie, my boy?" she said to her maid's son, who clung to the cart.

A groom emerged from behind the house. He touched his forelock and took the reins of the pony. Robbie jumped down and said loudly, "Milady was just wantin' to know, as she's going into town, does the mister want anything?"

The fellow shrugged. Anne, thanking heaven for Robbie's abundant good sense and quick mind, stepped down from the cart and said, "Thank you, my good man. I shall ask Mr. Grover myself, then, if you don't know."

Robbie took the reins of the pony, stating that was his job, as Anne sailed up to the house and employed the knocker. She was greeted by a maid who curtseyed, awed, it seemed, by Anne's excellent clothing, plumed bonnet, and riding switch. It was unconventional, to say the least, for her to visit a widower and stranger in such a hasty manner, but this was the country, not London, so country manners would be her excuse. Anne was shown directly into Mr. Grover's library, where he joined her a moment later, buttoning his jacket over his paunch.

"Lady Anne, how delightful to see you again!" he said, bowing deeply.

"Mr Grover, What a lovely house you have!" Mendacity had its reward in the smile wreathing his round face. He indicated a chair, but she declined, saying, "I just stopped on my way into Hornethwaite. I understand it's the only place nearby to purchase paper and ink."

"You will find a most helpful stationers. I am sure your ladyship is a prodigious correspondent," he said with another bow.

She hit her whip handle against her palm and said, "This visit is a little unusual, but I'm a country woman, Mr. Grover, and employ country manners. I thought I'd inquire if you or your housekeeper need anything in the village."

He stared at her, a puzzled expression on his fleshy countenance. "No, I don't believe so, my lady."

She glanced around at the sparsely furnished drawing room. With an arch manner, she said, "How graciously open your rooms are. One can see you have no wife resident, sir, for a woman would have filled every corner with furnishings." She could see in his eyes some kind of dawning knowledge, but she was astounded by his next words.

"I'm a lorn widower, my lady. If I could find a lady such as yourself, with taste, style, substance," he said with an insinuating softness in his voice, "I would rush back to the altar with abandon."

He thought she was husband hunting! As humili- ating an assumption as that was, it gave her the opening she needed. Never afraid to show herself in a less than flattering light, she said, "You widowers, sir, are very disarming." She simpered. "Flattery, of course, is never amiss." She tapped his arm with her crop in her best imitation of the empty-headed coquette she had once aspired to be, then added in a confidential tone, "Tell me, has any local woman designs on the marquess?"

An expression of distaste fleeted across his fleshy face. "His lordship has had his share of local women fall at his feet, and I say that in a figurative and literal sense."

She paused, trying to puzzle him out. Clearly he *wished* to be understood, but she must say just the right thing. Without a lying word, she said, "He is a most arrogant, infuriating man." He appeared to relish her criticism, so she leaned forward and added, "He alarms me with his violent fits."

Mr. Grover reached out and grabbed her free hand, holding it firmly to his chest. "Oh, my lady, be careful. Do! Too many young women have lost their lives near that place." He gave a great shudder that rolled over his hefty frame like a wave over water.

"Whatever do you mean, sir?"

He looked around, as if they might be overheard, and murmured, "Last year a young lady rumored to be intimately involved with the marquess died in a… hmmm, tragic *fall* from Staungill Force, on Darkefell land."

She did not have to feign shock. "My goodness!" She extricated her gloved hand from his grip and held it over her thumping heart. "That's terrible!"

He shook his head. "The local magistrate did what he could to investigate her death, but I fear he is in the marquess's pocket."

"What are you saying, sir?"

"I would never say anything to insinuate, to imply... in short, to give anyone reason to think the marquess culpable."

"Oh."

"But then in February, just two short months ago, young Mr. Allengate's sister, Fanny, died in exactly the same way!"

Anne's stomach clenched, and the scene she had witnessed between Richard Allengate and Lady Darkefell took on a dreadful new meaning. "She... jumped? Is that what you mean?"

Grover shook his head, his florid cheeks flapping. "No one quite knows what occurred. It is said... but no, I should not retail gossip."

Continuing her charade of avid spinster gossip, she said, "Tell me, sir, for I'm a stranger to all in those houses except my poor, dear Lydia, and I worry for her. She's such a child, still, though a bride of four months."

He lowered his voice, and his eyes goggled. "Miss Allengate had told some of her intimates that she would soon be engaged to the marquess, and then she tragically died. No one would say a word, except for the coincidence of the death occurring at the falls. The girl a year ago, Jacob Landers's daughter, Tilly—

"Jacob Landers, the postman?"

"The same."

"Well, that explains Mr. Landers's distaste for the family, if his daughter died on Darkefell land."

"The apple of Jacob's eye—he's never been right since her murder." He put one fleshy hand over his mouth, and his eyes widened.

"*Murder?*" Some London gossip came back to Anne. "I recall some gossip, sir, at the time—Lord Darkefell's brother was accused of causing her death."

"Yes, but some say Lord Julius Bestwick was covering for his brother—they were twins, you know, and very close. Someone saw the marquess at the falls, but Lord Julius claimed it was he and that he saw Tilly fall to her death. Lord Julius was about to be charged with her murder when he disappeared, then turned up in Upper Canada, and then died. Perhaps it all ended as it should. It troubles me to see the sons of that family cause their dear mother so much turmoil. It never would have happened if their father had lived."

"I had no idea of any of this," she said. "And I must daily face these people while I visit poor Lydia!"

He shook his head. "My lady, it troubles me to speak ill of my friends."

"Though you seem to have no friendship for the current marquess, sir," Anne said tartly. Grover drew back. Anne had allowed her real personality too much freedom. "I mean," she said, softening her voice, "the marquess, as I have said, is a difficult gentleman to like. Very high-handed. He claims you have reason to dislike him because he corrupted your son, Theophilus."

Stiffly, Mr. Grover said, "That is not true. He *tried* to lead my son astray while they were in school, but Theophilus was impervious to such debauched temptation—he's now a highly respected man of the cloth and will be bishop some day. Lord Darkefell's jest was poorly done."

"An ill-timed bit of humor," she murmured. "I must go, sir, for the pony has been left standing with my tiger long enough."

He walked her toward the door and said, "I did not mean to become pokerish, but Theophilus is the pride of my life, and the marquess has no right to make sport. He is a rash young man—I regret repeating such filth, but it is said that Tilly was at the falls that fateful day to tell him that she was carrying his child."

Anne did not try to hide her shock. "How can you say such a thing?"

"I'm sorry, my lady, for saying things unfit for your ears, but it's galling to hear him lauded as a good landowner and this and that, when the truth is that he is a fornicator and a trial to his mother. Ask him! Was he not Tilly's lover? That poor girl had fallen from grace with him and carried his child—just ask him to deny it!"

She felt sickened inside and regretted the worm of doubt about Darkefell that wriggled into her, but it did not escape her notice that, though Mr. Grover had said he would not speak of it, he did ultimately reveal some of the evidence against the marquess. Malice or honesty? "I thought it was Lord Julius who was seen near the waterfall that day?"

With a sly tone and raised eyebrows, he said, "Twins, my lady, and very close—'twas an anonymous note to the magistrate that exposed the marquess's presence there that day. Lord Julius may have thought he was saving the family name. Sometimes a ne'er-do-well will try to redeem himself with a grand gesture, and Julius was a bit of a ne'er-do-well. After his death, all talk was hushed."

"How convenient for the marquess that his brother died, then. What about Richard Allengate's sister?"

"Poor Fanny." He shook his head and made a tsk-tsk sound between his teeth. "A good girl led astray, I've always thought, by the blandishments of a powerful man." He opened the door for Anne.

"But her death cannot be laid at the door of Lord Julius," Anne said, strolling out into the sunshine and turning back toward Mr. Grover. "Was it suicide?"

"Her brother does not think so, I can tell you that. The poor fellow is distraught."

"I admit, sir, that I'm puzzled by all of this, how a family of such seemingly good character can have had such a rash of deaths and terrible events befall them. And now these werewolf sightings and sheep slaughter, and poor Cecilia Wainwright's murder, for such it must be called. I can't believe that was an animal act."

"I cannot explain it. The barbarity of such an action! It's deeply distressing." He sighed. "I have given it much thought and have decided that I will be leaving my home here."

"Leaving?" She stood on the doorstep and gazed up at him. Whatever she had expected to hear, it was not that.

"I can no longer live here alone. With my son about to marry, I think to sell and purchase a cottage near him and his lady. I no longer wish to be burdened with running this estate. I inherited when I was a lad and spent the best years of my life here, but the once-honorable marquessate has changed in the hands of such a man as the current Lord Darkefell." He paused and looked back into his house. "That is why you see my home so empty and with no butler or footmen. I have been selling or moving my possessions and letting go of staff. It is a long process and difficult, but I'm ready to move now."

"I wish you luck in your new home, sir. To whom do you sell?"

"I suppose it is no harm to tell, though it's not yet final. Lord Darkefell will be purchasing my home." He sighed heavily. "He's been after me for years to sell it to him. He'll get his wish."

Anne wasn't surprised; Mr. Grover's acreage was like a hole in the Darkefell estate, a hole that would now be filled. "What do you think is the answer to the mystery of the werewolf sightings, sir?"

"At first I thought it horseplay, but then sheep were slaughtered and left to rot, among them some of my own." He frowned. "Perhaps a pack of dogs?"

He took her arm and led her out to the pony cart and handed her up into it. He bowed, then, and said, "I have been heartsick, my lady, about these awful events. My greatest hope is that the perpetrator of these foul deeds shall be identified and receive his just rewards, a meeting with the hangman."

Eleven

THE JAUNT INTO HORNETHWAITE WAS UNEVENTFUL. She left the pony trap at the livery stable, and then, with Robbie, strolled to the village center. Hornethwaite was everything she had expected Staunby to be: quaint, active, and busy. The high street was built on a hill that climbed steadily to green vistas beyond it. Each building and bridge, parish wall, church, and spire was built of dun-colored stone with slate roofs, but far from appearing dull, it had a harmonious glow, the spring green of the surrounding countryside in the distance and village green setting it off nicely.

She bought unnecessary ink at the stationer's, superfluous ribbon at the dry goods shop, and gratuitous headache powder at the chemist's, engaging in polite conversation at every stop. Finally, she had exhausted her shopping and her feet. The people of Hornethwaite were closemouthed, and numerous sallies to try to pry information from the reticent Yorkshire folk shut them up tighter.

Even an arch reference to the werewolf did nothing but draw a frown of remonstrance and a barely

understandable rebuke that such talk was "trammel"—
Anne took that to mean nonsense or trash—though it
was acknowledged that some girls of the village had
been troubled by the creature. It was thought that
they were "gauvies"—simpletons, she guessed—easily
frightened. She was tired, discouraged, and thirsty.
The coffee shop was to be her last stop. Followed by
Robbie, she returned to the far end of the high street,
near the livery stable and inn.

There was a dirty-looking fellow lingering outside
of the taproom. As she strolled past, he accosted
her, begging for a pittance with which to purchase a
beverage. Never one to deny a thirsty man relief, she
dug in her reticule and handed him a farthing.

"Thank'ee, ma'am." Then he leaned in closer, his
sour breath making Anne's nose twitch. "I 'eard you
arskin' 'bout yon weerwolve," he said, his Yorkshire
accent broad. "If yer lookin', look no farver than yon
African, from t'markwis's castle—'e be stricken wi' an
African curse, turning 'im inta wolf at night."

Her brow wrinkled, Anne waded through his
accent and asked, "Are you speaking of Mr. Boatin?"

"Yers. 'E had no right," he said, then followed with
a string of unintelligible words.

He bumbled toward the taproom door. Anne
followed, grabbed his sleeve, and said, "Whatever do
you mean? What are you saying?"

His expression was blank, though, and he said,
shaking his head, "Niver you mind, marm." He
broke free of her restraining hand. His bloodshot
eyes widened, and he shook his head. "I niver said
nothink 'gainst yon blackamoor, but whut he's

doing what he oughtint wiv girls he oughtint tooch. I saw 'im."

He disappeared through the taproom door, and it was not an establishment into which Anne could follow. Puzzled by the man's oblique reference to Osei Boatin—his dialect was far thicker than any of the other Hornethwaite residents she had so far spoken with, but it sounded as though he was implying he'd seen Osei with a girl, Cecilia, perhaps. She pondered his words as she entered the dining room that was on the other side of the inn entrance. Robbie eagerly agreed to milk and cakes in the landlady's own kitchen, while Anne ate in solitary splendor in the dining room.

When the landlady, a Mrs. Haight, came to serve her, Anne looked her over. She was a comfortable-looking lady of middle years and clearly well-entrenched in local affairs, as was proved by her familiar greetings to many of the locals who entered.

"Thank you, Mrs. Haight," Anne said as the woman set down a tray of scones with creamy butter, a pot of preserves, and a steaming china teapot. "May I ask you a question?"

"Certainly, milady," she said, curtseying.

She appeared flattered to be spoken to on such familiar terms by the daughter of an earl. Anne knew villages; her exact lineage was common knowledge by now, as was her friendship with Lydia and her stay at Ivy Lodge. A woman in Mrs. Haight's position would dispense gossip along with the best Gunpowder Green and China Black.

"I'm visiting Ivy Lodge. My dear friend, Lady John Bestwick, has been sorely troubled by the goings-on in the area. What do you think of it all?"

The woman appeared to be taken aback by such open questioning, but Anne had little time and less patience for obliqueness. When Mrs. Haight was silent for a long moment, Anne added, watching her face, "She has been so frightened by talk of a werewolf, or a wolf, and I wish to set her mind at ease with what the more *astute* of local inhabitants think."

The flattery worked. The bosomy lady murmured, "Well, milady, we 'ave our suspicions." She glanced around, and when Anne waved at the chair opposite her, she sat on the edge of it. She leaned forward, her bosom resting on the edge of the table. "Haight an' me, we think the werewolf is joost local tricksters, harassin' the marquess an' his family."

"Yes?" Anne said encouragingly.

She glanced around the room and lowered her tone, saying, "But the murderin' savage whut has plagued us hereabouts… that's another matter."

"Three young women dead, whether by the same hand or different ones, is distressing. I see you separate the events—the supposed werewolf and the deaths—and I think that's wise, for given the difference in the gravity of the two affairs, they truly do not seem to be committed by the same person."

"Aye, milady."

"Three young local women dead. And all on the marquess's property!"

"An all wi' a man o' th'estate as a beau!" The woman's eyes widened, and she put her work-worn hand over her mouth.

Digesting what she meant, Anne slowly said, watching the woman's eyes, "All with a man of the estate as a beau… you believe the gossip about Tilly Landers and the marquess, then?"

She was clearly conflicted, but Mrs. Haight finally said, "Well, noow, he's a man, in't he? Can't be expected to do without, not but whut he normally keeps such affairs to London."

Anne's stomach turned. "Were they still… involved… at the time of her death?"

"Some says yes, some says no." She began to stand.

Her mind whirling with speculation, reeling from the unexpected confirmation that Darkefell was entwined with Tilly Landers, Anne searched for a way of inquiring further and finally said, "Do the people of Hornethwaite think the awful event of two nights ago is connected with those who live at Ivy Lodge or the castle?" It was the most delicate way she could think to ask.

The woman made a sound through her teeth and seemed undecided for the moment, but then sat back down and said, "I'm of two minds. I don't like to be th'one to say, but my window overlooks the high street—I saw wi' me own eyes a certain young man cooming back to his home in Hornethwaite in the airly hours of the morn' after that poor girl was murdered t'other night… tho' I didn't know it at the time, did I? I'm not one to gossip, but where was he? When we heard about the terrible deed the next day, I told Haight 'bout seein' him, walking down the high street in the dark, the moon shining down on him, like as if he were in a daze."

"What did your husband say? Of whom do you speak?" Anne asked when it appeared the woman had no more to say.

She frowned and shook her head. "Haight asked the young gent, an' 'e said 'e was out walkin.' Out walkin'? At that hour, I says?" She shook her head and straightened. "But Haight sees nothin' strange in't."

A young man of the village; could Mrs. Haight be speaking of Richard Allengate? He was the only one she could think of, but then she didn't know the local population. She opened her mouth to ask, but just then more customers came in and Mrs. Haight rose, her candid expression shuttering into well-mannered distantness with just a trace of regret.

"Good afternoon, milady," she said, with a hasty curtsey. "I'll be beggin' that you don't take whut I've said amiss. I know naught and shouldn't be flapping me gums on such things."

Anne, familiar from personal experience with the feeling of having said more than she ought on a subject, suspected that Mrs. Haight, flattered by her attention, had said more than she intended and wouldn't respond to questions about the identity of the young man. It was too late, anyway, as the landlady was moving away, returning to her duties.

Two genteel-appearing ladies who had just entered took a table near Anne and proceeded to gossip, throwing her occasional glances of avid curiosity. Unfortunately they spoke of people unfamiliar to Anne, so the conversation did not interest her. Never had she regretted the divisions that prevented her from starting conversations with strangers, and the reticence her position in society as an earl's daughter imposed. If she had been a shopgirl or servant, she would have learned more in two minutes than she had so far learned in two hours.

Not finding any reasonable solutions in her own mind for the crimes of which she had heard that morning, her mind drifted to the intolerably high-handed Lord Darkefell, the kiss he had inflicted on her the day before, and the indubitable perfection of his technique. Was she so simple, then, that a skillful kiss could knock good sense out of her? She still regarded him with suspicion, more so now that she knew of his reported affair with Tilly Landers, speculative though it might be. But still, her heart beat faster at the thought of his dark eyes and overtly masculine form, and that was the reaction of a silly woman, the sort she had disparaged more than once in conversation as beneath contempt. Perhaps in future she would not be so judgmental.

She abandoned that train of thought. His lordship would not physically impose on her again. He was mocking her, deliberately teasing her because he knew his effect on her. It was in his eyes when he spoke to her, and in his tone. He was a handsome man and aware of it. She was a foolish woman and feared he was aware of that, too. Thus the kiss. If he wished to mislead her, that was the behavior of a devious fellow with something to hide; she could not forget that.

Those thoughts led to another more painful train of thought in the wake of the information Mrs. Haight had given her. She had said all three girls were involved with those at the estate. Did that mean his lordship, as was the way with some men of power, dallied even with the maid, Cecilia Wainwright? Had she threatened him with exposure or told young Jamey? Or confessed her pregnancy and demanded…

something? Even if her interest was in Jamey, the groom, a marquess would be a greater catch even just as a lover, and she was a lovely young woman. She could have engaged in a tryst with him for the gifts and favors he could bestow upon her. If she had told Jamey she was moving on to another affair, would he have hurt her in retaliation? Or perhaps jealousy of his lordship was reason enough for Jamey to hurt her?

She didn't like the direction her mind was taking and turned away from those thoughts.

The tea was good, the delicate scones better, and the preserves indescribably delicious, but it was time she returned to Ivy Lodge. She was getting no further in Hornethwaite and had more unanswered questions than she had started with, thanks to Mr. Grover. How had Tilly Landers died? And Fanny Allengate? Were those deaths connected with Cecilia Wainwright? If it was Richard Allengate that Mrs. Haight spoke of, why was he coming back to the village in the early hours of the morning? She could think of no scenario that would cause young Allengate to murder an innocent maidservant, even if he was angry with or suspicious that one of the men of Darkefell Castle had hurt his sister. Too many questions and too few answers.

"Excuse me, my lady," one of the genteel young women said. They had both risen and stood by her table.

"Yes?"

"I believe we have an acquaintance in common," she said and named a young woman with whom Anne had gone to school, Miss Henrietta Copeland.

"Ah, yes! I remember Miss Copeland. How is the dear girl?"

"Actually, she is now Mrs. George Lange and lives in Leeds. George is my brother, a barrister there. I am Miss Beatrice Lange."

Anne eyed her with interest; she was a buxom young woman, very pretty, with rosy cheeks and a pert bonnet perched on dusky curls. She indicated the empty chairs at her table. "Would you sit with me for a few moments and tell me, how is dear Henrietta? As you can see, I have no other acquaintance here, and was just regretting that fact." As they chatted, Anne examined both young women. They were well dressed, their stomachers and petticoats fine brocade and silk, even if the lace trim was lower quality and the style of their clothes a year or so out of date. Addressing Anne as she had was wrong of Miss Lange—it was too forward an action—but Anne forgave her the impertinence, as it suited her own needs so perfectly.

"I'm temporarily resident at Ivy Lodge," Anne offered. "My dear friend Lydia is now married to the youngest son, Lord John Bestwick."

The two ladies exchanged significant looks; Anne had told them nothing they didn't already know. Anne almost rubbed her hands together at the prospect of a couple of local gossips. They knew some of what was going on at Darkefell and perhaps conjectured more, but drawing them out was a delicate process. Her first question, regarding Mr. Osei Boatin, provoked mostly silence; neither girl knew anything about him beyond his sad history, nor, they claimed, had they heard any gossip. He was only rarely in town and then went about his business and returned to the Darkefell estate.

The other young woman's name was Mrs. Lily Jenkins, and as Anne chatted with them, it became apparent to Anne that she, while duly flattered at the notice of a woman of Lady Anne's stature, was full of her own importance. She was the wife of the eldest son of a local brewer, and as such, one of the premiere families of Hornethwaite. She had too little learning to be interesting, but enough money to be frivolous, a deadly combination.

But useful. Miss Lange was more careful, wiser, more charitable; so soon Anne turned her full attention to Mrs. Jenkins. The young woman gleefully gossiped about Tilly Landers's death; the daughter of the local postmaster, Jacob Landers—of whom Anne had no good opinion—she was a barmaid at the inn's taproom, a vain, trifling, catty girl, and "no better than she should be," according to Mrs. Jenkins. It was rumored that she thought to trap one of the men of Darkefell into marriage by claiming to be pregnant with his child.

The marquess, perhaps?

A fool's plot indeed, for no man of stature would marry a barmaid because she carried his bastard babe; the usual method of dealing with such incidents was to provide a modest dowry, marry the girl off to some worthy local fellow, and secretly provide for the child's education in a respectable trade. Ladies knew of such dealings and turned a blind eye to it. But then, Tilly was accounted a foolish young woman.

The question was, and still remained, which gentleman was she targeting? Lily argued for Lord Julius Bestwick, but Miss Lange was vehement that it was Lord John. Neither thought she would dare try to trap the marquess, a formidable fellow, both feared and respected. But were they wrong? If Mr. Grover and Mrs. Haight were to be believed, the marquess had succumbed to Tilly's simple charms.

However, it didn't mean the child she claimed to carry was his nor that he was even still involved with her. "But *was* the child she carried one of theirs or not? I assume that the marquess is very… healthy in his appetites," Anne commented with a prim moue of distaste, feeling a pink flush mount her cheeks. "Perhaps it really *was* his."

"Coulda bin *anyone's* bairn," Mrs. Jenkins said, her careful accent slipping back into Yorkshire broadness.

"Lily, that's unkind. Poor Tilly didn't have our advantages," Miss Lange remonstrated.

"Doesn't mean she couldn't have kept her skirts down," Lily crudely stated.

"But Tilly's immoral behavior is not the case with poor Fanny Allengate, who was also found dead on Darkefell property," Anne said carefully.

"No," Miss Lange said, her brilliant blue eyes welling with tears. "Oh, no, poor Fanny! She and Tilly could not have been more different."

"So *you* say," Lily Jenkins murmured, turning her face away and staring out the window.

"Did you know her?" Anne asked Miss Lange.

"Since girlhood, though she is… was… a couple of years younger than I. The Allengate family and mine were very close."

This was the opening she had hoped for, but just then Robbie came in and stood nearby, waiting for her attention. "Yes, Robbie?"

He whispered, "'Is lordship's come into town."

"The marquess?"

He nodded. Her heart thudded. But she wasn't doing anything wrong. Resolutely, she decided to see this through and sent Robbie off to the confectioner's to get a few pen'worth of candies for himself, and to the butcher for some catmeat for Irusan.

"Miss Lange, you were saying that you were a girl-hood friend of Fanny Allengate. What was she like?"

"She was a sweet girl," Miss Lange said, her unshed tears trembling on her long lashes. "Innocent. I don't mean, uh, untouched, though I'm sure she was," the young woman hastened to say, blushing, even as Mrs. Jenkins gave an audible sniff of disbelief. "I mean naïve, I suppose."

A commotion near the door made Anne raise her voice to be heard over the din. "Naïve? Was she easily taken advantage of, you mean?"

"Yes, I suppose that's what I mean. She believed anything you told her. Girls used to tell her the most frightful lies," she said with a glance at Lily Jenkins, "and she would believe them. It may have been a joke but often ended in tears for poor Fanny."

"Was she involved with the marquess, too?"

A voice from behind said, "I am surprised, Lady Anne, to find you gossiping like a common dairymaid, and in the coffee house of all places."

Anne stiffened as Mrs. Jenkins and Miss Lange leaped to their feet, murmured hasty, tumbling farewells, and departed, their half boots clattering noisily on the wide-board floor. Turning slowly, Anne pasted a smile on her face and said, "Hello, Lord Darkefell. This is not the sort of place I would expect to meet you."

Twelve

"I WAS DRAWN BY YOUR PRESENCE," HE SAID WITH A mocking lift to his left brow.

She regarded him evenly. "Darkefell," she said quietly with a quick look around the room to make sure she could not be overheard, "you've driven me to seek out gossips simply because of your own reticence... *understandable* reticence. Painful family history is not what any of us likes to divulge, but if it has anything to do with the current troubles—"

"But it doesn't," he thundered, his smile dying. "You are dragging—" He stopped and glanced around at the customers in the dim dining room; they turned away hastily at his dark look. He leaned over Anne and growled, "You are dragging my family's name through the muck for no reason but your own incurable nosiness. I will not allow that."

His face was inches away from hers, and she noted the pulsing vein at his temple, highlighted by the weak light filtering in the window. "This is not the place to discuss matters," she murmured, her voice trembling. "If you wish, I will attend you at the castle—which you have promised to show me, and I'll hold you to that promise—and we can speak about the current problems and any solutions I may devise."

He stared into her calm gray eyes then straightened. "Though I don't recall promising to show you about the castle, I will do so if you wish." He took her arm, nodded to the befuddled landlady, and hastened Lady Anne outside, where her tiger awaited her with the pony trap. His horse was tied to the back of the trap as he had commanded. "I must insist you come away from Hornethwaite this minute, though, my lady," he said, tugging her toward the waiting vehicle. "You see before you an errand boy. I have been sent here with a message from my mother—she demands that you come back to Ivy Lodge at once and deal with the commotion caused by your maid and your… cat." He choked back laughter.

"Oh dear," Lady Anne said, climbing up in the trap with his assistance. "Has Irusan been making a fuss?"

"Is Irusan your maid or your cat?"

"My cat."

He thought for a moment, then looked up at her as she settled herself on the seat. "What, my dear lady, do you have against poets?"

Her gray eyes widened, and she laughed out loud, taking up her whip from the holder. "You know the old story!" she exclaimed, smiling down at him.

He was wordless for a moment; her swift, elegant movements and laughter showed her in a singularly flattering light. Young ladies, in his presence, tended toward simpering flattery, awed silence, or awkward coquettishness. Lady Anne appeared unimpressed both by his temper and his eminence; why that should be attractive, he could not imagine. Surely he should prefer the flattery or flirtation? But he didn't. Her cool indifference, mingled with the impression he had that she was attracted to him despite her better intentions, was fascinating. If he was to kiss her once more, would she strike him yet again or kiss him back?

She eyed him and said, "You are uncommonly silent, struck dumb by a simple question?"

He clutched the smooth wood of the cart seat and said, "I *do* know the old story of Irusan and the poet, Seanchan."

Robbie, the lady's tiger, had already leaped up to the back of the coach. Darkefell climbed up, the trap creaking under his weight, and took from her both the reins and the whip. She did not, contrary to his expectation, protest his assumption of command.

"I have nothing against poets, my lord," she said, folding her hands in her lap, "though I prefer straightforward prose. But from the old tale, I *did* admire the feline's ambitious behavior."

He laughed and started the pony trotting. Irusan was the main character in an old Irish folk story. "But the original Irusan was not just a cat, he was the king of all cats, and the poet, Seanchan, wrote a poem insulting him and his family, so Irusan attacked the poet and dragged him away. Am I right in my memory?" When she nodded, he went on. "So how does your Irusan merit such a name as the king of all cats?"

"You'll have to meet him. They say that noble men have a demeanor that prevents them from being taken as anything but a nobleman. Irusan, even as a kitten, could not be taken for anything but royalty on cat's feet. However, the story has a sad ending— poor Irusan was the one to suffer in the end, killed for his audacity."

They were soon out of the village. The marquess glanced over at Lady Anne. As irritated as he had been at her impertinent behavior—questioning strangers about his family's troubles—he had a sense that commanding her to stop would do little. She was a free woman, and though he could evict her from his property, it didn't strike him as a wise course of action if he wished the gossip to stop. He had already established, in a brief conversation with Lydia—more of an interrogation than a conversation, really—that Lady Anne was independently wealthy and stubborn. It did not seem to him that she would meekly leave Yorkshire if he cast her out of Ivy Lodge.

Abruptly, he said, "What do you wish to know, my lady?"

She watched him as he turned back to regard the road and guide the pony. "I wonder how much I should expect you to tell me? Don't you think it is odd that Cecilia's death should follow so quickly on the heels of Miss Allengate's on your property? Do you think Miss Allengate's and Tilly Landers's death a year ago are connected? Were you involved in any way with any one of those women—Tilly, Fanny, Cecilia—who died?"

"My, you've been a busy little gossip, haven't you?" he asked, bitterness lacing his voice.

"Not gossiping, Lord Darkefell," she said, her hands still folded serenely on her lap. "I'm looking for answers, and in that search discover extraneous information, most of it utterly useless in discovering the perpetrator of Cecilia's dreadful murder. It must be weeded out, considered, and dismissed if it has no bearing on the tragedy."

"I thought you were merely here to soothe my idiot sister-in-law's precious worries," he complained, nodding to a laborer who stopped, touched his cap, and bowed as they passed.

She was not distracted by his unkind characterization of Lydia, instead answering directly, "That was my quest, but in stumbling upon something so much worse… I cannot rest until I know what devil killed Cecilia." Her voice trembled with authentic fury but held no fear. "Are you going to answer my original question, my lord, about your involvement with those girls?"

"I don't think that is yours or anyone's business."

"Have you not considered that perhaps someone is targeting you, trying to make you look guilty of this string of deaths? Have you offended anyone, my lord, someone in your employ? Or someone in the village?"

He let a mile of countryside slip past them without answering. He supposed he had offended many people in his life and perhaps some without even knowing he had done so. Though he did not believe the deaths of Tilly, Fanny, and Cecilia were connected, still Lady Anne had given him much to ponder.

The day was golden, the sun coaxing brilliant green shoots to fatten and become lush grassy fields. The road from the village toward Darkefell property was lonely, and they encountered no other traffic on the way. "My lady, I'm pleading with you—don't jeopardize your safety. Trust me to bring this foul murderer to justice."

She was silent for a moment then said, sounding as though she chose her words carefully, "Lord Darkefell, I believe you will do everything in your power to solve this dreadful crime, but the closer one is to a problem, the harder it is to see it objectively."

"You believe I will be blinded by partiality or deliberately obtuse if the killer is someone in my employ or… " He reined in the pony abruptly. Robbie, on the back, held on as the carriage pulled to a full stop. "Do you imply," he muttered through gritted teeth, turning and staring at her, "that the perpetrator is a family member? You *cannot* mean that. You wouldn't dare!"

She regarded him intently, her brow wrinkled, her lips pursed. "You have a mercurial temperament, my lord." She lifted one finger and traced a line on his neck, saying, "And a vein that bulges dangerously on your neck and in your temple. I advise you to calm your temper and be wary of apoplectic fits, for many a choleric gentleman has died in such a manner."

Fury cooled in an instant, and he burst into a bark of laughter while quelling a startling jolt of pleasure from the delicate touch of her fingertip. "I'm quite sure that many have died in your presence in just such a manner, my lady." He clicked to the patient pony, and they continued their climb toward Darkefell land. He marveled how he had gone from wrath to laughter in a few seconds. "You do have a way, my *dear* Lady Anne, of puncturing my inflated sense of the dramatic. How can I possibly go on in that vein of self-righteous anger when you have so sweetly expressed concern for my health?"

"I have never had anyone call my comments 'sweet.'"

The moment they trotted up the gravel drive toward Ivy Lodge, the door burst open and Mary trotted out. "Milady, you must come at once."

"What is it?" Anne asked.

"Irusan give Lord John sech a claw on his cheek! And then he wouldna let the puir man out o' Lady John's room, an' there's bin a commotion ever since. I've bin watchin' for ya oot th'door."

Anne jumped down from the pony cart without waiting for Lord Darkefell's help and strode toward the open door. As always when she was agitated, Mary's Scots accent became more pronounced; it was a barometer of seriousness that she had slipped back into "wouldna" and cut short "ing" word endings. She could hear the marquess chuckling, but she didn't consider it a humorous situation.

Mary, with Robbie at her side, led Anne upstairs to Lydia's sitting room next to her bedchamber, but the sight, when they got there, was not what she had expected. Mr. Boatin was just leaving the room with a purring cat cradled in his arms. Anne, nonplussed, gaped in astonishment.

She looked past the secretary to find Lord John nursing a bloody cheek and Lydia cowering on a divan. "Mr. Boatin," Anne said, "you astonish me. Irusan is a difficult feline and seldom makes new friends."

"Cats are miracles from God, my lady," he said, his dark eyes glinting with humor behind his spectacles. "I think his highness, King Irusan, sensed an admirer and so allows me to serve as his palanquin."

"That cat is a devil," Lord John raged, holding a cloth to his cheek.

Anne entered the room and said, "I most humbly apologize and beg your forgiveness for Irusan's irascible temperament. He was supposed to be confined to my bedchamber. I can't think how he got out…" She trailed off, seeing Lydia's beseeching gestures behind her husband's back.

"He was in here," the man bellowed, "sitting on Lydia's lap when I came in. All I did was push him off, and he attacked me."

"John, dear, he was asleep, and you gave him such a whack!" Lydia said.

"Nevertheless," Anne said, refraining from upbraiding him for his behavior toward her cat, "I apologize most deeply for my cat's bad manners, my lord. If you need some cream for that—"

"No, Lady Anne, I do not," he said, pushing past her and out to the hall. He stomped away, muttering under his breath, and was soon gone from sight and sound.

"Goodness," Anne said, glancing between Lydia on her divan and Mr. Boatin near the door, who still held Irusan. Lydia looked pale but composed, and Anne said to her, "I will talk to you later, my dear. Right now, I think I should take Irusan back to my room and make sure he doesn't cause any more mischief. Mr. Boatin?"

"At your service, my lady," he said.

"Follow me, then." She had a second chance to talk to the secretary, and this time she was not going to let him escape without answering some questions.

She led Mr. Boatin to her room and asked him to set Irusan in a chair. "Mr. Boatin," she said, "how is it that Lord Darkefell came all the way to Hornethwaite to fetch me concerning my cat's bad behavior? Was this scene frozen for an hour or more, Lord John kept at bay all that time by my ferocious puss?"

He laughed, a rich, throaty chuckle. Petting Irusan, who still curled in his arms, he said, "No, I am told that *before* being cornered in Lady John's room, he led the footmen on a merry chase while your lady's maid, Mistress Mary, followed, remonstrating, saying if they would just leave him alone, the feline king would return to his quarters on his own."

"True. Left alone, he's well behaved. Unfortunately, like me, he misbehaves when people don't treat him properly. Please, Mr. Boatin, sit for a moment with Irusan. You seem to have a calming effect on him."

The man looked doubtful but was won over when Irusan stretched in his arms and butted the secretary's chin with his enormous, shaggy head. "He is a very big cat." He sat down in a chair and cradled the feline on his lap.

"He's almost two stone." *Trapped,* Anne thought, eyeing Mr. Boatin. As long as Irusan luxuriated in his arms, he would probably not move. "Why were you and his lordship here?"

"Some estate business required Lady Darkefell's input, for it involved Ivy Lodge. The marquess is diligent in consulting his mother on many points, as it is her home. We found chaos, and the marchioness commanded her son to find you and bring you back."

"You became involved involuntarily?"

"I thought I might be of assistance."

Deciding that the man, obviously intelligent and indubitably well mannered, deserved honesty, Anne told him gently about her venture into Hornethwaite, the smelly drunk to whom she gave a farthing, and what he said about Osei being under an African curse. She held back for the moment, not asking about the almost incoherent insinuation that he was seen with a young woman, possibly Cecilia. He had no comment, merely shaking his head.

"How did he get such an absurd idea?"

"It may have come from some of the younger members of Lord Darkefell's staff in their occasional visits to the taproom. Some of them make sport out of anything. Teasing a drunk with wild stories would not have been beyond them."

"I can only imagine, Mr. Boatin, how difficult your life here has been, even with your employer. As good as he is, still the marquess cannot be easy to work for. Have you not had run-ins with him?"

The secretary admitted it with a nod of his head. "But we resolve our differences quickly, and I never forget how much I owe him."

"Have you ever considered going back to your homeland?"

He nodded again, more slowly. "But I can never repay the debt of gratitude I owe to his lordship. He did far more than save my life, he saved my spirit. I came here with little comprehension of the world into which I had been thrust, and he gave me everything I required to save myself. He offered me language and knowledge, the two pillars upon which the fate of the world rest. And more than that… he gave me hope. My only wish is to find out if my sister survived and where she is. I wish I could rescue her from slavery, if she is so bound."

Irusan stretched in the gentle man's arms and purred loudly.

"You were friends with Cecilia Wainwright."

He nodded.

"And you were with her the evening she was killed?"

He nodded again. "We were walking and talking, no more than that, my lady. Serving staff are allowed a couple of hours each evening to walk outside or rest in their rooms after their duties are done. I walked her to the back door and saw her go in."

"You saw her go in?" She chewed her lip for a long moment. "Why would she go back out, I wonder?"

He was silent. She eyed him. He knew, or he thought he might know, she realized, judging from his downcast gaze and concentrated lack of response to her question. How could she reassure him that she didn't wish to blacken the girl's name or reputation? "Mr. Boatin, if there was any way you could help discover Cecilia's murderer, you would do it, as her friend, wouldn't you?"

He nodded, misery deep within his dark eyes.

"I think you have an idea why she went back out but don't think it involves someone who could be suspected of murdering her?"

He nodded again as he scruffed Irusan under the chin and behind his ears.

Anne leaned forward. "But what if you're wrong?"

Mr. Boatin stood and gently set Irusan on the chair he had just vacated. "But I am not, my lady." He bowed. "You must excuse me. I have work to do."

As Osei left, Mary entered Anne's bedchamber. "How did that man calm Irusan? Puss was yowling, taking on in sech a manner, and for him to go from that wild beastie to a purring puss in two minutes is beyond wonderful."

"Some people just have a way with animals," Anne said, staring at the door.

"Aye, like that Jamey, the lad all the girls are crazy for," Mary said, brushing cat hairs from the chair just vacated by the cat. Irusan had decided the bed was more to his liking for a midday nap and was now curled in the center of a pillow.

"Jamey, the groom Ellen walks out with? Does he have other flirtations?" She watched Mary as the woman bustled around, tidying small things put out of place.

"Indeed he does. And that explains a brangle between Ellen and Cecilia," she said, turning away from the dressing table. "Come, have your hair done properly, milady, for it's gang agley."

Anne obediently sat in the dressing-table chair. "A falling out? An argument? I thought they were best of friends. Who heard it? What was said?"

"Well, first, Jamey is new to his lordship's stable staff, hired at last Martinmas servant fair to work on the home farm, but Dandy Lincoln—he runs the home farm wi' his wife Peg—told the marquess that Jamey was a dab hand wi' horses, and so he came to th'castle in December, just afore Christmas."

"About when John and Lydia arrived at Ivy Lodge with Cecilia, from their bride trip. Whom did he work for before?"

"Now that's interestin.' He worked for Mr. Grover and so knew the ways o' the castle and some of the staff. During the holiday nonsense that always happens with extra time off and spirituous fluids, Jamey Spencer flirted with all the maids, from the tales I've heard."

"Among them Cecilia and Ellen."

"Aye. There was much foolishness at first between the girls, good-hearted, mostly. But that appears to have ended badly on St. Agnes' Eve." Mary twisted Anne's hair tightly, winding it into a neater style and pinning it, her face in the mirror a study of concentration.

"What happened on St. Agnes' Eve?" Anne finally asked. That was in late January, just three months before.

"Ah, well, Caroline, one of the maids, was there an' another maid who has since left service and married. The girls, Cecilia and Ellen, needed two more girls to do the love posset that would tell them who Jamey was truly meant to wed, for the fool girls went so far as to think the fellow serious about matrimony."

"What on earth is a 'love posset'?"

Mary sighed. "Have you no' ever bin a daft girl, milady? Called a 'dumb cake,' as well. Some girls did that even back home when I was a lass. I dreamt of my own dear Collin after such a thing. But these fool girls don't think they will *dream* of the fellow, but that his living spirit will actually *come* to them!"

"Oh, I know!" Anne cried. "I've heard of this, of course. Some of my friends did it. Four girls make a cake—when it's made, it's cut into four pieces, and each girl gets a piece and stands in a corner of the room. Then you do some nonsensical hocus pocus, and the spirit of your husband is supposed to take the cake."

"Aye, the key being the fellow is visible only to the maiden he'll wed. The lassies did this, and Ellen, being more gullible than Cecilia, so it sounds, believed her when Cecilia claimed to see the spirit of young Jamey walk right up and take her piece and eat it. That's when the trouble started."

"Hmm. But Ellen claims to have been a dear friend of Cecilia's. She was crying the morning after Cecilia was murdered."

"P'raps she was feeling that badly that the girl was kilt an' there bein' bad feelings still between them?" Mary finished her fussing and patted Anne's hair. "Better."

And indeed it was, Anne thought, twisting this way and that in front of the mirror. "You're a miracle worker, Mary. You should have seen the abomination foisted upon me by Ellen."

"I've heard of it. Begging your pardon, but it's become legendary in the servants' hall. Therese, Lady Darkefell's abigail, a French woman," she said with a sniff of disapproval, "said that Ellen ought to have been brought up on charges for murderin' your appearance. Not one o' the other servants, to their credit, thought that humorous, after the events that took puir Cecilia's life. But then, none o' them have any use for Therese, and most like Ellen."

"So Ellen, far from being a friend of Cecilia's, was her rival for the affections of Jamey."

"A rivalry that Cecilia is said to have won."

"I shall speak to Jamey. Perhaps he's the father of her unborn baby. I wonder if she had already told him? Perhaps she went back out that night to speak with him about what she should do once she started showing her condition. A girl would lose her position over that. I wish I'd known this before I spoke with Mr. Boatin just now." She thought for a moment then said, "How could I get to speak to Jamey?"

"I'll talk to Sanderson, milady—the coach and horses are kept up at the castle, but Sanderson is bedded here and eats his supper in the servants' hall. He might be able to tell us more about the lad."

"I did ask him to befriend Jamey, as I suspect he's involved in this werewolf business. And I'll speak to Ellen and even the terrifying Therese, the superior French abigail. According to Ellen, Therese said that she, too, saw the werewolf."

"Aye, I already asked her aboot that, but she claims 'twas just from a window."

"Mmm, that's not enough to question her on. I had hoped for a lucid account—French women are supremely rational. I suppose I'll get busy, then." But first... "Mary, this is dreadfully inappropriate to ask, but you're the only one who may know."

"Aye, tell me then. I've had a feelin' somethin' was amiss." Between them was a boundless trust and complete understanding. Mary and Wee Robbie were mired in destitution after her husband died in the Gordon riots. Catholic to the bone, Collin MacDougall had been protecting a priest from the mob incited by the rabidly anti-Catholic Lord George Gordon, and died shielding him. The church would have taken them both in after such a martyrdom as her Collin endured, but Mary preferred to work for her living.

"I wouldn't say it's anything amiss," Anne answered, pondering how to raise the topic on her mind. She touched her hair and glanced at it in the mirror one more time, though she already knew it was perfect. When Anne found out about Mary from a friend, the Scotswoman knew nothing of being a lady's maid, but Anne hired her anyway. It was just a few months after Anne's fiancé had died, and sequestered in mourning, anyway, she was beginning to realize she didn't wish to rejoin the marriage market, baiting a spinster's hook with her considerable personal fortune. Mary had repaid the kindness of a job for herself and a home for her child, Wee Robbie, by applying herself to the art of taking care of a lady and becoming proficient at it, even though she didn't truly care about such fripperies as bonnets and hairstyles.

Anne, still unsure how to go on, moved the brushes Mary had laid out precisely. "Mary, if a man has no interest in a woman, would he still kiss her?"

"Beggin' your pardon?"

Anne repeated what she said, adding, even as she focused her gaze on a spot above Mary's face, "Men, I've heard, use seduction to get what they want just as some women do. Do you think a man might kiss a woman he has no interest in, perhaps just to shut her up? Or confuse her and stop her from asking questions?"

"Are you asking, milady, do I think Lord Darkefell kissed you to silence you?"

Thirteen

ANNE GASPED.

Mary said, "D'you think you weren't observed?" Her rolled r's rippled with laughter. "In the servants' hall they're a'chatterin' about the master's behavior. E'en though Ivy Lodge is Lady Darkefell's domain, make no mistake, milady, the marquess is still master. They daren't cross him. I overhaird the chatter, for they wouldna have spoken to me 'bout such a thing."

Anne defiantly crossed her arms over her chest. "Since I have no secrets, Mary, what do you think?"

"A man's capable of anything, milady, some more'n others. I've no' had time to study the marquess, though a powerful handsome man he is. As far as I ken, he's no' in the habit of inflictin' such behavior on ladies of his acquaintance, leastways not at the lodge nor th'castle."

"Oh."

"So, what was it like, the marquess's kiss?" Mary asked, her eyes wide.

"It was adequate," Anne said, retreating to hauteur and disarranging the brushes on the dressing table yet again.

"Likely more'n that," Mary said under her breath, apparently recognizing that no amount of prodding would elicit a dram more of information.

"I'm going to visit Lydia and find out how Irusan happened to be in her room," Anne said hastily. "I suspect he was invited there and took umbrage when Lord John swept him aside as if he were a common cat."

She started out the door but, at that moment, heard a commotion downstairs. A loud voice shouted, "*They've got him—they've got him!*" She swiftly descended into the hall and found Hiram Grover joyously calling out to Lady Darkefell, who was approaching from the corridor as Andrew, the footman, stood back from the open door.

"What is it, Hiram?" the dowager marchioness said, her cold tone bell-like and echoing in the great hall.

Anne continued down the stairs.

"They have the murdering bastard who killed the maidservant, begging your pardon, my lady, for the coarseness. I'm that turned about with relief!"

"Who is it?" she cried, her hands clutched together and held out in front of her, an oddly beseeching position for so haughty a woman. "Who? Tell me, Hiram!"

"That drunken wretch from Hornethwaite, William Spottiswode."

As Anne watched, the woman staggered slightly, and her voice weak, she said, "Thank the good Lord!"

Hiram Grover guided her to the drawing room off the great hall. Anne followed, and Lord John, drawn by the commotion, followed too. Gathered in the drawing room, Hiram Grover helped Lady Darkefell to a seat and then held court, Lord John sitting by his mother, on the arm of her chair, her hand in his, and Anne standing nearby.

"I was in town to see about selling some of my horses to a fellow there," Mr. Grover said. "I happened to see Sir Trevor. I called out to him, but he was in a hurry, on his way to the alehouse, for something extraordinary was happening. I followed."

"Go on, Grover!" Lord John prodded.

"Patience, my lord," Grover said, his face even ruddier than normal. He mopped his brow with a cloth pulled from his pocket and sat down near the fireplace. After a moment, he said, "I followed Sir Trevor into the alehouse, and there was the most extraordinary sight! William Spottiswode—that fellow they call Spotted Willie, the disgusting drunk who begs outside the tavern—was sitting with a circle of young fellows surrounding him, and saying he murdered poor Cecilia Wainwright."

Anne gasped, and her legs felt wobbly. Was that the same fellow who had accosted her outside the alehouse and begged a farthing? Had she been that close to solving the murder if she had asked the right question?

"What happened?" Lady Darkefell said.

"Sir Trevor charged him with her murder, and Spottiswode is now confined in a cell below the guildhall. I heard him with my own ears—the fellow claims he was Cecilia Wainwright's lover and the father of her unborn bastard. He met her that night to discuss her demand that he marry her, and they argued. He had no money to marry, but she said that didn't matter, for she would not bear an unnamed child. He became enraged when she taunted him with talk of her new lover, Lord Darkefell's secretary, and murdered her." He put one hand over his heart and said, "How terrible! The poor girl. That her immoral behavior should lead to her death may seem a judgment from God, but I, for one, cannot find it in my heart to condemn the poor child's conduct, as disgraceful as it was."

"He confessed?" Anne asked, reflecting on the suggestion that Osei Boatin was named as her other lover rather than Jamey, the groom.

"He did. I heard it myself."

"And said he was the father of her baby."

"Yes."

"But she taunted him, saying she had taken Mr. Boatin as a lover?"

"Yes!" Mr. Grover said, fastening his walleyed stare on her.

"How could you tell all that?" Anne asked. "I spoke to that fellow, and his dialect was incomprehensible."

"But I have lived here many years, madam, and understand the language."

"It sounds like a lot to decipher."

"Thank God," Lord John said, sighing. "A confession. That poor girl—to have sunk so low as to try to force a man like Spottiswode into marriage!"

"It defies belief," Anne agreed, thinking of what she had heard of Cecilia's and Jamey's affair. None of that accorded with what Spottiswode apparently said, even about Cecilia supposedly having taken Mr. Boatin as a lover, but then, who was to say she wasn't lying to Spottiswode to make him angry? To hurt him? He had certainly been infuriated about Mr. Boatin when she briefly spoke to him.

"I thank you, sir, for bringing us the news," Lady Darkefell said hoarsely, rising on unsteady legs, her full skirts swaying with her movement. "If you will excuse me, I find myself in need of rest." She left the room, and Grover departed soon after.

It was only Anne and Lord John at the dinner table, for Lady Darkefell pled illness, as did Lydia. Lord Darkefell, after he dropped Anne off that day, had disappeared. With this new development, he likely had to confer with the magistrate.

Anne toyed with her whitefish, pushing it around her plate and eying Lord John. "You and I have not had much occasion to speak, Lord John."

He nodded.

"Lydia has been badly frightened by this werewolf nonsense. Do you have any idea what is happening? I understand it's not just your own people who have seen it, but villagers as well."

He blandly said, "Some dog is killing sheep."

"While that's possible, it doesn't explain the sightings of an actual werewolf, seven feet tall and standing upright like a man."

"Idiocy. If people are frightened, they should stay in at night."

His demeanor was truculent, and she began to wonder if she had been too hard on Lydia when she thought the girl imagined her husband's change of manner toward her. "Is that how you've comforted your wife, by telling her that?"

"My behavior toward my wife is no one's affair but my own."

They were both silent while a footman—not Andrew but a lesser fellow—made the change of courses.

"Do you deny that you have changed in your behavior toward her?"

He was stonily silent, eating his beefsteak, but his cheeks flamed.

"Where were you the night Cecilia was killed?"

"You saw me," he said.

"But you came from the back hall," Anne remarked. "Where were you before you entered?"

"I fail to see what business any of this is of yours, Lady Anne!" he said, rising.

"Will you not tell me what has gone on? I'm trying to help," she said. "What of Fanny Allengate's death? And Tilly Landers? What about your brother, Lord Julius, being accused of Miss Landers's death and disappearing to the Canadas? What say you of that?"

"Good evening, Lady Anne," he said, his face red, the blush extending down to his cravat. He bowed. "I'm going to see my wife. Apologize for my abrupt departure. Ask the serving staff for anything you require!" He bowed again and exited hastily, bumbling into the sideboard on his way.

Anne retired early to her room but sat up in the window seat. So Cecilia had been murdered by a lover, but such a lover as Spotted Willie, or whatever Mr. Grover had named him! Why, if Cecilia had been successful in winning the handsome–by-all-reports

Jamey as a lover, did she take up with the loathsome Spotted Willie? And was this same fellow also responsible for the slaughtered sheep and the deaths of Tilly Landers and Fanny Allengate?

The moon shone down on the lawn, and a movement drew her attention. Someone was stealing out a side door and moving stealthily, just as another figure moved toward the lodge from the opposite direction. Mindful that, though she had conjectures, she still was not sure of the identity of the prankster who was posing as a werewolf, Anne leaped into action. She recognized Ellen, draped in a shawl, her blonde curls escaping and illuminated like burnished gold in the moonlight. The other figure, moving toward her, was surely Jamey. Perhaps she would find out more about the werewolf hoax by following them. The young man had much to answer for, wooing both Cecilia and Ellen—who knew what other mischief he was up to?

She rushed into her adjoining dressing room. Mrs. Hailey had agreed that it would be least upsetting to the household if Mary and Robbie had cots in her dressing room. She crossed and found Mary's bed; the woman was not sleeping and sat up immediately, still fully dressed.

"I knew y'wouldna be asleep yet, milady. Do you wish something?"

"Yes, I wish your company," Anne whispered. "Let Robbie sleep, get your cloak and mine, and come!"

Mary, accustomed to sudden decisions, didn't protest. She helped Anne into a warm dressing gown and hooded cloak, donned her own, and they were soon outside Ivy Lodge and following the direction

Ellen took. Anne damned the time it had taken to find a discreet exit, creep from the lodge and, staying off the noisy gravel, steal along the lodge walls toward the open lawn where she thought Ellen and her swain would meet. Now she could see no sign of them, even as she and Mary were out in the open.

She peered into the dark, and it came to her in a flash; she knew where they would head. The tower! She grabbed Mary's arm and headed up the slope toward the structure, explaining in a hushed tone along the way, but then both fell silent as the rigors of scrambling through the night required all their concentration. It was fortunate indeed that her ankle had recovered quickly from her first night's misadventure. Anne blessed Mary's stalwart and loyal nature, for this was beyond what a lady's maid should be expected to do.

Happily, the moon was waxing, not waning, and the trees were still light of leaf. Being a countrywoman had its benefits; the terrain was hilly, and night noises would have made an inferior woman nervous. Anne occupied the time identifying noises. One in particular she recognized was the night sound of a moorhen. They must be near water. She remembered seeing the stream and waterfall from the top of the tower; the stream's path must meander close by.

Just then a howl rent the night air, silencing the other night noises. Mary gasped, and Anne reached back, grabbed her arm, and the two stopped. The small hairs on the back of her neck and along her arms stood straight up as Anne pushed her cloak hood back, whispering, "I heard that howl the night I arrived, just before I heard Cecilia Wainwright's death cry."

The howl echoed through the night again, and then a woman screamed.

"That must be Ellen! Come, quickly," Anne said, pulling Mary after her.

The howl split the night air again. As Anne and Mary crested the hill and found the tower, a black blot in the dimness of the shadowy grove, Anne heard a rustling sound then saw, in a clearing, a creature lope by, running to the top of the next hill, where it stopped and howled. It moved on, but a moment later Anne saw the indistinct shape of a creature on two legs… a man? But no—it had, outlined clearly by the moonglow, a long snout!

"What is that?" Anne cried, but by the time Mary turned and followed her pointed finger, it was gone.

"What?" Mary cried, gasping for breath.

"We must find Ellen!" Anne turned toward the tower, fearing the worst. Her stomach churned in fear.

"Who's there?" a male voice called out.

Anne, heedless for her own safety and concerned only with the young maid, headed toward the voice, breathlessly demanding that Mary stay in the open where she would be safer.

"I'll no' leave you on yer own, milady," Mary cried, following on her heels.

A wavering light flickered and fluttered, and Anne stopped, terrified into caution for just a moment. She dreaded what she might see—had poor Ellen suffered the fate of Cecilia? Did that mean they had the wrong man as murderer, and young Jamey was the culprit?

"Who's there? Where's Ellen?" she demanded again, her voice quavering.

"Lady Anne?"

A slim figure, illuminated in the flickering flame of a lantern, emerged from the shadows at the base of the tower, and Anne almost wept in relief.

"Ellen, you're alive!" she cried, falling on the girl and hugging her in an uncharacteristic display of emotion. She released her and set her at arm's length as a young man—Jamey, it seemed likely—emerged from the shadows after her. "What's going on here?" Anne asked. "I heard the howling and a shriek. Are you two cozening me?"

The young man, a fresh-faced fellow of about twenty, stepped forward and brazenly said, "Ow'd we do that when we din't even know you wuz there?"

Ellen stepped forward and pushed Jamey behind her, saying, "Excuse him, milady. We didn't mean nothing. Just some joshing on Jamey's part. You won't report me to Mrs. Hailey, will you? She'd let me go!"

Anne, her heart finally beginning to settle down, regarded her thoughtfully. "Did you not hear that howl? I saw the creature running, and it stopped and howled. A wolf, it looked like."

"We heard the sound, ma'am—that's what caused me to scream like that." She paused then continued. "Well, that and I was startled when Jamey, he was... he tickled me, see, and scared me—"

"Enough," Anne said, holding up one hand. She decided not to say a word for the moment about the two-legged creature. "I think you should come back to Ivy Lodge with me, Ellen. You'll suffer more than a damaged reputation if you persist in creeping out at night to meet this fellow. You've not been completely honest about your feelings about Cecilia Wainwright, and though her killer has been caught, I'm still interested to hear the story."

Her chin went up, a mulish expression on her sweet face. "We were friends, ma'am, weren't we, Jamey? Cecilia an' me were friends," she said, looking back at her beau with a significant look and digging him in the ribs.

He nodded. "Aye… friends."

She had handled them all wrong, Anne thought ruefully, giving them a chance to present a united front. "That's not what I've heard. Nevertheless, Ellen, I would strongly advise you to accompany me back to the lodge."

It was interesting how the meek girl Anne had met the first morning returned in an instant.

"Yes, milady, of course." She cast a glance back at Jamey. "You remember what I said, now, Jamey."

"Go along with Mary," Anne said to Ellen, "for I'd like to speak to Jamey for a moment."

Mary said, eyeing the sullen young groom, "I don't like leavin' ya alone just now, what with th'wolf an' all."

"Nonsense. That has to have been a dog, not a wolf, after all."

"Like no dog I've ever seen," she muttered, but at a look from her mistress, she took Ellen's arm and said, "Right, you come along with me, and we'll wait for her ladyship down't th' bottom of the hill."

Anne turned to the groom as the two women departed; he appeared uneasy. "You, young man, have caused quite a bit of trouble among the girls of Ivy Lodge with your flirtatious ways."

"Don't know nothin' 'bout that," he said, the sullen expression still on his handsome face.

He was a good-looking enough fellow in the flickering light of his lantern, with a broad face, even, unblemished features, good teeth, and a sturdy frame. Among the other farm workers and stable staff, he likely looked a prince. That was the only explanation for so elevated a creature as a lady's maid—Cecilia Wainwright—falling for him, that and her evident loneliness since coming to Ivy Lodge. A lady's maid would normally set up a flirtation with a footman, as they were, without exception, tall and handsome. Or a secretary, like Mr. Boatin, would be a catch for a girl like Cecilia.

"Do you deny that you had a flirtation or more than that with Cecilia Wainwright? And that you met her on the night she died?"

At that he looked genuinely frightened. "Look 'ere, yer ladyship, I were nowhere near Ivy Lodge that night. Wasn't me she met. You arsk that blackamoor whut he was doin' talking to a girl like Cece."

"Cece? A pet name?" she asked, watching his face. He wasn't as handsome as he first appeared, and she could see how coarseness was creeping in on him. Eventually he would become careless about his personal grooming, his beard would coarsen, his clothes fail to fit over a thickening belly, and one day soon he would be just a scratching, spitting, belching groom, and the girl who married him would sigh for the handsome lad he once had been and wonder where he had gone. He eyed her with ill-concealed dislike. A girl as refined as Cecilia had seemed to be, on the one or two occasions Anne had seen her when visiting Lydia's home, was wasted on him. Ellen, simpler of mind and heart, would be more his cup of tea. "What do you say to that? You had come so far as to have a pet name for Cecilia?"

He reddened. "Didn't say we wasn't friends, just said I din't meet 'er that noight."

"And she and Mr. Boatin were friends, too. If she could have you as a… *friend,* could she not also speak to Mr. Boatin?"

He didn't say anything.

"And the werewolf costume you and some friend devised—tell me about it, how you made it, what you've done with it? Come, tell me, for I know it was you all along posing as a werewolf. Did you and a friend not frighten the girls in turn, howling and running about? Who is your confederate in this? He's out this very evening, isn't he?"

But Jamey, a mulish expression on his face, turned, muttering, "Got to get back t'the castle." He turned on his heel, and without permission, bolted, racing quickly out of sight, taking the light with him.

"Dash the fellow!" she exclaimed as darkness closed around her. She could no longer hear Ellen and Mary but hoped she could find her way, orienting herself from the dark tower and heading off carefully in what she thought was the right direction. Once she was out of the brush, she would be all right.

A rustling nearby made her pause. "Mary?" she said. No answer, but more rustling. She tried to go faster, but she was afraid she had gone astray a little. She paused and called out Mary's name again. No answer.

Something was near, though, she could feel it, and her hair stood straight up on her arms again. A quivering, superstitious dread trembled deep in her belly and she stumbled, trying to move toward a faint hint of light… or at least a lessening of the dark shadows within which she was mired.

Out of the woods rushed a figure, and she screeched, but then a very human hand clamped on her arm and another over her mouth.

"Shhh, don't scream, and stop squirming!"

It was the marquess's gruff voice, and she wriggled around in his grip, beating at his arm, but he would not loosen his hold, so she bit his finger.

"Ow, damn you!" he grunted, releasing her.

"What do you mean by following me, creeping up on me, then grabbing me like that!" she gasped, panting.

"I didn't want anyone to know I was here. Then came you and your confounded prying. You almost ran into me in your blundering through the woods! You moved so quickly, and I wanted to catch hold of you before you hurt yourself in stumbling about in the brush."

"I began to move so quickly only because I heard you rustling around in the brush," she exclaimed. "Cecilia's confessed murderer has been arrested. Doesn't that mean the property is safe? What are you doing out this time of night anyway?"

"I should be asking you that, milady." He grabbed her arm and began to propel her forward. "Why *are* you out here in the woods?"

She ignored the question. "I saw that wolf you say doesn't exist," she said as branches whipped in her face and her feet seemed to barely touch the ground. She wrenched free of him after a few moments, exclaiming, "Let me find my own way, if you please, if you're going to be so violently difficult!"

"You were going in the wrong direction!" he exclaimed. "That's why I had to stop you, or you would have ended up on the other side of the woods near Staungill Force. I'm bloody well not going to have another woman take a tumble off that." He took her arm and more sedately helped her through the forest.

They finally came to a clearing, and a shot of moonlight silvered the darkness. She shivered and looked around, not recognizing where they were. "I didn't come out alone, anyway—Mary, my maid, was with me and will be worried sick if I don't join her."

He chuckled, a deep rumbling sound in his chest that was terrifyingly attractive. He moved closer to her, so close his body heat bathed her in warmth. "Are you saying that," he whispered close to her ear, "because you wish me to know someone will miss you if you disappear?"

Determined to keep her dignity intact, she shrugged away from his warm breath and said, "Sir, please do not play at being menacing. It only makes you appear foolish."

"You are a most unusual woman," he said after a moment, moving away from her. "Perhaps I'm flirting with you. Some women find mysterious men attractive. Have you considered that?"

"That you flirt with me? No, for I gave you credit for more sense than that, though I can easily change that opinion if necessary. But I have considered that you're trying to hide something, like who is perpetrating this werewolf hoax. Or what the real animal is, for I heard and saw something, Lord Darkefell, and it was *not* human. I also saw something else... something that perambulated on two feet!"

"Nonsense!"

"It is *not* nonsense." She turned, but he grabbed her arm and whirled her around.

"I must tell you again, please keep to your room at night."

"That sounded oddly like a threat, or a warning from someone who knows something. But the murderer has been caught," she said coldly. She regarded him in the dim light of the silvery moon; his handsome face gleamed with dampness, though the night air felt cold to her, and she wondered what caused such perspiration. A guilty conscience? "And I don't believe in werewolves. Is it simply more convenient for you if I stay in my bed, shivering, with the covers pulled up to my nose?"

He growled and released her. "Maddening," he said, thrusting his fingers through his hair and pulling at it. "Infuriating. Baffling. Unwomanly." He threw up his hands and retreated, saying, "Go, then... *go!* Devil woman."

She sighed, trying to settle her trembling as she watched him disappear. He really did have the most extraordinary effect on her, setting her heart to throbbing and her insides to quivering like quince jelly. She slid awkwardly down a damp hill and finally out to a broader clearing. Mary trotted toward her; Ellen, shivering, stood sullenly some distance away, her shawl pulled close around her.

"Milady, I was that worrit! I was just about to go back, for I thought I heard voices."

"Just me talking to myself," she said, savagely kicking at a tuft of grass. The marquess had to be the most irritating man she had ever met. He insisted on mocking her with his faux seduction, and then he called *her* maddening?

Mary eyed her but held her tongue, and in silence, the threesome returned to Ivy Lodge.

Fourteen

THE NEXT MORNING DARKEFELL DOURLY contemplated the state of things as his man, Harwood, completed his toilette, preparatory to Palm Sunday service and the church appearance that was required of him.

"Lift your chin, please, milord," Harwood said, expertly wielding the straight razor. "Now down, please, milord."

Darkefell closed his eyes; there was to be a special prayer of thanksgiving that Spottiswode had been "captured." Every crime of the last two years had been laid at his feet, starting with Tilly Landers's supposed murder on the Staungill Force, up to and including the poor-box money being pinched the previous Sunday after service.

The slaughtered sheep were believed to be sacrifices for a witch's rite Spottiswode performed. Cecilia Wainwright supposedly threatened him with exposure for moral lapses—though why anyone supposed Spottiswode had any moral standing left from which to lapse, Darkefell couldn't imagine—and so he had murdered her. Some of the more suggestible even thought the poor drunk was the "werewolf."

Perhaps Darkefell should be grateful the locals had decided Tilly Landers's death was a part of Spottiswode's criminality, since suspicion before that had fallen on his head or that of his brother, Julius, but he wasn't. The *facts* were clear: Tilly Landers's body was found below the waterfall after an anonymous note addressed to the magistrate claimed that the marquess had pushed her off the cliff. Darkefell denied it, and it likely would have been forgotten, but Julius, fearing his brother would be arrested, claimed it was he who was seen, that he had met her to offer her money to leave the marquess alone—she was apparently claiming that he had fathered her unborn child—but after meeting her, he saw her fall from the cliff.

Darkefell scowled as Harwood applied pomade to his dark hair and plaited his queue. Julius didn't kill Tilly Landers, but that's what many concluded after such an idiotic story as his brother had told. Now, of course, the villagers believed it was Spottiswode, even though that made no sense either. Her death was an accident, Darkefell thought, though the anonymous note, suggesting there was more to the girl's death, still troubled him.

Today the marquess had to stand up in church and praise the Lord that Cecilia Wainwright's killer had been secured and would be tried. Despite the confession, he wasn't convinced the fellow had done anything of the kind. If Spottiswode had been worth a damn, he would have protested, but the man had been headed for the hangman's noose since the day he was spawned. However, Darkefell had heard that vaguely worded threats were being bandied about; Spottiswode was not well liked, and some thought they should save the Crown trouble and just hang him. *That* Darkefell would not allow, and he would make sure everyone in Hornethwaite knew his feelings on the subject. Spottiswode would get his trial.

But Darkefell's foul mood had little to do with service. He would say the correct things and calm the upsets of his people with just the right mix of humbuggery and sententiousness that they seemed to expect from their lord. It was that damned fool woman, Lady Anne Addison! Last night's expedition had been the outside of enough, and he was ready to command that she be hauled away by her coachman and set down, with her wrists tied and a gag over her ever-flapping mouth, in her Kentish home, where she would be safe. Who would ever guess that she would wander out at night, following a maid who was trysting with her swain? Though she hadn't told him that was her object, he had guessed it, having spotted Jamey and Ellen together. He had had to confront Lady Anne, sweating like a lathered horse, to make sure she got back to her maid rather than wandering on in the direction she was headed, to fall into Staungill Pool, or something equally as ridiculous.

An unwilling smile tugged at his lips; perhaps he was being unkind. She wasn't foolish, but she *was* foolhardy.

"Done, milord," Harwood said, sweeping away the cloth used to protect Darkefell's clothes.

The marquess regarded himself in the mirror: his dark, glossy hair was swept off his forehead and tied back in a neat queue, his face was clean-shaven, and his neckcloth perfectly tied. Fortune and fickle fashion smiled on him, for with a full head of hair, he could eschew wigs for any occasion but Parliament, now that it was deemed acceptable. Harwood fetched his gleaming boots and helped him put them on. Darkefell then stood, and as Harwood held his blue brocade jacket for him, he slid his arms in; he then allowed his valet to perfect his knotted cravat and regarded himself for any flaw in his appearance. But no, he was perfectly groomed and attired.

"Have Mr. Boatin summoned, Harwood," he said, still looking at himself in the cheval mirror by his wardrobe. "He will attend church, and I don't give one confounded blast what people say."

"As you say, sir."

"And send a message down to the lodge. I want every single person at church service in Hornethwaite, including Lady John Bestwick and Lady Anne Addison. I will accept no excuses. Not *one*." He didn't dare leave Lady Anne alone on the estate; who knows what she would do without supervision?

"As you say, sir."

"And Harwood," he barked.

"Yes, sir?"

Darkefell regarded himself in the mirror, adjusting the intricate folds of his cravat and smiling at his reflection, trying to improve his expression. "Have Quentin," he said, naming the castle gardener, "send up a bouquet of posies. Nothing too showy. Tulips, I suppose. Yellow. Or… no, not yellow, purple. Purple goes with gray nicely."

His valet was quiet, and Darkefell caught his glance. "For the ladies," he said defensively. "We have already provided bouquets of tulips and daffodils to the church for the altar, and I thought the ladies should have bouquets. It is spring, after all."

"Then, should I have Quentin send up *three* bouquets, sir?"

"Yes, yes, of course," he said, waving one hand negligently. "One for each lady. In different colors. But definitely *one* purple."

A half hour later, Darkefell leaped down from his best carriage outside of Ivy Lodge and waited as the others came out the front door in a procession. First his mother, then John and Lydia, then the irritating Lady Anne. He presented a posy to each lady: yellow for his mother, pink for Lydia, and finishing with a flourish by handing the purple one to Lady Anne, who coincidentally was dressed in a becoming shade of lilac.

He handed her up into the carriage—Osei sat above with the driver—climbed in after, then hammered on the roof to indicate the driver to move on. The silence was stifling but for the rattle and creak of the carriage. "Did everyone sleep well last night?" he asked with a significant look at Lady Anne, who so far had refused to meet his gaze.

"I didn't," Lydia complained, leaning heavily on her husband, who was silent and gloomy. "I'm not well at all, but no one seems to care," she said with a sniff.

Lady Darkefell glanced over at her with little interest. "You must learn, *dear* Lydia, that not every complaint will be answered instantly with sympathy. Others are fatigued and ill, too. Just look at Lady Anne, who appears gaunt and sallow this morning."

Startled, Darkefell stared at his mother. Such rudeness left him speechless.

"Thank you for your evident concern for my health, Lady Darkefell," Anne said, examining her tulip bouquet with every appearance of enjoyment, "but if I appear gaunt and sallow to you, then it must be habitual, for I look today just as I always do."

He regarded the younger woman with admiration. It was a setdown both oblique and clever, leaving no stain on Lady Anne but pointedly referencing the marchioness's discourtesy. His mother had cowed every lady he had ever met... until this one.

"Indeed," Darkefell said, "I think you look particularly fetching this morning, Lady Anne, in that shade of purple. I chose your posy myself with great care, for the color goes well with the lovely dove gray of your eyes."

Everyone in the coach stared at him, after such a florid speech. He shifted uncomfortably. Silence returned and reigned until they arrived in Hornethwaite.

The church, a pleasant chapel constructed in the previous century from local stone, was full, the coughs, shuffling feet, and sighs of a hundred people or more echoing into the upper reaches of the vaulted ceiling. The vicar read the appropriate verses for Palm Sunday, spoke of the Savior's ride into Jerusalem, then preached a homily of thanksgiving, reading several piquant verses concerning the punishment of evil and seeking out wrongdoers. He reminded everyone that there would be a Maundy Thursday service and a special service for Good Friday. The next Sunday being Easter, a vigil and resurrection service would be held on the hill above the village.

Then it was Lord Darkefell's turn to finish the service. He had thought long and hard what to say. In the end, he decided to keep it simple. Osei Boatin sat with his family in their box, and Darkefell began with a Palm Sunday reading, spoke briefly about the meaning of Easter, the Resurrection and Ascension, but then surveyed the gathering. "Some of you," he said, sweeping his gaze across the congregation, "have decided, at last, on a guilty individual for all of the ill that has happened in our corner of this riding in the last few years. But before you did so, you cast aspersions on others, in particular a man in my employ, Mr. Osei Boatin."

Anne glanced around the church. Some churchgoers shifted uneasily in their seats, but many others stared at the marquess with stony expressions, while others glared at the secretary. Mr. Grover was not one who glared at all; he kept his gaze fixed firmly on the altar. When she glanced over at Mr. Boatin, pity flooded her heart. He looked most uncomfortable to be the cynosure of all eyes; though she didn't suspect Darkefell of deliberate cruelty, he should have imagined how his speech would affect Mr. Boatin.

"Now, though," he continued, "you have decided that William Spottiswode is guilty. He convicts himself with his own words. So be it. But I warn you, wait for the rule of law to be enforced. I have heard stirrings of unrest, the desire to effect what some would call righteousness but which I would call injustice, by taking Spottiswode from his cell and hanging him."

He leaned forward on the pulpit and swept his dark gaze across the audience. "I vow to you now, in this holy place and on this holy day," he said, his deep voice gruff with restrained anger, "that if one person dares to deny Spottiswode his day in court, I will bring down vengeance upon the man who crosses me. We live in a nation of courts, not a land of extrajudicial assault."

Spellbound, Anne watched him. Though she noted that, in invoking the rule of law, Darkefell made a personal threat of violence on anyone who violently broke the law, she was quite sure the irony of that escaped him. But she applauded his intent.

Whispers rippled through the crowd, and a few people abruptly got up and left. Mr. Sydney, the vicar, rushed up to the pulpit and babbled, nervously interrupting the marquess, to remind the congregation, yet again, that the next Sunday was Easter; they would gather, some for Maundy Thursday, but certainly for Good Friday service and then on the hill overlooking the village for an Easter Sunday vigil and service. He gave the homily even as others rose and made their way down the aisle to the big oak hobnailed doors.

One of the congregation who slipped out quickly was familiar to Anne; it was Richard Allengate, considerably cleaner and steadier on his feet than when she had first seen him. Why did he depart so hastily?

The service was over, the marquess mired in a heated conversation with the vicar, who seemed to be protesting Darkefell's usurpation of the pulpit to threaten the gathered congregation. Anne rose and hustled down the aisle of the church out to the brilliant spring sunshine.

She stood at the top of the church steps and scanned her unfamiliar surroundings: the village road, the long, low wall around the church property, the sweeping trees and greensward of grass. Where had Allengate gone? She saw a tall male figure shambling between the tombstones in the cemetery below the church yard, his pace slowing and the whole demeanor of the fellow sagging with every step forward. That was him.

Mrs. Lily Jenkins, who had evidently been one of those who left the service in a huff during Darkefell's unusual diatribe, stood at the bottom of the church steps with a young man who must be her husband. He was speaking animatedly with another young woman, but as Anne watched, Lily grabbed his arm and tugged it, hard. He stumbled sideways, swept a brief bow to the young woman, and obediently guided his wife toward a waiting open carriage. There was no mistaking the irritation on her face as she turned toward her husband and plainly, even from a distance, berated him. Perhaps about stopping to speak to the young woman, as innocent as the conversation appeared?

Anne was torn; she would have liked to speak again with Lily Jenkins but could not let Richard Allengate go. He was surely the better source of information about his own sister. She swiftly hurried after him, down the steps and across the grassy yard, threading through gray, lichen-encrusted stones toward newer ones as she got farther away from the church.

In the back corner of the cemetery, Allengate knelt by a tombstone near a weeping willow just showing delicate fronds of green. The engraving on the stone named young Fanny Allengate as the sad inhabitant of the grave. Mounded dirt in front of the stone was just beginning to sprout fresh shoots of grass. She paused and hung back. Now that she was there, it was impossible to interrupt his grieving. The young man's shoulders shook with grief. Anne turned to go.

"What do you want from me?" he asked.

She turned back and saw that he had stood up to face her. She regarded the tears standing in his blue eyes and trailing down his smooth, pale cheeks, and said gently, "I'm sorry. It wasn't right to follow you."

"I recognize you. You interfered when I attacked poor Lady Darkefell."

"Yes."

"I'm so ashamed," he said, hanging his head.

"You've had a difficult time since your sister died, haven't you?"

"We were close, for our parents are both dead. Now I'm alone, but that doesn't excuse my attack." He lifted his head and gazed at her, an open expression on his handsome face. "Thank you for interfering and saving Lady Darkefell from serious harm at my hands. You were very brave."

There was genuine gratitude in his tone. Anne examined him, his cheeks streaked with tears, his eyes clouded and red. "Why did you attack her? What did she say that upset you?"

He just shook his head, unwilling or unable, it seemed, to divulge his conversation with the marchioness.

"Why were you there?"

"I was wandering. I had too much to drink and went up to Staungill Force, but… " He trailed off and shook his head again. "I don't know what I was thinking."

She hesitated but then said, "I've heard things about your sister, *good* things. I've heard she was very sweet and trusting."

"You've doubtlessly heard that she was easily fooled. My poor, gullible Fanny."

"Yes, I had heard that." Birds chirped and sang, the sun breaking through the canopy of new leaves overhead and casting green light about them. A breeze swept through the graveyard, rippling through the jade green grass. "Mr. Allengate, it's not my place to say this, I know, but though you have been dealt a heavy blow, you're healthy, young, and have a career. Perhaps it would be best for you to move away, to try to forget—"

"Forget? No," he said, his voice hard suddenly. "I won't leave, and no one can make me." He strode past her and started zigzagging across the cemetery toward a gate that opened onto the road that ran past the church.

Anne followed and caught up with him, grabbing his sleeve and hanging on, her posy of tulips getting crushed in her haste. "Mr. Allengate, do you believe that someone killed your sister?"

"Yes.

"Do you believe that William Spottiswode killed her?"

"No."

"Why?"

"He had no reason. I don't imagine he even knew her."

"And despite the accusations put forth, you don't think Lord Darkefell did it?"

He hesitated but then said, "No. No, I do not believe Lord Darkefell killed Fanny."

Did it sound a little like he was trying to convince himself? "Who do you think did it? And how?"

"If I knew, that man would be dead," he said.

Anne frowned. "Do you have any ideas?" She tugged on his sleeve, but he kept moving, and she trotted to keep up. "Mr. Allengate, I know you've likely discussed this all before, but I have good reason to ask."

He stopped and turned, staring at her. "Why?"

"What?" She released his sleeve.

"You say you have a good reason… what is it?"

She took a deep breath. "I think you have been misled, perhaps, about who your sister was involved with. And even how she was involved."

"I'm listening," he said cautiously.

They were by the stone fence, and Anne saw in the distance, near the church, Lady Darkefell pointing her out to her son. The marquess stared at her, but then turned and spoke to his brother and Lydia.

"I've heard it said that your sister was naïve, and you confirmed that." Anne thought furiously and slowly continued. "I don't understand though, about what? What do you mean by that?" He said nothing, and she continued, watching his face. "Why was she at the waterfall the day she died? Who was she truly involved with?"

His expression showed his own bafflement, and he shook his head. "She didn't tell me, and yet I read her journal after her death, and in it she said she met the marquess on at least three occasions, and he kissed her. She hoped to marry him."

Anne felt a pain in her stomach. "The marquess?"

"Yes. I don't know what to make of it. Fanny was naïve, even fanciful at times, but she never lied… at least not to me. And yet the marquess denies meeting her there." The young man passed his hand over his eyes and shook his head. "I've known him my whole life. If I was so bold as to judge him, I would say he's not the sort who lies easily. But why would she write such a thing in her journal—her *journal,* the secret relation of what was in her heart—if it wasn't true? I'm so confused."

"This question… I feel I must ask, Mr. Allengate. Was there anyone else in Fanny's life? Any other beaux?"

"She was engaged once but decided against the marriage."

"Who was the gentleman?"

"Mr. Benjamin Jenkins."

Anne exclaimed, "Really? The same gentleman now married to a Mrs. Lily Jenkins?"

"Yes."

Was there some kind of connection? Reluctantly, Anne decided that in a village the size of Hornethwaite, it would be odd if a young man rejected by one young lady did not go on to marry another local girl. And it could explain Mrs. Jenkins's apparent dislike of Fanny Allengate, as a married woman will always dislike her rival or past rival for her husband's affections. "And it was she who ended the engagement?"

"Well of course," the young man said. "He would not jilt her. Benjamin is a good sort, but Fanny decided she did not love him, and she was a romantical girl. She wished to marry for love. I did my best to discourage her silliness, but there was no harm in her fancies, I finally decided, and supported her decision to end the engagement. She became engaged to Benjamin too soon after our father died, looking for the security of a settled situation, but then decided that was not a firm basis for marriage. Ben Jenkins was good about it, really, despite his disappointment."

"Do you think he cared for her a great deal, or was her dowry the main enticement?"

The young man appeared shocked at such plain speaking, but he answered quickly enough. "Benjamin always loved Fanny, from the time we were all children together."

Anne saw that the marquess was heading toward her. Her time with Allengate was dwindling. "Mr. Allengate," she said, turning away from the marquess and toward the fellow. "Did you know Cecilia Wainwright?"

"The maid who was killed? No. Why?"

How to raise the question of his nocturnal wandering, as witnessed by Mrs. Haight? Straight forward was often best. "Where were you the night of her death?"

"I beg your pardon, my lady?" He stared at her, the dark smudges under his long-lashed blue eyes deepening the impression of suffering.

Anne glanced over her shoulder; the marquess was swiftly approaching. "Mr. Allengate," she said hurriedly, "someone saw you the night of Cecilia's death, coming through the village at an early hour, long before sunrise. Where were you?"

He paled, if that was possible for such a pallid, tormented-appearing individual. "Are you accusing me of murder, Lady Anne?"

"Of course not," she said, casting another hasty glance toward the marquess. "But I'm curious.

"I have been troubled of late, ma'am, and often walk out of the village, along the river."

It was a reasonable answer, given with dignified suffering, and she could not take it amiss, especially since he answered with such sincerity and openness as left her feeling he had told the truth.

"Allengate," the marquess said easily as he joined them. "How are you? Better, I hope?"

He bowed. "I'm a little better, my lord. I would have approached, but felt my attentions could not be more ill-timed. I pray your poor mother does not suffer from my unconscionable actions?"

"She's hardier than she appears," he said. "And she recognizes that she insulted you when you spoke to her. She's heartily sorry for that. Rest easy—she's well, and none of us holds that aberration against you. I would not see you up on charges after an exemplary life, nor does my mother wish that. I hope you've been staying away from spirits in the meantime?"

"Yes. I cannot risk the awful repercussions of drink ever again. I'm one of those unfortunates who cannot tolerate it, it appears."

The marquess turned to Anne. "My lady, the carriage awaits, and the cattle should never be left standing, especially since storm clouds gather on the horizon."

"I would never be one to wish harm to the cattle," she rejoined dryly. "Good day, Mr. Allengate."

"Good day, my lady."

The marquess took her arm in his steel grip, and she felt herself almost lifted by his impatient tug.

"The horses won't suffer if another thirty seconds pass," she said, yanking her arm from his grip as she tripped on a tuft of thick grass.

A rumble of thunder overhead made them both look up. Anne stalked off, and the marquess caught up with her.

"I apologize, my lady, if I was overly forceful. Concerning what were you speaking to young Allengate?"

She glanced sideways, noting the grim set to his jaw line, and did not feel inclined to answer.

"You are really the most uncompromising woman I have ever met."

"I suppose most ladies fall at your feet, swooning in gratification after being assaulted?"

"I beg your pardon?"

He had stopped walking, so she paused and turned, regarding the warning signs of a nerve twitching at the corner of his eye and a vein pulsing in his neck. Overhead thunder rumbled again, seeming to reflect his darkening mood.

Choosing her words carefully, she said, "I think you should reserve your kisses for women who have invited such an indication of your… affection, my lord."

The twitch intensified. His neck began to redden. His physical being was a veritable barometer of his mood, and she could judge that he was getting more agitated, but his tone, when he replied, was mild enough.

"I must apologize, my lady, if the one time I kissed you seemed an assault as you so piquantly state."

"I'm at a loss to explain it, I must say, except as some kind of method of imposing your will or expressing frustration. Could it be either of those things?"

"You are positively the most unusual woman I've ever met." He sighed, flexed his shoulders, and smiled. "Shall we forget our previous disagreements, Lady Anne? As a peace offering—if the rain holds off—I would like this afternoon to take you on a jaunt over the estate and a walk through the castle, which you were so kind as to say interested you."

She watched his eyes and read only complaisance there. It accorded with her own wishes, so she said, "I would like that above all things, my lord."

Fifteen

I MUST HAVE BEEN MAD, DARKEFELL THOUGHT AS HE climbed up into the pony trap next to Lady Anne that afternoon after luncheon. The rain had splashed down for a while, but had then disappeared, and there was, unfortunately, no reason not to follow through with his offer. He wished, in truth, to control her view of his estate and perhaps keep her from annoying his people by wandering the estate, making awkward inquiries and discoveries. She was a most unpredictable young lady.

He expected a barrage of questions and was not disappointed on that head, though the direction of her inquiries startled him. It began immediately after he stated that they would tour the home farm first and clicked to Nip, the sturdy gray pony, to begin.

"I understand from Mr. Grover that you are purchasing his estate from him—is that true?" she asked, her hands crossed on her lap as he drove the trap along the lane past the Ivy Lodge stables, up the hill, and around the woods past the tower.

"How did that come up in casual conversation?" he said, guiding the pony along the path.

"He told me he was selling up and moving to be closer to his son, and I asked him who was purchasing his estate."

"He told you he was moving to be closer to his son?" Darkefell asked, his tone sharp.

"Yes," she said with a swift glance sideways. "I have to guess from your tone that he lied. He said his son was about to marry, and he wished to move closer to him."

Darkefell saw no reason to prevaricate. "He and Theo haven't spoken in… let's see… two years? Three, perhaps?"

"Really? Over what did they fall out?"

"Why would I be privy to that information?"

She still watched his face. "You do know, though."

"What makes you so sure?"

"Two things—first, you did not simply say *'I don't know,'* and second, you have a telltale nerve that leaps at the side of your eye when you are unsettled."

He followed the path away from places he didn't want her investigating, more aware than ever that she was an exceedingly observant woman. "That nerve must leap like a spring lamb whenever I'm in your presence, my lady. I should have said, then, that even if I have an idea, it is not my business to tell others why Mr. Grover and his son no longer speak."

She nodded. "I see I'm teaching you to be both more precise and more successfully evasive."

He chuckled and glanced sideways at her, appreciating both her wit and her concise way of speaking. She had a trim way of sitting, too, ankles crossed, wrists crossed, completely at her ease and yet with her spine perfectly straight, her lovely full lilac skirts perfectly placed, her waist trim beneath her gray caraco and embroidered lilac stomacher. She wore a dark gray cloak unfastened, just draped over her shoulders. Her simple elegance pleased him more than any allurements he had ever been thrown by any young lady, and he had experienced more than his share of enticing glances and gestures.

She had dressed her bonnet with some of the purple tulips from her crushed bouquet, and as they nodded above her shadowed face, she looked both absurd and oddly adorable. He glanced at the path, then back at her. It was true her nose was a little too long and her chin too pointed. There was a faint equine suggestion about the nose and generous mouth. Her color was good, though, and her dark hair glossy; she glowed with health and vivacity. She would never be accounted a beauty, but neither was she ugly, merely plain. She met his eyes, and her gaze was open and frank. He wished he could be honest with her, but there was much that was none of her business, and more that could lead to endless trouble for his family if it were discovered.

Ultimately, as much as he admired some aspects of her character, he didn't know her. Perhaps she could keep a secret, and perhaps she *would* keep a secret, but he couldn't depend upon it. Oddly enough, he longed to unburden himself to someone who didn't need him to guide them, but she was forbidden to him as a confidant by the very nature of his secrets.

"You can tell me anything, you know," she said, watching his face, her words oddly perceptive of his thoughts, "without fear of it being spread." Her gaze flicked between his eyes and his mouth and back up to his eyes.

He looked back at the path. They had followed the beck for some time but had climbed away from it and were now topping a rise; they overlooked the valley where the home farm nestled. It was a sight that filled him with pleasure, almost as much as staring at the castle. "I don't know what you mean, my lady. Tell you what?"

"Anything. I came here because Lydia asked me to, but—"

"I understand that you were engaged to her brother. Is that so?"

"Yes," she said, quietly. "He died at the siege at Yorktown in the colonies five years ago."

"Peace was bought at an awful price—we lost many of our bravest and best," he said, his manner awkwardly sententious. "You must have suffered, to have lost someone you loved at such a young age." He glanced at her yet again, and this time, with the carriage stopped, had no need to tear his gaze away. For some unknown reason, he longed to hear her answer. Would she say she missed him terribly and had never recovered? Would she say she could never love another the way she loved him?

"It was a difficult time," she said simply. "As I was saying, I came here because Lydia asked me to, but having stumbled across such an awful crime, I feel compelled to know what happened to that poor girl, Cecilia Wainwright. Do you believe that William Spottiswode is telling the truth and killed her because she was plaguing him to marry her? It seems unlikely."

"It's not up to me to make such a judgment. Why would the man lie, after all? Why would he confess to a crime he didn't commit?" It was a question that had beset him since first hearing of the confession, but he still had no answer. He did *not* believe the man had killed Cecilia but had no proof to back up his feeling.

He wouldn't let the man hang, but… he turned away from the problem in his mind. Darkefell swept out his arm, indicating the landscape. "This is the home farm, Rohnshire."

But Lady Anne would not be distracted. "I can't explain Spottiswode's confession, but I don't think he killed Cecilia," she said. "She was an attractive girl, beautiful even, and clean in her habits. Spottiswode would never have attracted her, no matter what he says. And in Lydia's service, she was confined pretty much to Ivy Lodge—how would she even have met the man?" She paused and looked over at Darkefell, every line of her body expressing anxiety. "Lord Darkefell, the only way I could believe she would… uh… lie with Spottiswode is if he attacked her, and I don't think that happened, either. She was not unprotected, nor did she go anywhere alone."

He sighed. "I take your point, Lady Anne."

"My lord, Cecilia was involved with Jamey, your new groom. The child she carried was likely his, but he says he wasn't with her that night, and if he's telling the truth, he didn't kill her. Mr. Boatin was with her but saw her go into Ivy Lodge—I believe him, too. So if it wasn't him, wasn't Mr. Boatin, and we don't think it was Spottiswode, then who did it?"

"I don't *know!* Damn it, if I knew, do you not think I would have flayed him alive and nailed his hide to the church door by now?"

She drew back; he regretted the curse word and his vehemence.

But before he could apologize for uttering such an oath in front of her, she broke back into speech. "I know you would have taken action if you knew who the perpetrator was. But is it not, then, all the more vital that every soul should try to find the villain out? That's all I'm trying to do."

He clicked to Nip, and they began the descent to the farm. How could he say that he feared her perspicacity because of the complexities of his family past? Delving into one secret might lead her on to others.

After a pause, she broke back into speech. "You referred to the old Dane skin legend, did you not, in your highly creative punishment?" she said primly.

He laughed out loud. She had a way of making him laugh even when he was in the foulest of moods. "Yes," he said, "I did refer to the Dane skin story."

"I cannot believe anyone would flay a human alive and nail his skin to a church door," she said, showing her knowledge of the old legend of the punishment meted out to those who desecrated a church in days long gone. It was said that those church doors still had the human skin on them, even in more enlightened times. "It's gruesome and inhuman."

"You have a better opinion of humankind than I do, my dear lady."

They pulled up to the farmhouse door, and a stout lady exited, wiping her hands on a white cloth and ducking her head.

"Good day, milord. How d'you do?"

Darkefell leaped down and put up one hand for Lady Anne as the Lincoln's eldest son held Nip by the halter. "Mrs. Lincoln," he said. "This is Lady Anne Addison, a visitor at Ivy Lodge."

The proper obeisance was made, and Darkefell showed Anne the farm, questioning the farmhands about the lambing, agreeing to changes, then led her back to the pony trap.

Through it all Anne had the sense that something was worrying him. She was sure that he knew or believed things that pointed to someone's involvement in Cecilia's murder, but that didn't necessarily imply guilt in the affair himself. He was hiding something, and that perturbed her. Though he didn't believe Spottiswode guilty, what could they do but investigate his claim?

They were in motion again, winding up a hill and into a forest. Anne said suddenly, "This is the way to that pretty waterfall I saw from the tower."

"It is," he said.

She glanced sideways at him. There was a grim set to his jaw, a regular occurrence. "It's where Tilly Landers and Fanny Allengate died."

"Where their bodies were found," he corrected.

It took her a moment, but she appreciated the subtle difference. "Ah, you think it is possible their deaths took place somewhere else, and the bodies were placed here?"

He shrugged. "Many things are possible."

"Surely the same person is responsible for all the deaths?"

He shook his head and sighed. "I don't think so. In truth, I do *not* believe that Tilly Landers was murdered and, though I would never say this to Richard, poor fellow, I fear Fanny Allengate took her own life. Too many things don't add up. She was imagining things, clearly." He gave her a quick look but then continued, "She'd lost her father just months before. She agreed to marry Ben Jenkins then broke it off." He shook his head. "She wasn't well, and I think she just… decided to end it all."

"Sad," Anne said. They trotted through a wood that was dappled yellow and green with sunlight filtering through the new greenery. It was a lovely sylvan spot, and amongst the trees she spotted drifts of primroses, their yellow flowers glowing like butter. "Stop!" she cried.

He pulled the pony to a halt. "What?"

She shed the cloak she had draped over her shoulders, jumped down from the pony trap without waiting for his hand, and lifted her skirts; she climbed a small rise into the woods beyond the primroses, sinking to her knees among the damp leaves. "Look!" she said, and stripped off her gloves then cradled the lovely perfect blossom on her hands.

"What is it?" he asked, crouching at her side.

"A wood anemone," she said softly, cradling the pinky white blossom and fondling the petals. "Isn't it lovely?"

"It is," he said, his tone husky.

She looked up, and he was staring directly at her. Overcome with shyness, she felt the blush mounting her cheek. What could he mean, saying such a thing while looking at her? Stuttering back into speech, she said, "I-I have heard it said that the wood anemone is found only in old, well-established woodlands, so this must have always been a forest?"

"I suppose," he said. He reached out and plucked one of the delicate blossoms then tucked it behind her ear under her bonnet. He let his hand linger, touching a loose curl that drifted down under her bonnet and caressing her neck. But then he stood and held out his hand. "Come, my lady, we have much more to see."

Grateful that he hadn't taken advantage of the solitary nature of the woodland copse to kiss her again—or was she sorry rather than grateful?—she gave him her bare hand and allowed him to pull her to her feet. He helped her back up into the trap and leaped up, taking the reins and clicking to the patient pony.

He was silent, and she felt awkward, so she began talking about the first thing that entered her mind, and that was oddly related, she supposed, to her thoughts of a few moments before. "It appears from our experience in the woods last night that Jamey has not mourned his lost love, Cecilia, for long, and has gone back to his other flirt, Ellen."

"I presume you have some source for this knowledge, that Jamey was involved with Cecilia?"

His manner was refreshingly normal, and Anne thought for a moment then said, "Well, yes." She told him about Mary's discovery of the love posset ceremony and Cecilia's claim that Jamey's spirit had taken and eaten her cake. "And the young man himself did not deny it when I asked him last night. That's why I don't believe she could have been involved with Spottiswode. Look objectively at both men. Which do you believe a young woman of Cecilia's intelligence and attractiveness would prefer?"

"I take your point." He was silent for a long moment then said, "I suppose that Osei, if he was sworn to secrecy by Miss Wainwright about the identity of the father of her baby, would respect that secrecy beyond the grave. Perhaps that's the secret he's keeping."

The path opened out just then to the riverbank and the sparkling vision of the waterfall above them. "How lovely!" she cried, clasping her bare hands together. She had neglected to put her gloves back on but didn't care about the impropriety, not in such company and on such a day. There was something about the marquess that encouraged a lack of decorum in her.

The bank was mossy and verdant, with a slender creeping vine that blossomed, opening trusting flower faces to the sunlight that filtered through the newly green branches of languorous willows. He brought the pony trap to a halt, jumped out, and lifted her down, pausing for a long moment with his hands at her waist, staring down into her face. Breathless, though she had taken no exercise, she turned and took a few steps away from him to regain control of her breath and to view the scene.

"How happy it makes me to see a view such as this, that has been left alone as the hand of the Creator made it," she said.

"I'm not one to tamper with what God and nature have conspired to create. I leave that to my mother, who never sees a patch of open ground without wishing to tame it."

"But cultivated gardens have their place, my lord," she said, ambling toward the eddy, a swirling, shadowed pool at the base of the waterfall. She stood on a humped hillock of moss and stared, admiring the sparkle of sunlight on the drops that scattered as a rivulet hit a rock. Mist billowed from the force of the falls and bedewed her cheeks.

"I still prefer the wild," he said.

She started and whirled; he was right behind her, his approach so silent that it took her breath away. He pulled her into his grasp and stared down into her eyes. His were dark, the sooty lashes long and striking, but the effect not the least bit feminine. So hard-muscled and masculine a man could never be thought of as effeminate.

"My lord," she gasped.

"I wonder," he murmured. "Would you strike me again if I kissed you?"

"I'm likely to, if you act without permission."

"Alas, I rarely ask permission." He bent his head and paused, then kissed her lips, the touch clinging, cloying at first, becoming firmer.

She closed her eyes; a light breeze caressed her cheek with the mist moistening them both, the sound of a lark somewhere not too distant fluted, and the trilling of the waterfall was music. And the kiss, his lips full, her own answering… she wouldn't strike him this time. It finally ended. She opened her eyes to find him still staring down into her eyes. Had he closed his eyes as she had, or kept them open?

"Why did you do that?" she asked, breathless.

"Because I wanted to."

"Do you always do what you want?"

"Always."

"Oh." She tried to work out how they had progressed from speaking of gardens to kissing in the dappled sunlight of an April Sunday afternoon drive, but it failed her, and she gave up trying to connect any action previous to the kiss with the caress itself. She didn't care to ask any further questions. "I suppose it's blasphemy to behave thus on the day our Lord rode into Jerusalem."

"I cannot consider so pleasant a thing blasphemous. That is the voluptuary in me." He turned her around and took her arm, strolling with her to the water's edge.

She had been thinking of something earlier and now gave it voice. "I hadn't realized before that there is a cart track right up to the falls. If Fanny and Tilly *were* murdered elsewhere, they could easily have been brought here and thrown in."

"You are the most extraordinary woman," he said.

She looked over at him in surprise. "I beg your pardon? Why do you say that, sir?"

"You have just been kissed and appear to have enjoyed it immensely, and yet, in another moment, you can calmly speak of murdered young ladies and discuss how and where they were possibly dispatched."

"What's extraordinary about that?"

"If you don't know, I must assume you know no other young ladies or that your acquaintance is made up entirely of extraordinary young women."

Indignant, she faced him, hands on her hips. "I take exception, my lord, to your taunting. I am not extraordinary. I'm no different than any other young lady."

"All right, then," he said, taking her arm in his steely grip. "You're quite ordinary. Let us climb."

"And another thing, Darkefell, I resent that you presume to say that I enjoyed your kiss immensely. How do you know such a thing?"

"I know."

She stopped talking, then, for she longed to offer him a setdown, but her honesty would not let her lie. She *had* enjoyed the kiss, thoroughly, deeply. He might persist in viewing her as an extraordinary young woman, but he was without doubt an extraordinary man and exceptionally skilled.

After a climb, they were at the top of the waterfall, and she saw why it might be an admirable meeting place for lovers. There was another rise, climbing up into humped rolling hills, but set in the steep hillside was a protected overhang. She headed for it, lifting her skirts and scaling the steep rocky incline, grateful that she had worn sturdy kid half boots, the soles scuffed from vigorous tramps along the Kent coast, for the moss was extremely slippery.

She entered the shadowy cavern and stood, staring. "Oh, my goodness! Darkefell, come quickly!"

Sixteen

DARKEFELL CLIMBED UP TO HER, PANTING FROM exertion, and stood staring into the mouth of the cave. "Somebody has been living here," he said, stalking into the cavern.

She followed. A shabby rug covered the floor, and in the gloomy depths, a half-broken chair listed by the remains of a fire. She shivered, a rush of air from the depths of the cave and the dampness from the water-fall's mist uniting with the scene to send a chill down her back. She should have kept her cloak on instead of leaving it behind in the trap. "Or at least visiting on occasion. When did you last see this cave?"

Moodily, he shook his head. "It's been months. I've had no cause to come here."

She glanced at his face, remembering their conversation about Fanny Allengate. As imperious as he occasionally seemed, finding the young woman's body had affected him deeply, she thought, making this spot one of horror. She could commiserate. "Who would do this?"

"It could be anyone," he said. "Could even be some of the lads from Hornethwaite."

"Really, Darkefell, would village boys dare live on your property like this? That doesn't seem likely." She took a few steps and stooped to examine the rug. It was old but had once been of excellent quality. Crouching by the fire, she poked a stick through the ashes then rose, dusting off her hands. She roamed the cavern, her gaze pausing on the rattan garden chair, a pile of blankets, and an old fur robe.

Fur. She laid it out carefully and examined it. "Darkefell," she said over her shoulder. "Could you please move? You're blocking the light from the cave mouth."

"I beg your pardon, my lady," he said with exaggerated politeness. He approached and knelt at her side. "What are you looking for?"

She glanced at him. To tell or not to tell? Information should never be given without some hope of recompense. In this case, that recompense should be in the form of information she knew he was holding back. "If I tell you, you must promise to answer one question from me, honestly and completely."

"You drive a hard bargain, my lady," he said, his dark eyes glittering. "How do I know that what you tell me will be worth the price? And what if I cannot answer your question because of a promise to another or because I don't know?"

"Really, Darkefell," she said, exasperated. "If you don't know, I won't hold it against you. And a promise… " Reluctantly, she sighed and said, "I respect a promise of secrecy. I'm willing to tell you what I'm looking for—and it's worth knowing, trust me—in exchange for one question. If you can answer with honor, do so." She looked down. Yes, this was it, she was almost sure.

"All right."

She parted the fur of the robe, isolating the spot she now knew was the one. "The other morning when you and your brother found me at the spot where Cecilia was murdered, remember the gold chain we found?"

"Of course."

"By the way, have you established to whom it belongs?"

"No. Was that your question?"

"Of course not," she chided. "Before you found me, I had just seen something else, and I… well, I hid it from you."

"You *what?*"

"I know, I have no excuse, except you startled me and—" She broke off.

"And infuriated you? Yes, I had that sense."

"Well, I had found a thick tuft of fur wedged in the crook between a thorn and the branch."

"Fur?"

"Yes, but it was not *torn* from its origin. It was, as my maid pointed out, cut evenly from a mantle or tippet, she suggested. Or from a fur robe like this." She moved her body out of the way but still held the spot where the fur of the robe had been evenly snipped, a sizable chunk missing. The color matched exactly; she was sure of it.

"Somebody planted those items in the thicket where Cecilia was found, then, to further the idea of a wolf attack," he said.

"No, not a wolf attack… an attack by something or someone *pretending* to be a wolf. Wolves do not generally wear gold chains."

He nodded his agreement. "But how could they count on them being found? It was dark when you found Cecilia."

"But if I had not been walking to Ivy Lodge just then and had not heard her cries, not alerted you, she wouldn't have been found until morning."

"So, whoever had these items, no matter to whom they originally belonged or were meant to point to, must be culpable in Cecilia's murder."

"It stands to reason." She thought for a long moment. Her legs were getting numb from crouching, so she sat down with a bump on the rug. "Unless we were meant to think that."

"I think you're giving the murdering villain too much credit for deep thinking." He stood and stretched his legs, walking to the mouth of the cave. He fiddled with his jacket as he walked, tugging it down. "I think we should look at it in a straightforward light," he added over his shoulder.

Anne could not speak at the moment. The marquess's perfect masculine form was outlined in the brilliant mouth of the cave, his figure shadowy, but the broad shoulders tapering to a solid waist and supported by thickly muscled legs all too evident. She was tongue-tied, feeling the flush of unwanted attraction overcome her, intensified by the memory of lips molded to hers in a warm, long kiss.

"Don't you think?" he asked, turning back and evidently regarding her, though his face, and so his expression, were shadowed, his back to the light beyond the cave mouth. He stalked back and stood over her. "Anne?"

His simple utterance of her name, unadorned, confused her. She opened her mouth, but nothing came out. He must have seen something in her eyes, on her face. He knelt by her and took her hand.

"Why did you kiss me?" she finally asked, staring at him.

He was silent for a long moment then said, "I told you the truth before. Because I wanted to."

"Nothing else?"

"No."

"Oh." She scrambled to her feet.

He rose, too, and put one hand on her shoulder as she turned away. "My lady," he said.

"Yes?" She looked back at him, but it seemed that was all there was to his sentence. "*My lady.*"

He brooded as he drove them away from the waterfall. She had swiftly become businesslike and distant, going back, as she always did, to the problem at hand: Cecilia's murder. Finding a possible link between the waterfall where Tilly Landers and Fanny Allengate had been found with the murder of the maid, Cecilia Wainwright, had left them both puzzled. She had asked who owned the fur robe, but he honestly did not know.

They agreed that he would send up two of his trusted men to remove what was in the cave and bring it to the castle without saying a word to anyone else. But now he was haunted by something else entirely. While she was busy with the fur robe, he had found something else, and it chilled him to the bone. He had found the weapon that he suspected killed Cecilia Wainwright.

"I still have my question to ask," she said.

"Yes," he replied abruptly.

"But I think I'll reserve it for another day."

"That wasn't our agreement."

"But there were no terms, and so *when* I ask the question should be immaterial to you." She glanced around. "We're going back by a different path," she said as they trotted over a stone bridge to the other side of a stream.

"There's someone I'd like you to meet," he said.

Unlike any other female he had ever come across in his whole life, she did not ask who it was. She didn't tease or plague him nor tug at his sleeve. She did not archly conjecture, nor did she pout, she simply waited, satisfied to find out in due time. A most unaccountable female.

He pulled the pony trap up to a tiny cottage made of local stone and roofed in slate. Hens clucked in the yard, and the first green shoots of vegetables and herbs pushed through the damp earth. A small fence enclosed the yard and was centered by a gate, which Darkefell held open for Lady Anne after helping her down from the trap.

But even before he guided her up the walk, the door flew open, and a rosy-cheeked girl of about thirteen trotted out, wiping her hands on her blue apron. Anne cast him a questioning glance, but he was enjoying keeping her in suspense.

"Is your mistress free, Moggie?"

"Aye, milord," she said with a curtsey.

Through the open door, ducking his head, Darkefell guided his captive into a large open room. An old woman sat in a comfortable chair by the fireside, but she was not still. Her hands worked at an incredible rate, knitting a blue blanket. She didn't look down at her work; in fact, she seemed to look at nothing. She stilled when she heard them, then her wrinkled mouth widened in a smile.

"Master Anthony!" she cried.

"Nan," he said, "I've brought someone to meet you."

She stilled. "Have you, now? An' oo would that be?"

Her voice was strong, still, though she was clearly of advanced age. Anne glanced at Darkefell then back at the woman, noticing her unfocused gaze. The woman was blind or almost completely so. Advancing toward her, she said, "My name is Anne, ma'am."

"Lady Anne Addison, Nan," the marquess said loudly. "She's visiting John's wife, Lydia, down at Ivy Lodge. Lady Anne, this is Mrs. Patterson, as she was known among the trembling servants of the castle when I was a child."

Anne stepped over to her, crouched, and took the woman's outstretched hands in her own. They were crooked with arthritis, and the joints were gnarled, but they were still warm and strong. She squeezed Anne's hands within hers.

"I was 'is lordship's nanny, you must 'ave figured." She cocked her head on one side and listened. "Would ee take some tea wi'me? Moggie was just putting up the pot."

Anne glanced at the marquess. He smiled and nodded, so she said, "I would enjoy that very much."

It was the most relaxed Anne had seen the marquess, sitting in the cramped parlor with his old nanny, talking loudly for her benefit as she went back to knitting, her crooked fingers speedily working the blue wool. Young Margaret, or Moggie as both called her, daughter of the Lincolns, Anne learned, was Mrs. Patterson's only servant, though the men from the farm split and stacked her wood, gardened, and repaired the cottage as needed, and a fellow both referred to as "Eddy" came regularly to tend to other needs.

After drinking tea, Lord Darkefell stood and said, "If you ladies will excuse me, I am just going to look around, make sure all the work is being done to my satisfaction."

There was a moment of silence between the two women after the marquess left, but then the nanny leaned forward, pausing in her incessant knitting, and said, "An' whut is there between ee, eh?"

"I beg your pardon?"

"'E's never brought a lady t'meet me afore."

"We were out for a jaunt, and he wished to look over the cottage. I suppose he's a conscientious landlord."

"Aye. That 'e is."

Anne was grateful that the woman did not continue to question her, and they proceeded to speak of other things. Eddy, it turned out, was another former estate worker, Edward Carter, the gamekeeper from the late marquess's day. He lived in a cottage on a hill, Mrs. Patterson said, and Anne recognized from her description the hut she had seen from the tower.

"Does he keep a dog?" she asked sharply.

"P'raps."

"And does anyone stay with him?"

The elderly woman's expression saddened. "Aye, soomtimes. Neddy, Eddy's son outta wedlock. Daft Neddy the cruel call him. Neddy's a sore trial to Eddy. 'E shows up outta nowhere soomtimes, and stays, but 'e's allus trouble when he does, an' 'e allus needs money."

Anne sighed deeply. That, it seems, was who she saw. It likely meant that what she witnessed was the marquess and his brother questioning the former gamekeeper and his wayward son about the maid's murder. "Trouble? What kind of trouble is he, ma'am?"

"Ooh, now, I shouldn't like t'say." And she meant it. Not another word would she expend on the topic of the gamekeeper and his troubled son.

Instead, the woman questioned Anne closely about her home, her past, and her marital status. Though Anne tried to ask about the marquess's past, the nanny became oddly closemouthed. "I understand from Mr. Boatin that, though in the painting I have seen of the family the twin boys looked remarkably alike, they were not identical as they grew older," Anne commented.

"I never thought they looked the same, nor did their mother. Lady Darkefell and I... we allus knew the differences, even when the boys was wee bairns. Though t'markwis—Anthony's da, y'mind—was dreadful thick 'bout that. Couldnee tell one from t'other for years!"

"I find the marquess a puzzle, ma'am, I must say. He clearly has a noble heart. I don't know if you've met Mr. Boatin, but I'm sure you know how the marquess saved his life."

"Aye. Th'lad cooms t'see me now an' agin, when they be at t'castle."

"Mr. Boatin?"

"Aye. 'E cooms and tells me tales o'Afric, where 'e's from, y'mind, while I knit. 'Specially in th'dead of winter, when it's fearsome lonely. I niver get tired o'listenin'. 'Ow I wish I was young again, when ee tells me tales o' the hot Afric sun, an' throwin' a spear at n'antelope, an' runnin' on the grassy plain. If I was young an' a man, I'd hop a ship t'Afric and niver look back." Her busy hands had stopped, and she turned her face to the window, the sun streaming in and lighting her pale, wrinkled face. Her white hair sparkled in the sunlight where it escaped her cap, and Anne wished she had her pencils.

"Why would you do that, ma'am?" Anne asked, genuinely curious. The longing in the old woman's voice was painful. A lump lodged in Anne's throat, and she couldn't clear it.

"So hot, so sunny. Mr. Boatin makes it sound like paradise. It gives 'im pleasure t'talk 'bout 'is homeland to someone whut likes to listen, I think. Winters is hard now, so long, so cold. Withoot Master Anthony and Mr. Boatin and me sweet Moggie, I'd be sore lonely."

"Ma'am, may I draw you some time?" Anne blurted out, still entranced by the woman's wrinkled face, the lines like roads on a map.

The woman chuckled, and her hands were back in motion, the blue blanket moving and shifting. "Aye, tho' what ee'd make a picture of, I dinna know."

There was silence for a moment, then Anne said, "Having met you, I have a sense that I now know how the marquess became such a fine man."

"Dinna count out the marchioness, milady. Lady Darkefell can be a fair difficult woman to coom to know, but she be good where it counts, deep in the 'eart of 'er, an' she's not 'ad an easy life."

"What do you mean?"

But the woman shook her head and would say no more. Darkefell returned, said good-bye to Mrs. Patterson, then assisted Anne into the pony cart and headed back to the castle. He had offered to take her back to Ivy Lodge, but she was not a bit weary. Dinner was to be at the castle that evening, but Anne was impatient by nature and knew that a family dinner was not a good time to tour the structure; she thus demanded her tour commence that afternoon.

As they rode, she raised a question she still did not have an answer to. "I asked earlier if it was true that you're buying Mr. Grover's estate?"

"I am."

"A wise purchase, I'm sure. It expands your property boundaries. How fortunate for him that he's not bound by an entail and has the freedom to sell."

"He inherited the estate from a distant relative when he was quite young. He was in trade," the marquess said with a disgusted expression, "but it was such as could be managed from anywhere, so he lived here and married a local lady."

His bias against someone in trade was not unusual. "What kind of trade was he in?"

Darkefell shrugged uneasily and said, "Whatever was profitable, I suppose. For a time it was the triangle trade."

"He was a slaver? You never told me that before!"

"It was his ship—well, he didn't own it, he leased it—that carried Osei. Julius and I were going to Jamaica to see if buying a plantation for him to run was a worthwhile investment."

"So, does this explain the animosity Mr. Grover feels for you?"

He shrugged. "Perhaps. But he has nothing to be angry about, so I don't think so. He wasn't even aboard the ship—he stayed in England. I did him a favor, really, prevented him from making a grave error. He's better off out of the triangle trade, for it's a risky affair. Aside from the human toll on the slaves, one bad crossing can wipe out a vast investment. I'm sure he knows that now."

"You know him far better than I. So you and his son grew up together—is he close to your age?"

"A year younger," he said, glancing over at her, amusement twitching his mouth. "I told the truth about Theophilus, you know. I did introduce him to many corruptions when we were in school together."

"I never doubted that, my lord," she said, her tone dry. "His father's resentment was avid and had the tone of disbelief, but your confession held the ring of truth."

"I should be insulted by your ready belief in my corruptive influence."

"I'd think that you would appreciate being believed."
She glanced over at him. "Unless you routinely
prevaricate and so expect to be *disbelieved*?"

"Don't you think the world requires one to lie?"

"If you mean agreeing that a friend's bonnet is
lovely when it is hideous, or that a woman's baby
is adorable when it looks like a gargoyle atop a
cathedral roof, then yes, I think skillful evasion of
the truth is requisite."

"Ah, 'skillful evasion of the truth'… what a lovely
turn of phrase."

She ignored the barb and asked, "Are you not still
friends with Theophilus Grover?"

"Oh, no, I'm too wicked a sinner for Theo, who
has his eye on a high post in the church. He really *is*
perfectly saintly. I don't object to his sanctity, only the
unbearable airs that accompany it. Ah, here's the castle!"

They topped a rise and looked down over the
structure. Anne was once again struck dumb. She had
stayed in many fine residences, and her own home,
Harecross Hall, the Harecross earldom's prime residence in Kent, was beautiful: large, lovely, gracious.
But Darkefell Castle was something more. To the
impression of size and age, it added a hint of gloomy
foreboding, a delicious melancholy mood that even
the brightest sun could not alleviate. It appealed to a
part of her she never suspected existed.

She was silent, always a good thing, Darkefell
reflected, though she didn't seem the sort who must
fill every second with chatter. That only added to her
other interesting attractions. He pulled up to the main
door and left the pony trap for his groom, guiding

Lady Anne into the castle through the twenty-foot tall double oak doors.

The main section was not made for modern comfort. He was loath to make any dramatic changes, for though he wasn't fanciful, still, he felt the ghostly hand of his ancestors reaching out to him, imploring him to preserve for future generations, if there were to be any, the Darkefell legacy untainted. It might be too late for that—recent years had spotted their reputation as much as any past barbarities—but he would persevere.

Lady Anne's enthusiasm was boundless, even for the gloomiest portal. "This place… it *seethes* with history," she said, her voice echoing in the upper reaches of one of the tower sections.

"An excellent description—this section, the old keep, was the defense against Scottish marauders centuries ago, when the clans to the north were fractious, but during the civil war it was useful, too. My family was Royalist," he said, guiding her through the great hall as his butler entered. "Lady Anne's cloak, Tanner."

"No," she said, waving away the hovering butler. "I can stay only a half hour and then must go back to Ivy Lodge, if we're to dine here tonight. I'll keep my cloak for the walk back to the lodge."

"Surely you are not one of those ladies who must spend three hours on her toilette?" he chided as Tanner bowed and retreated.

"I assure you, my lord, that the plainest of women require as much fuss and bother as the most sparkling of diamonds. Perhaps more—while they are merely gilding the lily, we are primping the weed."

He was silent, not sure how to answer, afraid that saying the wrong thing would hurt her, and he didn't want to hurt her. She was plain and aware of it—unnaturally so, it seemed to him—but how to admit that and yet compliment her many fine features? He stayed silent; there was no way that was not patronizing or insulting.

He directed his efforts to showing her at least part of the castle. It was too vast to do more than begin in the brief time they had. She was quiet, merely listening with that rare quality she had: absolute focused attention. He guided her to the armaments room, where he displayed the ancient weapons used by his ancestors in bygone battles, and then to a huge, virtually empty chamber with vaulted ceilings. "This," he said, "was the knights' hall. This is where the Barons Destaun met with their knights, ate, planned strategy. Plotted."

"Some of the work looks newer," she said, eyeing the stone corbels. Several did not have the natural patination of age.

"It was crumbling in places and becoming structurally unsound. I commissioned stonemasons to repair the foundation." He guided her through the hall, up some concealed steps, and through a door to an open gallery that looked out over the back. "This is the best view of the chapel on the hill over there," he said, pointing to a low rise with a stone chapel atop it, "and the cemetery just to the left. Ten generations or more of my people and their valued servants have been buried in the plot just beyond, and a mausoleum only for family members. It is guarded, my grandmother said, by the ghosts of my ancestors."

But Lady Anne wasn't listening to that last part. "Darkefell, I keep meaning to ask Lydia about this, but perhaps you know. Was it truly Lydia, or was it Lord John who objected to Cecilia's being properly buried in the servants' plot? What decision was made?"

He felt frozen to the marrow, and for the first time, did not admire her focus on the problem at hand. Why could she just not let it go for a time? "I'm sure I don't know, my lady, which it was who truly objected. Why don't you ask your friend?" He turned away. When he glanced back to see if she was following him away from the window, she was eyeing him with a quizzical slant to her eyebrows.

"To answer the other part of your question, Cecilia, poor girl, has already been buried in the plot we reserve for family serving staff. Yesterday, in fact. She will have a suitable memorial. I corresponded with her mother, sent all her belongings and also a considerable sum of money, but I did not tell Mrs. Wainwright that Cecilia was with child. I thought that would be too cruel, and if Cecilia had somehow already communicated that fact, unnecessary."

"You are a most unusual and thoughtful man, my lord."

"Thank Osei, not me," he said, curt from discomfiture. He could not allow her to praise him for qualities he didn't possess. "He made all the arrangements. My part was reserved to making decisions about where she would be buried, what would be told her mother, and how much money would be provided for the poor woman." The day had turned dull for him with the reminder of business he had yet to conduct. Lady Anne could not know it, he supposed, but he was dreading the confrontation he would have that evening when the family was gathered. He had to confront the owner of the murder weapon and find out when it had last been accounted for, and that haunted him.

Seventeen

THE NIGHT WOULD TELL ITS OWN TALES, AND HE couldn't predict the outcome. He took her arm and guided her onward. Finally they were back in the main great hall, a huge open square near but not directly opposite the doors, and he led her up steps toward a gloomy enclosure; he caught her by the arm when she would have surged forward. "No! Be careful, my lady, for headlong movement will send you somewhere I don't think you wish to go." He took her arm and led her sedately up the last two steps... to the pit.

She stood on the flagstone edge and looked down, a shiver passing through her body. "My, my, but your ancestors were a bloodthirsty lot, weren't they?" she said. "To have such a thing in their home?"

"This is the castle keep, and it was always more than just their home. It was my ancestors' protection from attack, their haven from enemies." They stood on the lip of a dark and deadly pit, thirty feet or more into the ground and lined with stone blocks. A cold breeze constantly swirled up from its depths. "Some say the present generation emulates the past," he said, still seized by the grim mood from her questioning.

She glanced over at him. "Do you refer, sir, to the awful gossip that your late brother killed Miss Landers?"

He shook his head and sighed, rolling his eyes. "Now why should I be obscure in my references, when you have so clearly pried into every dark corner of my life and have no restraint in raising the stories in my presence?"

"You forget, my lord," Lady Anne replied tartly, "Lydia brought me here to reassure her about the marauding werewolf, but finding Cecilia's murdered body set me on a different path. I won't rest until her murder is solved, and if that means prying into past tragedies and asking awkward questions, I'll do it. I'll not curb my tongue to save your delicate sensibilities."

"Would *anything* curb your tongue?"

She bridled, and her chin went up. "Kindness, sensitivity where it is due, love, compassion, appreciation—many things curb my tongue when necessary. This is not the time for that, and I did not think you the sort of man who needed coddling. Forgive me if I'm wrong and your sensitive feelings have been wounded. I want to know what happened to Cecilia Wainwright."

"But it's not your mystery to solve, my lady," he growled, irritated by her biting remarks. "And Cecilia's murder has nothing to do with Tilly Landers's unfortunate death!"

"How do you know? You may think it was an accident, and Fanny's death suicide, but I keep trying to find a pattern in the deaths on your property of three women whose only similarity seems to have been in age. I admit I've had no luck so far, and no one seems willing to help."

There was a long silence.

"The pit, my lady," he said, redirecting her attention and grimly clutching her arm.

She gazed steadily down into the pit. "Just what did your ancestors have such a menacing structure for?" Anne glanced over and watched his face. A sardonic smile quirked his perfect lips, and the effect was unsettling in the gloomy shadows.

"It depends upon who is telling the tale. My father maintained that it was a prison in ancient times, nothing more. As there was no way out unless someone threw down a rope ladder, it did not need a jail keeper."

"That makes sense. Your family was probably the only law three or four hundred years ago."

"Yes, but I came across an old drawing of the layout and was intrigued enough to bring it here and examine it, orienting it properly."

"And?"

He turned her about so she was standing with her back to the pit. Her head got a little light, and the impression of the yawning pit at her back, a cold breeze lifting her curls under her bonnet, turned her stomach. She was not going to let him see how it affected her.

"Look down the steps toward the wall."

"Yes?" She determinedly focused.

"Do you see a slight difference in the stone coloration there?" His fingers traced in the air a tall arch in the wall.

"I do," she said. "It looks less weathered."

"Once, long ago, that was a doorway. Unsuspecting enemies would break down what appeared to be an unguarded door and charge up what they thought was a stairway to the main part of the house. In the gloom, instead, they would be met by a sudden drop, and many of them would fall to their deaths down this pit. It is called a murder hole. I don't know of any other like it in all of England, and so I preserve it."

"Oh," she said. She stepped forward and turned to face him, taking in a deep, shuddering breath, forcing her stomach to settle. "And do you practice that story, with just that gloomy intonation, to frighten young women? Or to impress them with your melancholy fascination?"

He laughed out loud and stepped forward into the light of a high window above the gloomy pit. "I would never try such a trick on you—for you, my lady, are indomitable."

"That's not true, but I have seen your tricks and am therefore wary. I do think I should go now, my lord. I will see you at dinner."

"Let me drive you back—you should not walk so far, for I expect you to dance this evening after dinner. Nothing wears off a heavy meal quite so well as a country dance or two."

"I won't take you out of your way, sir," Anne insisted, stepping away from his troubling touch. "Though he is staying at Ivy Lodge, my coachman, Sanderson, is at the castle today mending a spring on my carriage. If you will loan him an equipage—the pony trap will do—he can drive me and bring the trap back."

Darkefell merely nodded. He couldn't very well refuse such a request.

"You've spent some time in the castle stables now, Sanderson—what's your impression of young Jamey?" Anne sat up next to her coachman in the pony trap as the burly man gloomily handled the reins. Such a vehicle was beneath his dignity, and he drove only because she asked. "Is he capable of murder?" She had absolute reliance on her driver's astute opinion as well as his discretion.

Sanderson shook his head. "Naw."

"That was my thought. But if Cecilia was carrying his child, and that threatened his position, then he *may* have. Men have killed for less." She thought for a long moment and sighed. "But I don't really believe that. He would not have planted those items I found where she lay. This was a deed of deliberation, not passion."

"Had no chance."

"I beg your pardon?"

"He had no chance, milady. Yoong Jamey were gambling th'noight of th'maid's morder, with t'other lads in th'castle stable. Playin' hazard."

"Hazard—they were playing dice! You're sure of this?"

"Aye. Two of t'other lads say so."

She blessed her surly driver's gift for drawing others out while he said nothing himself. She had not had to direct him as to what she needed. "So, she could not have crept back out to meet *him,* and that eliminates him from Cecilia's murder."

"Aye."

"Which leaves me still with the possibility that this murder is connected to the other two deaths of young women. Or wholly unrelated. Those most intimately connected with Cecilia and, thus, most likely to have reason to harm her, are Jamey, Ellen—jealousy will make a young woman do many awful deeds, though killing your competition seems a little extreme—and… well, I must include Lord John. He entered the great hall quickly after I came to the house after finding Cecilia, but still… I think he would have had time to kill her and return to Ivy Lodge. Lydia is firm in believing he doesn't care for her as he used to, and the young man does seem to be mired in unusual gloom. What if he has some dark side to him that she is only beginning to suspect?" She bit her lip as she thought. "And I cannot forget Mr. Boatin."

Sanderson was silent.

"I like Mr. Boatin," Anne said, staring off at the landscape without seeing it. "But after all he has suffered in his life, can I really say that his calm exterior is the true one? I've known people who seem, on first meeting, to be one way, only to show their true selves at some later date. If he was in love with Cecilia and she led him on, only to take up with Jamey… again, jealousy can be the motivation for murder. And he was with her just before her death—that we already know."

"Aye."

"But I don't want it to be him, Sanderson."

"Aye."

"Nor do I want to think it could be Lord Darkefell. But he's a deep man, Sanderson, one whose depths I have not begun to plumb," she said, thinking of his gloomy delight in the "murder hole."

She mustn't concentrate too much on the marquess—as fascinating as he was, he seemed to expect her to fall desperately in love with him. Ridiculous man. She noticed that they were in a part of the estate she had not yet seen; the gravel lane from the castle to Ivy Lodge wound through a lovely park. "How pretty this part of the property is," she said, delighted at the glades of young trees and drifts of spring blossoms arranged for the most picturesque display. Someone had planted clumps of Holland bulbs, and they burst forth in the vernal sunshine.

He was silent.

"Stop!" she cried. As the pony trap pulled to a quick halt, Anne stared into the wooded glade. She had seen movement. Of course, that was not unexpected; there were probably deer and other creatures afoot. But… no, it was not a deer. She saw something slinking through the underbrush. "What is that?" she asked, pointing.

"Don't see nuthin', milady."

She had forgotten how myopic he was. "Stay here!" she commanded as she shrugged out of her cloak and scrambled down from the pony trap. She lifted her skirts and sprinted across the grass toward the shady copse, but just as she approached, she saw the animal streaking away through the trees so quickly, it was a blur of gray and white. Panting, she put one hand against a tree and rested. The animal was gone. But she was fairly sure that it was the same creature she had seen from the tower, slinking away from the hut on the hill as Lord Darkefell and Lord John approached.

Oh, how her poor feet ached! She limped back to the gravel drive and climbed back up into the pony trap. "It must have been a dog," she said as Sanderson set the vehicle in motion again with the merest click of his tongue against his teeth and the slightest of movements.

"Not any kind I ever seen," he said.

"Exactly my thoughts." She looked over at him. "How well *do* you see, Sanderson?"

"Well 'nuff when it suits me, milady. It cooms and goes."

His vision seemed remarkably bad when having good vision would require effort on his part, yet remarkably acute when he wished to make a comment on something in the distance and for driving. Despite Sanderson's faults, though, he suited her.

"Find out for me, if you can, anything about Edward Carter and his ne'er-do-well son, Neddy. Carter was the gamekeeper for the last marquess and lives in a hut on the side of the hill about a half-mile distant."

"Aye, milady."

Back at Ivy Lodge, Anne stormed Lydia's bedroom, plunking herself down by her friend's bed and waiting. Lydia was sleeping, or rather, pretending to sleep. This had gone on long enough.

"What was going on with Cecilia, Lydia?" she said loudly. "Who did you suspect was the father of her child? I know you, my girl—Cecilia was at one time dear to you. You would not keep her out of a cemetery plot just for a moral lapse. Something personal prompted your pettiness."

Lydia's eyes flew open, and she leaped up, very awake for someone who was supposedly napping. "If I had known," she cried, pounding her fists on the silky bedcover. "If I had only known… oooh! Traitor!" She broke into tears, great, heaving, choking sobs.

Anne, genuinely concerned, hopped up on the bed, taking Lydia in her arms and soothing her with little noises and words: "Hush, Lydia, don't cry. No, it's all right, my dear, really. I didn't mean to upset you… hush, now." She pushed Lydia's curls back off her forehead, and the girl, her head on Anne's shoulder, wept as if her heart was broken.

Once she had calmed, her lovely blue eyes reddened and tear trails marred her creamy skin, Anne, her arm still around her friend's shoulders, said, "My dear, you know me. *Trust* me. Tell me what has been worrying you."

Lydia sat up straighter and moved out of her friend's protective embrace. Biting her lip, she gazed at Anne and said slowly, "All right. But I'm frightened what you'll think."

"You must trust me!"

"I do, but I know you, Anne. You won't bend for anyone. If… if someone I l-love has done something…" She trailed off and looked confused.

Anne felt a trill of concern in her stomach. What was Lydia going to tell her?

The girl looked away, composed herself, and then looked back at Anne. "John doesn't love me any more."

"I told you, Lydia, that's nonsense. He loves you. The night I arrived, he was there, worried to illness about your swoon."

"No, you don't understand. He's just pretending now for everyone else's benefit."

"Why do you think that?"

"Everything was grand while we were alone," she said, her eyes misty and unfocussed. "He was attentive, kind, l-loving. But then we came back *here*." Her tone held such loathing. "And his mother… she picked away until I felt I was not good enough for her son. It was awful. I felt… I felt as though John was looking at me differently, that he was seeing me as his mother does, a silly girl, a child with no sense. I'm not like you, Anne, with brains and sense and logic."

"Lady Darkefell doesn't seem to like me much either, my girl, so there you have it. You cannot let your mother-in-law's behavior worry you."

"But it's not just that. John… he stopped… stopped coming to my room after a while." Lydia looked away, and a pretty blush mounted her soft cheeks. "And then… he was seen kissing Cecilia."

Anne's stomach twisted. The vision of the poor dead girl being carried in by the marquess, her throat savaged, dripping with blood; the sense she had in the dark of death: it all came back. Had Lord John been the father of her unborn child? Did he kill her to keep it a secret? But wait—"You said he was 'seen' kissing her… you didn't see him yourself?"

Tears dripped down her face and off her chin, and she shook her head. "Of course not. He's too careful for that."

"So who told you about it?"

"One of the maids saw it and told Therese, Lady Sophie's abigail. She told me."

"And you believe her?"

"I didn't believe Therese, but I asked the maid, and she admitted she had seen it. She told me when and where."

"When did you hear this?"

"The day before you arrived. It's why... why I was so distracted and told no one you were coming. I was upset! I don't know what's wrong with me lately. I can't seem to think!" She broke down in tears again, great gusty, heaving sobs.

Anne watched her with a dispassionate gaze. So when Lydia asked her to come to Yorkshire, she had not known about her husband's indiscretion with the maid, though she *had* felt something was wrong with John. "John was seen kissing Cecilia—what did you say to her about it?"

"N-nothing," Lydia said on a choked sob. "I didn't know what to say! She did my hair the next morning, and I kept trying to figure out how to say it, but Cecilia had been so different toward me in the last weeks, and I... I was afraid. Afraid of what she would tell me."

"And you haven't asked him?"

"No."

That was Lydia, Anne thought, afraid to hear the truth in case it was unpalatable to her. "So which maid told you she saw your husband kissing Cecilia?"

"Ellen... Henderson, I think her last name is."

Ellen, Cecilia's competition for the attention of young Jamey, the groom. Much seemed to come back to those two young women. After her conversation with Lydia, Anne went in search of Ellen, but Mrs. Hailey told her that the maid had a half day off—they rotated half days off through the staff so not too many would be off on the same day—and had presumably walked to Hornethwaite, her usual destination. A conversation with her and an exploration of what she actually saw would have to wait until the next day.

Dinner at the castle was a formal affair. The magistrate and the reverend and his wife were once again invited, as was Mr. Grover.

Anne tried to imagine why the neighbor would attend, since he despised the marquess. The answer, of course, was his friendship with Lady Darkefell. He was attentive all through dinner to the aloof marchioness, while Darkefell watched, his dark eyes hooded by half-lowered lids, his lips permanently twisted in the sardonic expression she was beginning to understand. All of the cruelty, baseness, and villainy he had seen in his life had made him cynical about humankind, if she understood him correctly. Cynicism was a tempting path; she fought against it on a daily basis. There was much to criticize in human behavior and little to laud, but it did no good to focus on the debased among humanity.

The ladies moved to the castle drawing room after dinner for a languid half hour of conversation, but Lydia was withdrawn, and Lady Sophie kept darting glances at the doorway through which they could expect the men. It was left to Anne and Mrs. Sydney, the reverend's wife, to keep up the conversation. Anne learned all about the woman's many children and several grandchildren, and even some gossip about village affairs. If they had been alone, Philodosia Sydney would have been an excellent source of information, for a reverend's wife heard many tales, but Anne could not question her with everyone there.

It was going to be a long evening.

Darkefell sat in his favorite chair in the library, where he and the other gentlemen had repaired after dinner. The book-lined walls and leather furnishings, soft lamplight and carpeted floor, gave a sense of cocooned warmth. Tanner handed around port and cigars, neither of which he liked much. John kept darting him glances, for though John didn't know what his older brother had to do that night, he seemed to feel something in the air. Finally, appearing too restless to stay still, he got up and moved to a window, shoving aside the draperies and staring through the glass.

The reverend and Mr. Grover spoke in hushed tones about Spottiswode's arrest. Mr. Sydney had been to see him, and it appeared the fellow was beginning to have regrets about his confession.

"What did you say just now, Mr. Sydney?" Darkefell asked. He set aside his unlit cigar and untasted port.

"William Spottiswode is now claiming it was the drink that was talking, not him. He says he was seized by the devil, and it whispered in his ear, forcing him to mouth untruths," the little man said with a perplexed frown.

"Merely the regrets of a man who now knows how much trouble he is in. The hangman's noose will cure him," the magistrate said.

"May I remind you, Pomfroy," Darkefell said, "that you were quite ready to hang my secretary not too long ago."

"But Mr. Boatin did not confess, did he, my lord? William Spottiswode did. And I say, no matter how much a man drinks, it does not make him believe he killed a woman!" He glanced around the room, the dim light from the oil lamps creating gaunt shadows on his ascetic face.

Mr. Grover merely appeared troubled but stayed silent. Mr. Sydney, though, shook his head and said, "Gin is an awful thing, sir. Is it gin he has been drinking? I read a tract that said women in London ignore their children and resort to all manner of perversion once introduced to its seductive influence. The devil's brew! It leads to madness."

"I don't know about gin," the magistrate said, "but I have come upon him more than once with a bottle of wine clutched in his grimy hands. And he would never say where he got it. Stolen, most likely. I took stock of my own cellar after that, I can tell you."

Darkefell sighed. The conversation served only to remind him of what he had to do that evening. He had been planning on putting it off, but it wouldn't serve. "John, may I see you for a moment? If you will excuse us, gentlemen, we have family business. I'll leave you to your port, and please join the ladies as soon as you wish." With such a disparate group as Grover, Sydney, and Sir Trevor, they would find relief in the ladies' company, he had no doubt.

"What is it, Tony?" John asked as he followed his older brother out of the room.

"I'll tell you in a few moments. Just come with me." He strode down the hall to the door of the drawing room. They were, of course, in the modern wing, so the hallways were wide and well lit with lantern sconces every few yards. He entered and saw his mother sitting alone, as usual, apart from the clustered women, and he beckoned her. She rose smoothly and approached him. Lady Anne, ostensibly in a conversation with Mrs. Sydney, noticed Lady Darkefell leave, but she would never guess what their family meeting was about.

"What do you wish?" his mother asked in a whisper in the dim hallway.

"Come," he said. "I need to ask you and John a question." He led the way to a small office where Osei awaited them. The secretary heightened the wick, and the pool of light cast over the table expanded. His mother and brother, both with expressions of trepidation mingled with dread, approached. Darkefell had a cloth bundle on the table, and at a word from him, Osei unfolded the bundle.

His mother gasped. "Where did you find that?" she asked.

That was the confirmation he sought, even though he didn't need it. "It's yours, isn't it, Mother?"

"Yes, of course, but where did you find it? And what is that dark staining?"

He watched them both. John had been silent but appeared bleached of color. "John? Do you recognize this?" He pointed at the item.

"I suppose," he said. "But I don't know what this is all about. What did you bring us here for? Lydia's not feeling well, and I should see how she's doing."

Darkefell shifted his glance between his mother and brother. Both eyed the item on the table—a long wooden stake with a handle—that had been plunged, he believed, into Cecilia Wainwright's throat before her slender neck was savaged to make the assault look like an animal attack. Or that of a werewolf. It was a dibber, used to poke holes in the earth for planting bulbs and tubers. On the handle were the initials S. D., for Sophie Darkefell.

"It's the murder weapon used to kill Cecilia Wainwright."

Eighteen

"WHEN DID YOU LAST SEE IT?" DARKEFELL ASKED his mother.

"I don't remember," she said, her face drained of all color and expression.

"This spring?"

She shook her head, but said, "I don't know! Tony, are you sure this is the murder weapon?"

He watched her carefully. His mother was an intensely private person, and no one shattered her shell. When the news came that Julius, her favorite son, was dead, she allowed one single tear to slide down her face and retreated to her suite. She may have cried a river of tears there, but when she emerged a week later, she was calm. In the year since the news of his death had come to them, only her garden seemed to give her any solace. And now one of her personal garden tools, crafted by her order with her initials on the handle, had been used for such a vile purpose as the murder of an innocent maid.

"Doctor Younghusband," he said, referring to the family's trusted physician, "examined Cecilia's body before she was buried. He told me she was with child, of course, and confirmed what I already suspected—her throat wasn't savaged by any animal. Someone thrust something directly into her throat to kill her. It wouldn't take a lot of strength."

There was silence for a long moment. His mother began, "But that does not follow that my... my... " She broke off and looked away.

"I know," he said gently as John still stared in horror at the dibber. "And I can't say it was used thusly. But something about this size and shape pierced her throat," he said, indicating the thick wood stake, pointed on one end and with a metal handle on the other. "It killed her quickly, and then her neck was ravaged with a blade of some sort, and all to make it look like an animal attack."

"In your opinion," John said hurriedly.

"In my opinion," Tony agreed. "And that of Dr. Younghusband. So when I found this, where it had no cause to be, and with stains that I believe are blood...?"

He let that hang in the air, but his mother didn't offer anything else. Osei cleared his throat finally, and Tony turned to his younger brother. "John?"

"What?"

"Where did you last see this?"

"I've never seen it in my life. I don't even know what it's used for."

Tony eyed him; that was not what he'd said just a moment ago. He let it pass for the moment.

"Where did you find it?" the marchioness asked.

"The cave above Staungill Force," he said. "Lady Anne was with me, but I successfully slipped the dibber in my jacket. She didn't see it."

"Why did you take that woman anywhere?" his mother said, an expression of distaste pulling her mouth down.

"I thought it best to control her view of the estate," he said. "She's quite capable of haring up to the waterfall and across the countryside on her own. I didn't know the murder weapon would be concealed in the cave, nor did I know someone would be living there." Damn… he hadn't meant to say quite so much with his mother there.

"Who is living there?" she asked.

"I don't know," Darkefell said, exchanging a look with his brother. "That's beside the matter."

She stared at him, worry in her pale eyes, so like John's, then turned her gaze to the dibber, choking back an exclamation of revulsion. She then glanced at Osei and said stiffly, "Tony, does Mr. Boatin need to be here while we discuss this?"

Darkefell gazed at her in surprise. Osei knew every family failing and foible and had helped immeasurably over the last two tumultuous years, providing succor and support to him, his mother, and his brother. He supposed it was her private nature that objected to his secretary's presence.

Osei got up and bowed, his dark, thin face void of expression, and said, "I will make sure your guests are comfortable, my lord." He exited without another word.

"That was rude and unnecessary," the marquess said to his mother.

Her lips tightened. "You coddle him as if he's family, Tony, but he's not, he's your secretary and the source of a great deal of trouble for us."

"What do you mean by that?"

But she tightened her lips, shook her head, and would not be drawn out further. "Tony," the marchioness said, putting one hand on her son's arm. "Just let this alone. Spottiswode has confessed. Can you not leave it at that?"

He stared at her pale face in the lamplight. "If I thought he was guilty, I would, but there are too many unanswered questions. How would he get the dibber? I've told Pomfroy I'm going to speak with Spottiswode tomorrow, and if he seems to have no idea of how Cecilia was killed, then I'll have to tell the magistrate about the tool."

"Really, Brother, what do you think is going on?" John asked, his fleshy face pallid and filmed with a sheen of perspiration.

"I don't know," Darkefell said. "All I know is, young women seem to be dropping all around us, and I intend that it should stop."

"How reassuring to hear you say that, my lord," a new voice said from the door. "Excuse me, gentlemen, my lady," Lady Anne said as she entered, "but Lydia is not feeling well at all and asked me to find her husband."

Darkefell, behind his back, tried to rewrap the dibber in the canvas but instead knocked it off the table onto the floor.

Lady Anne advanced swiftly and picked it up, glancing down at it as she handed it back to him. "What…" She stopped and stared at the bloodstained implement, then looked up at him with questioning eyes. "What is this?" she asked, and her glance took in each one of them.

"This," the marquess said, snatching it away from her, "is none of your business." He looked to his brother. "John, go see to your wife. Mother, I've kept you away from our guests long enough."

Lady Darkefell, with a haughty look at Lady Anne, swept from the room, followed closely by John. The marquess wrapped the dibber back in the canvas then stowed it in the drawer of the folio table against the wall. He turned to meet her suspicious glance.

"You think that may be the murder weapon," she said, accusation in her voice.

"It's one possibility. I found it up at the cave today, and I wanted see if my brother or mother had ever seen it before."

She eyed him. "What is it?"

"Some kind of farm implement," he said. He took her arm and pushed her out of the room.

"May I see it?"

"Not right now, my lady. I've been too long from the others, too."

"Did Spottiswode have access to a tool such as that?"

"I don't know. I've not told Sir Trevor about this—I don't want him leaping to conclusions that are not warranted, something I think he does far too easily. Let me handle it, please."

Anne was restless and anxious after the dinner at the castle. Too many ideas, too many possibilities, roiled through her brain. Why had Lord Darkefell hidden the farm implement, if that's what it was? She was sorry now that she hadn't examined it more closely when she had it in her hands, but her first instinct was to hand it back to the marquess. Did he know where it was from? He had avoided her when they returned to the others, and there was no opportunity to question him further.

Still dressed but with her hair undone, Anne watched the rising moon from her window seat, with Irusan lolling half on her lap and half on the rest of the cushioned window seat. There had not, after all, been country dancing after dinner. They made up a couple of tables of whist, and Lydia played the piano, but otherwise, conversation, always difficult with such a mixed group, was the order of the night. Darkefell was brooding and morose for the rest of the evening, watching all of them, his dark eyes traveling each face as if he sought answers. Even from her; his gaze rested on her face at times, and she could not fathom him. What did he want from her?

They hadn't stayed late. Lydia really didn't seem well, but whether it was worry or something else, Anne couldn't tell. The marchioness had not appeared well, either; the reverend's wife was concerned, but Lady Darkefell claimed a headache. For both reasons, they returned to Ivy Lodge relatively early.

Mary, who had attended her to the castle dinner party, of course, said that castle maids were still nervous about the werewolf sightings. Some had seen a wolflike creature just two nights before and had been scared into staying inside in the evening, despite the improving April weather. Sanderson heard that some boys from the village were egging each other on with a bet as to who would have the grit enough to come up to Darkefell at night and "bag the wolf."

Anne still had not been able to speak with Ellen, and her earlier conversation with Lydia haunted her. If Lydia's husband had an affair with Cecilia, and she carried his child, he had a motive to murder her. As little as she could imagine the placid and pleasant fellow committing such a violent crime, it was possible. She feared even Lydia had thought of the awful possibility.

She ruffled Irusan's thick collar of neck fur. "Why was Lord Darkefell hiding the weapon, puss? Did it have some connection with his brother? And was he confronting him with that evidence at the dinner party?"

Irusan murmured a throaty rejoinder and stretched.

What if John *was* the guilty party? Lydia loved her husband, but if he was the killer… no, there must be another answer! She got up, dumping Irusan off, and paced, wringing her hands. He watched her with a disgruntled expression.

Something must be done to solve this awful crime. If Ellen had come back from her half day in the village, she would likely be up in her shared bedchamber at the top of the house; it was tempting to go up and demand answers, but Anne was afraid she was just looking for something to do to ease her own anxiety. She returned to the window seat and tried to compose herself. She must wait until tomorrow to speak with the maid.

Just then, through her window, she spotted someone stealthily creeping away from Ivy Lodge. She strained, staring through the glass, the angle awkward; the figure was cloaked, but a wisp of light-colored hair wafted out of the hood. It had to be Ellen slipping out to meet Jamey again. Anne bustled into the dressing room, but though Robbie was there and sleeping soundly, Mary was not. She had said something about going down to the kitchen to get a hot compress to ease her cramps—she suffered from women's complaints badly at her time of month—and Anne didn't want to wait, nor did she want to drag Mary away when she was feeling poorly.

She scrawled a note and left it on Mary's cot, then grabbed her cloak quietly, so as to not disturb the sleeping child, and fled from the room. Irusan followed, swift when he wanted to be. She tried to make him go back, but he yowled. He'd wake the house if she put him forcibly in her bedchamber and shut the door, so he'd have to go with her. She wouldn't mind the company.

She carried an oil lamp, and hidden under her cloak she had a penknife. Foolhardy it might be to follow the maid, but she did *not* believe in werewolves. Jamey and his friends were just playing tricks. Ellen knew something, she was sure of it, and Anne wanted to know what she was hiding.

Getting out of the lodge was easy, for the door had not yet been latched. Getting back in might be a problem, but she would deal with that when the time came. Anne held her cloak closed with one hand and the lamp in the other as she sped over the gravel drive, around the lodge, and across the green sward of grass that began to elevate toward the wooded glade that backed the property, being careful to skirt the chasm

Lady Darkefell was creating for her rockery. Irusan, a swift gray shadow at her side, seemed delighted with the adventure.

A howl cut through the sound of her own heaving breath, and she skidded to a stop, panting from exertion. If the howl was a dog, as it must be, then surely she was in no danger. She could just make out a movement in the woods; it *must* be Ellen, for the girl had vanished from sight and was gone by the time Anne topped a rise, yet she could not have gone far. Anne had to continue, for the image of Lydia's pretty, tear-stained face floated before her. Her friend was depending upon her. Either her husband was an adulterer and murderer—in which case, as difficult as it was, she would be better off *knowing* than *fearing* it—or he was incredibly stupid and unfairly maligned. Either way, Anne was going to solve this mystery.

Irusan made a funny little chirring noise of interrogation, and she looked down at him. "Yes, we're continuing on, my boy, and if you see a dog, I want you to go up a tree!"

She plunged forward, grateful she had at least thought of the oil lamp this time, instead of a flickering candle; the flame was protected by glass and burned steadily. *Where on earth was Ellen going this time?* she wondered. And where was she now? Anne stopped just inside the edge of the forest and could hear nothing, not a whisper of a sound, not even the howling dog.

But no, she was wrong... there was a faint rustling sound. As her breathing slowed and her heart stopped pounding in her ears, she heard it more clearly.

Someone—or something—was creeping through the woods. A trill of instinctive fear snaked down her back, but she refused to pay it heed. She did, however, get out her penknife. It might not kill any creature, but it would give it a surprise and some pain, perhaps enough to stop any attack.

She had been foolhardy, she admitted to herself, plunging into the wood after Ellen. It was imprudent, but now was not the time to flog herself for an error in judgment. However, as much as it pained her to admit it, she should retreat and rouse the household.

And tell them what? That she heard an animal, saw a figure, acted like a flea brain?

She held the lamp higher and looked around, commanding her nerves to calm. Looking about was not conducive to calmness, as all around her were shadows that could too easily be creatures poised to pounce. She shivered. Irusan had paused by her side but now hunched down, his ears flat back on his skull and his neck fur bristled into a ruff, tail like a bottle brush, his appearance when he saw a bird or mouse. The rustling had stopped, but she was not alone. The hairs on her arms under her cloak rose, standing to attention as her cat growled, a low, menacing sound. Her heart pounded, her breath quickened, and she considered backing away, but she was closer to a clearing on the other side of the woods, she knew, from her past expeditions. So she edged forward, listening and watching, determined not to be caught off guard.

Where was Ellen? she wondered, trying to distract herself from her mounting fear. How had she just disappeared as she did? The eerie howl had alerted Anne to Cecilia's death on the night of her arrival; what did it portend now?

"Come, Irusan," she said softly. Somewhere in the glade, something took footsteps that matched her own. No animal on earth would do that, she was sure. She sped up, and it/he/she sped up. If she were to be caught by an assailant, she wanted it to be out in the open, though that made little sense. She could be attacked there just as easily as in the woods.

When she and Irusan emerged from the wooded copse, she was near the tower, its dark presence blotting out the moon, leaving her in sullen shadow. She huddled close to its sturdy strength, the cold stone a poor substitute for human warmth. The memory of being clasped in the marquess's powerful arm crept through her. What she would not give for his warm embrace now!

Why couldn't she just stay put in her room? Why did she constantly need to push the boundaries of what a lady ought to do or be? The moment her mind said, "*That is not what a lady would do,*" then her feet began to take her there.

She shook off her moment of doubt. As comforting as the marquess's stalwart presence would be at a moment like this, she was no wilting flower, needing the shelter of a stronger soul. And she must never forget that he irritated her as often as he pleased her. She held up the lamp and swung it in an arc. All seemed quiet now, and even Irusan's fur had returned to its normal sleek appearance; she retired the penknife to a pocket on a string that hung inside her cloak.

Now what? Ellen had disappeared, as had Anne's grand notion of finding the solution to present to Lord Darkefell in the morning.

Aha! She stopped dead in her tracks, mouth open in astonishment. Was the root of her determination a desire to impress the marquess? She hoped that was not her motivation, for it would make her as foolish as Lydia.

A movement caught her attention, and she flattened herself against the tower base again, the cold stone oozing menace. If she had any nerve at all, she would have extinguished her lamp, but instead she tried to hide the light by cloaking it as Irusan huddled by her feet.

Through a pearly gray, moonlit opening in the woods, she saw something move—oddly human, and yet strangely animal. Her stomach clenched, but now was the moment when she needed to decide what she believed. Did she think, as the foolish maids of Ivy Lodge did, that there was a werewolf afoot? Or was she firm in her conviction that a mischievous human was responsible for the werewolf sightings?

It was a human, and he or she was upsetting people and possibly doing violence to a lot of innocent sheep. She had enough of speculation; if she saw it up close, she could destroy the myth. Foolhardy she might be, but she also had confidence in her ability to look after herself. She slipped after the thing, using her lantern to light her footsteps, and closely followed by her cat. The creature moved quickly, and she could catch only glimpses of it.

Should she call out? Show that, whoever it was, they were found out?

No, she decided, her curiosity fully engaged. She wanted to know what came next. If it looked back, it would see her there, following with the lamp, but it seemed dedicated to going wherever it was going.

Back into the woods!

With a moan she kept securely behind her teeth, she followed, anxious and ill but still determined. She was a foolish, *foolish* woman, but now was not the time to lament that fact. Quickening her footsteps, she plunged deeper into the woods. Voices! Quivering, she didn't know if she was most relieved or most afraid to hear human voices. It *could* be good, but given the number of women's bodies that had ended up being found on Darkefell property, she was not so sure. Danger came more from men than animals.

She hesitated but followed. Perhaps it was Ellen after all, with her beau, and Anne couldn't decide if she most feared for the young woman or suspected her. There was a clearing in the woods ahead; she could see a stream of moonlight and then… what was that, the voices? It sounded like drunken singing! She moved on and saw the creature more clearly now, the back hunched, ears pricked up. Her heart pounded.

There were some fellows ahead; she could dimly see moving shapes and hear their voices. They were singing "As I Walked Forth," and when they got to the line *"The Dead Man's Thumb, an herb all blue,"* someone drunkenly laughed out loud. They came to the chorus and shouted out, all together, *"Alas! Alas! There's no one e'er loved as I!"*

But that last was punctuated by the fearsome howl of the wolf-monster, which just then came upon them. The drunken fools screamed and scrambled, beset upon in their drunken state, and ran pell-mell away, some of them stumbling, one screaming, all shrieking, "Wolf! Wolf!"

Human laughter followed, but from whence it came, Anne could not tell. It had an odd, muffled quality.

She followed the creature, which now strolled more leisurely. It broke down branches and left a clear path, so though Anne could not see it at all times, she *could* hear it and follow, seeing the broken remains of branches along the way.

What was it? Or *who?* Was it the same creature she had seen in the wood by the castle? And on the hill by the old gamekeeper's shack? How could it be? That creature was doglike and moved on four feet, while this—animal though it was in appearance—seemed to move in a crouch but on two feet.

A trickle of fear warred with a desperate craving to know the truth.

There is a rational explanation for everything, Anne thought as she crept through the forest after it. Beside her, Irusan moved much more stealthily. She hoped they were headed for another clearing, because the dark, with only the flickering light of the lantern to show her the way, filled her with fear. Moonlight glimmered ahead. Following the creature's trail, she broke through the last line of tangled brush, and a beam of moonlight from the almost-full disc above glowed. The beast had stopped.

"There is no such thing as a werewolf," she muttered to Irusan under her breath, creeping forward into the clearing. Her words then proved terribly naïve, for the wolfish creature turned, staring directly at her with an intensity both human and bestial. "Though it seems I may have been mistaken," she murmured.

The creature started toward her. Irusan hissed and arched his back, yowling with piercing intensity. This was utterly ridiculous, she decided, for she had never believed in the supernatural and was not about to start at the advanced age of twenty-four. She steeled herself and stared, holding the flickering lamp aloft; the glimmering light glinted against something shiny. Was it…? Yes, *brass buttons!* Surely a werewolf did not hold its skin on with brass buttons! As the creature advanced, threatening her with outstretched claws and growling menacingly, Irusan adding to the din with his unearthly yowls, Anne made a swift decision. She pulled off the glass and threw the flaming lamp, spilling oil over the creature. The fur caught aflame immediately, and the air was rent by a very human voice shrieking, "Damn and blast! Devil woman… I'm burning! Help me get this cursed skin off!"

"I will *not!*" she shouted, well satisfied by the sight of the fellow hopping from one foot to the other, pulling blazing bits of stinking fur from him and flinging them down to the damp grass, where the flames sputtered and died. "It well serves you for frightening poor Lydia and trying to trick me!"

"Help me, *now!*"

Anne stopped in her tracks. The voice sounded familiar, grumpy and complaining, yet at the same time commanding and imperious. She dashed forward and pushed the imposter down, rolling him in the dew-laden grass, then pulled away the last bit of stinking, singed fur, and a papier maché mask that came away from his face whole. It was the marquess! "Lord Darkefell! *You* are the werewolf?"

"I *was*," he said dryly, gazing up at her, his face smudged with ash and soot, "until you destroyed my costume."

Nineteen

"HOW DARE YOU, SIR!" LADY ANNE CRIED, scrambling to her feet. It was dark now, her lamp extinguished by her rash action, and only the moon as illumination. "How dare you terrorize us all, your own people, your servants? What's the meaning of this?"

He stared up at her. Her eyes glittered, the pale gray of the irises faintly silver in the moonlight, outlining the black of her dilated pupils; her hood was thrown back, and dark wavy hair tumbled over her shoulders, long as her waist. Fury was delineated in every part of her, arms stiff at her sides, hands clenched, shoulders rigid with wrath. Perhaps he had been right when he yelled "devil woman" in his flaming ire. The stink of his cremated fur still reeked, filling his nostrils. He was weary of the masquerade and, in truth, glad the damned costume was incinerated.

Something about his scorched appearance must have touched her, for she sighed and shook her head, then offered him her hand and helped pull him to his feet. "I am fascinated to hear your explanation of this... this aberrant behavior, my lord. Why do you inflict this travesty upon your people?"

He kept her hand trapped in his and pulled her closer, gazing down at her upturned face, the pale skin gleaming nacre-bright in the moonlight. No other person, except for Osei, knew of this trickery, and he wanted it kept secret. But how to ensure it? Bully her? She'd laugh at him. Bribery? Information was a currency she might accept, but how much was he willing to offer? Seduction? An oddly appealing thought to him, but she had proven adamant in the face of his romantic persuasion so far.

She was breathing quickly, even with no exercise to prompt it. He bent to kiss her, but she backed away.

"You, sir, stink of singed fur."

His lips twitched. A bubble of hilarity welled up in him, and he burst into laughter. "And you, madam, are delightful," he said, tweaking her cheek. He swept her a gallant bow, aware how ridiculous he looked with bits of animal fur hanging from him, and sooty-faced.

"I don't know why you say things like that," she said crossly.

"I merely speak the truth," he said. "Help me get this off." He pulled at the remnants of the costume, discarding the pieces in a smoldering heap.

She examined the "paws" made of dark leather gloves, and the bits of fur. "If I hadn't found that fur robe with the bit snipped out of it already, I would be looking at you askance at this moment, my lord."

"Let's move away from this spot. I can still smell the fiery fur. Retrieve that lamp, first," he said, pointing to the extinguished oil lantern she had flung at him.

He felt a twinge in his ankle when he put his weight on it. Nothing he couldn't stand.

"Look, you've twisted something and are limping," she said. "Rest on my shoulder, and let us go… where?"

"There's a spot close to here where we can rest a few moments."

"Irusan!" she called out. The underbrush nearby rustled, and an enormous gray cat emerged, gave him a look he could only describe as disgusted, and moved to her side.

"*That* is Irusan?" he asked, eyeing the large beast, like no stable cat he had ever seen. It was at least twice as large and had a mane of gray fur framing its face like an Elizabethan ruff. It stalked to Anne's side with ponderous dignity.

"This is Irusan, King of the Cats," she said.

Without further comment, he pointed the way and leaned on her shoulder. "Those drunken fools from the village are thankfully gone now, frightened away by the werewolf, which has clearly made its last appearance, and good riddance. But the legend should be enough to dissuade others from venturing on my land for a while." They limped on. "At least until I can figure out what is going on," he added under his breath.

"I was hoping this wolf charade meant you knew all."

"No." It seemed that some measure of honesty was going to be required. "I must humbly admit to mystification on many points, including what you are doing out here in the middle of the night, yet *again!*"

She gasped. "Ellen!" she exclaimed. "In the hubbub, I forgot my purpose in venturing out—where did she go, I wonder? I followed Ellen Henderson, the maid from Ivy Lodge. Did you see her? Do you know whom I mean?"

"Yes, of course I know whom you mean, but no, I didn't see her tonight. Didn't I scare her enough when I caught her and Jamey kissing by the tower on a night cold enough to freeze a man's b… buttons?"

"That was you? I thought it was he and a friend who were being the werewolf."

He didn't answer. "Does anyone know you're gone from the lodge?" he asked.

"I left a note for my maid, telling her not to concern herself and to go straight to bed, as she was not feeling well," she said tartly.

"How considerate you are of your servants," he commented.

"No reason for you to be snide, my lord."

"I've been accused this evening of coddling my secretary, so you are, I feel, in excellent company. We both apparently lack appropriate frigidity toward our valued underlings. Up this hill and through those trees," he said as they slowly advanced, "there is a cottage with all the necessities."

It was a small wooden cabin, protected from view of the tower and everyone else by the woods surrounding it on three sides. They entered, Irusan before them, and the marquess lit a lantern with flint and tinder from a box on the table. Lady Anne glanced around as the light illuminated the interior. Her cheeks flamed as her eye caught and held on the bed made up in the corner. He would have enjoyed the sight of her discomfiture, but the place reminded him of painful things in the last couple of years. He shouldn't have brought her to the cabin, but it seemed the only place they could talk comfortably out of the chilly, damp evening air.

She didn't comment but pointedly took a rush chair near the table, angling it first so she did not need to look at the bed. Her giant cat made a slow circle, sniffing each crevice and corner of the small structure, then settled on the empty hearth and pointedly glared at him.

"Why did you never marry after your fiancé died?" he said suddenly, watching her closely as he turned up the flame in the lantern.

"That's rather far afield from the subjects at hand. Who do you believe killed Cecilia Wainwright? Do you honestly think William Spottiswode did it?"

He took her pointed rebuff in stride. "I don't, but I can't imagine why he would confess to it, knowing his fate. It makes no sense to me." He hesitated but decided to share what he had learned that night. He turned around a chair, straddled it facing her, and told her about Spottiswode's supposed recantation. "I'm inclined to think he's just now beginning to realize the seriousness of his predicament, and that would be reason enough for him to say he wrongly confessed, even if he truly is guilty. I'm going to question him tomorrow… or today, as it is after midnight." He rubbed his smoke-grimed eyes. "I cannot rest easy until I judge for myself whether he is lying now or lying before."

Her gaze fixed on his face, she said, "I'd like to be there, my lord."

Why did she have to continually "my lord" him? he wondered, irritated. "No," he said stiffly. "Absolutely not."

"Darkefell, I don't think you understand," she said, her voice softened. "I have known for some time that Lydia was upset about something more than the supposed werewolf. I suspect that was merely an excuse to call me to her side. She wouldn't tell me what it was that prompted her oft-asserted notion that Lord John did not love her anymore, but today I finally got down to the truth."

He felt a wrench in his gut. "What are you talking about?"

"You first, my lord. Agree that I may accompany you tomorrow, and I will tell you something of great import."

"You," he said with feeling, "are the most stubborn, wretchedly determined, and unfeminine female I have ever met."

Irusan growled from the hearth as if understanding his discourteous words.

"I suppose you call me unfeminine because of my curiosity." She sat forward on the edge of her chair and stared directly into his eyes, giving him an unsettling impression of her vigor. "Let me assure you, Darkefell, that my curiosity and need to know the truth are not unfeminine, nor is my intelligence, my determination, my strength. Those are false notions of femininity that you hold, encouraged by the legion of gentlemen who would feel less than men if their ladies were every bit as capable as they are. I did not account you to be one of those… those poor examples of masculinity, sir."

He jumped from the chair, knocking it over in his haste, took her face in his big hands, and kissed her. She wrenched herself from his grip and staggered to her feet, smacked him hard, and ran to the door, followed swiftly by her cat.

He advanced upon her, ignoring the feline's warning howl. "Go. Run, if you're afraid of me. But I know you want to kiss me. Admit the truth, and I'll think you the bold woman you claim to be."

Anne watched him warily; his eyes glittered in the dim light, and she put one shaking hand to her lips. "Quiet, Irusan," she said and put out her other hand. He calmed. Anne tried to calm her pounding heart so easily. Darkefell's kiss had been thrilling, but also a little frightening. How well did she know him? He would not be the first man to take advantage of a woman alone. She had heard the tales of lords and barons who made a sport of taking advantage of women, especially those in a vulnerable position. She had the protection of her name and status, though, and he shouldn't kiss her unless he wished marriage.

Marriage. With him. And her. She trembled.

He saw it, and his expression altered. "My lady, I'm sorry if I frightened you," he murmured, his voice hoarse. "I apologize. I will never force another kiss upon you, I promise it."

He had misunderstood her trembling. "I'm not afraid," she said. She proved it by walking over to him. Gently, she dusted away the last vestiges of the burned fur costume and sooty smoke from his cheeks, then put her hands on his shoulders, stood up on tiptoe, closed her eyes, and met his lips with her own.

After his first startled "mph" of surprise, he met her kiss with a deeper, more thorough challenge. His arms, powerful and thick, snaked around her and pulled her close, and she was lifted slightly from her toes, so that she felt as though she were floating. And his lips… soft, clinging, wet tongue darting… she pushed away and staggered back, panting. His dark eyes gleamed with challenge and delight.

"Do not start what you don't intend to finish, Lady Anne."

"Follow your own advice, sir. We started a conversation, and I intend that we finish it. Let me go with you tomorrow to question Spottiswode."

"Damn you! *Damn* your infernal single-mindedness," he growled and turned around, leaning against a nearby chair for a long moment.

"There's absolutely no need to curse. Are you quite all right, Darkefell?" she asked finally.

He laughed, but it was a harsh, grating chuckle. "I don't think so. I think I must be mad, because I'm going to say yes to you, my lady. Yes, you can come with me tomorrow when I talk to Spottiswode."

It was unexpected, and she hadn't even offered her information again. She had been willing to tell him, guardedly, the story that John was caught kissing Cecilia Wainwright, but she wasn't sure she would now, for he had not made it a condition. He seemed to have forgotten she had anything to tell him at all, an unexpected lapse in his acuity of which she was willing to take advantage. "Why the sudden agreement?"

He turned and shrugged. "I find myself interested in what you will ask him and what you will think once we've spoken to him. I hope you know I want the truth, nothing more, nothing less. And I don't want an innocent man to hang. Things are moving swiftly now, for the spring assizes are in two weeks, and I need to hurry my pace."

She understood his concern; within days of a guilty verdict, Spottiswode would be hanged, all chance of reprieve gone. There were many unanswered questions, but Pomfroy, the magistrate, had not seemed the kind of man to look further than a convenient confession. When the gentlemen joined the ladies after dinner, he had talked expansively of the efficacy of British justice, that it could so expeditiously seize, try, and hang a man.

She turned away from dark thoughts and back to her problem of Ellen and Lord John. It likely had nothing to do with Cecilia's death, that she had been seen kissing the marquess's younger brother, but Anne still wanted to hear the tale from Ellen's own lips. "Darkefell, I told you the truth. I *did* come out here following Ellen… or at least, I thought it was Ellen. I wanted to speak with her earlier, but she had her half day off. If it was her I saw leaving Ivy Lodge, where could she have gone?"

"I don't know. I didn't see her, but then I was single-minded in my purpose. I had heard about those young fools from Hornethwaite, coming up this evening to roust out the wolf, and I needed to get rid of them before they caused trouble. I suppose I could have confronted them in my guise of enraged master of Darkefell, but it suited me tonight to be the werewolf. For the last time, as it turns out."

Anne eyed him thoughtfully. "Are you sure you're the only werewolf, sir?"

He gazed at her in admiration. "Good question, and reasonable. However, to my knowledge, I am the only one."

"One thing that's troubling me. Who—or what—slaughtered the sheep? Mr. Hiram Grover and some others, I have heard, lost part of their flock, and for the animals to just be savaged and left to die does not seem the action of a reasonable person, but rather animal in nature."

"Any animal that would kill a sheep would presumably do so for food. The animals were not eaten. I saw the remains. Again, that's one of the many mysteries that have plagued us over the last few months. We've had our share of thieves in these parts, but a thief steals, he doesn't slaughter and leave the carcass to rot."

A rustling sound outside startled them both, but before she could be alarmed, Anne heard a voice softly calling, "Lord Darkefell… are you there?"

"It's Mr. Boatin," she said and undid the latch, opening the door.

The secretary entered with a wary glance between the marquess and Anne. "Good evening, my lady," he said with a proper bow. Irusan trotted to him immediately and leaped up into his arms, knocking him slightly off balance. "Oof… and Sir Irusan! I was concerned when his lordship did not return at the appointed time."

"And you're familiar with this place," she said.

"I know every spot on the estate," he answered, caution delineated in his expression and his careful answer. He stroked the big cat.

"The deception is over," Darkefell said, eyeing Osei and his purring armful. "She caught me in my bestial vestments and promptly set them aflame. Tomorrow we must retrieve the remnants of the costume. The werewolf—at least this one—is dead." He said the last with a significant look to Anne.

It was beginning to rain. If he could have saved her the walk, he would have, but he enlisted Mr. Boatin to accompany Anne back to Ivy Lodge, while he limped back to the castle.

Anne, Osei, and Irusan made their way speedily through the drenching downpour. She tried to question Mr. Boatin, but it was all they could do to keep their footing as they skulked through the woods and slid down the slippery hillside back to Ivy Lodge, the secretary carrying Irusan under his coat so the cat wouldn't get wet. Fortunately, he had a key to a garden door and could let her in without alerting the household to her scandalous late-night perambulation. She and Irusan went up to her room without creating any unnecessary commotion. Mary was nearly frantic, but Anne calmed her down without telling her much, brushing Irusan's bramble-knotted fur while Mary performed the same task for her. She was exhausted and confused, and just wanted to sleep, but feared slumber would elude her for quite a while.

Was it Ellen she saw walking away from the lodge? If so, where did the girl go? She curled up under her covers, with Irusan a weighty presence beside her, and fell quickly into a deep, troubled sleep filled with dreams of wild creatures and midnight terror, and Darkefell—always Darkefell—threatening her with sensual torment.

That same question was on her mind the next morning, so she was up early, and even before break-fast, she ventured to Mrs. Hailey's lair. The woman was short with her, but the answer to her question was, Ellen had apparently not returned. No one knew why. And now another maid had left; Caroline, one of the downstairs' maids, had disappeared.

Perhaps that was the blonde young woman Anne saw leaving in the night; if so, she left of her own accord. Anne said, "I'm going into Hornethwaite today, Mrs. Hailey, with Lord Darkefell. If Ellen has family there, I could check with them to make sure she's all right and find out what has happened."

The housekeeper reluctantly agreed, and Anne left with directions to Ellen's family dwelling. Lord Darkefell arrived at the gate of Ivy Lodge promptly at two, and they set out to Hornethwaite.

Anne, seated beside the marquess in the high-perch phaeton, suited to such a sunny day after the rainy night, was without the accompaniment of Robbie, since the poor child was still not feeling well, a bellyache brought on by too many slices of fresh bread slipped to him by a complaisant cook who doted on hungry little boys. Lydia, too, was not well and was confined to her bed. Irusan seemed content to stay with Robbie, after his adventurous nocturnal prowl.

As she and the marquess trotted briskly along the country road toward Hornethwaite, Anne kept casting glances at him, noting the firmness of his gloved hands on the reins, his strong jaw, his perfectly molded lips in profile. "Sir," she said with no preamble, "I cannot help but think that the continual kisses and caresses you inflict upon me are your way of distracting me from something—a logical mind will then proceed to the question: '*What is he hiding?*'"

"I have never had a lady reproach me in quite such a manner," he said, his lips twitching. "So I *inflict* kisses upon you, do I?"

She sighed. "Will we never have a conversation that does not consist of questions to answer questions to answer questions?"

"Do you notice that you have done the same thing yourself, just now?"

"So I have!" she exclaimed, gasping. "And so have you."

"Between us, we must have a surfeit of inquisitiveness."

"And we always come back to discussing it." She was silent for a while, watching the scenery. So far, her visit had been so full of turmoil that she had not had time for any of the things she normally did when visiting: writing letters, drawing, walking, exploring. And this was a place she would, above all, love to see. The Yorkshire landscape was unexpected in its variety, beauty, and appeal to her.

"I think," he said, glancing over at her, the reins slack in his hands as his handsome team trotted along the hard-packed road, "you should know that not all kisses are alike."

"I *have* experienced a kiss or two before yours, you know."

"Oh?" he growled.

"Yes. Even a plain woman, be she of good birth and ready fortune, will be importuned for kisses."

"I think you value your attractions too lightly," he said, his deep voice holding a gentle tone.

She glanced over at him and could not look away, examining his face, the dark shadow where his beard had been perfectly sheared, his exquisite tailoring, his long dark lashes. He was perhaps too hard and bold to be considered by society a beautiful man, but she thought him exquisite. His very beauty made her tremble inside, and she chided herself at the shallow nature of her attraction. However, on reflection, she was grateful; if her inner trembling could be explained by attraction to his handsome appearance, she would soon be rid of unwanted sensations. Even perfect beauty, when viewed too often, would become everyday.

He met her gaze, and she felt it, then, to the core. She was deceiving herself. Her powerful attraction to him had little to do with his looks, as perfectly suited to feminine appreciation as they were. There was something within him that called to her, and she was terrified to answer. She looked away, her stomach aching, her gaze misty and unseeing, all attention turned inward. What was it? And how could she defeat the irrational appeal he held for her? It was unthinkable to fall in love with such a man. Even if he should consider her for a wife, being wed to him would lead to her becoming completely besotted, she feared. Drowning in love was too terrifying a notion to contemplate.

She struggled to think of anything else, and as she stared at a distant rise and green fields trailing upwards, she said, "Darkefell, what role do you wish me to take in the questioning of William Spottiswode? I saw him once on the street, and know I will understand only one word in three that he utters, given his impenetrable accent. But what little I have seen of him and understand, I utterly despise." She turned to look at the marquess. "You, as a lifelong inhabitant of this place, will understand him, no doubt. I know I asked to come along, but I doubt myself now."

"I don't doubt you," he said, meeting her eyes. "I've come to appreciate the acuity of your mind, the steadiness of your character, and the depth of your understanding of people. I trust your ability to look beyond words, my lady, and would say, then, that understand what you can, ask your questions through me, and keep your eyes open. I will, despite my initial resistance to your accompaniment, be interested in your opinion."

And there he was again, appallingly fair-minded. She could not dislike him, no matter how much she tried.

But he had to stop kissing her; that was all there was to it.

Twenty

DARKEFELL PUT THE TEAM AND PHAETON UP AT THE livery stable and walked, with Anne on his arm, to the guildhall near the magistrate's grand mansion at the top of the village. The guildhall was a long, large structure built into the rocky side of a hill. In the basement, cells held prisoners until they could be transported to the assize court in York.

"A hundred years ago, when the woolen industry took hold and commerce with Scotland was unsteady, my ancestors built the guildhall and encouraged the people of Hornethwaite to create a local weaving guild. Hornethwaite weave is renowned for its fine texture and beauty."

She cast him an amused glance. "I would think you're trying to sell me something, sir, you're so persuasive."

He was silent for the rest of the walk, but she didn't blame him for his serious humor. They had spoken of it already; he couldn't bear the idea that an innocent man might hang but felt it even more terrible that a guilty one might go free, a threat to his people and the peace of his community. She should be probing him for what his involvement in this whole mess was—she strongly felt he was not telling the whole truth—but she absolved him of the most serious charge: murder upon Cecilia Wainwright. He said he was speaking with his mother when Anne arrived at Ivy Lodge that awful night, and if that was true, then it exonerated both of them, not that she had seriously considered the marchioness a suspect.

"Here we are," he said.

The guildhall was large, with a columned entrance flanked by elegant wings. Enormous glass windows reflected the afternoon sun and dazzled her eyes momentarily. He led her up the steps and inside, where proper obeisance was made to him by the custodian of the hall, a Mr. Conyngton. The man bowed and clanked his keys officiously, their footsteps echoing as he led them through a series of vast chambers then down some stairs to a dank passageway.

Lanterns were perpetually lit in the gloom, and the light flickered and danced up the dank stone walls. The smell—putrefaction, dirt, and human waste—invaded Anne's nostrils. She took a kerchief from her pocket and held it over her nose, the scent of lavender a welcome respite, and asked to carry a candle or lantern.

"My lady," Darkefell said as he took down a wall lantern and handed it to her, "I'll not think less of you if you wish to return upstairs. Mr. Conyngton could take you to a drawing room and fetch you some tea or other refreshment."

"Gracious lady, my wife would be honored if you would come up and partake of her tea and cakes… the lightest in this county, milady," the fellow said, bobbing his head. "Please, let me take you from this formidable place, for the delicacy of a lady should never be tested so severely."

That fussing was all Anne needed to steel herself. "I'm perfectly well, gentlemen," she stated, taking the kerchief away from her nose and holding her lamp high. "Thank you for your concern. Lead on."

The tunnels were narrow and oppressive, dampness seeping through cracks. Faint scuttling sounds from creatures sent chills up Anne's back. The marquess did not top six feet, but the ceiling was low enough that he had to duck his head in places.

They arrived at their destination, a row of cells. The first in the line was inhabited by a weeping woman. Anne paused at the cell door. "Why are you here, my dear?" she asked, her voice echoing oddly into the cell.

The huddled woman peered over at her, blinking in the faint light of the lamp Anne held.

"Don't pay no attention to 'er beefin,'" Conyngton said. "Widow Bess Parker… thief, she is. Stole a bolt o' fabric and lace trimming from the dressmaker she worked fer, Mrs. Holderness. Base treachery, to steal from yer employer like that!"

"Did not, Mister Tom, I didn't! 'Twas an accusation, but I didn't do't! Wouldn't dare steal from madam, now, would I? Not wi' three young 'uns to feed an' poor Jack dead."

"If you didn't do it, why are you accused?" Anne asked, holding the lamp close to the cell door and searching the woman's red-rimmed eyes. She seemed a clean sort, given her surroundings, and was even pretty in a work-worn way, with tumbles of red-brown hair, matted though it was and dirty from her time in the cell. But prettiness was no indication of character.

"'Twere that gossip, Mrs. Jenkins!" the woman said on a sob. She clapped her hands together in a prayerful attitude. "Oh! Pardon me, miss… ma'am… M-Mrs. Jenkins, she came t'the shop an'… an' accused me o' all manner o' filthy things."

"Mrs. *Lily* Jenkins?" Anne asked. The marquess surged forward, but Anne held up her free hand, and he stayed back in the shadows. His appearance might have been enough to frighten the woman into silence.

"Yes'm."

"You call her proper, y'mind!" Conyngton said, hitting his stick against the cell bars. "This 'ere is 'er ladyship, Lady Anne Addison!"

"Stop it, Mr. Conyngton," Anne said angrily. "Is that how you treat all of your prisoners?"

"It *is* a jail," the marquess murmured behind her.

"That doesn't mean we treat people like animals, sir," Anne retorted, turning and glaring at him. She turned back and peered through the cell-door bars. "Of what, exactly, did Mrs. Jenkins accuse you?"

The woman approached the bars more closely and whispered, "Foolin' wiv her 'usband, ma'am. She don't trust 'im, I s'pose, an' someone told 'er… 'e was wiv me. 'Tweren't me, I swear't! We talked oncet on the street, but no more'n that. She said summat to Mistress Holderness, an' next day I was up on charges. Found fabric in my room, they did, an' lace, too, but I *swear* I din't do't!" She broke down weeping.

The weight of the woman's franticness bore down on Anne. Clutching the greasy bars, disregarding the state of her fine lawn kerchief, she asked, "Where are your children?"

"Wiv me mum, but she can't keep 'em. They'll go t'almshouse! My poor babes."

Anne looked over at the marquess in the shadows and whispered, "Darkefell, I've met Lily Jenkins. I'd like to look into this."

"I know of Benjamin Jenkins, of course, and his wife. But we do have more pressing business, my lady," he said, his tone tense.

"Then I will do it myself once we are out of this place," she said, not willing to go into the reasons she doubted anything Lily Jenkins said right at that moment. If this proved to have been a false arrest based on Mrs. Jenkins's word, it exposed the woman as willing to twist people's lives to soothe her jealous heart. She had seemed irrational on the subject of Fanny Allengate, suggesting she was not as innocent as others thought her. Had Lily Jenkins had anything to do with the young woman's tragic end?

Anne was still haunted by Richard Allengate's consuming grief over his sister's death. All Anne knew was that Fanny had been found on Darkefell's estate, near the waterfall. If there was a connection to Cecilia's murder, it escaped her, but her curiosity was piqued now. She turned back to the woman. "I cannot promise anything, but I'll find out what I can." She pushed her kerchief through the bars, begged the woman to take it, and left Bess Parker weeping. She swept on down the line of cells, followed by the marquess and Mr. Conyngton, who had retreated to sulky, silent obedience after Anne's rebuke.

"This be 'is cell," Conyngton said finally as they got to the end of the row. "We 'ad to put 'im 'ere, 'cause he talks and yells and snores and makes such a clamorous noise."

Darkefell turned to Anne as Conyngton unlocked the cell door. "Are you certain you wish to come and speak with him?"

"I am," she said.

They both edged into the narrow cell, and the marquess said loudly, "Spottiswode, wake up!"

With a huff and grunt, William Spottiswode roused himself and sat up on his straw pallet. A rat scuttled away into a crevice as he shifted. He blearily stared up at them both, his bloodshot eyes dim with hopelessness.

Conyngton, who had edged into the cell, too, kicked his leg and said, "Say a proper 'ello to the marquess and Lady Anne, you worthless drunk."

"Conyngton, enough!" Darkefell barked. "Leave us with him."

"I can't do that, milord," the man said with a shocked expression on his fleshy face. "What if he'd fall upon you and morder you? It'd be worth my 'ide!"

"I think I can handle him," Darkefell said dryly, flexing his shoulder muscles.

Anne bit her lip at the unexpected humor of the paunchy warden, thinking he might need to leap to the marquess's rescue, half Conyngton's age, near twice his height, and three times his strength as Darkefell was.

The fellow bowed and backed out of the cell. "You 'oller good 'n loud if you need me, now, and tell me when I should lock 'im up again."

Darkefell squatted by the prisoner and said, "Spottiswode, do you know who I am?"

He nodded. Anne watched him. He looked like a beaten dog, cringing. He was covered in bloody sores, scratches, filth crusting his face and hair, a disgusting and pitiable sight. At that moment, a noise in the passageway alerted them to someone else's approach. It was Sir Trevor Pomfroy, his pompous voice the first indication as he browbeat Conyngton before arriving outside of Spottiswode's cell.

"My lord, I thought you would announce yourself to me first," Pomfroy said, a testy edge to his voice as he arrived at the cell. "If I hadn't seen your phaeton, I would not have known of your arrival." He entered the cell, too.

Anne swiftly glanced at the marquess; visibly annoyed, it was clear that he hadn't wanted the magistrate present. Darkefell stood and said, "I rather wished to make this less of a trial to you, Pomfroy."

"This is my duty, my lord, and I will always do my duty."

Giving into the inevitable, Darkefell crouched down to Spottiswode again. "Willie, isn't it? Willie, I understand you have expressed some hesitation about your memory of facts. Are you recanting your confession?"

The man just stared. Anne watched and saw his bleary gaze flick between the magistrate and the marquess.

"Darkefell, simpler words?" she murmured.

Startled, he glanced up at her and nodded. "Of course. Willie, do you still say you killed Cecilia Wainwright?"

But the man just stared.

"Did you murder the girl?" Pomfroy shouted. "Answer the marquess!"

Spottiswode, trembling, nodded and said, "Aye, but didn't mean ter."

Darkefell glanced over at Anne again and shrugged.

"How did you kill her?" Anne asked, speaking slowly and clearly.

Spottiswode held trembling hands out in front of him and wrung his hands together with a strangling motion.

"You strangled her?" Anne asked.

"Aye," he said, a shudder quaking his whole body.

"That's not how Cecilia died," the marquess murmured.

"What did you do then?" Anne asked.

He muttered a garbled string of babble as Darkefell listened intently. Darkefell then turned to Anne and said, "He says he strangled her because she would not marry him, even though she was carrying his child. She said she had someone else she planned to force to 'pay up.'" The marquess shook his head. "Anne, Cecilia was not strangled—I don't know why he says he strangled her. He says he took her body and dumped it, *just as he was told to do.*"

"What does that mean?" Anne murmured. Pomfroy was leaning in closer to listen, and she felt the intrusion.

"I don't know. I thought he was going to try to recant, but instead he's admitting it, and yet with details that do not fit the crime."

"Is he really admitting it, if he doesn't even know how Cecilia was killed? And who told him to dump Cecilia's body?" She shook her head. "I don't know, Darkefell—I was there. I heard her killed. There was no time to 'dump' her body anywhere. She died where she lay."

Pomfroy hit Willie's leg with his walking stick. "Spottiswode, you're just being clever. Trying to pretend you don't know how Cecilia Wainwright was killed."

Anne shook her head at the notion that Spottiswode could do anything clever.

"Come on, then, tell the truth. You killed the girl, murdered her because she was carrying your child!" Pomfroy bellowed, his thin face red with fury.

Spottiswode nodded.

"You slit her throat, like the animal you are, then savaged her and dumped her body in the bushes, isn't that correct? Spottiswode? Come now, isn't that correct?" He hit the man's legs with the stick again.

"Stop that *now*," Darkefell said, grabbing Pomfroy's walking stick.

The fellow on his pitiable pallet hesitated but then nodded and wept, tears making rivulets in the grime on his face and disappearing into his filthy beard.

"And that is that," the magistrate said with a look of disgust at the weeping man. "I told you all, he's just afraid of the hangman's noose now, but I'll have none of this indulging of my prisoner."

Anne glanced over at Darkefell, saw his neck go brick red, and knew he was close to exploding.

"Pomfroy," he said with great restraint through gritted teeth. "*Never* speak to me in that tone again."

Pomfroy's manner became immediately more conciliatory. "Of course, my lord. I… I apologize, but this crime disgusts me, and I cannot be easy with any suggestion that Spottiswode would be let off because he decided the hangman's noose frightened him too much." He bowed, then turned to his prisoner and

said, "I'll see you next at the assize court, Spottiswode."
Pomfroy hit the cell bars with his stick and called out,
"Conyngton, come lock up your prisoner."

Darkefell and Anne were ushered from the cells and
upstairs, then Pomfroy pleaded a prior engagement
and hurried off. That he was embarrassed at being
taken to task by the younger, but much-higher-in-
rank man, was Anne's strong sense. A gentleman of
such powerful self-love as he displayed would not be
inclined to listen to any suggestion that he had been
hasty in doing his duty.

"That was highly unsatisfactory," Anne said as
she walked on the marquess's arm down the street.
"Spottiswode's relation of the crime bears only a vague
resemblance to the facts. In fact, there is only his assertion that he killed her and *no* supporting facts."

"Still, he did repeat his confession."

"True. Where did Spottiswode reside?" she asked.

Darkefell didn't know, but after some discussion,
he said if she was really set on investigating further, he
could find out. Just minutes later they were let into a
dark, tiny room by his landlady. The slovenly but sober
woman admitted she never thought Spottiswode, after
drinking as much as he had in the last year, would
rouse himself to do anything so vigorous as murder.
And no, she said, in answer to Anne's question, she
had never seen the man with Cecilia Wainwright.
Yes, she said to the marquess, his drinking had been
markedly worse in the last year.

Her thick Yorkshire accent translated by Darkefell,
the woman claimed that a year and a half ago
Spottiswode, though a heavy drinker, had been

stable enough to hold a job as a carrier for the seed merchant. What had spurred his rapid descent into abject dissolution—not her word, but Darkefell's translation—she could not say, but in the last year he had lost his job, his horse, and most of his physical capabilities. So sodden with drink was he, that by sundown most days, he was incapacitated.

Anne advanced reluctantly into the room as the landlady rushed ahead to open the shade to allow in what light managed to filter down the alleyway upon which the room was situated. It smelled dreadful, not much better than the cell which was William Spottiswode's new residence. A few ragged pieces of heavily soiled clothing littered the floor, but other than a chair, a broken bedstead, and a decrepit wardrobe with no doors, the rest of the decoration consisted of empty bottles. Bottles littered every surface and lay drunkenly about the floor like soldiers on leave, some smashed.

"This one has a label," Anne said, holding one up to the stream of light, "but it has been torn off. There are remnants, though—the handwriting is rather good, what's left. It looks like it's in Italian."

"You read Italian?" Darkefell asked.

"Doesn't everyone?" Anne replied with a half-smile and a glance at him.

"Far too good a bottle for a man such as Spottiswode," Darkefell said and passed the empty under his nose. "A decent red wine, certainly Italian, perhaps from Valpolicella."

"Where would a man like he get a bottle of Italian wine?"

"From someone who didn't know what he was giving up, I would say. Or he stole it."

Anne shook her head. They looked around some more, but there was no clue as to the man's doings in the past year, other than the volume of bottles. The landlady was just waiting for permission before she sold the bottles to pay up Spottiswode's overdue rent.

They exited together, and Anne took in a deep breath of the fresh air then said, "Darkefell, I have a couple of errands to run. Be a good fellow, and find out for me where Madam Holderness's dressmaking shop is?"

"I happen to know without going looking," he said. When she looked askance at him, he said, "I do have a mother, you know, who uses Mrs. Holderness's services when she cannot get to London or even Leeds."

She wanted to get rid of him for a while so she could ask some questions, but he would not leave her side. All right, she thought—perhaps he had some answers. "Darkefell, from where did you get that ridiculous wolf costume? I cannot for the life of me picture you, by candlelight, sewing up a fur robe into a wolf costume and cleverly crafting the gloves into paws."

"Ah, but I am very domestic, my lady," he said with a wicked grin. "Actually," he said, growing serious again, "you had some of it right last night. Jamey and one of the other grooms were using it to torment the young women of the household. I took it from him when I figured it out."

"Where did *he* get it?"

"He said he made it. I didn't believe him, but he wouldn't say another word." The marquess shrugged. "I couldn't prove he didn't. I decided, when Miss Allengate was murdered and I didn't know · who had done it, to use the costume to distract people while I investigated. The fear of attack by a werewolf would, I hoped, keep other young women indoors. Despite Cecilia Wainwright's death, I have been otherwise successful." He gave her an expressive look. "Although nothing, so far, has managed to keep you indoors at night."

"But I do not believe in werewolves, my lord. Or perhaps my nighttime perambulations have to do with the salubrious Yorkshire climate. This means, of course, that James and his friend, and whomever they told, know you have been roaming as a werewolf."

He looked thoughtful. "I didn't tell them so, but they could know, yes. Are you implying that Jamey or his friend—though the other young fellow, Jamey's confederate, is a groom who accompanied my steward on estate business to London a month or so ago and is still there—could be guilty and pinned the murder on me by leaving the tuft of fur in place?"

"Sounds ridiculously sophisticated for Jamey, doesn't it?" Anne said.

"Yes; however, whom may he have told?"

"Hmm. Darkefell, I have two more tasks in this village. I don't require your agreement and will not brook interference."

He eyed her. "I *could* carry you away bodily," he said, "and no one in the village would stop me." His dark eyes were intent, at odds with the brilliance of the day.

"Why do you say things to try to imply that you're a dangerous fellow?"

"Why do you insist on thinking I'm not?"

She ignored his tone and the way it sent a chill down her back. "I'm going to Madam Holderness's shop to find out the truth of Bess Parker's trouble," she said, not relating what she had heard of Lily Jenkins and her willingness to "fool" someone as simple as Fanny Allengate was rumored to be, "and then I'm going to visit Mr. Richard Allengate. I feel we have not begun to look into Fanny Allengate's death, and I'm curious."

"Then I'll be going with you, my lady. I'll not have you wandering the streets of Hornethwaite, upsetting the locals, without at least observing."

She sighed heavily. He was a nuisance, but from experience, she knew there was no point in arguing with him.

Twenty-One

THE SAD HISTORY OF FANNY ALLENGATE WAS AMONG the things neither the marquess nor the magistrate had thought to consider, since the connection with Cecilia Wainwright's death, the only tragedy of interest at that moment, was seemingly nonexistent. But Anne could not get over the idea that the deaths of Tilly Landers, Fanny Allengate, and Cecilia Wainwright were connected. So she and Darkefell paid a visit to Richard Allengate's home—with his permission and using his key—and examined Fanny's journal, the source of much information regarding her last days.

Darkefell confessed that he had heard the gist of the entries from Richard himself when the fellow accused him of dallying with Fanny, and maintained that they were pure flights of fancy on the girl's part. The journal—a birthday gift from Richard, who had it made for her—was a blank book bound in kid leather, her full name engraved on the cover in gold. Anne, sitting in Fanny's girlish bedchamber, skimmed while Darkefell paced; there were sketches, poems, and entries, some dated, some not. At first they were vague and sweet, the story of a young girl falling in love for the very first time *after* a disastrous engagement to Mr. Jenkins, a connection that she deeply felt was a mistake. She related her emotions in pretty phrases and tender sentiments, and there was no hint at first of anything beyond admiration for a certain gentleman, and trembling hope. She never said a name but said she "saw her love from afar," and they exchanged few words.

Then there was a change. The last few entries, though in the same neat copperplate handwriting, were specific and graphic; she named the marquess, said what they did together, and Anne was intrigued—and a little shocked—by the language employed. Mr. Allengate returned home from his law office briefly while Anne and the marquess were still there. He was discomfited by his sister's words, but equally so by the marquess's denials, confused by whom or what to believe.

From Richard she gained a picture of the young lady that did not fit with the unseemly descriptions of her rapturous reaction to the marquess's attentions in the last few journal entries. Nowhere else in the seven months of journal entries, that Anne could see after the quick scan, did she employ such colorful and uncouth expressions.

It was puzzling. One thing drew her attention, though; it appeared to Anne that one or a couple of pages may have been cut out of the journal. What was on those missing pages? It was impossible to judge if there were days, weeks, or months missing.

Together and with Allengate's permission, Anne and the marquess looked over the solicitor's modest home. He was a neat gentleman of regular habits:

work every weekday and Saturday morning, church attendance on Sundays, whist Monday evenings with three other gentlemen, and a weekly courtesy visit to an elderly aunt every Saturday afternoon, taken up in place of Fanny's faithful visits after that young woman's untimely death. Nothing in the house gave them any clues to solve the mystery.

"What do you make of Miss Allengate's journals?" Anne said with a frown as they strolled together up the high street.

"I'm appalled," the marquess said grimly, "that she lied so viciously about her imaginary meetings with me."

"Really, Darkefell, can you see nothing beyond that?" Anne said, impatient with his lack of astuteness.

He stiffly replied that if he was being dull, then she ought to enlighten him, so she did as they strolled and had the satisfaction of having him agree with her conclusions. Anne was convinced that someone—she had a suspicion who, but no proof—ripped out some entries and wrote in the last few.

"I wish we could confront those I suspect with our deductions," Anne said wistfully.

"Why don't we?" Darkefell asked, his eyes glittering. "I would give much to confront certain people with our surmises. Let's do it tonight. We'll have a gathering and force someone's hand."

"You, my lord, have the soul of a gamester."

"Agreed. And you, my lady, have the devious mind of a solicitor. We make a fine pair, representing both ends of the moral spectrum. Then it's agreed. No one will refuse an invitation from me—they have too much to lose."

The second item of interest was discovered at the shop of Mrs. Holderness, the seamstress. Anne warned the marquess to enter the shop with her but not to interfere, no matter what the seamstress said.

"I would not dream of interfering in any of your plans, Lady Anne."

The shop was near the top of the high street, a superior address with a superior shop owner. Mrs. Holderness was an older woman, spare and bony, with blue veins close to the surface on her neck and hands. She had a way of holding her head high, which meant she must quite literally look down her prominent nose at anyone with whom she spoke, but whether it was hauteur or bad vision was not clear.

She welcomed the marquess, who introduced Anne as they had agreed, using her full name and antecedents. Lady Anne Addison of Kent, daughter of the Earl of Harecross, and good friend of the new Lady John Bestwick, he said. Anne lounged around the showroom with a bored expression, lifting pieces of fabric and dropping them with a sniff of disgust.

Mrs. Holderness became more and more agitated. "May I help you with anything at all, my lady?" she said in painfully strangled accents, badly copied from upper-crust clients, as she clasped her bony hands together and followed Anne about the shop.

"Oh, no, I doubt if I would buy anything *here*," Anne said, careful to place the stress on the most insulting word. "Although one of my favorite bonnets was sadly mashed on the way to Darkefell Castle, and I *could* have it sent down to be repaired. Do you have anyone skilled in millinery?"

"I would account it my honor to take care of your bonnet myself, my lady—we have some very fine ostrich plumes just now, and some lovely green and pink grosgrain."

"Perhaps," Anne said with a great show of reluctance. "My friend told me you have a rather good helper by the name of… what was it?" she said, turning slightly toward the marquess, who though appealed to, stayed silent. "A Mrs. Parker, I believe?"

A noise like that made by a strangled chicken emanated from the shop owner, and she said that was impossible. Anne insisted it would be Mrs. Parker or no one, to dress her bonnet.

"Mrs. Parker had, unfortunately, to be let go," Mrs. Holderness admitted at last, giving a sketchy and highly suspect relation of the circumstances of Bess Parker's arrest. When closely questioned by Anne, Mrs. Holderness admitted that Mrs. Parker claimed not to know how the fabric got in her home.

Anne fixed her with a gimlet stare. As a girl of eighteen, she had been bullied by her mother and many a seamstress into unbecoming dresses by the score. Her Season had been one long, mortifying sequence of spring green, frothy confections, mauve monstrosities, and pink, plumed headdresses. Her court dress aside—one must be presented to the queen in a full gown of excessive size—no woman needed to wear a skirt so full she couldn't enter a door, or stays so tightly laced she couldn't breathe. The excesses of fashion were for the vain or the frivolous. A woman must have utter confidence when dealing with seamstresses, she learned, for the tribe seemed to delight in foisting on their clientele ugly but expensive frills and furbelows, especially on plain women.

"Do you mean," she said, horror dripping in her tone, "that you accused the woman *before* you knew the entire story and without taking her denials—those of a competent and loyal worker—into account?"

Mrs. Holderness hesitated, but one long look at Anne's perfectly tailored serge caraco over a figured gown and stomacher and the expensive froth of mechlin trim, and she made a desperate attempt to justify her behavior. "What choice did I have, my lady?" she whined, wringing her hands in a gesture oddly reminiscent of Bess Parker in her cell. "I was threatened with embargo by Mrs. Lily Jenkins, and she is capable of enforcing such a thing. I would have no customers inside a week if I did not do as she wished."

The marquess made a smothered sound of fury, but Anne shot him a halting look and said, "How can such a young lady have so much power?"

The shopkeeper's expression was dark. "She makes it her life to… to know things… anything. Everything. About people." She edged forward, speaking to Anne in a hushed, confidential tone. "She's a… a *harpy!* A horrid young woman! And she'll not stand any interference in her and her husband's relationship, even so far as destroying the reputation of any woman who so much as catches his attention."

"And you helped her!" Anne said, not concealing her disgust.

"I did nothing, my lady, truly! 'Twas Mrs. Jenkins who did everything."

"I would advise," Anne said, with the same gimlet stare still fixed on the seamstress, "that you revisit the circumstances surrounding Mrs. Parker's arrest. Theft is a hanging offense, madam, as I am sure you are aware, and if Mrs. Parker suffered that fate, I would not want to have to say that I knew a murderess. *You,* to make my point perfectly clear. That would be more harmful to your reputation than any embargo, I think."

With that, and not a single glance at Darkefell, she swept from the shop.

He followed, and once outside, storm clouds darkening the sky over their head, he swept her an elegant bow. "Never, my lady, have I seen such a complete rout! She was flanked, outmaneuvered, and defeated on the field of dishonor."

She paused on the walk and glanced up at the storefront. "I would like nothing better now than to confront Mrs. Jenkins with her culpability, but it's far more important that she attend our little surprise soiree tonight, and if I tell her what I think of her, she won't."

"You're wise to leave it for the moment. Let me deliver the invitation to Benjamin Jenkins, for no matter if his wife hears what you have done to Mrs. Holderness, she still will not go against her husband, and he'll accept any invitation from me."

"Is it wise to invite them?" Anne asked.

"Regardless of our other suspicions, I wish to see her confronted with your work today, and for her to know she's uncovered as a jealous, troublesome wench," he said grimly.

At Anne's request, they stopped at a modest cottage on a back street in Hornethwaite, the home of Ellen

Henderson's widowed mother. Mrs. Henderson, a careworn woman of about fifty, with a couple of grandchildren clinging to her skirts, told her, with wide and frightened eyes, that Ellen had not visited them at all the day before. She hadn't expected her, the woman said, as a young girl had other things to do on her half day off than visit with her poor old mum, so she had thought nothing. Of course, Anne's visit and questions now had her worried. Anne did her best to reassure the woman that her daughter would be fine.

After a few more stops, they began the journey back to Ivy Lodge. Some of what had gone on lately between Darkefell estate and the village finally made sense, but as Anne said, "If our suspicions are correct, much of this has nothing to do with Cecilia Wainwright's murder."

"I think you've hit on some truths, my lady," the marquess said, "and some mischief or worse done, but it doesn't surprise me that there is no connection. I've never felt the matters were intertwined."

"Hmm," Anne murmured. "We still have a few questions I would like answered for sure."

"And you will have what you desire before the night is done," he answered. "It will all be out in the open before long, I hope."

She glanced over at the marquess, whose mouth was set in a grim line at what they had conjectured. He was an admirable companion when he kept his mouth shut in the right places, but then, he would likely say the same thing about her.

At least now they had some suspicion, as shocking to both of them as it was. The next twenty-four hours would tell the tale.

The clouds were thickening as they approached Darkefell estate along the hard-packed road. A distant rumble of thunder and light patter of rain warned of a deluge to come, so the marquess smartened his team's pace. Just for a moment, Anne wondered if this was what it would be like to be mistress of this estate and to be wed to the man beside her, this amiable silence and the preceding hours of working together effectively. She glanced over at him and was surprised that the thought unnerved but did not disgust her. He was surprisingly agreeable when he chose to be.

Of course, her good sense chose that moment to assert its dominion over her imagination; *when he chose to be* was the phrase that must be heeded. He could not command her. She was free, independent. As his wife, a woman would be at his command, and he struck her as having an iron will. He would not be conformable to feminine impulses, she thought, nor would he be even the slightest bit bendable. Once the courtship was over and the ring thrust upon the appropriate digit, the ball would be over. That saved her from anything like regret that such a union never would be.

He would never want to marry someone like her anyway. She was willful, stubborn, a "devil woman" as he called her in his angry moments. She was plain and proud and nosy. Brisk. Contrary. She sighed. If anything, this trip to Yorkshire had shown her that kisses, even those visited upon her by the same man, could have various effects upon her; they could make her swoonish, wary, angry, and on occasion she experienced a new sensation she could name only "lusty," for want of any more accurate term. This was an uncomfortable sensation for a determined spinster.

His kisses were likely not going to trouble her further, anyway. Darkefell, she had always suspected, kissed her to confuse her, and now that she knew his secrets, especially that he was the dreaded werewolf, there was no need. That thought came with a pang. She rather liked the unexpected nature of his kisses. How like life to teach her a new enjoyment just as it was to be taken away from her. She glanced sideways, and her mouth twisted in a smile as she noticed that part of his thick eyebrows had been burnt to frazzled crisps from her incineration of his werewolf costume the night before.

"I hesitate to ask, but of what are you thinking as you glance toward me so frequently, my lady?"

She bit her lip but decided to share at least one of her thoughts, the one safe for him to hear without making him vain about his masculine charms. "I was admiring how your thick and unruly eyebrows have been singed. It gives them an interesting piquancy. I had a maid once, when I was young, who burned my fringe just that way with an overheated curling iron."

"You seem to suffer hair torture from time to time, judging by your torment at the hands of the maid the first day at Ivy Lodge."

"Ah, yes, my gorgon style; alas, I was hoping to set a new trend in classic hairstyles, but Mary will have none of it, and any intelligent woman is a servant to her abigail, you know. That style was the work of Ellen Henderson," Anne said, brought back with a thud to the problem at hand. Where was Ellen? As the carriage still rumbled swiftly along the road to Darkefell, Anne frowned off into the cloudy distance. "I'm worried about Ellen," she said aloud. "She seems to have disappeared completely."

"No doubt she stayed with a friend in town overnight and made her way back to Ivy Lodge late," the marquess said. "Mrs. Hailey will reprimand her, and all will be done."

"I hope you're right, but I have an uncomfortable sense about it." At least the mystery of the other missing maid, the one Anne had followed away from Ivy Lodge, had been solved; Caroline had run away with one of the grooms from the livery stable in town, they had learned when the marquess retrieved his carriage. It was a juicy scandal, and all the world loves a scandal.

It was beginning to rain. Anne absently scanned the open field as they passed a wooded copse and saw a flash of movement. "What was that?" she asked. It was a creature loping through the lush green grass of the field surrounding the woods; as she caught sight of it again, it stopped and howled. She grabbed the marquess's arm. "Darkefell, stop the carriage!"

He pulled on the reins. Anne jumped down even as the carriage was still moving, stumbled, and staggered back onto her feet, but by the time she regained her balance, the animal had disappeared into the woods; the bushes moved just on the edge of the glade. Determined to establish what the animal was, once and for all time, she lifted her skirts and began down the raised embankment and across the grassy field.

"Lady Anne! Anne! *Stop!*"

But she bolted, an anxious fluttering in her stomach. Dog? Wolf? Killer? She had thought she was sure of her and Darkefell's conjectures, but her mind churned with questions. All she wanted was to see more closely.

"Anne, get back here, *now!*" Darkefell shouted.

She looked over her shoulder; he was bounding after her. She put on a burst of speed, secure in the knowledge that he would follow, concerned only that he would catch her, being much swifter and unencumbered by skirts and a cloak. She reached the perimeter of the woods just as the rain began in earnest, pouring down as if someone was emptying a bucket over her; she paused a second then pushed through the thick brush at the edge, moving in. She could see movement in the shadows. Her bonnet was roughly pulled off her head, and thorns and branches caught at the cloak she wore over her caraco, but she would not stop, not while she could see that movement ahead of her. What was it? She was so close to an answer!

The woods were dim and damp and cold, but they were protected from the deluge. She shivered and stopped, peering into the dank shadows. Where now? She saw another movement, and a howling bark cut through the silence, shivering down her spine with the unaccustomed sound. Instinctive fear roiled in her stomach, but something else caught her attention besides the animal movement she could detect and the yip and howl of the creature.

Something blue… an unnatural blue never seen in the middle of a woods. She pushed through as she heard the marquess call her name in commanding tones. Bluebells? Violets? Not in the middle of the woods!

She yanked her cloak out of the greedy grasp of the tangled brush as she found the source of the blue just beyond the thorny bush. Was it a heap of clothes or perhaps an abandoned cloak or blanket? Breaking off a branch that impeded her progress, she used the broken branch to prod the pile of clothes, trying to grab it with the hooked end of the branch.

"Ooooh!"

Anne jumped back and screamed at the movement and sound emanating from the bundle.

"Anne! Anne!" Darkefell cried, crashing through the bush like a draft horse in a pony stall.

"Here! Darkefell, someone is here!" She had used an indefinite word, but she knew who it must be. "Ellen! It's Ellen," she said, pushing past the last brushy obstacle, animal forgotten, her worry for the girl paramount. She crouched by the cloaked figure as the marquess, panting, reached her.

"Do not *ever* disappear on me again!" he bellowed.

"It's Ellen Henderson, and she's hurt but alive." Anne, on her knees, pulled the maid's cloak hood back and gently turned the girl over, the maid's golden hair catching on her brushy bed. Anne gasped in horror; Ellen's round, pallid face was bruised and cut, crusted blood matted into the hairline and flaking in dried rivulets. Her lip was cut and swollen, and one eye sported a dark purple, swollen bruise under it.

Ellen moaned and stirred. "My money… want my money… my Jamey… " She groaned and fainted.

"We must get her back to the lodge," Anne cried.

Darkefell didn't hesitate a moment, and Anne blessed both his vigorous nature and his physical strength, for he put his arms under Ellen's knees and back and gently lifted her as if she was a light as a lamb. Anne glanced around, for though haste was clearly needed for the girl's well-being, Anne was also aware that finding the maid had been merest luck, brought about by seeing the dog-creature and following it. What was it doing so close? Ellen did not appear to be ravaged by the creature, nor was there any sign of animal attack.

Even while Anne looked about, she wondered about Ellen's words: money, Jamey?

Anne saw another flash of movement and longed to follow, but Darkefell was single-mindedly moving back toward the road, and she knew she must follow. "Darkefell, I thought I saw a person back there," she said breathlessly, looking back over her shoulder as she followed him. "It could be whoever attacked Ellen."

"They waited around for twelve hours until she was found? This girl has been lying there some time. The wounds aren't fresh."

"How do you know?"

"The color of the blood and the smell," he grunted but did not elaborate.

She eyed his broad back as she reluctantly followed him. One always had a sense, with the marquess, that there were hidden depths, things of which he did not speak. How he came to know what a wound smelled like after several hours was one of those things.

The rain still poured down. Fortunately, they were only minutes from the lodge by carriage, but still, they were soaked by the time they got there. There was a rush of activity as they pulled up and the marquess carried Ellen in. The maid was soon in the competent hands of Mrs. Hailey. Anne turned to the marquess, but he was rapidly heading toward the door. She swept after him; they had things of which to speak, and she wasn't about to let him go without some acknowledgment of how this latest twist fit with their idea of what had been happening.

"My lord, wait!" she said, exiting the lodge after the marquess, followed by the curious gaze of the footman. Darkefell leaped up into the seat of the phaeton. "I am about to get a crick in my neck from looking up at you," she complained, the rain splattering her cheek. She wiped drops out of her eyes.

"Did you follow me merely to say that?" he asked.

"Of course not."

"Then go back in and dry off. Our plans stand."

"Despite finding Ellen?"

"Yes," he said.

"Good," she said, determined to be his equal in brevity. "Until this evening, then."

She reentered the house and headed for Mrs. Hailey's chamber, where Ellen had been taken, but the maid was still unconscious and had not said another word.

Twenty-Two

THE MINUTE HE ENTERED THE CASTLE, DARKEFELL headed for his library and summoned Osei. Harwood brought him a towel, and he dried as best he could. Armed with new suppositions raised by his enlightening conversations with Lady Anne, he was able to ask pointed questions and demand answers of Osei. In truth, Osei appeared relieved to be able to tell what he knew of Cecilia Wainwright's actions. With child by Jamey, desperate to marry and gain an establishment, she had played a dangerous game, and if Darkefell and Lady Anne's conjectures were correct, had reaped the unfortunate consequences.

Brooding, Darkefell sat and stared into the empty fireplace after their conversation. Osei finally stood and said, "If that is all, my lord?"

"What? No, sit for a moment longer." He watched his secretary for a long few moments. "Tell me the truth—were you in love with Cecilia Wainwright?"

Osei's dark eyes clouded with pain, and he looked away. "I do not know, my lord. She listened to me as no one else did, and I came to care for her." He shrugged as if there were no adequate words for his emotion. "I do not understand the workings of my own heart, I think. Perhaps that comes only with more years than I have yet lived."

Darkefell nodded. "And your last minutes together were spent as you have said?"

"Yes."

"Why did you say nothing afterwards about what she said she was going to do?"

"I never suspected such a conclusion as that to which you and Lady Anne have come. Ellen did not tell me whom she was meeting or when, just what she hoped to accomplish, so I thought I would have time to convince her of the folly of her plan. I pointed out the dishonor of blackmail, and we argued. She said only men thought that way, and when I had a child, I would understand the need to provide a better life, no matter what it took."

"So you knew she was with child and who the father was?"

"Yes."

"Why, then, did you react as you did to the news the morning after her death?"

Osei shook his head. "The public exposure of her condition and conjecture of her character—she was dishonored, as well as dead... a terrible moment."

Darkefell nodded. Knowing Cecilia in a way none of them did, as a cherished friend, Osei was hurt deeply by what was said about her. "You agree that evening must have proceeded the way we imagine, after you and she parted?"

"Yes, though it fills me with sorrow. I am sorry that man is so lost to the world and heaven that he would do it."

The marquess watched Osei for a moment; the fellow had turned to Cecilia, another person who felt alone in Yorkshire and at his estate, for solace. Darkefell had been remiss, perhaps, in not making efforts to ameliorate his secretary's loneliness, but his mother already considered that he "coddled" his secretary. Though he did not guide his actions by her measure, he must have taken some of her axioms to heart and behaved accordingly, as he had with his father's harsh tutelage.

But he was approaching thirty. It was past time to act according to what he felt and thought down to his core. The most powerful thing he had learned in his brief acquaintance with Lady Anne Addison was to guide oneself according to one's deepest feelings, as she did. He admired her more than he could express in words, for in her he saw a vigorous honesty, tempered by flashes of charm and wit, boundless energy, and beneath her asperity, great kindness. Her beauty was the sort that emanated from within, and every moment spent in her company, he saw it more clearly, glowing through her skin. She attracted him in a way no other woman ever had.

"I miss her so very much," Osei said, his voice thick and strange.

Darkefell looked up; his secretary stared toward the window but not through it.

"In Cecilia," Osei continued, "I saw the prospect of a life beyond what I had imagined for myself. It was not that I thought I could have that life with *her*—she was in love with another—but I saw what it would be like to have a woman with whom to speak, one who sympathized and yet added her own thoughts, allowing me to see from another's perspective. She shared her emotions in a way men seldom do."

Against every bit of training from his youth, the strict discipline of his father, Darkefell could feel the seductive pull of just that... having a woman to talk to and in whom to confide. Women—or one woman, at least—offered an openness missing in daily converse with any other soul. Was that what marriage could bring if one selected wisely... a deep, all-trusting, all-confiding friendship?

A wife, among his acquaintance, was an indispensable nuisance, a legal necessity to produce an heir. Affairs of the heart and delights of the flesh were to explore with a mistress. With men, one shared opinions and ideas. But could one woman unite all of that?

This was far too close to the bone and marrow of him for comfort. "Osei," he said, anxious to change the subject, "they are talking in London of sending Africans back to their various homelands. I don't know if you've ever thought of it. I've been meaning to raise this subject for some time but never found the opportunity. If you wish help in finding your family, I would offer what I could. Even if you would like to return to your homeland... I will help."

Osei stood and bowed, his spectacle lenses glinting in the lamplight and concealing his eyes. "Thank you, sir, but my home is here."

"Good," Darkefell said, feeling awkward and so resorting to the hearty mannerisms his father had employed in such a situation. "Good, good. No need to speak of that again, then!" He rose and clapped Osei on the shoulder. "I must go and dress for dinner at Ivy Lodge. Is everything prepared according to my instructions?"

"Yes, sir."

"Good."

Agitated, Anne paced, viewed sternly by Irusan, who sat atop her vanity table among the brushes and pots of cream. Mary sat in a chair by the fire, trying to mend the damage done to Anne's cloak by the brush Anne had pushed through. Robbie, who had been helping the Ivy Lodge stableboy, entered just that moment; by the excited gleam in his eyes and triumphant grin, Anne knew he had information.

"You know something," she said to the child, who went directly to his mother. "Robbie, you have the look of a fellow with a head stuffed full of information. Out with it!"

He nodded as he leaned on his mother's shoulder. "Bertie—that's Gilbert, mum, 'oo is stableboy 'ere—'e sez Miss Cece gave 'im a note, and 'e took it to the fella like you sed. 'E can't remember rightly if it were that day, but 'e got in bags o' trouble from Mister Lisle—'e's the head groom—'bout missin' 'is chores that afternoon, then remembers you comin' milady, so 'e thinks it *were* that day."

Anne sat abruptly on the edge of her bed, deep in thought. Irusan leaped down from his perch and gracefully up to the bed, then padded across to her and settled half on her lap and half on the bed. He flexed his claws, tangling them in the fine fabric. She picked his claws from her skirt and smoothed the threads.

"'E's scaret o' you, milady—'e sez 'e shut you inta the tower by mistake an' is afraid of a hiding if 'e sez he did it."

Well, that solved that little mystery, too, Anne thought; so the boy had accidentally locked her into the tower and run away out of fear. "All right," she said and suddenly stood to pace again. Irusan, dumped unceremoniously from her lap, let out a squawk of disapproval and leaped to the vanity table, knocking down a bottle. The resulting crash made him even more cross, and with a chatter of fury, he leaped swiftly down from the vanity, up to the bed, and then, with one mighty leap, up to the top of a bookshelf. Robbie clapped and laughed. "All right, m'boy," Anne said, "you've done very well. You shall have the entire bag of boiled sweets I promised you, so you can make yourself as ill as you please. But off with you, now. I must dress quickly for the evening."

Robbie headed off to the dressing room where he and his mother slept, and Irusan, with one reproachful look at Anne, leaped down from his perch and followed the boy. This, of course, was his action whenever he wanted Anne to know that he was especially peeved with her; for to prefer the attentions of a small boy was a "catty" way of expressing extreme indignation.

Anne ignored him. Once the door was closed behind them, she was just about to strip down to her chemise, but a tap at the door stopped her. "Who is it?"

"It is Hailey, milady. Ellen is awake an' asked for you in particular."

With an exultant hop, Anne raced to the door, flung it open, and faced the housekeeper. "She asked for me by name?"

"Yes'm," Mrs. Hailey said. "Wants to tell you something."

Anne was gone for a half hour. Ellen spoke with some difficulty, because her throat was raw, but what she had to say was worth hearing. Anne would now have to hurry to dress appropriately, she realized as she returned to her room. However, the rush was worth it. She wondered if she ought to send a message to the marquess; but no, she would see him soon enough and would let him know that their conjectures were fully supported by Ellen Henderson's information.

She explained what she had heard to Mary, and then, trembling all over as she stood in the middle of her bedchamber, said, "Mary, I wish to look my absolute best tonight. Despite the odd mix of dinner guests, I expect fascinating conversation and scintillating revelations." She sat in the vanity chair.

Mary began with her hair. "This interest in your attire wouldna be because of his lordship, would it?"

Anne twisted and stared up at her maid, giving her a sour look but not saying anything. Of course, Mary was partly right. As much as she wished it were not so, she did care what the marquess thought of her. "All right, then—I wish him to think well of me, if nothing else. Make me as attractive as is possible."

The grin on her maid's face was broad, and she rubbed her work-worn hands together. "Aye. Now there's a challenge to sink ma teeth into."

"Thank you very much," Anne said, on the edge of being insulted. Her sense of humor reanimated, and she finished with a laugh and said, "I expect wonders, then. Make me as pretty as Emma Hart." Though she had never met the young woman— of course no lady *could* meet such a woman as the notorious mistress of the Honorable Charles Greville—she had seen a couple of the paintings Romney had done; they were rhapsodic, and Emma must be a glorious creature. Anne admired beauty, whether male or female, though she never confused pulchritude with politesse.

"I'm verra good, milady—but I'm no' a miracle worker."

"I should sack you for impertinence," Anne said tartly.

"No one else would put up wi' your captiousness." With that last sally, Mary set to work in earnest.

Though Anne had decided on her favorite green sarcanet, Mary was firm; she had been given free rein and had her own idea of what Anne must wear. Once the elaborate hairstyle was done, it was time for Anne to begin dressing.

"First, scent," Mary said, spraying Anne's chemise with fragrance of hyacinth. "Then your stockings and stays." She firmly laced in Anne, pulling hard until Anne could barely breathe.

"Why so tight?" Anne wailed, tying her garters with some difficulty.

"We're going to make the most of your figure, because you've got a verra good one, and there is not a man alive who doesn't like to see a nice pair of upthrust breasts." Mary's rolling r's drew out the last two words.

Anne began to feel the first quivering of anxiety. She was going to look like a trollop, she just knew it! She would have huge upthrust bosoms under her chin and a pinched expression on her painted face, her eyes bulging from the tightness of her stays; she'd frighten everyone but Irusan.

"Now, rump pad, and petticoat," Mary said. She tied the little roll around Anne's waist, then fetched a silver-tissue petticoat from the wardrobe, pulled it down over her mistress's head, and laced it, too, around Anne's waist, along with a pair of pockets. "And now the gray tabby silk," she said, fetching the dress from the other room then dropping it over Anne's head and lacing her up, "and silver-embroidered stomacher." Finally, lilac damask slippers with silver buckles, the matching lilac damask fan with silver fittings and amethyst cabochons, and a fine jeweled mechlin collar around her long neck.

When they were done, Anne, afraid to look at herself, turned away from the cheval mirror. "I can't do it," she said, shivering. "I can't look."

Mary briskly grabbed her shoulders, saying, "Don't be daft," as she whirled Anne around.

Anne stared at her reflection. Her hair was glossy, the rich brown color illuminated by pomade and lilac feathers; it gleamed like silk in the lamplight. Her bosom was creamy white, and a single silver locket hung from a glistening chain and nestled in the décolletage below the mechlin lace band. Overall, the silvery dress and petticoat was elegant and lovely, her figure perfection, and tears welled up in her eyes. She had never in her life looked better. She should have known she could trust Mary.

"I will never be Emma Hart, Mary, but you've made me a modestly attractive woman. Thank you."

The abigail's eyes glittered, and she smiled. "His lordship values the woman beneath the attire far more, if he's wise, for never have I met a woman wi' a heart like yours." She paused then tagged on, pragmatic as always, "But borrowed feathers willna hurt you for one night."

"Why have you never done this before, this, this...?" She broke off and gestured to her reflection in the mirror.

"Ah, nouw that'd be whisperin' tales to a birdie, wouldn't it?" Mary said with a wink.

"I have no idea what you mean."

"Good. It's time to go down, milady. Have a good e'en, and don't muddle wi' a murderer."

The family gathered as the guests arrived. Lord John and Lydia sat in the drawing room while Lady Darkefell stood near the door, greeting people as they arrived: Sir Trevor Pomfroy, the vicar and his wife, Richard Allengate, Hiram Grover, Mr. and Mrs. Benjamin Jenkins, Miss Beatrice Lange. It was an odd assortment. His mother had complained, but the marquess overruled her objections in ordering this impromptu dinner party.

But where was Lady Anne? Darkefell fumed, glancing at the clock in the hall. She was necessary to their plan, for she was the only one he trusted to play her part perfectly and to catch things he might not. Out of the corner of his eye, he saw a movement on the stairs and turned.

Lady Anne descended, and as she emerged from the dimness of the wide staircase, he was assaulted by the vision of elegance she had become in the few short hours since he had last seen her. He leaped up the three steps remaining and grabbed her arm. "Why the devil did you make yourself over into some kind of society diamond? What are you thinking?"

"What do you mean? Unhand me!" she said in clear, frigid tones, yanking her arm from his grasp.

"I mean," he muttered, "how are you going to melt into the background and watch the exchanges we hope for if you stand out like a bird of paradise among hens?"

"Don't be ridiculous, Darkefell. I'm simply wearing appropriate clothing. To dress otherwise would be to invite derision. I assure you, I shall blend in far better dressed thusly than as some fright, as you clearly prefer."

She stalked down the last three steps, leaving him fuming. He followed, regulating his facial expressions as his mother guided guests who had never been to Ivy Lodge—Mr. and Mrs. Jenkins and Miss Beatrice Lange—to the appropriate room.

The play was about to begin.

Anne burned in silence as she strolled toward the drawing room. How dare the man take exception to her style of dress? Just because he had not seen her in proper attire, did he think she didn't own any beautiful clothing? That was the perfect example of how impossible he would be to whatever unfortunate woman married him. He could be all charm and appeal when he wished, and then become, in the next moment, imperious and unbearably high-handed.

She entered the drawing room and paused, glancing around at the gathering. The first face that drew her attention was Lord John. He was pale, appeared ill, and she felt a qualm as to their procedure. Lydia, too, looked ill, and in fact appeared to be faint. She sat in a chair but leaned heavily on her husband, who stood beside her.

What was wrong with those two? Lydia looked up at her, and their eyes locked. Anne thought she mouthed, "I'm frightened," but couldn't be sure, and her attention was demanded at that moment by Mrs. Lily Jenkins, who flounced over to her.

"What is going on here?" she asked.

Anne was ready for this and replied, "Lady Darkefell thought it would be kind to have a little dinner party for me, as I will be here only another few days. She invited everyone I mentioned having met and found congenial in the last weeks."

The young woman appeared mollified and said with exaggerated politeness, "I beg your pardon, my lady, for my tone just now. I was just *that* taken aback at finding so many others arriving."

Anne watched her eyes as she said, "Are you

uncomfortable with any of them, Mrs. Jenkins? I would not want you to feel ill at ease."

"La, of course not, my lady," she said in light tones but with hard eyes. "I am perfectly accustomed to every upper level of society, I must say, for my husband is of the most elegant family in town, I assure you."

"Speaking of elegance, I understand Mr. Jenkins aspired to the hand of Fanny Allengate once, but that she turned him down or broke off her engagement with him?"

"Well," the young woman said with a sour expression on her narrow face, "he proposed *only* out of kindness, you know, to an old family friend, for she had just lost her father. But he was *so* relieved when she released him, for he had been in love with me forever, he was just shy to say it. He knew I had refused more eligible offers, you see, and did not have confidence in his ability to attach a woman of my spirit and strength."

Anne was not fooled for one tick of the clock by Lily Jenkins's bluster. Her words were those of a determined shrew who will always characterize herself as spirited rather than shrewish.

Richard Allengate and Mr. Benjamin Jenkins were talking affably at that moment, and Anne watched while Richard played his part. He frowned and leaned into Mr. Jenkins, asking him the question and giving the salient information with which he had been supplied by the marquess. Mr. Jenkins looked surprised, then glanced toward his wife. Mrs. Jenkins's eyes widened in alarm and swept across the room toward her husband.

Mr. Hiram Grover, attired in an old-fashioned,

wide-sleeved jacket and bag wig, was sitting by the fire when Mr. Osei Boatin walked into the sitting room. Anne noted the watchful gaze of the gentleman and his increasing agitation as Mr. Boatin walked steadily over and took the chair opposite him by the fire. Mr. Boatin said not a word; he merely sat, gazing calmly into the fire. Grover moved so he was facing slightly away from the secretary.

The stage was set.

Lord Darkefell, with a significant—and dare she say sheepish?—look to her, took a position near the fireplace by the mantle. "Ladies and gentlemen, may I have your attention?"

The majority of the people gathered turned their attention toward the marquess, but there were a few notable exceptions. Hiram Grover, his face and neck showing a brick red color as his wig slid askew, stared into the fire. Lily Jenkins, also red-faced, clasped her hands together and stared up at her husband, who bore the shocked expression of a man who had just had mist cleared from his gaze and seen horror. Lord John seemed concerned only with Lydia, who still looked faint and ill.

Anne faded into the background and watched each one in turn, waiting.

Lord Darkefell cleared his throat and began: "I have been remiss in addressing the concerns of my people, the people of Hornethwaite and Staunby, for the last year or more. I have no excuse, not when people were laboring under fears I ought to have soothed and instead exacerbated."

The vicar, who stood with his wife and Miss

Beatrice Lange, spoke up, saying, "My lord, as much as you are responsible for the people in a corporal sense, it is I who bear the responsibility of caring for their spiritual needs and immortal souls, and I feel—"

"Not now, Mr. Sydney," the marquess said, holding up one hand. "In an effort to clear the air and to inform all of you—for each one of you has your sphere of influence and can disseminate what comfort I have to offer—I am going to reveal the truth about some things that have been, until now, clouded in a shroud of doubt and suspicion."

Anne watched Benjamin Jenkins, his frown deepening as he threw a questioning glance at his wife, who gazed at him in mute appeal. She tugged his sleeve and said something, but he shook his head and firmed his lips. It looked, to Anne, as if she was pleading to leave. She put one trembling hand to her forehead in a feign of illness, but he was unmoved, folding his arms over his chest.

"I don't have solutions to everything," the marquess went on, letting his gaze travel over the gathering. "I cannot say who killed Tilly Landers, nor do I know who was responsible for Fanny Allengate's unfortunate death. I believe I *do* know who caused that poor girl much torment before her death, though, and loss of her sterling reputation after."

Richard Allengate still bore the look of solemnity he had ever borne, but now there was an added element of anger directed toward only one individual.

"But Cecilia Wainwright, whose well-being was my responsibility in a way not one of the other unfortunate girls' was... well, I know how she died. Ambitious, but foolhardy in that ambition, she aspired to a life beyond what she could ever have as a lady's maid. She was brutally and foully slaughtered, not by a wolf nor a werewolf—there never was any werewolf but some frivolous fellows and myself—but by a human hand. She was murdered by someone in this room."

Twenty-Three

THE EXPECTED GASP WENT AROUND THE ROOM, AND
Lydia wavered, her husband's firm arm the only thing
that kept her upright. Several voices called out, *"Lord
Darkefell is the werewolf?" "Is that true?"* and *"Killed… by
someone in this room? Surely not?"* but they stopped when
Lady Sophie Darkefell stepped out of the gloom.

"This is enough!" she said, approaching the
marquess. "Tony, you cannot invite people to dinner
and then accuse one of murder."

"Aren't you curious," he asked, watching his mother's
face, "as to which of your guests I consider guilty?"

"No!" she cried, her hands balled into fists, her
gloves bunching. "No!"

Darkefell's brows knit together, and he stared down
at his mother.

Her eyes glittered oddly in the candlelight, and
Anne's stomach twisted. Had they got it wrong? Why
was the marchioness so distressed?

Mr. Grover stood and approached Lady Darkefell,
grabbing her arm and supporting her while he glared
at the marquess. "You should be ashamed of yourself,"

he bellowed, shaking so much that his old-fashioned wig skewed even more sideways. "Ashamed, I say. To bring us all here and to bring in that... that son of Canaan," he said with a furious gesture toward Osei still sitting by the fire. "It's disgusting! If that trollop, Cecilia, had not consorted with him, she wouldn't have died. Shameful strumpet got what she deserved!"

Lady Darkefell pointedly removed her arm from his grasp and said, so quietly Anne had to strain to hear, "Hiram, that's enough."

"No, Sophie, I'll not let you be shamed by your son. A whoremonger, lying with barmaids and town girls like Tilly Landers and Miss Allengate... he may do as he likes, but I'll not have him slander his neighbors by accusing one of murder."

"How interesting, Mr. Grover," Darkefell said in steely tones, "that you so strenuously revile Mr. Boatin's presence here, and yet he is silent upon the subject of your presence, which he has had to suffer innumerable times over the last few years."

"You compare us, sir?" the gentleman roared. "You *dare* compare me to that... slave of slaves?" Grover dropped back down into a chair and passed one shaking hand over his bulging eyes.

"See here, Darkefell," the magistrate said, eyeing Grover uneasily but then turning his attention fully to the marquess. "Am I to understand that you believe someone in this room to be guilty of the murder of Cecilia Wainwright? William Spottiswode is *not* guilty?"

Darkefell cast him a look of patient derision as he said, "Ah, Sir Trevor, you've finally joined the rest in catching what I said and what I meant… both the same thing, I assure you. Someone in this room foully murdered Cecilia—I do not see Spottiswode in this room."

The magistrate turned red, so that made three people in the room suffused with the color. It was increasingly difficult to watch all that was occurring, but when Anne again looked at Lydia, her gaze was riveted, for her friend was rising, pulling herself from her husband's grasp. She dashed across the room and threw herself at her brother-in-law.

"He didn't mean to do it! I'm sure of that," she cried.

"What on earth…?" Darkefell grunted, set off balance; he cast a look of appeal to his younger brother. "John, come get your wife! Unhand me, my lady!"

"Nooooo," she keened, clinging to him, her knuckles white as her fists bunched in the fine fabric of his jacket sleeves. "John didn't mean to kill Cecilia. You cannot prove it!"

Anne watched in horror, dizzy with doubt. Did Lydia know something they had not considered? But Lord John appeared mystified and horror-struck in a way that left no doubt—in her, at least—as to his innocence.

"My God," Lady Sophie cried, both trembling hands up to her forehead, "John, I said you would regret marrying that foolish featherbrain!"

Weeping, Lydia whirled away from the marquess and glared at her mother-in-law. "You've always hated me," she sobbed. "You tried to turn John away from me and succeeded."

John made it across the space in three steps and took Lydia into his arms. "My love, don't be silly! Mother could not turn me away from you."

The babble in the room, consisting of confused murmuring and questions circulating from person to person, grew. Sure as she was of John's innocence of the worst suspicions, Anne spared a moment to shake her head at Lydia's absurdity. The girl was truly shatterbrained, but at least her husband was gentle with her, taking her into his arms and murmuring to her as she wept against his chest. Anne glanced over at the marquess, to see that he was going red-faced himself, now. Four red-faced folks. To forestall further speculation, she stepped into a pool of lamplight and said, "Calm, everyone, please! Despite my friend's fears, her husband is not the culprit Lord Darkefell spoke of just now. *Please* listen to the marquess."

"Thank you, Lady Anne. John, perhaps you should take Lydia to her room," he said, raising his voice over her sobs.

"No, we'll stay, Tony," the younger brother said grimly, his arms still around his wife, her head against his shoulder. "We'll stay if just to see in what folly you're engaged. I thought I was the foolish son, Mother, but perhaps Tony has decided to usurp my position."

"Very good, John!" Darkefell said with a flash of a grin. "Congratulations on the best sally I have heard from you in many a year."

Lord John fell silent, his cheeks burning with a crimson stain at his brother's teasing. Anne was beginning to suspect the red-faced malady was infectious, from the number who now sported scarlet flags on their cheeks. She was pleased to see that the marquess was regaining *his* normal color, so perhaps the infection spread quickly but was as soon defeated.

Darkefell exchanged a brief glance with Anne, and she nodded once; he scanned his audience. "I cannot tell you the entire story, I'm afraid, but several things have united to give me confidence that I now know the culprit of at least that one terrible crime, Cecilia Wainwright's murder. She was guilty of ambition beyond her status in life, but who can blame her? She was with child when her life was cut short; that much is commonly known," he said over a few gasps. "But much speculation has been bandied about. My secretary's name has been posited as the hopeful father."

"Disgusting," Grover grunted, his arms crossed over his paunch. "The taint of that unnatural union is what got her killed, for what is the fellow but a savage, a beast plucked from that sinister continent for the purpose of servitude, his natural state since Ham first dared make a jest of his revered father, Noah!"

Anne longed to answer as Osei, speechless and ashen, could not, for Grover's twisting of the mythic biblical curse of Canaan revealed him to be a sophist of the most degraded and dangerous type, willing to misuse Bible verses to justify any kind of foul behavior.

But the marquess was prepared. "Grover, you've revealed yourself to be a biblical hypocrite, for doesn't that Book also tell us not to bear false witness? Your implied accusation against Osei is a sham."

"Do not use the good Book against me, you fornicator," Grover said, rising with difficulty from his chair. "You, who bedded that bar wench, Tilly Landers, and likely killed her, too?"

"Be careful, Grover," the marquess said through gritted teeth. "You tread on dangerous territory."

"Sophie, despite the friendship I bear you, I will not stay to be insulted by your son. He is not fit to wash my feet nor those of my son."

"Your son, your *only* son, the same one who will no longer speak to you, Grover?" Darkefell said, his tone deadly soft. "The son who has severed ties with you, despite your lies to the contrary?" he went on, his tone rising. "Theo wrote to me, you know, to apologize for your wickedness, and told me he no longer considers you his father. Perhaps he suspects something we should know about? Something *besides* your willingness to kill innocent Africans on their terrible voyage to slavery in Jamaica?"

"You… you have *never* proved I had anything to do with that!" Grover said, jabbing his finger in Darkefell's direction.

"No, perhaps I cannot tie you to it by a specific order given, but if I had not come forward with what Julius and I witnessed, you would have recovered for damages from lost slaves, slaves that your crew tossed overboard. You knew about that, for I told you myself. Yet you tried to recover their monetary value from your insurer for accidental death, even knowing your case was a lie from start to finish. Your crew performed actions that any civilized nation—and I do not count our country among those civilized nations, not when we can wink and turn our face away from this—would call murder!"

Grover began toward the doorway, pushing past horrified guests.

But John leaped in front of him and grabbed him by the shoulders, saying, "Do you want him to stay, Tony?"

"Yes, Brother. I have one more crime to lay at his door, one that both his biblical studies and the law of this land *do* condemn, the murder of Cecilia Wainwright."

Lady Sophie gasped and put one trembling hand over her mouth.

"What proof do you have of this infamous accusation, my lord?" Sir Trevor shouted.

"Sit down, all of you, and I'll tell you," Darkefell said. But the crowd could not so easily settle, though they gathered in tightly around the chair in which John had forced Grover to sit. "Lady Anne, will you join me?" he asked, putting out his hand.

She advanced and took his hand, which he used to pull her close and tuck her arm in his.

"This lady," he said, covering her hand on his arm with his free hand, "was the inspiration for every bit of evidence I discovered—"

She cleared her throat.

"That, uh, *we* discovered, and she reasoned out, with me, the sequence of events."

Mr. Grover tried to rise, but Lord John put one hand on his shoulder, saying, "Do get on with it, Tony, if you have proof. Grover seems restless."

"Sophie," Grover said, staring up at the marchioness with beseechment in his goggling eyes, "stop your sons, please, for they're tormenting an old man."

She mutely shook her head, but there was confusion and fear over her face. "Tony, do you have proof that he had anything to do with Cecilia's death?"

Anne met the marquess's gaze. Because of their tiff on the stairs, she hadn't told him of the confirmation she had received from Robbie about Cecilia sending a note to Hiram Grover on the very day she was murdered, a note Anne suspected asked him to meet Cecilia, to accede to her blackmail. They had earlier deduced that Cecilia figured out Grover was responsible for the slaughtered sheep, a crime for which Jamey was afraid *he* would be blamed because of his use of the wolf costume. Nor had Anne had time to tell him of her speaking with Ellen and her confirmation of their theory of what happened to her.

She leaned close to his ear and murmured to him briefly all she had learned. He squeezed her arm in exultation, and Anne stared up at him, distracted by just how dangerously attractive she found him in that moment, handsome, as always, but triumphantly doing what was right.

He turned to his mother and said, "Yes, madam, I do have proof."

"He's lying, Sophie," Grover cried. "You, above all people, should know my measure." He stared at the marchioness with an unwavering gaze, and there was something in his eyes that Anne thought was different than the appeal one might expect; it almost seemed a threatening expression, but the woman shrugged and shook her head. It was an odd little exchange, and Anne stored it in her memory to mull over later.

Tony turned toward the door and said loudly, "Sanderson, bring them in!"

Anne's burly groom pulled in, by the scruff of their necks, William Spottiswode and Jamey. Some of the ladies fell back and gasped, while the men turned angry stares toward the marquess.

"What do you mean by subjecting our wives to the foul presence of this... this monster?" Benjamin Jenkins asked, flinging one hand out toward Spottiswode.

"Darkefell, you have gone too far," Pomfroy blustered. "How can you justify stealing a prisoner away from my cells? Who authorized such a thing?"

"No one. But if you listen, you'll agree that I have, indeed, brought a murderer into the midst of this gathering, by inviting Hiram Grover."

Several voices began speaking at once, clamoring, asking questions, demanding answers. The marquess put up his hand as Grover, pale now, sweated in his chair, John's heavy hands still on his shoulder.

"Let's leave, Jenkins—I want to go home," Mrs. Lily Jenkins said, her voice clear but trembling.

"Go if you wish, Jenkins," the marquess said. "But remember what you have heard from Mr. Allengate of your wife's dealings with Mrs. Holderness and how she's responsible for an innocent woman, Bess Parker, being held on a charge of theft. Mrs. Jenkins broke into that woman's home and planted the only evidence of her supposed thievery, just because you happened to speak with Mrs. Parker one day on the street, and someone told her about it."

The marquess paused, then with a quick glance at Richard Allengate, said in a softer tone, "And then ask her about Fanny Allengate and the girl's diary, which she purloined from Allengate's home and filled with poisonous lies about that inoffensive young lady's supposed 'affair' with me. During a bereavement visit after Miss Allengate's tragic death, she returned the tainted journal to its hiding spot. I invited you both here tonight because I wished Miss Fanny Allengate publicly vindicated." He swept his gaze over everyone gathered. "She and I were not involved in any illicit affair, nor did we meet secretly. She was innocent in every sense of the word. Mrs. Lily Jenkins is a young lady who will stop at nothing where she fears her husband's emotions engaged. She was jealous of Miss Allengate, and she was jealous of Bess Parker."

Lily Jenkins shrank next to her husband. "Lies, Benjamin, all lies."

Darkefell said, his voice hard with anger but his manner restrained, "Not lies, madam, the truth. You fail to recognize it, perhaps, because you abuse it, and so it is no friend of yours."

"I'm the one who told Lily Jenkins about Fanny's admiration of you, my lord," Miss Beatrice Lange spoke up, staring at him. "I n–never thought she'd use it so... never suspected..." She trailed off and covered her face with both her hands. The vicar's wife rushed to her side and held her.

"Miss Lange," the marquess said gently, "even if you had not told her such a thing, she would have figured it out or found something else to use against Miss Allengate, so vicious was her jealousy. But enough about Mrs. Lily Jenkins's sordid behavior. It bears repeating only that Miss Allengate and I had no affair. She was an innocent maiden, who merely indulged in the kind of daydreams in which girls will apparently indulge."

He cast a wicked glance at Anne, and she coolly returned the look. He would not make her blush, she was determined.

He then swept his gaze around the company. "Tonight's gathering would serve several purposes, I thought, but the most important is still extant—the guilt of Hiram Grover in the murder of Cecilia Wainwright." He turned and summoned Jamey to him. Sanderson, for the time being, stayed a respectful distance away with Spottiswode still in his powerful clutches. "Jamey," the marquess said as the young man approached him, "did I not catch you and one of the other stable lads frightening serving girls with a hideous wolf costume?"

"Yes, sir," he said.

His youthful good looks appeared jaded and coarse by candlelight, Anne thought.

"It was an elaborate charade, indeed, for the costume was more than just a pelt—it had a full mask made of papier maché. I know, since I was wearing it when it was incinerated," he said with a sideways grin at Anne. "And where did you say you got the costume?"

"Told you we made it, milord."

"And that was a lie, was it not?" The groom nodded, and Darkefell went on: "And where did you really get it, as you *finally* told me just yesterday?"

"From Mr. Grover, milord."

"Mr. Grover, for whom you worked before my farm tenant, Dandy Lincoln, hired you? Mr. Grover, who paid you to leave his employ and wheedle your way into mine as a spy and informer?"

The stablehand nodded.

The marquess turned to Hiram Grover. "I do wonder, sir, where you got such a costume?"

"If that costume came from my home," he said

with an attempt at nonchalance, "then it is an old one from when my son and you and your brothers engaged in amateur theatrics."

"The wolf from Perrault's Red Riding Hood," Lady Darkefell gasped. She turned to her son. "Tony, do you not remember? The wolf costume that Mrs. Grover made."

"I do remember, now that you speak of it," he said.

"Then that farmhand stole it from me!" Grover thundered, pointing at Jamey.

"No, I din't!" Jamey hollered. "Squire Grover give it t'me an' tolt me t'be seen a'wearin' it couple'times."

"But why?" Darkefell said, stabbing his finger at Grover. "Why pass it to onto your former stablehand?"

Grover remained silent and turned his face away, assuming, from what Anne could see of his fleshy countenance, an expression of dignified loathing and distaste.

"I'll tell you why," Darkefell said, glancing around the room. "He has waged an insidious war against my family, and more specifically, myself and Mr. Boatin, in his anger over my stopping his nefarious scheme to collect insurance money to which he was not entitled."

"Lies," Grover bellowed.

"Not lies! The truth, and well you know it," Anne said, her voice cold.

"Ridiculous to imply that I would willfully attack a friend in such a base way," Grover said into space. "For how could I harm him without harming his mother?"

The marchioness stared at him, her eyes wide with terror.

Darkefell went on, "The fact that you did not

have the wolf costume in your possession does explain, though, why a tuft of fur found by Cecilia's Wainwright's murdered body was *not* from the wolf costume but from another fur, a robe found in the cave by Staungill Force."

"That proves I had nothing to do with it!" Grover cried. "I have *never* been up to those falls."

"It doesn't prove any such thing, even if we believe you," Anne said. "Just because the fur robe was found up at the falls does not mean it was there when the piece was cut from it, does it? It is a movable object. You cut the tuft but then discarded the fur robe, as you did not want it associated with you or your house. Unfortunately, some poor wretch—Neddy Carter, perhaps—found it and carted it up to the cave to use for warmth."

"A framework of lies!" Grover said.

"I don't understand what any of this means," Pomfroy said impatiently. "And I don't know why, my lord, you have gathered us all here to listen to such things that make no sense to any of us."

Darkefell motioned to Sanderson, who dragged Spottiswode forward. "William Spottiswode, you have publicly stated that you murdered Cecilia Wainwright. Do you affirm that statement now?"

Shivering, the wretch shook his head. "No. No, I dint do't."

"But you did kill, did you not?"

"Sheep! Nobutt sheep!" he cried out. "Squire Grover tolt me I could 'ave whatsomever I wanted out t'wine keeper, so I kilt sheep, his'n, some others, an' I drank an' drank 'til I was near 'nuff blind. Den I heard about t'girl being kilt up here t'markwis's place, I t'ought… did I kill'er? So I sed it in me cups, but I dint, I swear't. I kilt sheep, but niver yon maiden. Squire tolt me yon blackamoor kilt 'er."

"How *could* you have killed Cecilia?" Darkefell said. "Your landlady, after close questioning, was able to state with some assurance that you were lying in your room that night, passed out from drink, one of those bottles of potent wine that Mr. Hiram Grover so obligingly gave you clutched in your paw—some of the finest wine I have seen in England, brought from his Italian odyssey when he was a traveling purchaser for a wine merchant before his fortunate inheritance of his estate."

"So I gave the drunk some bottles of wine!" Grover said, lumbering out of the chair, driven to defend himself against the mounting evidence.

Lord John stood back as his wife called out to him, her faint voice quavering.

Grover's cheeks burned red, but his clenched fists showed white knuckles. "I'm leaving this dreadful county, this dark corner of benighted England. I might as well dispose of the wine, for how can I store so much in the cottage to which I have been forced by this powerful man's ravening hunger for my land?" he said, waving one hand toward the marquess.

Murmuring among the crowd broke out.

"Aye, ask him about that," Grover said, glancing around at his neighbors. "His lordship has agreed to purchase my land for a pittance after driving me purposely into bankruptcy with his evil vengeance for some imagined slight."

"Imagined slight?" Darkefell shouted, his voice

hoarse with emotion. "I imagined no slight, nor did I imagine the slaughter of a score of Africans by your own men on the high seas near Jamaica and then your insolent attempt to collect insurance money on them." He stalked over to Grover and shook his fist in his face. "*Horrors* I have suffered in the night and in the day, the remembered screams of dozens of helpless, ill, enslaved humans ringing in my ears... yes, I say humans... *people!* And if I've suffered, I can only imagine the nightmares Osei Boatin endures after seeing his fellow slaves murdered *en masse*."

Darkefell turned to the vicar, who stood with his wife and Beatrice Lange. "Those people, the slaves... they're our brothers and sisters, are they not, Reverend?" he said, his voice ringing out in agitation. "Is this man," he said, flinging his hand out toward Osei, "not the living embodiment of God's grace?"

He whirled, the fierce anger in his dark eyes, frightening to see for some, Anne supposed, but thrilling to her, for it was clean anger, burning bright through the filthy deeds of Hiram Grover, and it shone as powerfully as a lamp lighting a revolting, dirty corner.

"You," he growled in Grover's face, "followed the murder of a score of Africans with the murder of a girl who did nothing more to you than foolishly demand money in exchange for silence." He stopped abruptly and glanced around. "Cecilia was a clever girl. She figured out about the sheep that Grover paid Spottiswode to kill, you see," he said to the others, his tone calmer. "She carried this fellow's child," he said, pointing his finger at Jamey. "And she wanted more than the life of a shamed maid carrying a bastard child—she wanted the honored position of wife and mother, and money to purchase a livery stable so that Jamey could use his talent with horses.

"She didn't know Grover was bankrupt—none of us did—so she threatened him with exposure of his sheep killing. She sent him a note by an illiterate stableboy to meet her, and Grover did, but instead of giving her money, he murdered her and left behind things he hoped would make it look like either I or my brother were guilty: a tuft of fur from a robe he hoped would be taken as the wolf costume he already knew I was using in my charade as the werewolf, and a bit of gold chain filched from John's pilfered pocket watch. And to kill the girl, he used my mother's own garden implement, stolen from her greenhouse."

Lady Darkefell turned, a look of horror on her face. "Hiram, you did this?"

"I did not! It is the basest lie."

"It was a fool's plot, and only an abject fool would think it could succeed," Anne said, speaking up finally. "But he might be able to deny it if Ellen Henderson, who thought to take up blackmail from Cecilia, had died at his hands, as she was supposed to and as he thought she did. But she's alive," Anne cried triumphantly. "She's alive and has pointed out Mr. Hiram Grover as her attacker."

Grover went white, and for a bulky man, reacted swiftly. He bolted for the door, but Sanderson, quick moving when he cared to be, tackled him and threw him down.

Twenty-Four

CHAOS ENSUED; ANNE FELT AS IF SHE WAS THE CALM center of a maelstrom.

Lydia screamed and fainted. Darkefell leaped to Sanderson's aid, bending Grover's arm behind him and hauling him to his feet. The murderer still blustered, but Darkefell shouted that it was over; Ellen Henderson was conscious and had confirmed everything they had just said. If Grover had not killed Cecilia, he would have had no reason to try to kill *her*.

Pomfroy shouted questions while the vicar prayed aloud, raising his voice to be heard over the din. He must believe God to be hard of hearing, Anne thought. Lady Sophie sat in the chair Grover had vacated, her head down; Miss Beatrice Lange, concern writ on her pretty round face, advanced to the woman and hung over her, finally kneeling by her and gazing up into the older woman's face. The vicar's wife approached Miss Lange and Lady Darkefell, and ordered Andrew, the hovering footman, to summon the marchioness's abigail and have the housekeeper bring cool water and a cloth.

She took charge of the large household with remark-able efficiency, earning Anne's admiration.

Lily Jenkins stood with her husband away from the chaos, and the two spoke earnestly. Finally the young woman threw herself into her husband's arms, and he hugged her.

Anne's primary concern was Lydia, who regained consciousness as the commotion calmed—Sanderson bundled Grover away as Darkefell explained every-thing to the magistrate and vicar. This time Anne thought Lydia's faint real, not manufactured to avoid answering awkward questions or distasteful visitors. Anne hesitantly approached the married couple and said to Lord John, "I'm concerned about Lydia's health. She should see a physician. If you do not like Doctor Younghusband, with whom Lord Darkefell is acquainted, I will gladly accompany her to Bath to consult my mother's physician, a gentleman famous for his cures."

"Oh, for heaven's sake," Lady Darkefell said, rousing herself enough to look up from her misery, the pool of lamplight shed on her showing her ravaged face swollen with emotion and wet from tears. "Lydia is well."

"I don't think so, my lady," Anne said, frowning over at the heartless woman. Who could gaze at poor, pale Lydia and think she was in perfect health? "She's excessively fragile and so full of sensibility that—"

"Pish-tush," the marchioness said briskly, shrugging off Miss Lange's comforting hands. "She's with child, nothing more."

With child. Those words from the marchioness stopped the remaining hubbub—Sir Trevor querulously harangued the marquess while Spottiswode pleaded for mercy—and all faces turned toward Lady Darkefell.

The marchioness sighed deeply and said, "If the girl had a jot of common sense, she would have known. Cecilia suspected, just as she knew *she* was enceinte. She whispered it to Mrs. Hailey, who asked me. Given the signs, I said it likely was true and have been watching since, waiting for the featherbrain to realize it. Why should she need to be told every little thing? I knew almost immediately when my boys were given to me. She will be quite, *quite* all right, if she will just realize it." She sighed with great weariness and put her hand over her eyes, slumping back in her chair. Miss Lange tactfully withdrew from a family moment.

Lord Darkefell advanced to his brother and took his hand, shaking it heartily. "Congratulations, John. Have a girl, first, will you?" He winked at Anne, who was still in some shock.

Looking back at the nausea and faintness, Anne wondered why it had never occurred to her that Lydia was going to have a baby. She looked up into her friend's face and was surprised to see fear. "Lydia," she said, reaching out and touching her arm. "My dear, don't be afraid. You're a healthy girl and will be fine." With a firm look, she took in the marchioness in her glance and said, "And you have your mother-in-law, who is experienced in such matters, to help. Isn't that so, Lady Darkefell?"

"Yes, of course," the woman said, not uncovering her eyes. "Of course."

It had been an eventful night, but it was finally over. Pomfroy had been threatened into taking Hiram Grover into custody, though he seemed reluctant and still expressed doubts even after Darkefell took him over their reasoning, step-by-step. Even the evidence of Ellen Henderson, who had met Grover to demand blackmail and was almost killed for her effrontery, did not convince him. Murder, in Pomfroy's eyes, was a crime of the lower classes. Grover, even in trade as he was, was still closer to being a gentleman than the servants who accused him.

Lydia rested comfortably now that she knew her husband was not only not a murderer but, more importantly to her, had never kissed Cecilia. Ellen Henderson had tearfully admitted she made that up just to get her rival for Jamey's affections, the lovely and intelligent Cecilia, in trouble and, she hoped, banished from Ivy Lodge.

Dinner, such as it was, was not much in demand. The marchioness did her best, herding those left into the dining room, but appetites were not large, and some simply sat in mortified silence, Mrs. Lily Jenkins the most noticeable of those. She would speak to no one except to deny the worst charge against her, of pilfering Fanny Allengate's journal and altering it; the couple left first, directly after the last remove. The vicar and his wife were the last to leave, and Mr. Sydney, at the door, murmured his good-byes to Lady Darkefell. As Anne hung back in the shadows, watching, he trailed off as he began to expound on a "delightful evening with congenial company." That polite social fiction was absurd, even when offered by the stuffy little vicar.

There were still a lot of questions in Anne's fevered brain. It was late, but as the marquess said good-bye to his mother, Anne took him aside. "I'm still confused on a couple of points, Darkefell," she said as she walked to the door with him.

He glanced toward his mother, who was speaking with Mrs. Hailey, and murmured, "As I know you are fond of late-night strolls, meet me outside once the household is quiet."

And so, as the full moon rose in the sky, Anne slipped from the house by way of the garden door, a method of egress that led one through the kitchen garden and beyond. Her heart began to pound uncomfortably as she spotted the marquess standing alone near the end of the garden, moonlight touching his gleaming dark hair with spots of brightness.

"You've come," he said softly as she approached. He took her hand and led her through the kitchen garden and into his mother's rose garden.

"How much are we really sure of?" she asked as they strolled down a graveled path. She was acutely aware of the feel of his warm hand enclosing hers. "There seems to be so much left unsolved. Starting with Tilly Landers's death at the falls. And Fanny Allengate… how did *she* die? Can we lay these other crimes at Hiram Grover's feet?"

He frowned, his strong features softened by the glamour of moonlight. "I've always wondered if Tilly was simply meeting someone, as she ofttimes did, and fell to her death. The cave above the falls is not so far from town, you know, by way of a commonly traversed pathway and suited, as you saw, for a lovers' trysting spot."

"So…" She hesitated; she was treading on delicate ground here. "Why did your brother claim he saw her fall?"

"He was trying to protect me."

"How did that protect you, to say that he had seen her fall?" He was silent; she stopped and withdrew her hand from his. She already knew the answer but wanted him to say it. "My lord, why did he think he would be protecting you? What had you to do with Tilly Landers?"

His expression was grim, and he said, "Do you know, in general I don't give a damn what people think of me." He turned and gazed down at her. "But I care about your opinion, my lady. I care what you know of me, what you think of me."

"Is not the simplest way to ensure I understand your past and your present, your motives and your actions, is to explain them to me?" she said, her heart throbbing at the idea that he should care so greatly what she thought of him. She searched his eyes.

"Perhaps. I've never deigned to throw the cloak of godliness over my actions. I'm just a man and cannot claim an unblemished past."

"My experience has been," she said tartly, "that those who *do* claim an unblemished past are those most likely to have much of which to be ashamed. Hiram Grover claimed virtue, but his hands are stained with blood. I deeply distrust that 'cloak of godliness,' as you call it."

Silence. The moonlight was just strong enough to delineate his profile, the saturnine twist to the lips, the grim set of his square jaw. She prodded him, saying, "Was there a connection between you and Miss Landers? Is that why your brother thought he needed to protect you from the accusation that you had contributed to the young woman's death? Is that why Jacob Landers hates you?"

"How perceptive you are," he murmured, "and how I wish, at this moment, that you were the dullest, least-imaginative creature on earth."

"But how pleased I am that your wishes are not fact. I shouldn't like to be dull, my lord."

He laughed out loud and shot her a glance of appreciation. "Always, even in my grimmest moments of self-flagellation, you can make me laugh."

But she would not be diverted. "You openly stated that you had no connection with Miss Allengate, and so it was easy to see that, if she did not write the journal entries herself, they must have been writ by someone else. We now know that is so and that Mrs. Jenkins, in her jealousy over an old rival, did so."

As Anne had whispered to Darkefell in the Ivy Lodge drawing room, that was one puzzle Ellen Henderson was able to solve; Grover, as he throttled her, gloated over his various actions to destroy Darkefell's reputation and peace of mind. Among them, he subtly directed Lily Jenkins, suggesting to her that, as Fanny had already confessed her infatuation with the marquess to her, perhaps Lily could make a fool of the girl she feared her husband still loved, by using secret letters. Fanny, an imaginative and sensitive girl, believed the anonymous notes she received to be from the marquess and saw their secret correspondence as that between star-crossed lovers, unable to openly acknowledge their passion because of their differences in status.

Anne could only imagine that Grover thought to accuse the marquess of misleading the girl, forcing him to publicly repudiate her, but she tragically died before that scheme bore fruit. Lily, after Fanny's death, had taken it a step further with Grover's suggestion that, to be sure she was not caught as the writer of the anonymous notes, she should cover her tracks. So she pilfered the journal, ripped out two pages, and added a few entries suggesting that Fanny and Darkefell had finally met and consummated their affair. This was to throw suspicion on the marquess if any of Lily's fake letters to Fanny were ever found. It was a vicious, disgusting scheme that could only have come from a depraved mind, Anne thought. She hoped someone would find a way to make Lily Jenkins pay for the attempted destruction of two reputations: Fanny's posthumously, with the disgusting journal entries, and Darkefell's, by suggesting he had taken advantage of a fragile and innocent young woman, perhaps leading to her suicide.

Anne absolved Lily Jenkins only of *knowing* she was being used by Hiram Grover, who had his own desire to destroy the marquess. Lily Jenkins had much to answer for—her cruel plot against Bess Parker was tantamount to attempted murder—but that was not Anne's responsibility to prosecute.

The marquess had been silent, brooding, as he stared at the ground, and Anne went on, "Your unwillingness to be equally frank about Miss Landers as you were about Fanny Allengate leads me to believe… to conjecture… " She trailed off, watching him and waiting for him to confess his involvement with the barmaid.

He finally said, "She was my mistress, yes, for a couple of autumnal weeks. My sensual needs sated, my fastidiousness would not stand more than that."

In a low and trembling voice, Anne said, "Do not criticize the young woman whose favors you no doubt eagerly sought while the fever was upon you. It's not fair! Nor is it gentlemanly."

"How perfectly you judge, my lady," he said, his voice harsh with anger, "that about which you know nothing."

"I know people," she said, facing him and glaring into his eyes. "I know women and serving girls, and I know they have hearts to break and spirits to crush." She turned away, ready to go back in, and said, "I have no stomach for this conversation now, my lord."

"Stop! We've wandered away from my point," he said, grasping her arm and turning her back. He stared down at her in the faint moonlight. "I am loath to damage myself in your eyes. I fear you're a harsh judge and may not give allowance for male weakness. I would never say to a woman that she must have only one bonnet in her life and that she should never sample other bonnets, trying them on, even purchasing one or two."

She examined him dispassionately then pointedly pulled her arm from his grasp. "If you think to entertain me with your glib tongue, you're misguided. Such an analogy is specious and immoral, and for the first time, I question your principles. A flaw sincerely confessed and honestly abjured I would excuse—a love affair is no more than a weakness. But to compare the poor girl to an inanimate object, to be used and tossed aside… *that* I cannot countenance."

"Self-righteousness ill suits you, madam," he said through gritted teeth.

"And idiocy ill suits you, my lord. Be a man, not a boy." She started to walk away, but he grabbed her, turned her toward him, and pressed his lips to hers, pulling her so close she could not breathe.

So she bit his lip.

He reared away from her with a loud yell of pain and touched his bleeding lip with two fingers. "Why did you do that?"

"For the same reason Irusan scratches when he's being held against his will. I did it to get loose."

"Don't try to tell me, my lady, that you dislike my kisses," he said with a throaty growl, "for I know very well that's a lie." He took a step toward her.

She took a step back. "I like strawberries, my lord, but they make me break out in red patches. They're bad for me, so I have concluded that I can live without them." She whirled and strode away.

He didn't follow.

Blindly, she wandered out of the garden along a gravel path, climbing above the Ivy Lodge gardens. Her abject misery surprised her. Hot tears bubbled in her eyes, coursing down her face in thick streams. Some women were blessed with the ability to cry prettily, with trembling lips and delicate sobs, but Anne's throat closed, and great choking sobs sounding like the cries of a wounded animal emitted from her, while mucous clogged her nose and dribbled out, hanging in ugly strings. She had no choice but to wipe her nose with her lace tucker.

But after a few moments, anger overtook her wretchedness. What was she crying about? Yes, he had disappointed her, but she had lost nothing. And *she* hadn't done anything of which to be ashamed. Unblemished reflection on her own behavior must be her solace. She straightened her back, stopped weeping, and strode a ways, for she could not go back to Ivy Lodge until she had cleansed herself of her unhappiness.

So as the gravel path changed to pounded dirt under her feet, then became narrower as it wound through a copse and grassy beyond that, she walked, blessing the brilliant moonlight and taking full advantage of her anger to speed her. Clouds now shrouded the moon, but the effect was to spread the white moonlight into a glowing ceiling above her, giving the effect of a brighter light. What hold did that man have on her? Nothing more than physical attraction, she decided. Yes, he made her weak when he kissed her, and she loved to look at him; he was gorgeous, as much as any sculpture of David or depiction of Zeus, but that was the full extent of it.

And yet… she slowed as she reconsidered. There *was* more to him, to be completely fair and honest. He was witty, intelligent, thoughtful. She could make him laugh, and that gave her pleasure. He was deeply sensitive to the plight of others, as exemplified by his care for Osei, but could be maddeningly obtuse at other times.

Why had he kissed her yet *again?* She had concluded that he used his intoxicating power of attraction to confuse her; but was he a born philanderer who would use that power just because he could? She had seen Irusan kill a snake once, not for food and not because the creature was a threat, but just because it amused him to do so and because he could. Did Darkefell kiss her for the same reason? Did it amuse him to feel her tremble in his arms?

Infuriating man. Maddening man!

She strode on but looked up finally to find that she had come quite a distance, and she was lost. The area looked vaguely familiar, but somehow different. Had she even been down this path before? She stopped and tried to take her bearings; the roar of rushing water warned her that she was near Staungill Force. She had approached it from a different direction last time in the pony cart with Darkefell. How far she had come! It would never do to trip around up near the falls in the middle of the night.

She turned, orienting herself so she would head back to Ivy Lodge and not get lost again, grateful that the trees were not yet in full leaf and so didn't block the moonlight or throw much beyond spidery, dark gray shadows. She took a step, but a sudden noise in the bushes near the woods startled her. She lost her footing on damp leaves that littered the path, tripping over a branch and landing on her bottom, her skirts tangled about her legs. A disheveled man lurched out from among the trees and, as she tried to rise, she skidded, her feet slipping as she tried to get a purchase on the muddy ground. He was dirty and wigless, his clothes askew and missing his jacket, but she knew in an instant it was Hiram Grover.

She screeched and gasped the first thing that came to mind, shouting, "How did you escape?"

He stared at her, mumbling something that at first she didn't understand; it became clearer as he repeated it: "… and thank You for delivering mine enemies into mine hands, oh, Lord, amen."

His face gleamed with perspiration, and his eyes protruded even more than usual. With the absence of his wig and his cheeks beet red, his face looked like a horrible mask. "I'm not your enemy, Mr. Grover." She untangled her skirts with one hand and propped herself up with the other; her skirt caught on the branch, and she tugged unsuccessfully, trying to free herself.

"The friend of my enemy is my enemy," he said. He lurched forward and enveloped her in a hug, yanking her to her feet and marching her up the path. The sound of the falls became louder, a dull roar in her ears.

"Let me go," she shouted, kicking as best she could with the damnable weight of skirts around her ankles. He was throwing her off balance.

Her horror grew as the sound of the falls became louder in her ears. She was not going to let him toss her from the top of Staungill Force, and that was what she feared he intended to do. She elbowed him in his paunch, and he expelled a loud gust of air, but his hold didn't loosen. As portly as he was, she never expected him to be so strong. In another few moments, they'd both go over the falls!

"Let me go. Let me go!" she screamed, thrashing about.

The keening howl she had heard twice before rent the night air; it had always before signaled a woman attacked! Grover stilled momentarily but then launched into action with greater vigor, dragging her and lugging her as she struggled to get free and made herself a dead weight in turn, desperately trying to break his manic hold on her.

Nothing helped. *Reason,* her brain implored her, *reason with him.* "Grover," she said, her voice strangled by his choke hold. "Listen to me. You're free—you should run! Get away. I'll help," she said, desperation lacing her choked voice. "My driver will take you anywhere."

He seemed beyond the sound of her voice, driven so far within himself by rage that he was single-minded in his actions. The keening howl again cut through the night, and the sound of his wheezing breaths and her own gurgling choking joined with the roar of the raging waterfall. Her blood pounded in her ears. Despite the brief pause the howl invoked in her captor, he was determined still, and now they were above the falls.

"God have mercy on your soul!" Grover shouted, his voice hoarse with exhaustion.

"I am *not* going to die!" Anne stepped on his foot, hard. When his grasp loosened momentarily, she twisted away from him and began to run, but he threw himself at her and caught her skirt. She fell on the lip of the slippery, mossy precipice and cried out in terror.

The next few moments were a welter of confused sensations.

Some kind of animal leaped out of the bushes and tackled Grover, who yelped in fear. A man or men—it was hard to tell in the dark among the shadows of the overhanging bushes—moved forward. Amidst the barking, shouting, howling, tangled confusion, Anne crawled away from the lip of the waterfall, the torrential sound filling her head until she couldn't even hear her own labored breathing.

She rolled over on her back and could finally see that Darkefell had hold of Grover. They rolled over and over, Grover grunting and Darkefell shouting at him to give up, until they were close to the falls. Anne struggled to her feet, but just as she was bolting toward the pair, her foot slipped sideways on some moss dampened by the spray of the waterfall; she began to slide down the slope toward irrevocable doom.

Darkefell saw her slip, and the horror on his face, shadowed by moonlight, twisted it out of recognition. He wrenched himself free from Grover, who stood, staggered sideways, and, with a terrible yell, trembled on the cusp of the precipice for one agonizing moment; then he disappeared, falling into the torrent.

But the marquess didn't hesitate for one moment, pelting over to Anne and pulling her to safety. She landed on top of him, and he clutched her close, smothering her with a breathless kiss. She hammered on his shoulder and turned her face away. "Let me breathe, you idiot!"

He stood then and pulled her to her feet. "I thought you were gone," he said. He pulled her into his arms and held her against his pounding heart. "I thought you were gone," he said, a guttural note in his husky voice.

For a long few moments they stood thus, one of his arms holding her close to him and the free hand threaded through her tumbled hair. She didn't want to move; his grasp was warm, powerful, reassuring, and she did not want to face the awful fact of Hiram Grover's fall from Staungill Force.

He held her head against his shoulder and said gruffly, "You'll marry me now, I've made up my mind about that. You *need* marital shackles just to keep you out of trouble."

She pulled away from him. "What are you talking about, Darkefell?"

His expression grim, he said, "You'll marry me. Soon. We'll go see Sydney in the morning and have him arrange it. Or I'll ride over to Richmond and get the bishop. I don't care which."

She swallowed. It seemed indelicate, after what they had just been through and how he had pulled her back from the brink of disaster, to tell him he was being a fool. But marriage? "We must go and find out what has happened to Grover," she said, pulling out of his arms.

But he held her arm firmly as they descended through the encroaching darkness. The moon was traveling across the sky, and the light filtered through the still-bare tree limbs, shaded to darker gray, as they picked their way along the treacherous path. It took all of their attention, and so neither spoke until Anne remembered the moments before Grover's dive off the waterfall.

"Darkefell, what was the creature that launched itself at Grover? It was too big for a dog. And... was there someone else with you?"

He paused for a moment as they negotiated a tricky hump in the path then said, "That was Eddie Carter's son—Daft Neddy, he's called—and the fellow's dog, that's all, a mastiff named Bull. Enormous beast, even for a mastiff. Pure luck he's been around lately. Neddy has had his troubles, but he's a good fellow at heart. Shy though. He disappeared once he knew I had taken care of everything."

How convenient, Anne thought, and how glib the marquess's explanation. Did she believe it? Her tired mind was too weary to con it over. They reached the bottom of the waterfall, but it was too dark to find anything or anyone. She glanced around fearfully. "Could Grover have survived?"

"No," Darkefell said, putting his arm around her shoulders. "Let's not speak of that. You're shivering—I must get you back to Ivy Lodge."

"How did Grover get away from Pomfroy's custody?" Anne asked as she let him lead her away. He was right; no one could search for Grover's body as the moon set and the dark closed in around them.

"I don't know, but I'll find out tomorrow," he answered grimly. "I gave strictest orders to have him confined and watched. Too late now."

Returning to a silent house after the drama of the evening was an anticlimax for Anne. She knew she wouldn't sleep a wink, but Darkefell would have much to do, and she must let him go. In the shadowed alcove that sheltered the garden door of Ivy Lodge, he took her in his arms and gazed down into her face. "Do you wish me to speak to your father," he said quietly, "or do you wish to just get married and take in your parents as a part of our wedding journey?"

She pulled herself out of his grasp and pushed him away. Either he was toying with her, in which case she despised him, or he was serious, and in that case she thought him the greatest fool who had ever walked the earth. By his own admission, the only reason he wanted to marry her was to keep her safe; as ridiculous as that seemed to her, she supposed it must be true, for he certainly hadn't given any other reasons. They barely knew each other. "Go home, Darkefell." She turned away.

"What do you mean? Don't turn away from me!" he said, roughly turning her back around.

"I mean, go *home!*" She pulled out of his grasp and entered, closing the door firmly behind her.

Twenty-Five

"Good-bye, my dear," Anne said, hugging a tearful Lydia at the door of Ivy Lodge the next morning. "Since you and John are coming to Bath in two months to consult Dr. Haggerty, I will go to my grandmother's then, and we'll have a lovely visit. Mother will be there, delighted to see you as always, and will fuss over you and make you take the waters." She set her friend firmly away from her and stared into her lovely eyes, keeping her hands on her shoulders. "Until then, listen to your husband and go visit Mrs. Patterson, the Darkefell nanny," she said with a little shake. "It was she who nursed Lord John and his brothers through all of their childhood injuries, and she was also midwife to Lady Darkefell. You'll find no wiser, nor any more suited informant, to give you all the reassurance you need about having a baby."

"Do you have to go," Lydia said, her voice clogged with unshed tears, "so hurriedly after that dreadful scene last night?"

Anne had visited Lydia first thing after a sleepless night and told her all about the evening before, leaving out, of course, all that related to dealings between herself and Lord Darkefell. Luckily, Lydia was either the most incurious of creatures, or it just never occurred to her to wonder why Anne went walking so late at night or what Lord Darkefell was doing out at the same time. "I *do* have to go. I came here for a purpose that is now satisfied. I'd like to go away for a while and forget last night's violence."

"Are you sure you were not terribly hurt?" Lydia said, searching her eyes. "I should be in hysterics if that was me, up on the waterfall with that dreadful Mr. Grover."

"I'm perfectly fine. A little sore on the bottom, and a few bruises, but otherwise fit as a fiddle."

The marquess had not yet found the man's body, those at Ivy Lodge had heard at a late breakfast, and so he and others were searching farther along the rain-swollen river, thinking Grover could have been swept quite a ways downstream. It gave enough time for Mary to pack Anne's trunks, and for her to get away. Cowardly she may be, but she didn't think she could bear another scene between her and Darkefell after his shattering announcement the previous night. She had left a brief note for him with Mrs. Hailey.

"If you stay, we could enjoy time together." Lydia sniffed as tears rolled down her smooth cheeks. "You could recover here. Why go *now* just when I need you most?"

Anne just shook her head. What could she say? A shouted proposal of marriage from an enraged marquess was not something she could easily explain. It wasn't even a proposal really, more like a command.

Nor could she explain her curious reaction to it. For one dreadful moment, held firmly in his arms, thoroughly kissed, drugged with the warmth of his arms, she had contemplated saying "*yes*." That both alarmed and infuriated her. After all that Darkefell said, to still be attracted to him?

No, she *had* to leave, if just to save herself from herself. When she was young and foolish, she had been swept into an engagement when she wasn't sure, but never again. She had been saved from that disaster by her fiancé's death; she could not count on such luck a second time. Darkefell seemed the kind of fellow who would live until eighty or beyond.

"I'm going now," she said firmly. "Go back to your room and rest."

Lydia said a final, tearful farewell and was guided upstairs by her doting husband. Anne watched the footman take her trunks out to her carriage, grateful that Lord Darkefell would not know she was gone until afternoon.

At least there was no witness to his "proposal," or whatever one called it. In the eyes of the world, he was a perfect matrimonial prospect: wealthy, titled, healthy, attractive. But despite her obvious attraction to him, he was not the kind of man she had pictured marrying. He was no scholar, nor a crusader, and as much good as he had done in saving Osei Boatin's life, they just wouldn't suit. She was not going to marry for an establishment of her own and to satisfy the requirements of a society that ridiculed unmarried women. There would be benefits to marrying Lord Darkefell, and they didn't stop at his wealth and position, for the man had an undeniable physical attraction. Being initiated into the delights of physical intimacy by him was a temptation beyond almost any other.

But… she was *beyond* irritated by his assumption that he could just cavalierly demand her hand and expect to be accepted. Why on earth did he think she would go along with such lunacy? No, though she was grateful that he had changed his mind about going back to the castle and had gone looking for her after their quarrel, arriving just in time to save her life, gratitude was not the basis of a good marriage, especially for two such irascible people as she and the marquess.

Lady Darkefell drifted into the entrance as the last bags were loaded, along with Mary, Robbie, and of course, Irusan; the King of Cats sat awaiting her in the carriage door.

"I wish you a pleasant journey, Lady Anne," she said stiffly.

Anne, standing by the open door, examined her curiously. The marchioness appeared drawn and weary, her face lined. But there was something more fatiguing her than the awful events of the last twenty-four hours, though Anne couldn't figure out what it was. With Anne's departure, it would remain a mystery to her. "Good-bye, my lady," Anne said with a curtsey. "Give Lord Darkefell my best wishes. Thank you for your hospitality during my stay."

Lady Darkefell examined her. "I will look after Lydia, you know, despite my poor opinion of her." She then clamped her lips tightly shut, her expression stony.

"I know you will," Anne said gently, adding, "I suspect that you will always do your duty by your family, my lady."

Tears welled in Lady Darkefell's eyes and the woman nodded, then turned away.

Anne walked out into the sunshine, a sense of freedom sweeping through her. She took Sanderson's hand, heaved herself up into the carriage, and he shut the door after her. Irusan climbed into her lap, turned once, and fell asleep as the carriage pulled away.

It was late afternoon, the sun glinting brilliantly off the diamond panes of the castle windows. Darkefell wearily descended from the pony cart and limped up to the new section of the castle as Tanner, his butler, opened the door and bowed. The other men—Dandy Lincoln, his son Ronald, and some others—were going their separate ways, but Tony had warned them to keep looking for Grover's body. Pomfroy said he'd ride down to Whaw, and a couple of villages beyond, the next morning, to warn residents about the body that had been swept downstream and have them on the lookout. There was a deep—some said bottom-less—pond a few miles downstream; if the body made it so far, it might not be discovered for some time.

Pomfroy! Darkefell could still barely bring himself to speak civilly to the old fool. It was his fault Anne's life had been endangered. The stuffy ass had been offended by Darkefell and Anne's investigative work, and when he took Grover away—he refused to confine the man to a cell at the guildhall—allowed the murdering bastard to go home until suitable quarters could be arranged. He clearly had never believed Grover guilty and took his word that he would stay at his own home, which would allow him to finalize the sale and packing of his personal goods.

Even now, Pomfroy thought that Darkefell and Lady Anne had gotten it wrong and that Hiram Grover had been driven to act "out of character," as he put it, by their cruelty. Osei, who Darkefell had judged should not be searching for Grover's corpse, given his past uneasy connection with the man, met him in the hall and helped him off with his jacket; Harwood, his valet, came hastily down the main steps just then and took the jacket, tut-tutting at its filthy state.

"The library, Osei," Darkefell muttered. "I need brandy and a chair."

"You did not find Mr. Grover?"

"No, but we'll keep looking. I have to dictate a letter to Theophilus. Despite his estrangement from his father, this is going to be a very difficult time for the fellow. Theo and I have had our differences over the years, but he's everything his father was not, in sincerity and a deep moral conviction. Telling him of his father's awful deeds and subsequent death is not an easy task."

Osei nodded, not needing any more information. The younger Grover's revulsion at his father's slave-dealing, and his horror over the incident on the ship, had been expressed in formal terms in the letter Theophilus had written to the marquess. In it, he sincerely apologized for his father's actions and moral lapses, and ended with his sincere best wishes to Osei Boatin. Darkefell had given it to Osei to read.

Osei took down the particulars of Darkefell's letter to Theophilus. It began with the delicately phrased announcement of Hiram Grover's death, but that his body was lost in the rain-swollen Staungill, and followed with the news that Darkefell would visit Theophilus himself to tell him the details. Osei suggested some better phrases and polished it with an eloquent expression of sympathy for the younger Grover's grief. He then rose to retreat and leave the marquess to his brandy.

"I'll be dining at Ivy Lodge this evening, Osei. I have particular news I wish to share with my family, but you may as well be the first to know," he said, swallowing hard. As much as this decision was all his, it still unnerved him. Though he always knew he would marry, it hadn't been in his plans for the immediate future. But as he pulled Anne back from the lip of the precipice, he knew he couldn't imagine living without her. This odd fevered emotion he thought must be love overwhelmed him; marriage was the only cure. He would practice saying it out loud: "Lady Anne Addison and I are to be married, soon."

Osei didn't appear startled so much as confused. He took off his glasses then pulled a letter from his vest pocket. "Perhaps that explains this letter, sir. I was to give it to you when you came in, but you were later than expected and I forgot. Did Lady Anne leave to go home and prepare her parents for this news?"

"What?" Tony said, frowning up at his secretary. "What are you talking about? Anne left? I don't understand."

Boatin's expression shuttered, and he said, "Lady Darkefell's housekeeper sent this note over with the stableboy and said, in a separate note to me, that Lady Anne left this morning first thing, but that she had left this for you. I suppose it explains her intentions."

Tony felt the first hint of trepidation. Had she actually agreed to marry him? He had assumed she would, even though she seemed irritated by him. She hadn't said "no," at least. What woman would say no to him? And surely she would not have let him kiss her so often, nor would she have reacted as she did if she didn't intend to accept his hand.

But she'd left? "Ah-ha," he said suddenly, sitting up straight. "She means for me to follow her! She wishes to prolong the chase, to be wooed. Very well, I'll chase her."

"Perhaps, sir," Boatin said hesitantly after Darkefell explained how he had left things with the lady, "she does not mean to marry. There are some ladies who do not wish to. Or perhaps she has been hurt some time in the past and has not yet recovered?"

Darkefell groaned and slapped his hand over his eyes. "You know what this means, don't you?" He took his hand away. "I shall have to speak to Lydia. Lady Anne was engaged to Lydia's brother several years ago, and the fellow died in battle, presumably a heroic ass. I shall have to pry from Lydia, if she can manage to string together three words that make sense, how Lady Anne feels now about her late fiancé."

First, he read Anne's note. It was little more than a stiff note of thanks for saving her life and the hope that he did not suffer any repercussions. She wished him well. It was insulting in its brevity, but he would not take it amiss.

He bathed and dressed then rode to Ivy Lodge, demanding an audience with Lydia the moment he entered. John had to be present, of course. He hung over his wife as if she were on the verge of death instead of merely enceinte, and he filled in words for her when she was tongue-tied. When Darkefell peppered Lydia with questions about Lady Anne's departure, she pouted and constantly deferred to John.

"She didn't say anything, Tony," John finally said, exasperated. "She wished us well, and when we get to Bath in June to consult Dr. Haggerty, we are to visit her at her grandmother's home there."

Darkefell stared at his brother and sister-in-law. If she had said anything at all about marriage to him, they would have said so immediately. He drilled Lydia with one of his focused looks. "Lydia, I know you were young, but think back and tell me—was Anne excessively devoted to your brother when they were engaged?"

Lydia's huge eyes filled with tears that spilled over and coursed down her cheeks. "Oh, yes," she said in breathless tones, clasping her hands together. "You've never seen such devotion. When she looked at Reggie, there was such *love* in her eyes. It was like… like someone who has seen perfection for the first time and cannot take their eyes from it," she said in a rare flight of fancy.

Darkefell had known Moore slightly and had thought him vacuous, vain, frivolous, and unbearably insipid. The man had no opinions but on fashion, gambling, and society. None of that fit with his opinion of Lady Anne, but in a rare flash of insight sharpened by a knife-thrust of jealousy, he saw how, as an eighteen-year-old girl in her first Season, Sir Reginald Gladstone Moore, a member of the Horse Guards, may have seemed the epitome of beaux. His death, not even a year later, may have wounded her deeply, as a first experience with tragedy will.

So that was what he was up against; his Anne was a determined spinster who mourned so deeply for her first love that she would not allow herself to find happiness, even if a far-superior suitor arrived to court her. He could mount an offense that would defeat such a foe. No dead fiancé could rival his determination, and he had one thing on his side, besides the little matter of being alive while Moore was dead. She was sensually attracted to him already and wanted him almost as much as he wanted her. There, at least, was a place to begin. He would storm the battlements of her chaste fortress. He strode from the room without another word to his brother and sister-in-law.

Anne drifted near sleep, gently lulled by the rocking motion of the carriage. They had been traveling for three days already, with a day-long stop for the holy day, Good Friday, and were almost at their destination, just in time for Easter service the next day.

"The sea!" Robbie cried, bouncing up and down on his seat.

Anne, jolted into complete awareness, sat up. "It's not as if you haven't seen the ocean before, Robbie," she said with an indulgent smile and wink at Mary, who was knitting a muffler for her son.

"But this be different from Kent, milady!" he shouted, peering out the glass.

Anne glanced out. It was a lovely scene, she thought, staring out the glass. This was Cornwall, and the high bluff which the road traveled told her they were almost to their destination, St. Wyllow, a village near Hell's Mouth on the north coast of Cornwall. The blue sea sparkled in the late-day sunshine. Sanderson turned the carriage around a bend in the road, angling away from the bluff, and within twenty minutes, they pulled up a lane to a manor house that was tranquil in the Cornish sunlight.

"Here, at last!" she said as Sanderson opened the carriage door and she climbed down to stretch her legs. Two days before, from a Shropshire inn, Anne had sent a note to her friend, Miss Pamela St. James, by Royal Mail, to say she was accepting Pamela's long-standing open invitation and coming for a visit. She needed a change in scene after her upsetting time in Yorkshire. Home at Kent with her father did not beckon, nor did Bath and the company of her mother and grandmother. But Pamela, as sensible as she, if many times prettier and a complete contrast to Lydia, was the kind of companionship for which she longed.

The front door of the gray stucco manor house opened, and Pamela emerged into the brilliant sunshine, accompanied by a smartly dressed gentleman.

"Pamela! St. James!" Anne cried as she swept up the steps. Her friend embraced her as her friend's dashing brother bowed, but then he, too, took her in his arms for a long hug.

"How good to see you, my lady!" he cried, holding her by the shoulders and examining her. "What a dashing bonnet! At long last, someone worthy of my expert flirtation."

Anne smiled and laughed.

"Ah, and so lovely, pink cheeks, eyes sparkling… you have been flirting with someone," he accused. "Nothing like admiration to improve a lady's color. I'm deathly jealous! Whom shall I challenge, my dearest lady?"

Oh yes, this was just the place to forget dark, thrilling Yorkshire and dark, thrilling Lord Darkefell, as well as his insulting, sublimely strange proposal and the events of the last week. Cornwall, serene and sunny, with her dear friend Pamela and St. James, a notorious but engaging flirt, who had an entertaining line of patter guaranteed to lift her spirits. "Shut up, St. James—you get more ridiculous with each passing year. Pamela, I hope you don't mind my descending upon you for a long visit."

"Not at all. We have all kinds of things to keep you busy," she said, "for with St. James's regiment billeted in St. Ives, there are assemblies, balls, picnics, strawberry-picking, parties… oh, we shall have a gay time, indeed."

Anne sighed. This was far from her preferred studious and calm life, but it would take from her mind the sensations she so desperately needed to forget: Darkefell's kisses, his powerful arms about her, and the thought that marriage to him still sounded like an adventure. She must put it all out of her mind.

She draped her arm over Pamela's shoulders and squeezed as they entered the house, followed by Irusan, who had exited the carriage and was nudging St. James's legs as he followed. St. James was a favorite of Irusan's for some reason; Anne thought the officer bribed him with treats. "You're just what I need, Pam. And you, St. James," she threw back over her shoulder, "are what *else* I need." She laughed. "So bring on your officer friends—I shall flirt and break all of their hearts," she finished with facetious sarcasm.

She sighed. One thing she could guarantee; not one of those officers would make her tremble with yearning. Thank heavens.

The End

Author's Afterword

Dear Reader,

I believe that most readers of historical novels, whether the books be mystery, romance, or straight fiction, are interested in the historical basis of the plot. With that in mind, I'd like to offer some pertinent information to those interested in knowing if there is any fact behind *Lady Anne and the Howl in the Dark*.

First: though the characters in this book are wholly constructed out of my imagination, the tale Mr. Osei Boatin tells Lady Anne about his experience on a slave ship has a factual, historical counterpart. The Zong was a slave ship owned by a Liverpool slave-trading firm. It sailed from Africa in September of 1781 overloaded with slaves. Malnutrition and illness had already claimed quite a few lives when the captain decided to cut his losses and toss the rest of the sick Africans into the ocean to drown, keeping only the still healthy on board.

Shockingly, this was not an illegal act, nor was it considered murder; the slaves were chattel, and in court proceedings later it was pointed out that this was no different than throwing horses overboard. The only illegal act was when the shipping company attempted to collect insurance money for the losses. Insurance would not cover those lost to disease, malnutrition, or suicide, nor did it cover the slaves thrown overboard. However, the ship owners argued the slaves *had* to be killed, as there was not enough water on board for everyone; that exigency would have made it an insured loss. The claim of inadequate water was proved to be wholly false; they had plenty for everyone.

The Zong Massacre became a rallying point for abolitionists in their attempt to put an end to slavery and the slave trade. It took many more years to achieve that goal.

Second: Hiram Grover's repeated mention of the Curse of Ham or Curse of Canaan is also inspired by real historical perspective. Misinterpretation of an Old Testament tale of Noah and Ham, his son, gave rise to belief in the so-called "curse" that some used to justify the African slave trade and racial segregation.

An Internet search of the keywords "The Zong Massacre" and the "Curse of Canaan" or "Curse of Ham" will turn up a wealth of information for those wanting to know more, or your local library will have informative books providing a more detailed relation of these subjects.

Fond regards,

Donna Lea Simpson

Read on for a preview of

Lady Anne
AND THE
GHOST'S
REVENGE

Available from Sourcebooks Casablanca in
August 2009

One

"What does Darkefell mean by following me to Cornwall, Mary? Why is he plaguing me so?" Anne, pacing the length of her small room in the upper reaches of Cliff House, Pamela and Marcus St. James' rented house, did not need to tell her maid what she meant, for they had already spoken of the Marquess of Darkefell at some length.

As she put away some sheets of paper into Anne's traveling desk and closed the lid, Mary gently said, "A man in love will do many a strange thing, milady."

"He's not in love with me," Anne declared, contemptuously, though the woman's words sent an odd thrill through her. "He doesn't even know me, and a man in love would not promptly try to change everything about the object of his affections, as Darkefell is trying to do to me."

Mary paused in her tidying. She hesitated for a long moment, but then said, watching Anne, "I think it would be well for you, milady, to lairn more about the man, before tossing him aside. P'raps he's just such a one as you *should* marry."

Anne gave a snort of derision, but a sound outside drew her attention; she leaned on the windowsill and stared out into the darkness. From her window she could only see a small portion of the back garden, and none of the sea. A moving shadow angled across Pamela's terrace. "Who is that?" she gasped. "And what are they up to, creeping around outside the house like that?"

With the imperious marquess's commands fresh in her mind and heart, Anne impetuously decided to do the opposite of everything he said. Even as she made the quick decision, she felt how foolish it was to be guided by negation, but an anxious trembling within her would not let her stay still. She did not want to think of what Mary had just said, that she should give serious thought to marrying Darkefell.

"I want to know what, or who, that is," Anne said, retrieving her cape, and heading for the bedroom door.

"You'll not go without me, milady," Mary said as she followed, throwing a shawl over her shoulders.

As Anne unlatched the garden door, feeling the rush of cool sea air on her face, she murmured, "Cliff House is certainly easier to leave than Ivy Lodge was." She referred to the dower house of the marquess's Yorkshire estate, where she had stayed while visiting Lydia; it was a much larger house with a regiment of servants and variety of locked doors.

She led the way out onto the terrace and paused, glancing around, her heart pounding in agitation. Whatever or whomever the shadow belonged to, it was gone now. Who could it have been? "Stay here, Mary," she whispered, putting out one hand and touching her maid's cloaked arm. "I'm just going up to the cliff to see if anything is going on."

"I'm not letting you go alone," Mary insisted, following her.

Anne crept down the garden in the moonlight, through the rickety gate and up the grassy slope to the bluff, huffing and puffing by the time she got there. She crouched and urged Mary to do the same, as they crept closer to the edge, near a stunted and twisted tree that clung to the edge of the cliff and shadowed the lip. It was too dark to see anything other than an impression of movement below. But when a lantern flashed for a moment, Anne could see that the beach was full of men.

But seconds later both Anne and Mary reared back in amazement as, out of the murky void on the cloudy night, a figure rose from beyond the edge of the cliff. It was the Barbary Ghost, so close they could almost reach out and touch it, if it truly was a substantial being! Mary shrieked in terror and started up. The Ghost whirled, howled in rage and drifted closer to them, the air between them lit up with fireworks, smoke, and flame blazing.

Mary grabbed Anne's arm and yanked her back from the cliff edge, but Anne pulled away and strode closer, just in time to see the ghost flailing, men below on the beach scuttling away from a rowboat, as on the cliff opposite Anne and Mary—the bluff that topped the other side of the deep cut—men rose from the shadowy murk and swarmed down toward the beach.

"Milady, come away, please!" cried Mary, her voice a thin wail of terror.

"No, I have to see—" Anne's words were drowned out by a burst of gunfire, then more fireworks. She tottered close to the edge, but the ghost was gone, disappeared in the drift of smoke that the sea breeze tugged and pulled, this way and that, particles glinting in the faint moonlight that peeped from behind a cloud.

"No more, milady," Mary gasped, as some more shots rang out, and shouting alerted them to a tussle on the beach. "We've got to go back. Please!"

"Where did that ghost go? Did you see anything?"

"Nooo!" Mary wailed. "Please, milady, come away!"

At the bottom of the cut, Darkefell had been lurking in the shadows of the scrubby shrubs at the base of the cliff. Above him explosions crackled, echoing off the cliff face, while beyond him, in the open, the smugglers beetled up the shore, abandoning wooden crates, dumping whatever they carried in their haste to get away.

He had followed Johnny Quintrell as the young man snuck from the Barbary Ghost Inn that night, and this was his destination, directly below the St. James's rented house, if he judged correctly. That answered Joseph's questions about his son's involvement. Darkefell was looking for an opportunity to snatch the boy back before the revenue men, who swarmed out of the cut, got to him, and arrested him.

But shots rang out again, and when he looked up in a flash of light from some explosive, it was to see Anne—*his* Anne—tottering on the edge of the cliff! After he had told her to stay out of it! That made his decision simple. Johnny would have to fend for himself; Darkefell was for rescuing Anne.

He slunk into the shadows and up the jagged cut, struggling against the wet sand, willing himself to not break out into the open. He was aware of men just to his left who were working their way down, likely the revenue men in a pitched battle with the smugglers. Shouts and confusion surrounded him, but he went unnoticed in the fray. There was only one direction for him, and that was up, toward Anne.

He finally topped the cliff face, and saw Anne, not alone, he was happy to see, but with her faithful maid, Mary. He raced to her, pulling her down. "What the devil are you doing out here?" he growled.

"Darkefell?" she cried.

He put his hand over her mouth, "For God's sake, madam, keep your voice down. Mary, go back to the house," he said, for in the ghostly light of the rising moon that slanted its pearly rays across the surface of the ocean, he could see that the Scottish maid was frightened out of her wits.

"Aye, milord," she said, and scuttled away. But then she paused, looked back and said, "Take care of her, milord, please!"

"You know I will." Once Mary was gone, he pulled Anne down to the ground, and whispered in her ear. "I'm going to let go of your mouth, but keep quiet!" He took his hand away.

"If I didn't know better," she hissed, gulping in air, "I would think you were trying to smother me."

In answer, he pulled her toward him and fastened his mouth over hers, grimly determined to silence her.

He half expected her to bite his lip—she had done *that* before—but instead she returned the kiss, pushing him onto his back. The dormant sensuality he kept ruthlessly subdued roared to life as he felt her long hair streaming about him, and her warm, soft body covering his hard angularity. The sensation of her full lips pressed to his raised his heart rate to pounding. Hungry for more, he grabbed her hips and pulled her close, but she resisted.

"Happy?" she gasped. "Now, *let me go*." She pushed out of his grasp and rolled away from him, then slithered to the edge of the cliff on her elbows and knees.

He rolled onto his side and cupped himself, adjusting, trying to make himself more comfortable, but to no avail. He would just have to let his turgidity subside naturally. Trying to ignore the physical discomfort her passionate kisses and voluptuous body had ignited, he crept to her side and collapsed.

"Darkefell, I saw it again, the Barbary ghost," she muttered. "Then Mary shrieked, and I swear, the ghost stared right at us and howled!"

The scramble below was dissipating, but a shot rang out, and Darkefell pulled Anne back from the lip of the cliff. Holding her close, he murmured, "Do you think Mary's scream alerted the smugglers to the revenue men?"

"I don't know," Anne whispered, in his ear.

His eyes rolled back at the intimate feel of her warm breath on his neck and ear, the murmur of her beautiful voice, and he supposed he unconsciously dug his fingers into her arm; she protested. He forced himself to relax. "I… I beg your pardon, my dearest Anne." He nuzzled her thick veil of hair. "I had no idea your hair was so long," he whispered, tangling his fingers in it, his voice oddly gruff. "And it smells so lovely." He put his hand on her back and stroked, down to her bottom.

"Darkefell!" she said, swatting at his hand. "Stop being an idiot. What are you doing here, anyhow?"

He rolled away from her, cleared his throat and summoned coolness. "I was down on the beach watching the smugglers," he said, deciding not divulge his reason for being there yet. He pushed himself up on his elbows and looked over the cliff edge. The beach below appeared deserted, from what could be sensed with the wan moonlight. There could be a battalion of men hugging the cliff, in the shadows, though. "Then I heard an altercation," he whispered, "then the fireworks, and the excise men came swarming down from the cliff opposite here, on the other side of the cut. I saw you flailing about on the cliff's edge, and began up the cut, staying in the shadows."

"I wondered where you came from."

"You were tottering about on the edge of the cliff, so I came up to make you heed common sense."

He thought she would retort angrily, but her tone was thoughtful, when she said, "I hope no one was hurt."

He remembered Johnny Quintrell, and fervently said, "I hope that too. But what the devil were you doing out? I specifically told you to *stay in*." Even as he said it, he knew it was wrong; would he never learn that to command her was to alienate her? Or did he just enjoy being censured by her?

But again, she reacted coolly. "And I told you I had no intention of being bullied into doing what you think is suitable. Are you going to help me discover what this ghost is all about, or not?"

He made a quick decision. "I am indeed going to help you." *To stay out of trouble,* he finished in his mind.

"But we can do nothing right now," she said. She peered over the edge of the cliff. "All's quiet. They're gone, I think, but it's too dark right now to detect. I do hope no one was hurt." Anne got to her feet and dusted off her dress. "Come back tomorrow, Darkefell. I want to have a look at this cliff side, and figure out how the ghost does his disappearing act. Then I want to find out what—or who—it is, and what his game is."

"Kiss me," the marquess said, taking her arm, "and I will agree to anything."

So she did.

Acknowledgments

No author finishes a novel without incurring debt, and I owe many people heartfelt thanks:

Michael, I deeply appreciate the time and care you take with every project, from start to finish; it's the sign of a true professional, and you conduct yourself throughout with grace and perfect honor. Thank you.

Deb, there is no better moment for a writer than when she realizes an editor "gets" her, and I can't thank you enough for sharing the enthusiasm I feel for Lady Anne.

Mick, there would quite simply be no published books without your love and support. You were the first to see a smidgen of ability, but without your encouragement, it would have stayed buried. There just aren't enough words to express my appreciation to you, but I'll say it anyway; thank you, from the bottom of my heart.

About the Author

Donna Lea Simpson is a nationally bestselling romance and mystery novelist with over twenty titles published in the last ten years and over 400,000 copies sold. Donna believes that a dash of mystery adds piquancy to a romantic tale, and a hint of romance adds humanity to a mystery story. Donna lives in Canada.

A *Duke* TO

Die For

BY AMELIA GREY

THE RAKISH FIFTH DUKE OF BLAKEWELL'S UNEXPECTED AND shockingly lovely new ward has just arrived, claiming to carry a curse that has brought each of her previous guardians to an untimely end…

Praise for Amelia Grey's Regency romances:

"This beguiling romance steals your heart, lifts your spirits and lights up the pages with humor and passion." —Romantic Times

"Each new Amelia Grey tale is a diamond. Ms. Grey…is a master storyteller." —Affaire de Coeur

"Readers will be quickly drawn in by the lively pace, the appealing protagonists, and the sexual chemistry that almost visibly shimmers between." —Library Journal

978-1-4022-1767-8 • $6.99 U.S./$7.99 CAN

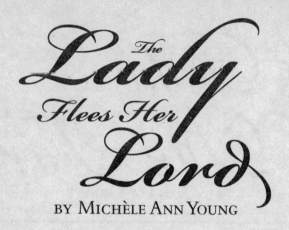

The Lady Flees Her Lord

BY MICHÈLE ANN YOUNG

DESPERATE FOR PEACE AND SAFETY…

Lucinda, Lady Denbigh, is running from a husband who physically and emotionally abused her. Posing as a widow, she seeks refuge in the quiet countryside, where she meets Lord Hugo Wanstead. Returning from the wars with a wound that won't heal, he finds his estate impoverished, his sleep torn by nightmares, and brandy the only solace. When he meets Lucinda, he thinks she just might give him something to live for…

Praise for Michèle Ann Young's *No Regrets*

"Dark heroes, courageous heroines, intrigue, heartbreak, and heaps of sexual tension. Do not miss this fabulous new author." —Molly O'Keefe, *Harlequin Superromance*

"Readers will never want to put her book down!" —Bronwyn Scott, author of *Pickpocket Countess*

978-1-4022-1399-1 • $6.99 U.S. / $7.99 CAN

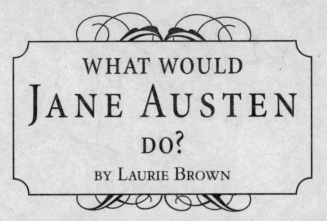

WHAT WOULD
JANE AUSTEN
DO?

BY LAURIE BROWN

Eleanor goes back in time to save a man's life, but could it be she's got the wrong villain?

Lord Shermont, renowned rake, feels an inexplicable bond to the mysterious woman with radical ideas who seems to know so much…but could she be a Napoleonic spy?

Thankfully, Jane Austen's sage advice prevents a fatal mistake…

At a country house party, Eleanor makes the acquaintance of Jane Austen, whose sharp wit can untangle the most complicated problem. With an international intrigue going on before her eyes, Eleanor must figure out which of two dueling gentlemen is the spy, and which is the man of her dreams.

978-1-4022-1831-6 • $6.99 U.S. / $7.99 CAN

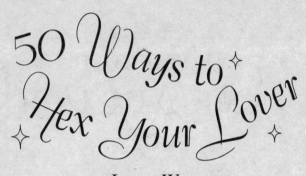

50 Ways to Hex Your Lover

BY LINDA WISDOM

"A magical page-turner...had me
bewitched from the start!"

—Yasmine Galenorn,
USA Today bestselling author of *Witchling*

**JAZZ CAN'T DECIDE WHETHER TO SCORCH HIM WITH A
FIREBALL OR JUMP INTO BED WITH HIM**

Jasmine Tremaine is a witch who can't stay out of trouble.
Nikolai Gregorivich is a vampire cop on the trail of a serial
killer. Their sizzling love affair has been on-again, off-
again for about 300 years—mostly off, lately.

But now Nick needs Jazz's help to steer clear of a maniacal
killer with supernatural powers, while they try to finally
figure out their own hearts.

978-1-4022-1085-3 • $6.99 U.S. / $8.99 CAN

Hex Appeal

by Linda Wisdom

"Kudos to Linda Wisdom for a series that's pure magic!"

—Vicki Lewis Thompson,
New York Times bestselling author of *Wild & Hexy*

Jazz and Nick's dream romance has turned into a nightmare...

Feisty witch Jasmine Tremaine and drop-dead gorgeous vampire cop Nikolai Gregorovich have a hot thing going, but it's tough to keep it together when nightmare visions turn their passion into bickering.

With a little help from their friends, Nick and Jazz are in a race against time to uncover whoever it is that's poisoning their dreams, and their relationship...

978-1-4022-1400-4 • $6.99 U.S. / $7.99 CAN

Wicked by Any Other Name

BY LINDA WISDOM

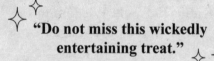

"Do not miss this wickedly entertaining treat."

—Annette Blair,
Sex and the Psychic Witch

STASI ROMANOV USES A LITTLE WITCH MAGIC IN HER LINGERIE shop, running a brisk side business in love charms. A disgruntled customer threatening to sue over a failed spell brings wizard attorney Trevor Barnes to town—and witches and wizards make a volatile combination. The sparks fly, almost everyone's getting singed, and the whole town seems on the verge of a witch hunt.

Can the feisty witch and the gorgeous wizard overcome their objections and settle out of court—and in the bedroom?

978-1-4022-1773-9 · $6.99 U.S. / $7.99 CAN

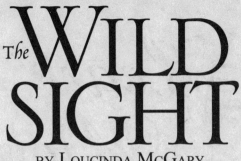

The WILD SIGHT

by Loucinda McGary

"A magical tale of romance and intrigue. I couldn't put it down!" —Pamela Palmer, author of *Dark Deceiver* and *The Dark Gate*

He was cursed with a "gift"

Born with the clairvoyance known to the Irish as "The Sight," Donovan O'Shea fled to America to escape his visions. On a return trip to Ireland to see his ailing father, staggering family secrets threaten to turn his world upside down. And then beautiful, sensual Rylie Powell shows up, claiming to be his half-sister…

She's looking for the family she never knew…

After her mother's death, Rylie journeys to Ireland to find her mysterious father. She needs the truth—but how can she and Donovan be brother and sister when the chemistry between them is nearly irresistible?

Uncovering the past leads them dangerously close to madness…

"A richly drawn love story and riveting romantic suspense!" —Karin Tabke, author of *What You Can't See*

978-1-4022-1394-6 • $6.99 U.S. / $8.99 CAN

Heart of the Wolf

BY TERRY SPEAR

A *Publisher's Weekly* Best Book of the Year

"A fast-paced, sexy read with lots of twists and turns!" —Nicole North, author of *Devil in a Kilt*

THEIR FORBIDDEN LOVE MAY GET THEM BOTH KILLED

"Red werewolf Bella flees her adoptive pack of gray werewolves when the alpha male Volan tries forcibly to claim her as his mate. Her real love, beta male Devlyn, is willing to fight Volan to the death to claim her. That problem pales, however, as a pack of red werewolves takes to killing human females in a crazed quest to claim Bella for their own. Bella and Devlyn must defeat the rogue wolves before Devlyn's final confrontation with Volan. The vulpine couple's chemistry crackles off the page, but the real strength of the book lies in Spear's depiction of pack power dynamics… her wolf world feels at once palpable and even plausible."

—*Publisher's Weekly*

978-1-4022-1157-7 • $6.99 U.S. / $8.99 CAN

Destiny of the Wolf

BY TERRY SPEAR

Praise for Terry Spear's *Heart of the Wolf*:

"The chemistry crackles off the page."
—*Publisher's Weekly*

"The characters are well drawn and believable, which makes the contemporary plotline of love and life among the lupus garou seem, well, realistic." —*Romantic Times*

"Full of action, adventure, suspense, and romance... one of the best werewolf stories I've read!" —*Fallen Angel Reviews*

ALL SHE WANTS IS THE TRUTH

Lelandi is determined to discover the truth about her beloved sister's mysterious death. But everyone thinks she's making a bid for her sister's widowed mate...

HE'S A PACK LEADER TORMENTED BY MEMORIES

Darien finds himself bewitched by Lelandi, and when someone attempts to silence her, he realizes that protecting the beautiful stranger may be the only way to protect his pack...and himself...

978-1-4022-1668-8 • $6.99 U.S. / $7.99 CAN

call of the highland moon

BY KENDRA LEIGH CASTLE

A Highlands werewolf fleeing his destiny, and the
warm-hearted woman who takes him in…

Not ready for the responsibilities of an alpha wolf, Gideon
MacInnes leaves Scotland and seeks the quiet hills of
upstate New York. When he is attacked by rogue wolves
and collapses on Carly Silver's doorstep, she thinks she's
rescuing a wounded animal. But she awakens to find
that the beast has turned into a devastatingly handsome,
naked man.

With a supernatural enemy stalking them, their only hope
is to get back to Scotland, where Carly has to risk becoming a werewolf herself, or give up the one man she's ever
truly loved.

**"*Call of the Highland Moon* thrills with seductive
romance and breathtaking suspense." —Alyssa Day,
USA Today bestselling author of *Atlantis Awakening***

978-1-4022-1158-4 • $6.99 U.S. / $8.99 CAN

DARK
HIGHLAND
FIRE

BY KENDRA LEIGH CASTLE

A werewolf from the Scottish Highlands and a fiery
demi-goddess fleeing for her life…

Desired by women, kissed by luck, Gabriel MacInnes has
always been able to put pleasure ahead of duty. But with
the MacInnes wolves now squarely in the sights of an
ancient enemy, everything is about to change…

Rowan *an* Morgaine, on the run from a dragon prince who
will stop at nothing to have her as his own, must accept
the protection of Gabriel and his clan. By force or by
guile, Rowan and Gabriel must uncover the secrets of their
intertwining fate and stop their common enemy.

**"This fresh and exciting take on the werewolf
legend held me captive."**

—NINA BANGS, AUTHOR OF *ONE BITE STAND*

978-1-4022-1159-1 • $6.99 U.S. / $8.99 CAN

SLAVE

BY CHERYL BROOKS

"I found him in the slave market on Orpheseus Prime, and even on such a god-forsaken planet as that one, their treatment of him seemed extreme."

Cat may be the last of a species whose sexual talents were the envy of the galaxy. Even filthy, chained, and beaten, his feline gene gives him a special aura.

Jacinth is on a rescue mission… and she needs a man she can trust with her life.

PRAISE FOR CHERYL BROOKS' *SLAVE*:

"A sexy adventure with a hero you can't resist!"

—Candace Havens, author of *Charmed & Deadly*

"Fascinating world customs, a bit of mystery, and the relationship between the hero and heroine make this a very sensual romance."

—*Romantic Times*

978-1-4022-1192-8 • $6.99 U.S. / $8.99 CAN

WARRIOR

BY CHERYL BROOKS

*"He came to me in the dead of winter,
his body burning with fever."*

EVEN NEAR DEATH, HIS SENSUALITY IS AMAZING...

Leo arrives on Tisana's doorstep a beaten slave from a near extinct race with feline genes. As soon as Leo recovers his strength, he'll use his extraordinary sexual talents to bewitch Tisana and make a bolt for freedom...

PRAISE FOR THE CAT STAR CHRONICLES:

"A compelling tale of danger, intrigue, and sizzling romance!"
—Candace Havens, author of *Charmed & Deadly*

"Hot enough to start a fire. Add in a thrilling new world and my reading experience was complete."
—*Romance Junkies*

978-1-4022-1440-0 • $6.99 U.S. / $7.99 CAN

ROGUE

BY CHERYL BROOKS

Tychar crawled toward me on his hands and knees like a tiger stalking his prey. "I, for one, am glad you came," he purred. "And I promise you, Kyra, you will never want to leave Darconia."

"Cheryl Brooks knows how to keep the heat on and the reader turning pages!"

—Sydney Croft, author of *Seduced by the Storm*

Praise for The Cat Star Chronicles:

"Wow. Just…wow. The romantic chemistry is as close to perfect as you'll find." —*BookFetish.org*

"Will make you purr with delight. Cheryl Brooks has a great talent as a storyteller." —*Cheryl's Book Nook*

978-1-4022-1762-3 •$6.99 U.S. / $7.99 CAN

SEALed
with a Kiss

BY MARY MARGRET DAUGHTRIDGE

THERE'S ONLY ONE THING HE CAN'T HANDLE, AND ONE WOMAN WHO CAN HELP HIM...

Jax Graham is a rough, tough Navy SEAL, but when it comes to taking care of his four-year-old son after his ex-wife dies, he's completely clueless. Family therapist Pickett Sessoms can help, but only if he'll let her.

When Jax and his little boy get trapped by a hurricane, Picket takes them in against her better judgment. When the situation turns deadly, Pickett discovers what it means to be a SEAL, and Jax discovers that even a hero needs help sometimes.

"A heart-touching story that will keep you smiling and cheering for the characters clear through to the happy ending." —Romantic Times

"A well-written romance...simultaneously tender and sensuous." —Booklist

978-1-4022-1118-8 • $6.99 U.S. / $8.99 CAN

SEALED

with a
Promise

BY MARY MARGRET DAUGHTRIDGE

NAVY SEAL CALEB DELAUDE IS AS DEADLY AS HE IS
CHARMING.

Professor Emmie Caddington's quiet intelligence and
quirky personality intrigue him. When he discovers
that her personal connections can get him close to the
man he's vowed to kill, will their budding relationship
be nothing more than a means to revenge… or is she
the key to his salvation?

Praise for *SEALed with a Kiss*:

"This story delivers in a huge way." —Romantic Times

*"A wonderful story that will have readers experiencing a
whirlwind of emotions and culminating with an awesome
scene that will have your pulse pounding."* —Romance
Junkies

*"What an incredibly powerful book! I laughed and sniffled,
was turned on and turned inside out."* —Queue My
Review

978-1-4022-1763-0 • $6.99 U.S. / $7.99 CAN

Romeo, Romeo

BY ROBIN KAYE

Rosalie Ronaldi doesn't have a domestic bone in her body...

All she cares about is her career, so she survives on take-out and dirty martinis, keeps her shoes under the dining room table, her bras on the shower curtain rod, and her clothes on the couch.

Nick Romeo is every woman's fantasy— tall, dark, handsome, rich, really good in bed, AND he loves to cook and clean...

He says he wants an independent woman, but when he meets Rosalie, all he wants to do is take care of her. Before long, he's cleaned up her apartment, stocked her refrigerator, and adopted her dog.

So what's the problem? Just a little matter of mistaken identity, corporate theft, a hidden past in juvenile detention, and one big nosy Italian family too close for comfort...

"Kaye's debut is a delightfully fun, witty romance, making her a writer to watch." —*Booklist*

978-1-4022-1339-7 • $6.99 U.S. / $8.99 CAN

Line of
SCRIMMAGE

BY MARIE FORCE

SHE'S GIVEN UP ON HIM AND MOVED ON...

Susannah finally has peace, calm, a sedate life, and a no-surprises man. Marriage to football superstar Ryan Sanderson was a whirlwind, but Susanna got sick of playing second fiddle to his team. With their divorce just a few weeks away, she's already planning her wedding with her new fiancé.

HE'S FINALLY FIGURED OUT WHAT'S REALLY IMPORTANT TO HIM. IF ONLY IT'S NOT TOO LATE...

Ryan has just ten days to convince his soon-to-be-ex-wife to give him a second chance. His career is at its pinnacle, but in the year of their separation, Ryan's come to realize it doesn't mean anything without Susannah...

978-1-4022-1424-0 • $6.99 U.S. / $8.99 CAN